THE WOMEN AND THE GIRLS

THE WOMEN AND THE GIRLS

Laura Bloom

ALLEN&UNWIN
SYDNEY·MELBOURNE·AUCKLAND·LONDON

This edition published in 2022
First published in 2021

Allen & Unwin
83 Alexander Street
Crows Nest NSW 2065
Australia
Phone: (61 2) 8425 0100
Email: info@allenandunwin.com
Web: www.allenandunwin.com

A catalogue record for this book is available from the National Library of Australia

ISBN 978 1 76106 704 4

Set in Garamond Premier Pro by Midland Typesetters, Australia
Printed in Australia by McPherson's Printing Group

10 9 8 7 6 5 4 3 2 1

The paper in this book is FSC® certified. FSC® promotes environmentally responsible, socially beneficial and economically viable management of the world's forests.

For Melita Smilovic

1

Libby

FOR A CERTAIN KIND OF PERSON, there's only one thing less welcome than a bill—and that's an invitation.

'Oh no,' Libby groaned, as she picked up a thick brown envelope from the pile of letters in her lap. She was sitting cross-legged on the couch in her living room, surrounded by her family.

'What is it?' asked Ben.

Neither of the children looked up as she ripped it open. 'Anna Wotcek has invited us to a dinner party.' She winced. 'On scented paper.'

'Who?' asked Ben.

'You know exactly who I mean. "Dinner for eight at eight," it says. I bet she'll serve fondue, and make us talk about abstract art.' Libby groaned and looked over at her husband. 'She must have loads of people to invite. Why us?'

'Probably because you invited her to our house for a dinner party last week,' said Ben mildly, going back to the balsa-wood model aeroplane he was gluing together under Jasper's intensely interested gaze.

'That wasn't a dinner party, darling,' explained Libby kindly. 'That was dinner.'

He squinted up at the ceiling as if he were about to sneeze. 'The food was fancy.'

'It was chicken! With just a splash of red wine. And the only reason I invited them—at the last minute, mind you—was because Summer and Michelle have become friends. I never meant for this to happen,' she added in a whisper, glancing down at her daughter, who was lying with her back to them on the carpet, a pair of giant headphones covering her ears.

'Well, you've done it now.' Ben handed the plane over to Jasper, who took hold of it as tenderly as if it were a kitten, his small face bright with wonder. 'She's paying you back for your hospitality.'

'She's paying me back all right,' muttered Libby. 'I bet you that she's already thinking up conversation topics to introduce, and then once it's over she'll expect us to invite them here again, and then they'll invite us, and so on, like a tennis match that never ends.'

'I believe it's what is called a social life.'

'It's what is called a pain in the arse, is what it is,' said Libby.

Ben looked pointedly in the direction of the children.

'Oh, honestly,' sighed Libby, 'they're not interested in what we say.' Nevertheless she went over to Jasper and hugged him tightly—careful not to touch his plane—until he politely detached himself to hold it back up to the window. 'Anyway, I'm not going. She's like your old friends from uni.' Her tone took on a lightsome, gracious air. '"Oh Libby, what a pretty frock, you must give me the pattern. And what delicious yoghurt! Did you *really* make it?"' She shuddered. 'As if that's all I can talk about.'

'Maybe she won't be like that this time,' said Ben, as he drained the last of his coffee and opened up his paper. He was wearing the short green terry-towelling bathrobe he liked to wear around the house on weekends, and tennis socks.

'Of course she'll be like that,' sighed Libby, picking up his cup off the floor and taking it over to the table. 'She's being herself.'

Libby sank down into the beanbag next to the fireplace and stretched her arms above her head. She and Jasper had been up twice during the night, and even though he'd gone back to sleep quickly each time, she hadn't been able to. Now her head throbbed and her muscles ached, as if she had a hangover.

'Anyway, I know why you're keen,' she said. 'You just want to see what they've done to their house.'

'That's not the only reason.' He shook his head at her knowingly.

'Why then? Because she's *leggy*? Isn't that what you said?'

'Because, you keep telling me, you're lonely.'

'Not that lonely,' she shot back, stung that he'd bring it up so casually, when to her it felt so private.

He kept smiling at her, imperviously. 'What's wrong with becoming friends with another mum?'

'What are you talking about? I'm friends with all the other mums!' But she wasn't. Not really. What with picking Summer up from one side of the playground and Jasper from the other, where the special-needs kids were *corralled*, it felt like to Libby, she kept missing out.

'You know what?' she sighed, taking off her cardigan, which she was wearing over her white cotton nightie. 'People like Anna just make me feel *more* lonely. "You were a bartender? Why how *original*. And Ben's an architect? That's so *interesting*." Which, as we all know, is code for good catch.' She looked over at him, expectantly. *I got the catch*, he was supposed to say, but he was absorbed again in his paper.

'"So Summer's nine, and Jasper's seven,"' she continued quietly, to herself. '"And he's only just started at school?"' She gasped and covered her mouth with her hand. '"Isn't that a bit late?"'

'Libby.' Ben frowned at her, giving her his attention at last.

'It's what she said to me! As though I forgot to put it in my diary. And she's such an over achiever.' Libby yawned. 'The other day—did I tell you? I went around there to pick up Summer, and Anna was standing on top of a seven-foot ladder in their living room, hand distempering the walls.'

'She's a monster, obviously,' Ben muttered, shaking out his paper.

'Nope, that's it. I've decided.' Libby hauled herself upright and pushed her feet into her clogs. 'We have to nip this in the bud, so there can be no question of it happening again. But what will we say to get out of it?' She looked around their living room, at the giant floor cushions covered in Indian cotton saris, Ben's huge aquarium humming in the corner, and the macramé hanging pot plants at the window, as though they might offer up an answer.

'Why don't we say that we need to stay home in the evenings, just for now, until Jasper gets settled into his new routine,' said Ben, 'but that we look forward to having Michelle come over again soon?'

Libby stared at him in amazement. 'That's perfect!'

'But do we?' he whispered, ruining the effect. 'Look forward to having Michelle over, I mean?'

'Of course we do. Summer adores Michelle—don't you, Summer?'

But Summer was lying with her cheek flat against the rug now, as if she were asleep.

'Okay, stop the presses, I have an idea.' Libby clapped her hands together, but nobody looked up. 'Why don't I invite Michelle over here this afternoon? Along with Colette, that new girl? They've formed that little group at school together, and I have some exciting news.'

'Hmm?' prompted Ben. 'What news?'

'I won seven free tickets to the ABBA concert in that recipe competition for *Epicure* magazine, and I think we should invite the girls.'

Ben squinted up at the ceiling. 'Why seven?'

'I don't know,' said Libby, deflated. 'That's how many they had to give away, I suppose. It's their first ever concert in Australia.'

'Quite the historic event,' smiled Ben, raising his eyebrows. 'But hey, good job winning with that recipe.' He gave her a thumbs up, and at last he looked genuinely impressed. 'Why didn't you tell me?'

'It's not that big a deal,' said Libby, but her cheeks felt warm with pleasure. 'We can have a disco this afternoon, to celebrate, and Devonshire Tea on the balcony.'

'Just so long as you don't make too much noise, okay?' said Ben, going back to his paper. 'I have to work this afternoon.'

'On a Sunday?' It was ridiculous, but for a moment Libby wanted to cry. 'I wish you'd told me earlier.'

'I wish I'd *known* earlier! But you'll be all right, won't you?'

'Oh, I think we'll cope.' Her voice sounded sharper than she'd intended. 'And Jassie's going to love it,' she added, brightening at the thought. 'What do you think, Summer?' She prodded her daughter as she sat down at the telephone table, but Summer lay stubbornly inert. 'Well, *I* think it will be fun, anyway,' said Libby determinedly, as she looked up Anna's number. 'And why don't we go for a picnic brunch at the beach this morning?'

A cheer went up from Jasper, and Summer finally looked up and smiled.

'You know what this means don't you?' said Libby, beaming, to Ben, who groaned. 'You're going to have to get dressed.'

Libby was a planner—this was her dirty secret. Even though it was her loosey-goosey ways that everyone admired her for, of plucking a tray out of the oven and bringing it straight over to the table when visitors dropped by, or whipping up scones in minutes, it was only possible because she was so organised. You had to have a well-stocked pantry and the recipe in your head to make scones that fast, let alone be capable of mixing them up while making conversation at the same time. You had to have the beach bags packed and the picnic hamper ready to go for a spontaneous beach outing, as well as to know and to be managing how each of the children—and Ben—were feeling.

'Why can't we just stay here and relax?' asked Ben now, looking longingly at his paper.

'Because it's the weekend and I want us to have fun,' said Libby. Now she wanted to cry again. Or throw a clog at him. 'Together, as a family.'

'We're together now, aren't we?'

'Please Ben.'

Their eyes met.

'I thought this was fun,' he grumbled as he hauled himself up from the couch.

He was only half joking, Libby knew.

'And ABBA—my god,' he continued as he shuffled out the door. 'How can you like music like that? They're so bland.'

'Well, I love ABBA,' Libby yelled after him as he began walking up the stairs. 'I love them! Oh, hello, Anna. It's Libby Kinsella here. How are you?'

Libby crossed her eyes at his retreating back as she began speaking into the receiver.

~

It was just a ten-minute drive to Colette's house and, keen to get away, even for just a little while, Libby insisted on being the one to drive her home. The disco hadn't gone as well as she had hoped, but she'd been so overwhelmed with catering to Michelle's surprise allergies and skirting a mini-meltdown from Jasper, that she couldn't think how to fix it. *Tomorrow*, she told herself, as she nosed their brown Kingswood station wagon down their street. Tomorrow she would talk to Summer about respecting other people's taste in music and the importance of taking turns. Although maybe by tomorrow Summer wouldn't care about her cassette player anymore, and she would look at Libby blankly, and say 'Obviously,' which seemed to be her new favourite word these days.

Without Ben here to disapprove, Libby let the car gather momentum once she had turned the corner, picking up speed as they began the descent down Church Street. She had only just got her driver's licence and driving without anyone sitting next to her to supervise still gave her a thrill. 'Weehee!' she sang out, as they became weightless for a moment at the bottom of the hill, but Colette remained silent in the back. Libby's eyes flicked to the rear-view mirror. The little girl looked exhausted, her head resting against the window as the car began toiling up the steep incline. The houses were smaller and meaner on this side of the hill, tightly jammed against one another, with concrete yards and outdoor bathrooms. They had been built over a century ago to house the workers who built the fine villas and lovely terraces where Libby and Anna lived, on the other side of Sandgate. As she pulled up next to Colette's house, Libby shuddered at the idea of having to go outside to the toilet at night. What if there were slugs on the path? Or spiders hiding under the lid? But these houses were well designed and made of brick, Ben would have argued, if she said this to him—he never seemed to just let her simply have an opinion—and once again she felt glad to be on her own.

Colette's house sat on the corner, looking just like the ones next to it, except a little neater, maybe, with lace gauze curtains and a thick hedge shielding the front room from the road.

'Thanks, Mrs Kinsella,' said Colette, jumping out of the car as her father appeared in the doorway to greet her. Steve certainly was handsome, noted Libby dispassionately, as she waved. Almost too handsome—his red hair too perfectly wavy, his denim outfit too perfectly coordinated, like a model in one of her knitting pattern books.

She was about to ease back out into the traffic when he put his hand up to stop her and she stalled, earning the blare of a car horn swerving to avoid her and the yell of 'Lady Driver!' as Colette's mother appeared next to him on the step. Half Steve's height, and curvy, Carol looked gorgeous, as always, and a little bit as though she'd dropped in from another planet. Planet Glam, maybe, thought Libby appreciatively. Today she was wearing a purple satin shirt and mini skirt, with yellow cork heels. At home on the weekend! Libby marvelled. Carol's legs were so pale they were glowing, and as she bent down to talk to Colette her mop of blonde curls glinted in the last of the afternoon sun. Then she skipped out to Libby's car, opened the passenger-side door and climbed in.

'Is something wrong?' asked Libby, taken aback. The accepted etiquette after a play-date usually was that a drop-off was enough.

'I just wanted to catch a moment with you, away from the kids.'

'But I'm double-parked,' objected Libby. All she wanted now was to get home and get the kids into bed as soon as possible, so she could have a glass of wine and an hour of mindless television on the couch with Ben.

'Please. It will only take a minute. Could we not just go around the corner?'

Her Cockney accent was so charming, and her crooked smile so sweet, what was Libby supposed to say? *No! Get out of my car!*

She released the handbrake and put the car into gear, feeling a little self-conscious as she turned another corner and pulled up against the kerb in the side street. She knew that Carol and Steve had emigrated with Colette from England just before Christmas, and that Colette was allowed to wear make-up, and buy lollies for afternoon tea. Apart from a few quick hellos and goodbyes in the playground, she and Carol had never actually talked.

'It's about Colette,' said Carol as soon as Libby turned off the engine. 'I'm worried that she's not fitting in.'

'Oh. Oh!' Libby undid her seatbelt, playing for time. She hadn't been expecting this. 'But Colette's only just started school this term, hasn't she? It's only been three weeks.'

'Her teacher said she got into a fight with Nell on Friday, but I can't get anything out of her. Do you know anything about it?' Carol's voice was high and breathy, like a child's.

'It was probably just a one-off,' said Libby carefully, not sure how much of what Summer had told her about it had been in confidence. 'I mean, kids are always ratty on a Friday, have you noticed that? And it's been revoltingly hot.' Libby shifted in her seat, the skin of her under-thighs on the vinyl making a sucking sound as she moved. She thought longingly of the breeze on her balcony, where she could be sitting right now. 'I have sweat running down my legs in a *rivulet* and it's well past 6 p.m.,' she added meaningfully, hoping Carol might take the hint.

'A one-off *what*, though?' insisted Carol, circling right back.

Carol had a right to know, Libby decided, sighing, no matter what Summer might have to say about that. 'Rumours have been going around the class apparently. Accusations were made.'

'*Rumours?*'

'Oh sweetie, don't look so horrified! That's just my word for it.' Libby touched Carol's arm. Her skin was surprisingly soft, like a baby's. 'Summer said there's been a gang of them who are suggesting that … well, that Colette, and Michelle and Summer, too, mind you, might be, well, a little bit spoiled.'

'*Spoiled?*'

Libby leaned back in her seat and closed her eyes. 'It's never simply about what they say it's about, though, is it, with nine-year-olds? I mean, Summer's hardly stuck up. If anything she feels defensive sometimes, because of Jasper, but that's another story.' It felt as though the weight that had been circling her ever since Friday afternoon, when Summer told her about the argument, had finally settled across her shoulders like an iron bar. 'Apparently they were all screaming at one another by the time the teacher came around.'

'Screaming?' echoed Carol faintly.

'Colette answered the teacher back, though, and so she was the one who got the blame.'

'But Colette's never been in trouble before!'

'If it's any comfort, Summer's been having issues, too.'

'What kind of issues?'

'Nell, her best friend—or ex best friend, I should say—dropped her just before Christmas, no warning, and now she's just really touchy all the time.' Libby was trying for a light tone, but it was the first time she'd talked about this with anyone apart from Ben, and now she realised how much it had been weighing on her. 'Summer's changed so much over the holidays, some days I think she's nine going on nineteen.'

'That sounds just like Colette. Steve says I'm being stupid to be so worked up about it, though.'

'Ben says I'm fussing, too. He says I should be more worried about Summer crossing the road without me, or catching the flu.' But for Libby this conversation felt real, and all those other conversations she'd been having with Ben all weekend about the house and work and dinner invitations—that was the superficial stuff. 'He says that to get any more involved in her drama will only feed it more.'

'But if we can't even talk about it, then how are they supposed to learn how to get along?' asked Carol.

Libby stared at her, surprised. Finally, here was someone who got it; who understood what having the wellbeing of your children as your overriding purpose in life was like. How exhausting it was, and how preoccupying, to do that impossible yet necessary thing of making sure that your children were *happy*, as well as safe.

'Sometimes I think the only reason Ben can be so calm about everything is because he knows he can count on me to do all the freaking out,' said Libby. The weight on her shoulders had lifted, somehow, and now she felt almost light with relief.

'Steve says I'm being neurotic,' said Carol.

'Well, it does drive you mad sometimes, doesn't it?' Libby laughed.

Carol wound her window down with jerky movements, allowing a waft of fresh air into the car. 'Ever since I heard about the fight on Friday I've been so homesick,' she sighed. 'I've been wishing we could go back home to London. But that's silly, isn't it? Steve says it's nuts.'

It was odd enough that Carol was asking Libby for reassurance about this considering they'd barely said a word to one another before today. What was even more peculiar was that Libby desperately wanted to give it.

'Sydney's the most wonderful city,' she said warmly, even though only last week she'd been telling Ben how much she wished they could live overseas. 'And Sandgate's the hippest part of it.'

Carol looked at her doubtfully. 'Really?'

'Oh yes!' she enthused. 'It's full of artists and students and interesting people, and there's so much going on . . .' She paused, a little embarrassed now. It was probably nothing compared to what Carol was used to in London. 'And Sandgate's a wonderful little school, too,' she said brightly, changing to a different tack. 'I'm sure Colette's going to love it here, once she's had a chance to settle in.'

'You're right. I'm sure you're right.' Carol hiccupped, and then she started to cry, her shoulders shaking as she pushed a balled-up tissue into her eyes.

Libby took Carol's hand in hers. It was small and soft, like a cat's paw.

'Thank you so much for having Colette over today,' said Carol, calming a little. She ran a knuckle delicately under first one eye and then the other, leaving her thick blue eyeliner intact. 'This is the first time she's been invited to anyone's house since we moved.'

'What's taking you two so long?' Steve's face suddenly appeared in the window, making Libby jump. 'Don't tell me we have the waterworks again! What is it this time?'

'We've just been having a little chat,' said Libby, but Steve was gazing hard at Carol, who was staring straight ahead through the windscreen, her fingers kneading the material of her skirt against her thighs.

'You've been going on again about that thing at school on Friday, haven't you?' he demanded.

'I just . . .' Carol's voice wavered as Steve began drumming his fingers on the windowsill, impatiently.

'I was worried, too,' Libby jumped in. 'But we've talked it over, and—'

'Then you're both fools,' he interrupted. 'Like chooks, the two of you, clucking and squawking over nothing.'

He disappeared from Libby's side and a moment later his leather belt and tightly fitted jeans appeared in the window on Carol's. 'Come on, Chook. Get out,' he said, opening the door.

Carol looked wordlessly at Libby, her blue eyes wary, her expression set.

'Are you okay?' asked Libby, putting her hand on Carol's arm.

'It's his tea time.' Carol's voice was flat. Her eyes were dry. 'Thanks for the chat.' She flashed Libby a glassy smile and climbed out of the car.

Steve leaned down to look at Libby through the window. 'You invited Colette to the ABBA concert, she said.'

'I have. I mean I did,' Libby stuttered. She had to stop herself from flinching away from his piercing gaze. 'I won free tickets with a recipe.'

His face took on a sceptical expression.

'Teriyaki Pork with Pineapple *en flambe*,' said Libby, clicking her fingers in the air. Instantly she regretted it. 'The judges always love it when you set something on fire,' she said sheepishly.

'Oh.' His face showed no reaction.

Well, after all, what did she expect? 'My friend Strauss made me go in it, so it's thanks to her, really, that we can go. She lives in London,' Libby added, irrelevantly. You're gabbling, she despaired. 'Anyway, the girls have been dancing to ABBA so much recently, I thought, why not invite them along?'

'Nice of you,' said Steve, in a tone that suggested it was anything but.

Libby sat up straight and put her hands on the steering wheel, catching her eye in the rear-view mirror. 'I'd like to invite Carol, too, actually, if she'd like to come.'

Steve brought his arm up to rest on the edge of the window, and stroked the stubble on his chin consideringly. Libby felt her temper start to rise.

'You know what?' he replied, just as she was about to say something; she wasn't sure what, but something witty and cutting. 'We'll all come.' He shrugged. 'It will be fun.'

As if he were doing her a favour, realised Libby, appalled. This was not the plan!

'Me and the missus used to go to gigs all the time, didn't we, babe?' Steve relaxed against the windowsill and began ticking off his fingers. 'Last year we saw Queen, Rod Stewart, David Bowie.'

'David Bowie? Wow,' said Libby. Okay, now she was impressed.

'Bette Midler—she's a wild one. And, who was it, the one you fancy, babe, that I can never remember?' Steve clicked his fingers and cocked his head as he waited for Carol to answer.

'Marc Bolan,' said Carol faintly from somewhere behind his head.

'That's right.' He nodded, smiling now with a distant look in his eyes, as if he were filled with fond memories. He straightened, rapped on the car roof and disappeared from view. 'Put us down for three.'

'Hang on! Wait!' Libby lunged over to call out the window, but Steve was already walking away with Carol just in front of him, his hand resting possessively on her bum. 'You're not invited,' she muttered, collapsing in her seat.

'Bye, Carol!' she called out loudly, as she drove past them on the way to the corner, but maybe Carol didn't hear her, because she kept her head down as she walked through her front gate ahead of Steve and disappeared out of sight.

~

'I'm going to be friends with Carol,' announced Libby that evening, sitting cross-legged on their low double bed. The French doors opposite stood wide open, the balcony with its wrought-iron lacework framing her view. They could see the city skyline from here, strung like a necklace of emeralds and sapphires and rubies over the glittering harbour. 'Maybe I can help her.'

'Help her do what?' asked Ben, from behind their Japanese changing screen. Libby had found it in one of the junk shops on Sandgate Road, and lugged it home to place in front of their wardrobe. There was something nice about saving each other from the sight of bum cracks and bra straps, thought Libby, as Ben emerged, his body seeming extra hairy and tanned in contrast to the thin material of his white cotton T-shirt and boxer shorts.

'Maybe I can help her fit in.' Libby felt shaken from what she'd seen, the way Steve spoke to her still resounding in her ears, and his possessive hand on Carol's backside as he walked away playing in her mind as she put the children to bed and cleaned up the kitchen.

'But listen, Lib,' said Ben, padding across the floor and climbing into bed next to her. 'If Steve's coming to the concert, does that mean I don't have to?'

'Ben!'

'It just seems like a waste for us both to have to go,' he said, as he pulled his mane of thick black hair into a ponytail.

Libby stared into her lap, willing herself not to give in to the disappointment she felt, like sap rising, in her veins. 'Summer needs it, and Jasper needs it, too.'

'Didn't the specialist say he needs to spend time with other boys?' Ben stretched, still oblivious to the effect his words were having on her.

'Find me some boys, then, Ben,' she said acidly.

'I don't know any boys,' he said, drawing an enormous book of architectural photos onto his lap.

'Neither do I. You know, when we had that little boy from Jassie's class over last week, they just played side by side all afternoon, and when I asked Jassie later whether he'd liked having Tim here, he said, "Who?" Well, this evening in the bath when I asked Jassie how his day was, he told me he'd been playing ABBA all afternoon with the girls.'

'And had he?' asked Ben curiously, looking up from his book.

'No, not at all! He'd just been watching them. But inside himself he was. And he loved it. He loves having things happening all around him without him having to be the centre of attention, and that's what Summer's friends can bring.'

'Well, good.'

'But you know, in any case, we talked about this,' said Libby, as he flipped through the pages. Home after home skidded by, each as empty and perfectly maintained—and devoid of the people who maintained them—as the next.

'About what, exactly?' he asked.

Libby paused. The few times she and Ben had talked about this so excitedly and heatedly they'd both had a lot of red wine. It felt very different to be raising it in her nightie, stone cold sober, in bed.

'About you being more supportive.' She felt his body tense. 'About me leading a more fulfilling life.'

They had gone to a couples' consciousness-raising group only a few times before the children made it all too complicated, but that had been enough to get the two of them—she thought—seeing things from the same point of view. Was it odd that you were meant to be liberated but could never speak? Libby wondered now. That you could agree that things had to change but then simply never talk about them again? It seemed to Libby that it should be the other way around. Well, it would be this time, she vowed.

'You know,' she said carefully, 'it's very difficult keeping everything going, with you away at work all the time.'

'I know, Lib. I don't know what I would do without you.'

'But this isn't just about you, is it? It's also about me.'

'Wait.' He cocked his head suspiciously. 'Is this Strauss talking?'

'No, Ben, it's me!' Although, as a matter of fact, she and Strauss had been writing to each other about it in the letters they wrote to each other regularly, once or twice a month, but only in the way they always did.

Ben took a deep breath, and put on his listening face.

'You hold yourself apart from me and the children, you know you do,' she said.

'Oh, Lib!' His voice rose passionately. 'You know I have to work hard if—'

'If you're ever going to be promoted, yes, I know,' Libby sighed. It was like a catechism that had been repeated so often it didn't mean anything, anymore.

Ben would say on a Saturday morning, 'I have a lot of work to do this weekend'. Or, he'd say, as they were planning Sunday afternoon, 'If we can get that done in time I'll be able to get some extra hours in. I have to . . . x or y or z.' It was always something time sensitive. Always something due, if not tomorrow, then very soon. Always something urgent and important to give tension and suspense to the question of 'would Ben get enough work done this weekend?' For years she had believed his stories, until lately she had come to the realisation that none of these buildings or projects or emergencies he talked about so convincingly were the point. The point was that he liked to be busy and absorbed doing his own thing, and all those deadlines and projects and excuses were nothing but holding patterns to keep her and the children at bay.

She didn't think any of this was on purpose. She knew enough about Freud and Jung and the unconscious to know he probably didn't mean for her to feel this way. But whether or not it was on purpose didn't matter to her anymore. He was doing it anyway.

'Let's talk more about this in the morning,' said Ben, putting his book on the floor with a thump.

Which meant talk about it never, thought Libby. He left for work so early on weekday mornings, they barely saw him.

'What's she doing now do you think?' yawned Libby, as she pulled on the long-sleeved cotton top she wore to sleep in. The cool change that had finally come through was bringing with it the smell of burning sugar and spice mix from the biscuit factory on the hill.

'Who? Strauss you mean? Probably in the most squalid bar in London, arguing with some poor sap fool enough to take her on.'

'I wish she'd been here this afternoon,' said Libby wistfully. 'The disco would have been much more fun, if she had.'

'Hmph,' said Ben, hardly hiding his relief that she wasn't.

He turned off his bedside light and lay down with his back pressing against her thigh.

Libby stayed sitting up, though, looking out through the French doors to where the lights of the city still glowed, and beyond, across the harbour.

Park Ridge was out there somewhere across the harbour with its shady streets and comforting routines, and a life so safe and predictable that it would be quite possible to be born and die there without anything interesting ever happening to you in the meantime. Even as a child, Libby had been sure there must be a better place, maybe in Sydney, or maybe somewhere else. She stayed home to do the nursing certificate her father had insisted on, and then hightailed it over here to the inner city as fast as she could, where abandoned ship-yards and streets filled with stray cats and boarding houses sat cheek-by-jowl with the life she had come to find: young people bursting out of pubs, deep in intimate conversations or loud arguments, interesting little cafes and delis filled with the exotic foods she hungered after, and all kinds of people living all kinds of lives, so different from the thick and constant sameness she had lived in growing up.

She found a job as a barmaid, first in a workingman's hotel near the fish markets down by the harbour, and then at the university, which lay at the top of the hill past the biscuit factory, at the end of Sandgate Road. She got to know shearers and wool graders and cargo men, and budding journalists and actors, and Strauss, whom she'd met at a Gathering held by a witch in the attic of the rundown terrace house she was living in at the time.

They'd kicked off proceedings by sitting in a circle and describing their relationships with their vaginas.

'My vagina is a pathological liar', said the woman next to Libby, when it was finally her turn, after woman after woman had recited something bland about its wisdom and its love. 'She only fancies sociopaths and liars, and so I have had to learn to ignore pretty much everything she says.'

The woman got up to go over to where an array of snacks had been laid out on a trestle table in the corner of the room soon after, and Libby, muttering something about her vagina always being hungry, had followed.

'My name's Evelyn, but I hate it,' said the woman, baring her teeth delicately to remove the pieces of frankfurter and canned pineapple from a cocktail stick. 'I just can't work out what to change it to.' She was wearing overalls with no bra, her bleached blonde hair cut short in a crewcut.

'What's your surname then? Or your mother's maiden name?' asked Libby, taking a shot in the dark.

'Smith,' she replied as she chewed. 'And D'Agostino. Oh, and Strauss.'

'Strauss,' said Libby thoughtfully, tasting the name on her tongue. She could already tell that it suited this woman, with its wild, brilliant energy, and surging moods. 'Your name should be Strauss.'

'You're a genius. But this food is disgusting.' Strauss glanced furtively back at the circle as she spat her mouthful back out into her napkin. 'This food woman's a genius!' she shouted, grabbing Libby and raising her hand in the air, like a prize fighter. 'Shh!'

the witch hissed, pointing at them with her finger, and they ran, laughing and whooping down the stairs and out into the street.

No one ever called Strauss Evelyn again after that, except for her father, and she and Libby had been talking and laughing about everything ever since.

Libby had been saving up to go to Greece for a holiday when she met Ben, who wandered into the bar one day when his lecture was cancelled. 'What's good?' he asked, looking up from his novel, which he'd placed on the bar. 'Me,' said Libby, smiling into his warm brown eyes. They'd pooled their money and gone to Indonesia instead, where they toured temples and palaces on a motorbike and Libby insisted on visiting every market, and talking to the cook at each roadside stall or restaurant they went to, until Ben managed to drag her away.

They were married in the park across the road from the university two months after. They both went barefoot and Libby carried a white lace parasol, and when she became pregnant two months after that, they had both been thrilled. This was going to be an even bigger adventure, Libby kept exclaiming, an even more fulfilling embrace of the life she had come to find.

But even her mother, whose idea of perfect happiness had been to be a perfect housewife—or so it had seemed—was taken aback.

'But you're so young, Libby!' she'd protested.

'I'm not that young,' said Libby sulkily. 'You had three kids by the age I am now.'

'I had no choice,' her mother had coolly replied.

Her life was going to be nothing like her mother's, Libby reassured herself, throughout the long months of her pregnancy. She was going to be a cool, hip mum, doing it not the way her mother had—with dinner on the table every night at six on the dot, and weekends spent with her husband rustling through the paper—but with creativity and flair. She was going to keep up with Strauss, who had headed off to London where she was training to be a social worker, and having mad affairs. Libby had tried having mad affairs herself, before Ben. She'd had two, plus a phoney engagement and a broken heart—it turned out he had a wife stashed away in the suburbs—and it convinced her she wasn't cut out for such things. But she was cut out for Ben, who from the first had made her feel as if she was particularly special and attractive, not to mention particularly good at the things that up until then she had simply just done—like the cooking and the sewing and the gardening. She had done them because they needed doing—in her share household no one else bothered and everyone admired you so much, she discovered, when you could do such simple things. She hadn't realised until it was too late that this was a trap, and that the praise was mostly just laziness dressed up as flattery. But she liked ruling over a household, she discovered, just as at work she had liked ruling over a bar. It made her feel capable and generous, as though she were in charge of her life. Like the Empress card in the Tarot pack which Strauss had given her when she passed the first trimester, and which Libby always seemed to pull, ruling over the top of everything, whenever she gave herself a reading.

'You are beneficent and loving, a natural mother,' she read out loud to herself and her unborn baby, from the back of the card. 'You create worlds.'

And then she had Summer, followed by Jasper three years later, and somehow all of that had fallen away. Not her love for the children, of course, but her feeling of excitement about life, which up until then she'd had no idea could be so fragile. It had taken her by surprise to discover how completely a family's needs could dictate every facet of the way you lived. It had been almost a relief when Jasper was finally diagnosed with developmental delays at two years old, and she'd had to accept that very little about this was going to be within her control. 'It doesn't mean he won't get there,' Ben kept saying calmly, when Libby had been bewildered and frightened, taking him to doctor after doctor who never seemed to be able to actually help. 'It just means he'll get there more slowly.' That's when Libby realised that she would get there, too. Both children were wonderful, and she was a wonderful mother. Yet on some days she found herself fighting a losing battle against the feeling that she was living a life very much like her mother's, except with a smaller yard and better décor in a different location. And it was lonely. So lonely. How had she never realised how lonely her mother must have been?

'What are you sighing about?'

Ben's voice in the darkness startled her.

'Oh, nothing. I thought you were asleep.'

'Are you thinking about how you're going to take the kids and run away to India? Or go and join Strauss in London?'

'Don't joke about it, I might,' said Libby, lying down. 'Not that you'd notice'.

He turned over so his face was directly level with hers. 'I think I might.'

'Or I might take a lover. You know, we talked about that.'

'We did,' said Ben carefully.

'Or I might get a donkey,' she added dreamily. 'They've got such soft ears.'

Ben moved his pillow closer so that now it was squashing into hers. 'We could.'

'We could take it on the Pilgrim's Trail across the south of France,' said Libby dreamily.

'Me and the kids could fling roses in your path, as you walked,' he teased, tracing his finger lightly down her neck and over her shoulder. He paused just above her breast, in implicit invitation. But Libby was tired now, too, sleepiness stealing over her like a spell, along with the scent of jasmine wafting in from the balcony. She picked up his hand and kissed it, before firmly giving it back.

'You know what?' she yawned. 'You don't have to come to the concert, if you don't want to.'

'Oh, Libby.' His voice was heavy with sympathy.

'Oh, nothing,' she said irritably, exhausted by herself as much as by anything. 'I don't care anymore.'

'If it will make you and the kids happy, then I'll come.'

'Really?' replied Libby doubtfully, allowing herself to be hugged by him.

But still she felt let down, and a welling of that dark emotion she'd felt each time after having the children—and the consciousness-raising group had only made it worse—stirred inside her. And each time after it lifted, Ben had said she should talk about her difficult feelings more openly, even though, apart from announcing that, he had never encouraged her to talk about them since.

'I love you,' said Ben. She could feel the hairs of his arm tickling her through the thin cotton of her top, and a moment later, his head resting lightly on her shoulder.

'I love you, too,' said Libby, turning over to look out over the harbour again. 'I do, I love you,' she repeated, more softly this time. But what if that wasn't enough?

2

Anna

IT WAS THE TIME OF THE day Anna loved best, when her work was done but she wasn't quite ready to head home. She had twenty minutes to spare and could take her time as she walked around the empty conference room, picking up the feedback forms her doctors had left for her, scanning them for a score, or a compliment. Market research could be pressured at times, but then there were these moments of calm, like oases of cool water, where, for a blessed interval, she was left entirely alone with her thoughts.

Interesting discussion. Lovely presenter, one doctor had written. Anna snorted. Presenter? She wasn't the presenter. She was a partner in the marketing division of Swenson Davis, the country's leading ad agency, and she had briefed the client, surveyed the data, formulated the questions, and conducted all the initial interviews. But the 'lovely' was nice. She'd accept that.

Drugs should not be forced on patients, another had scrawled in thick black lettering. Anna raised an eyebrow. Not even if it were a drug that would help a man just like him avoid a heart attack? In any case, there was no question of force, the only issue was whether the government would decide to fund it, but some people just loved to sniff out a conspiracy, even if they had to make one up.

The thick carpet felt soft under her high spike heels as she wound her way through the forest of chairs to pick up the forms. On the table at the back of the room lay the remains of the buffet they had offered as part of the deal for coming here tonight. Anna knew that after a busy day in their hospital clinics and surgeries, doctors needed to be lured with the opportunity to have their opinions heard, and to be wined and dined in luxury with their colleagues. Now, half-drunk cups of coffee and glasses of port were scattered among the half-eaten platters of biscuits and cheese. The evening had gone well. Some of the doctors had lingered over the goodbyes, chatting and laughing together until she'd had to tell them she needed to close up the room for the night. It made her wonder if they had anything to go home to.

She picked up a chocolate-covered strawberry, closing her eyes as her teeth bit through the crust of chocolate into the soft flesh of the berry. She stood perfectly still, her attention focused on the explosion of sharp wet sweetness as she slowly chewed. Then she stuffed the thick wedge of papers into her leather satchel, swung it onto her shoulder and walked out of the room, leaving the mess satisfyingly behind her for someone else to clean up. That was something a man could never understand, she contemplated idly as she walked past the lifts and trotted briskly down the stairs. She eyed herself in the mirrored columns of the hotel's glorious atrium as she waited in line at reception. Her new aqua argyle polyester suit worked well with her pearl accessories, and the heels were worth it for the extra height they gave her, despite the slippery discomfort she felt on the parquet flooring.

'Was everything to your satisfaction, Mrs Wotcek?' asked the girl behind the desk.

'It's Ms Wotcek, actually. And yes, thank you, except the coffee was only lukewarm when it was brought in. Don't they have little stands now that can keep the coffee hot while it's sitting there?'

'I don't know, Mrs Wotcek.'

'*Ms* Wotcek. I saw them on sale in David Jones this morning. It's the kind of thing that would work well for the meetings. Please make a note and tell your manager about it, won't you?'

'Yes, Mrs Wotcek.'

Anna sighed as she handed over the room key.

In the taxi on the way home she eyed the wodge of papers in her satchel warily. She wouldn't let herself flip through them; if she did, she would want to go straight upstairs as soon as she got home and start working again, analysing, calculating, possibly even ringing her statistics expert, and having to apologise to his wife for it being so late. It would be like a force impelling her, and she had other things she had to do tonight. She sat back, letting her head loll against the car seat, and closed her eyes.

This morning while Anna waited in the hotel's reception she had flicked through the pile of magazines set out for visitors, and amid the fashion tips she came across a story that claimed half of all women had an imaginary lover. She had wondered about this throughout her morning, as she finished typing up a report. How would you even create a survey for that? You couldn't come right out and pop the question—*Do you have an imaginary lover?*—because it would startle the interviewee too much, encouraging them to exaggerate, or deny. You would need to creep up on it slowly—*Are you satisfied with your current lover?* you'd have to say. But would you say 'lover'? Did any woman really think of her husband as her lover? Then again, what if the woman you were interviewing wasn't married? More and more women lived that way these days. *Do you sometimes think of being intimate with another person?* perhaps. The whole thing was just ridiculous, she'd decided by the early afternoon, when she was meant to be finalising tonight's materials.

There was no way a statistic like that could be real. It could only be the result of bad science, or bad journalism, or both, and Anna had been half tempted to phone the publisher to find out.

By the time her meeting started, with doctors arriving harried and stressed from work, she was trying the idea out on herself, and attempting to cast one of them in a starring role in her fantasy. Simon Lieber was an attractive man—smart, well groomed and, most importantly, well mannered. Paul Oxenborough was nice too and, even more importantly, he obviously liked her. 'My lady,' he said, clicking his heels and kissing her hand in a playful way, which made her shake her head at him in only partly mock-disapproval. But even now as the taxi bounced and roared through the back roads of the city towards home and she tried to encourage her fantasy—imagining herself kissing first Simon, and then Paul, and now both at the same time—she couldn't bring herself to feel even remotely interested.

Idly she wondered if Myles had ever cheated on her, as the taxi turned into her street. She very much doubted it. He wasn't the type. And she had never cheated on him. If she ever took a lover, she would have to leave Myles immediately. She wasn't like those hypocritical friends from college, who made sure they were virgins when they married and then considered their wedding the doorway to freedom at last. And she wasn't like the students at university now, some of whom slept with just about anybody, from the reports she'd heard. They didn't do it because they were in love, they did it for fun! It was hard to understand how removing the fear of pregnancy could also remove the fear of being thought loose, but something made this new generation brave—all of them at the same time—and it seemed to have nothing to do with how they'd been brought up.

She stepped carefully up the front path through the plantings, which had only gone in a week ago, their fresh dirt smell pungent in the warm evening air.

'Good evening, darling,' said Myles, swinging the front door open just as she reached the verandah. He'd already changed into his pyjamas, which he wore with a summer-weight dressing gown and slippers. He smelled of sweet talcum powder, and his short dark hair looked freshly washed. He was taller than Anna, and slim like her, so when they stood together in the doorway like this she couldn't help noticing, as she always did, that they were a perfect physical match.

Anna caught a whiff of the wood-smoke smell of his pipe as she kissed him.

'How were the girls this evening?' she asked as he took her satchel and hung it on the umbrella stand next to their antique Chinese spice chest in their gleaming black-and-white-tiled reception area. 'Did Nanny say anything about their afternoon?'

'Nanny had an early mark today, because I got home early from work. Michelle has a new pet rock, and Leanne made homemade slime. You should have seen the mess! And, now, how about a nightcap?'

The entire house glowed, thought Anna, following him into the kitchen. The cork tiles, copper art and Scandinavian shelving creating exactly the homey effect they had been going for, in perfect contrast to the stunning marble and damask of the reception areas. It had all turned out exactly as she and Myles had planned for all those years, sitting across from one another in the rattly little kitchen at their old place.

She accepted her cup of tea gratefully and took a sip. 'Would it be all right with you if I had a quick soak?'

Anna saw a flicker of disappointment cross Myles's face, but he said warmly, 'Of course.'

'Are you sure? I just . . .' She grimaced, and he grimaced back, no words needed for her to express and him to understand how much she needed a brief pause.

As she ran the bath and undressed, Anna looked around her bathroom with satisfaction. She had wanted a striking colour scheme, and one of those bathroom mirrors with light bulbs all around it, like Liza Minnelli's in *Cabaret*, but now she was glad Myles had talked her out of it. This was more tasteful, the light more flattering for her no longer quite young skin. Not that she dared look too closely tonight after such a long and difficult day. She stepped into the bath—steaming hot, despite the weather being so warm—and visualised dropping all of her worries, as she'd taught herself to do when she'd gone back to work after the children. She let them fall to the floor, and then mentally she swept them into boxes, some marked 'Urgent', some marked 'Tomorrow' and some straight into the bin. It amused her to see these questions, so alive all day in her thinking, now shrugged off, as easily as she'd shrugged out of her slacks. For a woman to have it all, she had to be able to do this, she liked to tell her female trainees. She had to be able to draw those lines separating there from here, and being able to switch off was just as important as being able to switch on.

Anna glanced at the clock as she lowered herself into the bath, letting the water lap at her chin.

So, what was her problem with the idea of an imaginary lover? She closed her eyes and rested her hands lightly on the edges of the bath. Well, for a start, she didn't like that she couldn't imagine one. There must be someone, somewhere, surely, who must once have taken her fancy? It was just so difficult to remember.

And what about the odd answer one of the doctors had given in that multiple choice section, on the fourth question? Her mind wandered. *No, stop it. Stop it!* She must focus. This was her time to think about how she was going to initiate a conversation with Myles about making love—or, rather, about the fact that they almost never did. The magazine article had reminded her, and then a quick scan of her calendar had confirmed, that tonight was the only opportunity for them to talk about it—with no deadlines looming or other distractions—for the next few weeks. As she soaped herself thoroughly with her giant sea sponge, she tried out opening lines. 'Myles, we must talk.' No, too direct. 'Myles, this simply cannot go on.' No, too critical. And not even true. It would keep going on and on and on, if, once again, she failed to get them to talk about it.

Anna slumped back in the bath, discouraged by the memories of their previous awkward encounters. Either Myles was very shy or very dim, or she wasn't making herself clear enough. But she knew he was in fact very straightforward and very smart, so it must be her who was the problem. Perhaps she simply wasn't sexual enough, as proven by the fact that she didn't have an imaginary lover.

She put down her sponge and closed her eyes. A man was materialising before her in her mind's eye. In corduroy pants and a thick white linen shirt, a pipe in his hand . . . Ugh. She slapped her hand against her thigh in irritation, sending water sloshing over the edge. She had just visualised Myles.

What was so significant about a lover, imaginary or otherwise, anyway? she asked herself exactly five minutes later as she towelled herself dry. Even more to the point, who spends all day being bothered by a random survey? Let alone one which doesn't even cite its sources? She felt much better as she threw on the terry-towelling bathrobe hanging over the back of the bathroom door as if it had been waiting for her, and expertly slipped in her hot rollers. Who was so insecure and easily influenced, that just by reading about a supposed 'fact' like that a person feels worried by it all day? It was ridiculous.

It was only when she was curled up on the sofa in the living room, as Myles handed her a fresh cup of tea, that her little voice of truth poked at her. She relied on that little voice; it had been her mentor and her taskmaster throughout her life. *It's not that you can't imagine having an imaginary lover that bothers you*, the little voice said. *It's that you can't imagine even making love.*

It was true. The idea of there being women out there so lustful, let alone imaginative, floored her. What's more, neither she nor Myles seemed to miss it. Was there a reliable statistic on what percentage of the population was in that situation? *Shut up!* she told herself, and taking a sip of her tea she said out loud, 'So, honey, how was your day?'

'I talked to council about fencing restrictions for Avon Street,' he said, settling comfortably into the sofa next to her and picking up his pipe. 'It's all fine.'

'Oh, well done. Did you get a chance to talk to the plasterer?'

'He says another four weeks maximum and then we can get some tenants in there.'

As soon as they had finished this house, they'd bought an investment property eight blocks away in Avon Street, on the other side of the hill leading down to the harbour. And now, once again, they would be spending all their free time discussing interest rates and rental returns and bedrooms versus storage areas.

'Let's talk about something different,' she said abruptly, just as he was getting started on whether or not they should consider new plumbing.

'All right,' he said equably, puffing away. 'I got that report into the head of the department this morning,' he offered. Myles worked as an accountant for the tax department. 'I re-did the table of annual benefits as you suggested, and . . .'

They were like colleagues, thought Anna, as he talked. Such a good team in every area, so dogged and productive—but maybe that was the problem.

'Myles, I was thinking,' she said, when he finally wound down. She tried to keep her tone casual, even though her heart started beating faster. 'Do you ever wonder if we're normal? As a married couple, I mean. The way we talk about these things?'

'I don't know,' he said, putting his glass down carefully onto its coaster. 'Does it matter?'

'I mean, not just the way we do talk about some things, but also the way, about other things, that we don't?' She was blushing now, and she looked down to pick at a loose thread in her bathrobe.

Myles froze for a moment, and then, very deliberately, he reached over and snapped it off.

'Not really,' he said lightly, settling back in his seat and flicking the piece of thread away. 'I mean, we all make our own version of normal, don't we? And who's to say what's normal and what isn't, as long as we're happy?'

'But are we?' She looked around at the living room, with its beautiful hand-distempered walls which she had slaved over, and thought of her diary, so packed with appointments and deadlines, and the girls upstairs, sleeping soundly in their newly decorated rooms. She couldn't think of anything she had particularly enjoyed for ages. Renovating, school activities, entertaining—it all just seemed like work. Her actual work at the office, weirdly, was the only thing she looked forward to. *But what about the girls?* she prodded herself. They made her happy, didn't they? No. They made her something much deeper, and more crucial. But not happy. Not lately.

'What a strange thing to say,' said Myles, frowning quizzically. 'I would say we have everything we ever dreamed of. That's what's important, isn't it?'

Anna nodded. He was right. And she had so much to be grateful for. This house, for a start, which could not be more different from the one she had grown up in, just ten blocks and a universe away from here, in the slum housing along the waterfront. *Imagine what Mum would say*, she reminded herself. It was her favourite way of making herself feel better about things, even though her mother had died five years ago. Her mother would have slouched into the room, and leaned against the doorway; one hand tucked into the strap of her petticoat and the other holding a cigarette. She would have been dressed in something loose and floaty and—inevitably—a bit dirty. She would have stolen furtive glances at the French Provincial sideboard, Shaker chairs and gilt clocks which Anna and Myles had gathered together on all of those antique-hunting expeditions they'd gone on with the girls over the years. She would have done a double take at their sleek high-tech standing ashtray which they'd had imported from France, and she would have whispered, 'Fancy!', her tone suitably impressed. But tonight Anna wondered if she really would have been. Tonight, for the first time, Anna could imagine something else apart from admiration like a question for Anna, in her mother's eyes.

'I hope you've been feeling smug about last night,' said Myles, busying himself with his tobacco and matches and relighting his pipe, as though nothing had just happened.

'I don't know why it feels so stuffy in here all of a sudden,' said Anna, standing up and walking over to the window, which she threw open, letting in the cool night air. She felt slightly nauseated at the way their conversation had just gone. All that preparation, and then, within a minute, the whole thing had fizzled out. Obviously, that wasn't the right way to deal with these things. Instead of talking, or *not* talking, she would *do* something, she promised herself. Something fresh, and new, and different, as soon as she got the chance.

'Anna? Darling? Our dinner party,' prompted Myles.

He smiled at her, and after a moment's hesitation she smiled back. After all, this was what they did well—skirting neatly around the things that weren't working, to focus on the things that did.

'The house looked beautiful,' he said encouragingly. 'It was a lovely night.'

'But . . . do you think our guests enjoyed themselves?' She sat back down on the couch. Myles always loved to debrief about these events, whereas Anna found them somewhat exhausting, a necessary social evil.

'What's got into you tonight?' Myles looked shocked. 'Of course they did. It couldn't have been more perfect.'

'I thought, maybe, the conversation was a little bit stilted,' said Anna. 'All that talk about houses. We promised ourselves we wouldn't talk about the renovation, and then that's all anyone wanted to talk about!'

'They didn't know each other,' Myles shrugged. 'The food was perfect.'

'Which I had catered.'

'You knew where to buy it, though, and what to pick. That seafood mousse, and then the orange–chocolate fondue. Amazing.'

Anna nodded gratefully as he took her hand. He really was the perfect husband. Understanding, supportive, handsome— everything her ten-year-old self had decided her future husband should be.

'I just wish Libby had been here,' said Anna wistfully, resting her chin in her hand. Libby would have come striding in, her lively face twinkling with curiosity as she entered the room. No doubt she would have worn something crazy but wonderful, like the cheesecloth harem pants Anna had seen her in at school this morning, or those striped woollen socks with toes in them, that she wore with those Birkenstock sandals that you could buy in health food shops—definitely a fashion *don't*, but Libby carried it off.

'I know, sweet,' Myles murmured, 'but Jasper needs his routine. Next time we won't do it on a weeknight.'

'Do you think that was really the reason? Sometimes I . . . I wonder if Libby likes me.'

There was a pause, in which Myles was supposed to say, *Of course she does!* and, *Who couldn't like you?* But, instead, he said finally, 'No, I don't think she does.'

'What?' It felt as if she had just been stabbed, beneath her ribs on the left side.

'Summer told Michelle, who told me.'

36

'And what did you say?' she asked sharply, pressing her hand to the pain.

'I told her that not everyone has to like everyone else, and that it's normal not to like a person sometimes. And that the most important thing is to be kind.'

'But why doesn't she, though, do you think?' she couldn't stop herself from asking. 'Like me?'

'I think she probably thinks you're . . . you know . . .'

He flapped his hand around the room, at the Limoges china collection in their glass cabinet, and the crystal whisky decanter and glasses standing on a tray on the sideboard as if ready to be served at any moment. Even though, it occurred to Anna for the first time, neither she nor Myles drank whisky.

'. . . a bit much,' Myles sighed.

'What's that supposed to mean?' Her voice came out as a squawk.

'A bit conventional, maybe. Middle class.'

'But they're middle class!'

To be middle class had been the goal of Anna's life ever since fourth grade, when the Department of Social Services finally ran out of patience with her mother's excuses and she finally got to go to school. It was there that Anna realised that the way her family and their neighbours lived wasn't normal. That it wasn't normal to go to sleep hungry, in a house that was cold and dirty. Her mother tried hard, but with so little money and so much work to do, it was a losing battle.

Libby was the kind of woman who would have been like the girls Anna went to school with, who were normal; who were cared for and doted upon, as though they were incredibly precious; who ate Sunday roast dinners in their carpeted homes, like the little girls on television, and whose mothers planned holidays and paid the bills on time, and never, ever argued with their husbands about their gambling debts, let alone Other Women.

Well, now Anna had achieved all that and more for her daughters . . . and yet. Something was still missing.

'Do you think we are? A bit much?' Anna demanded.

'I think maybe we got a bit carried away, ordering stationery,' said Myles. 'But what does it matter, if that's what we like?'

Anna stared down at her hands, mortified. The thing to do with a dinner party was to just casually announce it, as Myles had suggested at the time. The thing to do—she knew this!—was to pretend, no matter how much you wanted something, that it was no big deal.

'To hell with Libby and her hippy names for her children and her homemade chicken eggplant!' Myles burst out. 'What do we care, anyway?'

'It was chicken marsala,' said Anna, her voice small.

'To hell with her chicken marsala, then. It's all so petty!'

But so revealing, thought Anna, suddenly overcome with despair.

'If we're happy,' Myles continued, 'and the girls are happy, then what does it matter what other people think?'

'But what if we're *not* happy?'

'Anna! Sweetheart! What's got into you this evening? I've never heard you talk like this before.'

Anna stared out the window, remembering the dinner at Libby's house at the beginning of term. Libby had spontaneously invited them the day before, and it had been so simple yet so sophisticated. The way they'd sat around the table in the kitchen shelling peanuts and drinking beer while Libby finished roasting the zucchini, and then the way she'd piled all the food onto a platter and brought the whole thing over to the table in one go. 'I'm just obsessed with pine nuts,' she'd said, scattering a handful over the top. After dinner they'd lounged around on giant floor cushions in the living room, listening to Motown and helping themselves to homemade fudge, which Libby served straight from the pan.

'Your outfit was stunning, and it was a lovely party,' said Myles, poking her lightly on the thigh. He was always affectionate, but never passionate, thought Anna. He was like a brother to her in his casual sureness. 'We'll get the hang of it, you'll see.'

Libby knew the secret. Not just to how things should look, but how they should feel.

Anna stood up and began to pace the Persian rug in front of him. 'I'm going to take Leanne to the ABBA concert. I've just decided.'

'What? But darling,' Myles frowned. 'We haven't been invited.'

'So what? It's a public concert. And it's unfair for everyone else to be going, and for Leanne to have to miss out.'

'Everyone?' he echoed, baffled. 'It's just Summer and Jasper and two friends.'

'And I want to go with Leanne,' said Anna stubbornly, turning her face away so he wouldn't see how much this hurt.

The decanter on the sideboard looked golden suddenly, in the lamp's reflected light, and on impulse Anna walked over and poured out a finger of whisky into one of the heavy crystal glasses—which, she realised too late, was a little dusty.

'What are you doing?' cried Myles, leaping to his feet as she threw it back, coughing and spluttering and dodging away from his helpful claps on the back as the alcohol burned its way down her throat.

'Anna, darling, you can't force someone to like you,' Myles said coaxingly, once she could breathe again.

'I just think Libby would if she really got to know me,' said Anna, leaning against him weakly as he took the glass out of her hand and put it back on its silver tray.

'But darling.' His expression seemed almost sad as he looked at her. 'There are so many people in the world who would love to be your friend.'

'I don't care,' Anna said. It showed how much he loved her that he really thought that. 'I want to be friends with Libby.'

3

Carol

NO ONE ELSE HAD A PERM like hers in all of Sandgate, Carol told herself dreamily as she walked Colette to school the next morning. Most likely nobody in this whole country. She'd got hers in Carnaby Street, and even there, in the coolest salon in London, she had caused a sensation. A professional photographer had taken her photo and blown it up and put it in the window of the salon where she worked in West Ham. People stopped to stare and talk about it as they passed by, and Steve had been ever so proud, kissing her and laughing with such delight when he first saw it that she'd wondered for a moment if he might be making fun of her. She did look different. She had gone in with long, straight brown hair that fell down past her shoulders in a waterfall, and come out with a strawberry blonde afro, the tone of her hair making her pale skin and blue eyes as vivid as a porcelain doll's.

It was wearing off, though, and her roots were growing out, so now it was a slightly too-orange blonde. The question was, how

41

long would it last before she would have to get it done again, or else think of something completely new to do? Usually she would have loved thinking about this; loved looking through magazines and watching people on the street for inspiration, but at the moment she just felt tired by it.

Maybe it was because she still hadn't decided on a salon. Carol was meant to be finding a job here in Sydney, and so whenever she passed a salon she'd loiter and watch, like a secret audition. Today she had been planning to go into one down the road called Velvet and Lace for a consultation. Every time she walked past there was a huge caramel-coloured hound sprawled in the middle of the floor, and candles in copper holders burning in the window. If she liked their ideas for her hair, she had been planning to ask if they needed any help, but that wasn't going to happen today, and possibly not this week.

'I can't get a job just now,' she'd said to Steve this morning when he mentioned it. 'It's not the right time for Colette.'

'It's been weeks now, babe. You're being neurotic.' He was standing in front of the mirror in the bathroom, looking like an executive in his cream slacks and safari jacket, even though he'd taken a position—just for now—on the warehouse floor. 'Anyway, I made you an appointment for an interview with Mr Harold, this morning. Why not go in and have a chat? Get you started.'

'Mr Harold? You mean that big place at the top of Sandgate Road?'

His salon, The House of Hair, was like a factory, and she would never want to work there. She had said as much to Steve when they'd walked past the other day and saw a 'Help wanted' ad in the window.

'I sent in your résumé.' He sprayed himself generously with Paco Rabanne, lifting up first one arm and then the other to get good coverage.

'I can't today. Please,' she pleaded. 'I just need a few more weeks to get used to things.'

'You keep saying that, and it's been months now,' he said, glancing at Colette, who was crouched over the record player in the living room, all set for school in her uniform. 'Why not see if they'll let you work shorter shifts so you can leave early at least?'

'It hardly seems worth it.'

'We've discussed it, and it's worth it. Christ!' He lowered his voice to a whisper. 'We need the money.'

'But what if I'm running late?'

'Then she can walk home and wait!'

'I just can't,' she cried, bursting into tears.

Steve had been patient with her, fetching the tissues and boiling the kettle for another cup of tea, but it was a long trip through the traffic to his job in the city, and he got fined if he was even five minutes late, so he'd had to go, leaving Carol lying on top of the duvet trying to calm herself down. The idea of not being there to greet Colette after school on top of everything else that had happened lately made it hard to keep breathing, and she finally gave in and swallowed one of the pills the doctor had prescribed for her anxiety. She'd had another one before they left the house just now to walk to school, and she had to admit, it was helping.

Sandgate Primary School looked a bit like the asylum for the insane she'd once visited with her mother to see her Aunt Susie on the other side of London, thought Carol as they approached it. The asylum had been terrifying to approach that time when she was ten years old, a dark Victorian squatting monstrosity—but when they went in, it turned out to be very pleasant. The carpets and windows were clean, and they had eaten jam roll and drunk tea with her aunt as though they were just at home. Her mother had been so pleased when they left, and light-hearted for weeks after.

And so now, every morning when Carol came to the school with Colette, she would think of that and feel fondly towards it, even though she also felt nervous. 'Of course you'll make friends with the other mums,' Steve had said dismissively when they first arrived here from London, as though it were the easiest thing in the world. They'd built the special-needs school right next door, and Carol always tried to make eye contact and smile at the kids and the parents going in and out, but so far they were still just a blur—except for Libby, of course. Now Carol craned her neck to see if she could see her waiting in the playground with Jasper, but today she wasn't there.

'You have a good day now, Cookie, you hear me?' She knelt on the asphalt to kiss Colette, who seemed to be wearing lip gloss, Carol suddenly noticed, and to have teased her hair. 'Is that mascara?' She leaned in to peer at her daughter, and lost her balance for a moment, clutching onto Colette's arm.

'No, Mama,' said Colette sweetly, helping her get back on to her feet. It most definitely was though, and eyeshadow and liner too, but Colette was flying away across the playground before Carol could think of what to say.

Once she got home, Carol opened the fridge to get some chilled water, and her eye happened on the bottle of Steve's cider he'd brought home last Friday. Just a little sip, she decided. Something sweet and fun and naughty to remind her of happier times, when they would go out clubbing or meet up at the pub with friends. She unscrewed the lid, sighing with the bottle as it released its pressure, and poured herself a glass. She took it out to the front steps, where she sat with a sunhat shading her eyes and her legs stretched out in the sunshine, watching the cars race by. A woman wearing bright blue houndstooth pants and a tight orange skivvy was toiling up the hill towards her. Carol watched her sympathetically—houndstooth was so difficult, you really needed to have legs like a giraffe, or else the patterns went every which way.

'Carol?'

She lifted up the brim of her hat. 'Libby?'

'Is that lemonade?' asked Libby, panting dramatically and leaning on the gate.

'It's cider.' What would Steve say if he knew another mother had seen her drinking on the steps at 10 a.m.? 'Would you like some?'

'Thanks anyway, but if I did I'd be snoring in minutes,' said Libby. 'I wouldn't say no to a cup of tea, though, if you've got time.'

'Of course!' She was still blushing furiously as she led Libby into the kitchen.

'Listen, I wanted to warn you.' Libby lowered her voice portentously as she sank into a chair. 'Someone else is coming to the ABBA concert. Another mother, I mean.'

'Is it Pat?' asked Carol, filling the kettle and turning on the fan.

'Oh, that's bliss,' sighed Libby, leaning over to put her face directly in front of it. 'Who?'

'Nell's mother. I don't think she approves of me.'

'Patricia? Pat doesn't approve of anyone. No, it's Anna, Michelle's mum.' Libby flicked her a testing glance.

If you don't have anything nice to say about someone, don't say anything at all, her mother had taught her, and Carol found it almost physically impossible to break that rule. Not that she knew much about Anna anyway, except that she always seemed to be extremely busy.

'She wears beautiful clothes,' said Carol hesitantly.

'That cost a fortune,' retorted Libby.

'I guess when you go to work every day, you have to always look good. I used to have to get dolled up where I worked as a hairdresser. I have photographs,' Carol added quickly, because she could tell Libby was about to disagree. 'Look, I can show you.'

She jumped up and went into the living room, where she pulled a thick blue album out from the little bookcase underneath the television, and took it back to the kitchen table. 'That's me, just after I got my perm done for the first time.' She was staring at the camera against a bright blue studio background, her blue eyes open wide and her glossy pink lips parted, as if in shock. 'Those were some of my clients,' she said as Libby turned the pages.

'These pictures are . . . Wow! Did you really do all these?'

Carol nodded, absurdly pleased.

'Did you do your own hair, too?' asked Libby, taking a sip of her tea.

'You could never do your own perm,' said Carol, scandalised. 'You wouldn't be able to get the tension right.'

'I tried to iron mine but I think I burned it. Look.' Libby pulled her combs out and tipped her head back, so that her long dark hair fell down lankly over the back of her chair.

It would have been beautiful once, thought Carol with regret. It had a natural wave in it, and even though the ends had been dyed a harsh black, the roots were a lovely brunette that flattered Libby's dusky skin tones. 'Why don't you let me fix it for you?' she offered impulsively.

'What, now?'

'I've got my scissors . . .' Carol's gaze wandered over Libby's round face and slightly flat cheekbones; her warm brown eyes with their extra-long eyelashes that she didn't seem to be aware of, because she didn't wear so much as a touch of mascara, and wide, full mouth. She had a sprinkling of freckles across her nose that Carol would have killed for, and thick, rather definite eyebrows, that thankfully hadn't been plucked. 'I could do you a shag, and get rid of all the burned ends,' said Carol. 'Unless . . .' She blinked and swallowed, coming back to herself with a thump. 'You must already have a hairdresser. You should probably chat to them first.'

'Oh, god no!' Libby shuddered. 'Mr Harold will kill me if he sees what I've done to myself.'

'From The House of Hair?' A shiver went down Carol's back. She was meant to be there doing that interview, she remembered, right now.

'He's awful,' said Libby, 'but they employ so many girls you can always get an appointment, and I've been going there for years.'

'I understand if you'd rather think about it,' said Carol, her voice trembling. What would Steve say if he knew she was lounging around here, socialising? Let alone giving out haircuts for free? 'I mean, it's a big decision to cut your hair.'

'The thing is, I went and ruined it anyway on that dratted ironing board,' said Libby, picking up a lock of her hair and then dropping it in disgust. 'There's nothing I can do to save it now, is there?'

'Just cut it off,' said Carol, sure about this, at least.

Libby sat with a towel around her shoulders on a chair in the bathroom, while Carol moved around her, snipping and grimacing and pulling back to study Libby's face again each time before making another snip. Each time a big lock of hair fell to the floor, she had to take a deep breath to steady herself, before raising her scissors again.

'Do you have a job?' she asked Libby, once the back section had all been done.

'Oh no. I've been at home with Jassie full time until five weeks ago.'

'You didn't want him to go to kindergarten?' asked Carol, distracted for a moment by her curiosity about how things were done here.

'Are you kidding? I would have loved him to. And he would have absolutely adored it. But there's no creche or kindy or anything like that for kids like Jasper, who need extra support.'

'But he's so sweet,' said Carol, pausing in her snipping for a moment. Their eyes met one another's in the bathroom mirror.

'Oh it's nothing to do with that,' said Libby, shrugging dismissively. 'It's just the funding for the extra staff they'd need that they care about. But anyway, he's thrilled to be at school, finally, and look at me, a lady of leisure!'

That's what Steve had called Libby the other week, after she dropped Colette off and they'd talked in the side lane. 'What does a woman like that know about anything?' His voice had been filled with scorn.

Once she finished the sides, Carol paused for a moment to refill her cider and offer some to Libby again, who once again refused.

'How do you drink cider and stay so slim?' asked Libby, once Carol came around to do her fringe.

'I don't eat,' said Carol, squinting with concentration. 'But even so, I've put on weight.'

'How much weight?' asked Libby, disbelieving.

'Five pounds, Steve says.'

'Five pounds?' Libby scoffed. 'I put on thirty pounds two years ago and Ben didn't even notice. The last thing you should do in these matters is listen to your husband.'

'Steve clocks every pound.'

'No need for the scales then.' Libby's smile was kind as Carol tidied up the side sections, but he'd been calling Carol 'thunder thighs' out of Colette's hearing, and he'd joked about her 'love handles' when they were in bed last night. It made her stomach clench now just to think of it.

'There,' she said, putting down her scissors.

'Already?'

Carol's stomach clenched again, so sharply this time that she couldn't help wincing.

'Carol, what is it? Are you all right?'

'Oh, I'm fine,' Carol said. 'Let's talk about your hair. I think it looks beautiful, but . . .'

Libby's hands flew to her head. 'Is something wrong? Tell me.'

'What if you don't like it?' Carol gasped as her stomach clenched again.

Libby jumped up to look in the mirror, her expression serious as she turned her head from side to side.

'Well?' asked Carol from the doorway, weak with fear.

'What have you done with my ears?' cried Libby. 'And where have these gorgeous cheekbones come from?'

To Carol, the woman looking back at them in the mirror now had a natural, earthy beauty; her thick fringe and feathered layers whispered around her face in a gentle frame, and the few longer locks that Carol had allowed to remain drew the eye down to her beautiful décolletage. But clients didn't always see things the same way.

'Does that mean you like it?' asked Carol. Libby was just staring into the mirror, turning her head this way and that.

'I don't like it. I love it!'

'Oh thank goodness for that at least!' said Carol, sinking against the doorframe. And then she put her face into the crook of her arm and burst into tears.

~

Dear Mum, she wrote, and then paused.

It was long past time. Carol sat staring at the page, her pen tapping. She had been trying to write to her mother for weeks now, but until this morning she hadn't felt happy enough. She reached for a cigarette, and Sampson—the big ginger Tom cat who'd come with the lease on the house—jumped up and settled on the chair next to her, purring luxuriously. Carol gave him a stroke as he arched his back sensuously and gave her encouraging meows. Between the cat and her cigarette and, most of all, the success of Libby's haircut, this was the happiest she'd been since . . . well, since she'd celebrated her twenty-fifth birthday six weeks before they got on the boat. And thank goodness for the cider, because without it she would never have had the courage to cut Libby's hair.

I think it might work out here, I really do.

She didn't like lying to her mother, but the postman said this letter might take up to ten days to arrive, and who knew what might happen in that time? Maybe her luck was turning.

'I wish we could ring her,' she'd said to Steve last night. 'Just to say hello.'

'If you waste your money on ringing your mother again it will come out of your housekeeping,' he'd replied, and so that was that.

He'd cut it down again last payday, and there was no way she could make it stretch any further.

Everything is different, here, especially Steve.

Especially Steve. She paused again.

They had first met when they ran into each other, literally, in the corridor of the technical college where she was studying hairdressing, and he was delivering office supplies. He was wearing white slacks—to work in!—and Carol had never seen anything so sexy in her life. He'd known from the minute he saw her that she was going to be his girl, Steve told her later on. He was eighteen, and already quite experienced. She'd been going out with Eliot Farquar at the time, who was forever correcting her grammar and pronunciation. Steve had taken her out to the pub on that first night, even though she was only fifteen, and convinced her that god didn't exist. Over a beer for him and a Shandy for her he'd explained that all those rules, like keeping herself a virgin and not using the pill, and everything she'd done so half-heartedly at mass on Sundays was merely a pointless show, to hold up the old system. She'd been so impressed by his intelligence. She had wondered later though, without all that, what were they left with? Football. And dancing. Always dancing. And him.

He had long hair then—she hadn't yet convinced him to feather it—and an easy charm that never deserted him. Not when he was expelled from his training college for something he would never explain to her, or when he lost his apprenticeship in a mechanic's workshop, and then his next one with an electrician. He had a way, her mum said, sighing, when Carol had told her they were getting married, and again when she'd told her she was pregnant. She'd wanted to have another baby right away, to keep Colette company, but Steve had said that he wanted them to find their feet first.

He didn't want them to keep living with her mother in her tiny council flat. He wanted their kids to have a better life, and that's when he started to talk about coming out to Australia.

As the years went by, though, it began to seem like just another one of his distant, never-to-be-realised dreams. In the meantime Carol was working, and Colette was thriving, and Steve found a job in a camera shop where he finally got promoted and became manager of the sales team. They never did move out of her mother's flat, even once they could afford it, because Carol didn't want Colette to be separated from her grandmother, and this gave them a lot of freedom as a couple, as Carol kept pointing out to Steve. Then one day, out of the blue, he came home and said that it was time. She didn't realise until later that, once again, he'd lost his job. 'We're going to have an even better life now, babe,' he said. 'But how will we do it without Mum?' she asked. 'We don't need your mum,' he'd replied.

They'd been here four months now, though, and so far no football, and no dancing, and Carol was amazed how much she missed her. And even church sometimes, too, these days. She wished she still did believe, just so she'd have somewhere to go with Colette on Sundays, and other people to talk to. Of course, they might be seriously uptight. Her mother's parish friends were always being scandalised by what Carol was wearing, or something supposedly shocking that she had innocently said.

Right now, Steve was in sales and distribution for a TV channel, which was a big step down from the job he'd left in England, but it wasn't forever, he told her, and this way he could move into production. And they wouldn't live in this house, on this busy road forever, either.

'But there's only one child's room,' she'd objected when they first saw it.

'It will get better,' Steve had said. 'We'll do better. This is only for now.'

The house was dingy and had cockroaches, but Carol was good at making a silk purse out of a sow's ear—as her mother had reminded her, when they spoke on the phone that one time. Carol had the uncomfortable feeling that her mum might not just have been talking about their house.

Everything is different, she wrote, *since I lost the baby*.

Carol stared at the words, remembering that night on the boat: the ugly white walls of their cabin, and the lurching motion that Steve said was all in her head; and the cramping, as bad as labour, and the kind doctor who'd taken one look at her in the tiny bunk bed and turned to Steve and softly suggested that he and Colette leave the room. He stayed with Carol the whole time—that kind doctor—until she was sure he must be starving, or dropping from exhaustion, and she kept saying she'd be all right, but he stayed with her until it was over.

Two days later, when she finally emerged on deck so weak and changed Colette had come running up to her. 'What's happened, Mama, are you sick?' she'd cried, and Carol had shaken her head. That was all she could do, even when she was alone with her, later. Just another shake of her head. She'd felt so alone and ashamed, and the loss seemed so enormous. It was as if once she'd lost the baby she'd been left stranded in the middle of space, with no umbilical cord for oxygen, or any way to get back to earth.

Carol still felt that way some days, out in the street, or here at home—it didn't seem to make any difference where she was, it would hit her like a wave and she would have to sit down or hold onto something until it passed. Being with Colette helped. Letting her daughter out of her sight was hard, though. And doing anything else, like working seemed impossible, even though back at home she had always loved it. That's where she got to express her glam side; all the girls who wanted to be rock chicks came to her. They called her Caz, and she'd made a name for herself locally by convincing her boss, a rather dour man who was in Rotary to try eyeliner.

Everything's changed. Especially me.

Carol stopped writing again, staring at the words for a long time before she tore off the page, scrunched it up, and threw it in the bin.

~

'Is this your drink?' asked Steve that evening, his face twisting in anger.

Oh god. Carol mentally smacked herself. She'd hidden the empty bottle in the garbage before Steve came home, but she'd forgotten about the glass Libby had taken from her when she burst into tears, which she must have put on the shelf in the bathroom before putting her arms around Carol.

'I thought we talked about this,' said Steve, scowling at her behind his new moustache. 'I thought you weren't going to drink during the day.'

'I wasn't going to,' said Carol, everything inside her shrinking. 'I just got so lonely this morning and—'

'Save it.' He slammed the bathroom door so hard she was afraid he'd break it, and poured the remains of her cider down the sink. 'I don't understand what's happened to you, Carol. You never used to drink like this back home. You've changed.'

'Colette, just five more minutes and then the TV goes off, okay?' she called weakly into the living room.

'Your peas might be nicer with a bit of tomato sauce,' she chattered, trying to sound conversational as she turned the chops underneath the grill. Sometimes she could jolly him out of a mood if she just kept on going as though nothing was wrong, but tonight Steve sat motionless, his arms folded across his chest, simply watching her as she brought their plates over to the table.

'Colette. Tea,' she called out, over the sound of the TV.

'Just one more minute!'

'We may as well get started,' said Carol, sitting opposite Steve and covering up Colette's plate.

'I don't want Libby coming around here if you girls are going to drink. She's obviously a bad influence.'

'It's nothing to do with Libby, she drank tea,' Carol laughed lightly, reaching for the salt. 'Why don't you put some butter on your potato while it's nice and hot? And that lamb isn't getting any younger sitting there.'

'You know what? Stuff ABBA. We're not going to that concert.'

Carol was so shocked she forgot to keep smiling. 'What? Why?'

'They're not the right friends for Colette, or for you.'

'But Colette has only just started to fit in at school.'

'Then it won't matter if she leaves, will it?' he replied triumphantly, reaching for his packet of cigarettes.

'Leave?' gasped Carol.

'Leave where?' asked Colette from the doorway. She was wearing her favourite Mr Fox pyjamas, and with her hair combed down flat over her ears like that she looked so young and vulnerable.

'Your school,' said Steve.

'No!' gasped Colette, her face pale.

'We're just discussing it,' said Carol brightly. 'Nothing's been decided yet. Isn't that right, darling?'

Steve frowned as he lowered his head to light his cigarette, and with every fibre of her being Carol regretted ever opening that cider.

'Colette, can you please go to your room?' she asked, bracing herself for an argument, but Colette was already walking off down the hall. What? No backchat? Carol stared after her daughter as she heard her bedroom door click shut.

Be cool, Carol told herself as she turned back to Steve. That was the key here, no matter what, to stay cool.

'I was asking around at work today,' said Steve, his cigarette resting on the side of his lip as he cut up all his food into bite-sized pieces, as though nothing in particular was the matter. 'Colette's a smart girl, and there are some very good schools, private ones, out of the area. We should try her for a scholarship.'

'But it's a very good school. It was recommended to us, remember? That's why we moved to Sandgate.'

'Yeah, well, that's before we knew better. I think it's ordinary. And Colette only got a B minus on that last test.'

Oh god. Carol mentally smacked herself again. She shouldn't have left Colette's homework lying around. 'That was just a quiz,' she said, trying to sound light. 'She's only nine years old.'

'What was the point of coming to Australia if it wasn't for the better opportunities?' He transferred his fork to his right hand and began to scoop the food into his mouth, smoking and chewing busily as he spoke.

'But how would she get there?' asked Carol. 'Would you let me take the car? I'd have to learn to drive.'

'The last thing the world needs is another lady driver.' Steve laughed mirthlessly. 'She can get the bus.'

'But she's only nine years old!' Carol repeated.

'When I was her age I was already making my own way. It's time she did, too. Will you pass the mustard? This meat is underdone.'

'Please, let her stay at Sandgate, at least for this year. I'll . . . I'll do anything,' said Carol in a low voice. Just the thought of Colette getting on buses and walking down streets on her own made Carol want to throw up. Let alone what she and Colette would both go through settling into a new school, so soon after they'd just done it at Sandgate. 'I won't see Libby anymore. Or anyone you don't approve of, I promise,' Carol jabbered. 'Just don't make me hurt Colette.'

'Hurt Colette? What do you take me for?' He stared at her. 'This is for her benefit.'

'Don't make me!' Carol screamed, slamming her fists on the table so hard the plates jumped.

'I can't handle this,' he muttered as he threw down his knife and fork and stubbed out his cigarette on his bread plate. He slung his safari jacket over his shoulders and picked up his car keys. 'You're acting neurotic again, babe, and this house is a pigsty. I'm going out for a walk.'

'Knock, knock, can I come in?' The room was dark, the curtains drawn, and it took Carol a moment to find Colette curled up on her bed by the wardrobe.

'Cookie, you know mummies and daddies fight sometimes.' She sat down as close to her daughter as possible, wedged against Colette's knees on the edge of the bed, but Colette wouldn't look at her. She just kept rubbing the lace edge of the duvet between her fingers, and tickling it against the tip of her nose.

'And sometimes, when we fight, we say things we don't mean. You know that, don't you, darling?' Carol crooned. Everything felt muffled in here, including her own feelings. She put her finger underneath Colette's chin and with her other hand stroked her cheek. Colette's shoulder-length hair, becoming thicker and darker as she got older, and her long lashes and blue eyes, reminded Carol of herself at that age. They would look almost identical, actually, if it weren't for Carol's hair.

'He means it,' Colette said, looking up at her.

'No, he—'

'I should have done better on that test.'

'Oh, no, darling, that's not what—'

'Everything he says, we have to do, don't we?' Colette said flatly, interrupting.

Carol couldn't lie to her daughter, so she stayed silent.

'We didn't want to leave,' Colette continued. 'We didn't want to move so far away from Nan.'

'That's true.'

'We didn't want to come here. But because Dad wanted to, we did.'

The weight of all that Carol had lost felt as if it might explode inside her chest, or take her down with it, drowning.

'So how will you stop him now?' Colette's tone was almost scornful.

'I don't know exactly, but I will, all right?' said Carol, but it didn't sound reassuring enough to be ending this conversation with a question. 'You have to trust me,' she added firmly. She stroked Colette's face, tempted to curl up beside her, but what would happen when Steve came home? What if he wanted to keep fighting? Or make love the way he pleaded her to sometimes, after a fight? And so she forced herself to get up and kiss Colette and walk to the door. 'I just will.'

'Baby, please, we need to talk,' said Carol when Steve finally came home, smelling of cigarettes and air freshener. She had been waiting for him in the living room. Soothing music was playing softly on the stereo and she'd left the mood lamp on, which cast a blue and purple tinge on everything, as if they were on Mars. 'We shouldn't be fighting like this.'

Steve narrowed his eyes, looking at her closely. She hadn't allowed herself to take another Valium or have so much as a sip of his abandoned beer, and she'd forced herself to swallow down every bite of the lamb and potatoes, which had gone cold by then, to give her strength.

'There's nothing to talk about,' he said finally. 'I've decided. We'll all go to the concert, seeing as we have free tickets. And then Colette's changing schools.'

'But,' Carol began rising to her feet, her heart pounding, 'I've thought of a way we could—'

'That's enough!' he shouted, making a karate-chopping motion in the air with his hands and stepping forward, so that his hands would have collided with her face if she hadn't stepped back. The two of them froze, suspended for a moment by the shock of what had almost occurred.

'I've decided,' Steve said, breaking the silence. Then he turned and lurched away down the hall and into their bedroom.

He was asleep, fully clothed on top of the duvet, when she followed him in. She loosened his belt and took off his shoes, placing them neatly side by side underneath the bed.

Carol changed into her nightie and took off her make-up sitting at her dressing table, like always. She didn't look any different—a bit drawn, maybe, but that could just be because it was so far past midnight. Another day had gone by without writing to her mother, because she had no way of putting what was happening to her into words. She looked deeply into her own eyes as she rubbed in her cold cream. She was going to have to deal with this on her own.

She picked up her pillow and dragged at the duvet, pulling it out from under him. She paused in the doorway. 'I've decided, too,' she told his sleeping figure, and turned out the light.

~

'I don't feel well,' she told Steve when he arrived home from work early on the day of the ABBA concert.

'Oh babe.' He seemed genuinely disappointed for her. 'I'll stay at home with you, then.'

'No need for that,' said Carol swiftly, trying to keep her tone light. 'I'm just going to take a migraine pill and lie down. Colette will be so disappointed if you don't go with her.'

'But babe . . .' He frowned with what seemed like, for once, real concern.

'It's your first big concert together!' said Carol brightly. She must appear sick but not too sick.

'It's raining pretty hard,' he said doubtfully.

'ABBA won't cancel,' said Carol firmly, even though they'd been speculating about it all afternoon on the radio. 'And whatever happens, Colette can still go to Summer's for the night. Libby said she'll make sure they all have a great time anyway.'

'Well, bully for Libby,' said Steve. 'We'll have a great time at the concert, won't we, Cookie?'

Colette, who had been watching them anxiously while they talked, beamed.

Like Carol, she obviously thought it was possible that Steve might cancel tonight at any time, even though since the night of their big argument, no one had mentioned it. The topic of Colette's schooling hadn't come up, either. That didn't mean Steve had backed down, though. If anything, he probably thought the way he was being so nice about tonight confirmed it. As if he and Carol had a deal.

She helped Colette into her lace-up boots and French-braided her hair. 'Goodbye, Cookie,' she said, handing her daughter a raincoat and giving her a light kiss. 'You will be one of the most freaky and fabulous girls there. Definitely.'

'Take care of yourself babe, yeah?' said Steve, as she handed him Colette's little red overnight bag.

'Yeah, I will. Thanks babe.' Carol smiled briefly and then raised herself on tiptoe to kiss the spot he was pointing to on his cheek.

She waved at them from the front step as Steve's red Mazda pulled slowly into the traffic. Once she'd seen it turning at the traffic lights, the tail-lights winking at her through the rain, she went back inside.

The cat was waiting for her in the hall, his face turned up accusingly. He liked to be on the duvet when it rained, but so far today she hadn't made the bed. 'Sampson, I am really going to miss you,' Carol said. She took off her thick gold wedding band and the square-cut diamond engagement ring Steve had given her in front of the Houses of Parliament, on her eighteenth birthday, and left them in the bowl on her dressing table. Then she went into the bedroom and pulled down the suitcases from on top of the cupboard.

It wasn't hard deciding what to pack, because she'd already winnowed down her things coming here from London, and in the few months they'd been here she'd hardly had the chance to make the house her own, and so now it wasn't hard to say goodbye.

It was just Sampson she worried about leaving, and as she petted him once again in the hallway, she wondered how she might transport a cat. It was pouring now, the rain battering against the front windows, and arcs of lightning crackling overhead. ABBA might still cancel, which meant she didn't have much time before Steve might be coming back. She didn't have time to be worrying about the cat.

But when the taxi arrived, she was busy fashioning a carrier out of a cardboard box, punching air holes in the top with a knife and tying it closed with pipe cleaners. She could feel him scratching and moving around heavily inside as she transferred it to the car, along with both their suitcases.

'Where to?' asked the driver, seemingly unconcerned that she was obviously running away.

'The Travellers Hotel on Broadway,' she said, trying to make sure her voice didn't shake.

'Right-o,' he said, but when they got there the receptionist said they had no vacancies. Carol berated herself, standing at the counter as she slid the notes back into her purse and clipped it shut. How could she not have booked in advance? And how was she supposed to smuggle in a cat?

'The Youth Hostel in Haymarket,' she told the taxi driver next. The three of them had stayed there for their first few nights in Sydney, while they were waiting to move into the house. But it was full, too, it turned out, when Carol finally made it to the front of the line to talk to the lone person on duty.

'How about that women's shelter in Parnell Street?' the driver asked her then. He hadn't said a word to her up until now, sitting impassively, waiting for her each time she came back to the taxi, defeated. Sampson remained silent in his box.

'Oh, it's not that bad!' Some of the children at school were from the shelter, and she could always tell who their mothers were, even from a distance, because they looked so wrecked.

The driver shrugged and swung the taxi into a layby, the engine idling, the rain pouring down so hard she could barely see, as she tried to make a decision. She could go to a hotel, one of the proper ones in town, but the money her mother had given her 'just in case'—she'd probably been thinking along the lines of a broken appliance or an emergency operation—wasn't going to stretch very far, and she had to work out a survival strategy before she spent it.

She could go home, simply say to the driver, 'Take me back.' Sampson had begun to meow in low tones of protest, and the taxi meter was already at a week's worth of housekeeping. Any moment now it would click over again.

'Where to then?' the driver asked, glancing at her in the rear-view mirror.

'I don't know,' said Carol, in a small voice.

He turned around, and she saw his face properly for the first time. He had thinning dark hair, neatly groomed, and a thick silver chain around his neck. He looked Greek, or Italian maybe. 'What about that women's shelter?' he asked again, more softly this time.

Carol met his sympathetic gaze. 'But my husband doesn't hit me.'

'You have kids?'

'A little girl.'

'I don't know any other place that will take a cat.'

Sampson! Carol cradled his box protectively.

'Is there somebody you can ring?'

'No, not really.' In West Ham there would have been so many people. But in West Ham she wouldn't have even needed to phone.

She could simply have turned up at half a dozen places. Here she didn't even know anybody's phone number by heart. 'We haven't been in Australia very long, you see.'

'I can lend you money, if you like. Pay me back later, when you want.'

Stupid! Carol scolded herself as she furiously brushed her tears away. She was just as Steve had said the other night, always brimming.

'No, thank you,' she said, forcing herself to sit up straight, 'but I couldn't possibly.'

'Do you have somewhere you could go, just for tonight?' He was talking softly and gently to her, the way she'd been speaking to Sampson, who had been trapped for all this time, not knowing what was happening, in his dark and airless box. 'A friend, maybe?' he suggested.

'You know what?' said Carol, wiping her face with her handkerchief and cracking open the window. It was still raining, but not as hard now, and the fresh air would do her good. 'You should take me home again. It's really not that bad.'

'Yes, it is.' The driver nodded vehemently. 'If it's bad enough for you to pack up and come out in this rain, then it is.'

At that moment Sampson yowled, his cry muffled and desperate. A claw appeared through one of the air holes, but the driver didn't seem to notice.

'Can you think of someone?' he asked, gently smiling at her as though he had all the time in the world.

'I can, actually,' said Carol and, under his encouraging gaze, she tremulously smiled back.

4

Libby

'GOODBYE, DARLING, I'LL SEE YOU TONIGHT,' said Libby to Ben that afternoon. She was leaving early to reserve them all a place in the queue.

'Oh god, I wish I didn't have to come,' he muttered.

The kids had been grumbling, too, before she got them off to school this morning, and Libby was beginning to regret ever thinking of Teriyaki Pork with Pineapple, let alone setting it *en flambe*, as she wrote out her final list of instructions.

'I just don't know how you can like music like that,' said Ben, when she came into his study, humming 'Tropical Loveland' under her breath.

'You said,' said Libby, heroically resisting the urge to pour the bowl of soup she'd just made him into his lap.

'I'm still saying,' said Ben, leaning over to inhale the aroma of his soup. 'And don't forget to pack extra towels, okay? We're going to get soaked. Unless they come to their senses and cancel,' he muttered.

'They won't cancel,' said Libby, wishing she felt as serene about all this as she sounded.

This was the Family X Factor, that Libby had never known about until she had her own family: that not only did you have to manage and organise things, you had to manage and organise people, and that was far, far harder. She didn't mind it, with Summer and Jasper. After all, learning how to manage your feelings was part of the job of developing into an adult. So why wouldn't she help them understand they were feeling grumpy because it was almost the end of term, and want to help them unwind by making sure they had everything they needed to have fun at the concert tonight? But she minded it with Ben. She had had no idea that when she became a mother, he would also expect her to mother him, and that his feelings would become a source of concern and interest in their household, in a way that hers never were. And that he would have moods, and be up and down, and feel like doing this and not feel like doing that, just like the children. But unlike the children she couldn't order him to do it anyway. Or even know what it was that he should do. She didn't have the authority, or the knowledge, and it dismayed her, and put her off him in a deep, deep way.

Even worse, her management and organisational skills seemed to turn him off her, too, she thought, as she watched him eating his soup. He didn't like it when she told him what to do, but he didn't like it when the kids were unhappy, or there was no routine, either. As far as Libby could see this was a lose-lose proposition— as Ben's marketing textbooks used to say—for both of them. She was somehow meant to organise and lead everyone and ensure they all had all that they needed—and not just in some emotional, significant way, but also down to a 'Where are my socks?' and

'Why can't I do a poo?' way. Ben had actually asked her that this morning, in a slightly accusatory tone, as though she was with-holding the answer!

So now Libby could organise and manage them all without being overt about it. She knew how to subtly yet strongly get everyone out the door and on the same page, looking forward to the same things and going to the same place. Yet, somehow in all this she seemed to have misplaced herself. She was always the manager, never the participant, and now she wanted to participate again.

'Don't forget, we love ABBA,' she called out as she raced out of the house to catch the bus. 'And we're all going to have a brilliant time tonight.'

~

'You have got to be kidding me,' muttered Libby under her breath, as she climbed down off the bus an hour later.

There stood Anna, waving at her madly, standing over what looked like a year's worth of camping supplies, right at the front of the line next to the turnstiles which led into the Showground.

'Why, hello, Anna. What are you doing here?' asked Libby, walking over to her.

'I heard about the queue on the news this morning, and I decided we should do everything we could to get a good spot.'

'*We?* It looks like it's all been you,' said Libby drily.

'Actually I meant me and my secretary. I sent him out for supplies.'

Libby counted two camping stools, nine umbrellas, an enormous blue foam Esky, what looked like a tarpaulin and a thick folded blanket. Anna looked dressed for camping, too—or for a *Vogue* shoot about camping, anyway—in tight blue jeans, thick-soled boots and a khaki button-down shirt, with a pair of yellow-tinted aviator sunglasses perched on top of her glossy blonde head.

'I always come prepared.'

'I can see that.' Libby was dressed in her classic concert wear: long denim skirt, gym boots with long socks, and the mustard-yellow T-shirt she'd won along with her concert tickets, which had the band's name written in bubbly lettering over a close-up of their four heads, which were lit like a religious painting. She was soaked already, because she'd accidentally packed her raincoat and umbrella with the rest of their stuff that Ben was bringing in the car, later on. As for supplies, she'd brought a pack of Life-savers and the latest Jackie Collins sex-and-shopping blockbuster.

Anna smiled shyly. 'Would you like to wait with me?'

Libby looked up at the looming thunderclouds, and then at the line that snaked away from the turnstiles down the hill and around the corner. When Anna told her that she'd bought tickets as well, Libby had accepted they'd be at the concert together. But not *together* together, necessarily, the whole time. There were thirty thousand other people coming tonight, after all. Now Libby resigned herself to the fact they were going to be side by side the entire night.

'Thanks,' she said, sinking down onto a camping stool.

'Cup of tea?'

'You brought a thermos?'

'And fruit.' Anna proffered a plastic container. 'I have biscuits and cheese, too, if you're hungry. I also brought face masks and surgical gloves, just in case we don't want to touch the turnstiles.'

At that moment a bolt of lightning ripped through the sky, and it began to rain again. Libby rested her chin in her palm as Anna opened an umbrella for her. It was going to be a very long night.

~

'We want ABBA! We want ABBA!' The chant surging towards them from the back of the stadium wasn't just a sound, it was a *feeling* breaking over Libby like a wave and then rolling on towards the stage, which stood waiting, just six rows in front of them, shrouded in darkness.

'You okay, hon?' Libby asked Summer, who'd finally taken her seat directly in front of her, alongside the other girls

'We want ABBA!' She turned to stare at Libby accusingly.

'I've been waiting in the line for the past six hours so we could get these good seats, you know,' said Libby, handing her a sandwich.

'I thought that was Anna,' said Summer, sceptically. 'We'd be all the way at the back, Dad said, if it wasn't for her.'

'Actually, Summer, I said that when you arrived, and do you know what? It's true.'

Summer shimmied a little dance move at her from underneath her poncho.

'It is, you know,' said Libby to Anna, who was seated next to her.

Anna shrugged and waved her hand as though it were nothing.

'No, seriously. Thank you,' Libby repeated. She and Anna had read, mainly, crouched on their camping stools underneath their umbrellas, occasionally putting down their books to stare worriedly at the sky. They were forecasting a hurricane, people in the crowd were saying. Was the concert really going ahead?

'I enjoyed it, actually, rain and all,' said Anna, raising her voice as another chant rolled by.

'You know what?' shouted Libby. 'So did I.'

What am I saying? she mouthed at Ben, who sat on the other side of her, with Jasper seated in between, but he was distracted by something he was looking at in his pocket diary. There was actually something quite special about a person you could sit in comfortable silence with for that length of time, especially in the rain. When they did talk it was easy, and it made Libby realise how nervy Anna usually was—around her, anyway.

'I'm still having a great time,' she turned back around to say, but Anna was leaning down to attend to Michelle, who was admiring Colette's white crocheted mini-dress underneath her see-through plastic raincoat. *What was Carol doing right now?* Libby wondered, examining the back of Steve's neck. He was seated next to Colette, his wet hair dripping onto his shoulders, which looked muscular and lean underneath his red satin shirt. He definitely gave off a vibe; a kind of intense and concentrated energy that could be attractive, she supposed, to some women.

'All good?'

Libby started as he turned around. Those blue eyes really were piercing.

'Fabulous.' *Arsehole*, she added silently. Every time she looked at him she thought of the way he'd spoken to Carol that day.

'You should put something warm on,' said Steve, his eyes on her arms, which were goose-pimpling, Libby realised, looking down.

At that moment a guitar chord sounded from the sky-high speakers on either side of the stage, jangling up and down Libby's spine, and Steve turned back around. Another chord sounded, followed by a crash of drums, and then the driving rhythm of the lead guitar going up and down the scale. The crowd roared, even louder this time and—finally—here came the band, running out on stage, dressed like priests in their golden robes, and the excitement and emotion coursing through the crowd was suddenly almost too much to bear.

'We want ABBA!' Libby screamed, as Benny and Björn ripped off their cloaks and picked up their instruments, and Agnetha and Frida took their places behind their microphones at the front of the stage

They launched into 'Tiger', which, thanks to Summer, Libby knew all the words to. She sang along, encouraging Jasper to make claws with his hands whenever Frida and Agnetha did.

Anna leaned forward to squeeze Leanne's shoulders during the chorus, nuzzling her on the cheek. The next time she did it, on impulse, Libby squeezed Anna's shoulders when she bent forward, making Anna jump. 'Sorry, I got carried away,' Libby was about to say, when Anna whirled around and pounced at her, teeth bared. Libby exploded into laughter.

She turned to Ben, claws at the ready to pounce on him, but he was frowning at his pocket diary again, which he was illuminating with a pocket flashlight.

'What are you doing?' yelled Libby into his ear, leaning over Jasper's head.

He looked up at her, his face creased in worry. 'I have to make a telephone call.'

'What?' Libby swapped places with Jasper and leaned her head close to Ben's. 'Has something happened?'

'I just realised. I have to go make a phone call. There's a telephone booth in the lobby.'

'What? Now? But it's only just started!'

'I'm sorry.' He shook his head at her, obviously contrite. 'I forgot we have a—for Monday.'

'A what?'

'I forgot we have a—'

'It's okay.' She waved his explanations away. Even if she could have heard him, what difference did it make what the details were this time? 'I'll save your seat for you.'

He slipped into the aisle and disappeared into the crowd. Libby turned back to Anna and Jasper, and for the rest of the song they made pouncing cat moves and claw hands at each other as they sang along in unison, ignoring Steve's puzzled backwards glances, the three of them laughing at one another in delight.

Even though she said she loved them, up until that night, Libby had never given ABBA's music much thought. It was fine for the children, but she was more into Patti Smith and Fleetwood Mac. And she'd been to plenty of great concerts, too, but this one was very different. Half the audience, it seemed, were little girls, and they generated a special kind of excitement and magic, Libby quickly learned. They gave their love so generously, screaming their approval at the end of every song and beaming with such sincere excitement at the adults around them that it was impossible not to fall under their spell. Even her cynical Summer had thrown off her poncho and was boogying down. Libby clapped along and swayed in her seat with a kind of girlishness she hadn't thought she was allowed anymore, let alone capable of.

And the girls and Jasper were all being so nice to each other! It was as if they had been replaced by different, even nicer kids— her dream children. Looking from their faces up to the stage, Libby could see it all through their eyes, and when 'Knowing Me, Knowing You' began she found herself reaching for Anna's hand.

Anna glanced at her, frowning quizzically, but her hand stayed in Libby's, and sometime, during 'Tropical Loveland' Libby felt what was left of the walls between them melt entirely away. In the light of this pure beautiful energy she and Anna, and everyone here, were all the same, and everything she'd ever needed was right here.

'Is this real life, Mummy?' asked Jasper as the orchestra began to play the swooping opening bars of 'Dancing Queen'. Summer turned around, and Libby braced herself to hear her say something along the lines of, *Of course it is, you dope!* but instead Summer reached up to hug him, and said, 'Yes it is, Jassie! Isn't it wonderful?' and Libby's heart almost exploded. This was the way she had thought—before she had kids—that family life would always be. Except for Ben not being here, of course. She noticed Anna glancing quizzically at Ben's empty seat, and Libby shrugged her shoulders exaggeratedly at her, and smiled. Anna shrugged exaggeratedly back.

Jasper began to twirl in circles, faster and faster until Libby had to drop Anna's hand to catch him and hold him tight to help him cope with his excitement. Libby's euphoria kept mounting, too; the feeling of hope and optimism that this band, along with the girls and Jasper, were fuelling in her, reminded her of her own innocence and beauty at their age.

'I forgot this feeling existed,' she said to a beaming Anna during a brief pause.

With each song it kept building, until she was wafting on a cloud of joy.

~

Three hours later, as Ben nosed the Kingswood into a parking spot in front of the house, she was still in that state of tired exhilarated wonder that makes you feel as though you will be content forever, and the girls in the back all agreed. Jasper lay fast asleep in the middle of the front seat, his head cradled in Libby's lap.

'Wake up, Jassie,' she whispered.

He opened his eyes dreamily and then closed them again. If she played her cards right she could get him upstairs, out of his soaked clothes and straight into bed without him really waking, Libby calculated. Ben was helping the girls out of the back as she and a stumbling Jasper began walking up the path.

'Mummy!' Colette yelled.

'No, darling, she's at home,' Libby turned around to say, but Colette was pushing past her, slipping dangerously on the path.

'Careful!' cried Libby as Colette hurtled up the stairs and over to the corner of the verandah where Carol sat, surrounded by suitcases and holding a very large cat.

'*Carol?* Are you all right?' Libby peered into the darkness. Had she forgotten to give Colette something? 'What on earth are you doing here with Sampson?'

Carol whispered something to Colette and the two of them came forward to greet them at the top of the stairs.

'Libby, can I talk to you for a second? Privately?'

'Of course,' said Libby, 'as soon as we get all these kids into bed.'

Whatever was going on she seemed calm, Libby saw with relief as she unlocked the front door and they all spilled inside.

'Daddy bought me an ABBA d-d-dress,' Colette was saying as they trooped up the stairs. She was soaked, her dark hair matted against her head and her go-go boots, sparkling white at the start of the night, streaked with mud. 'F-F-Frida!' In her tiredness and excitement Colette had begun stuttering. 'F-Frida f-f-fell over on stage.'

'Oh, dear,' Carol murmured, shepherding her daughter into the bathroom and covering her head with a towel. 'Was she all right?'

'She was incredible,' sighed Colette, when she emerged.

Carol looked pale but clear-headed as Libby knelt beside her on the bathroom tiles to pull Jasper's sopping jumper over his head. *What on earth was going on?*

~

'How are you doing?' asked Libby, knocking lightly before stepping into the guest bedroom, which Strauss had left as neat as a little cell. Carol was sitting upright in the single bed, wearing pink candy-striped pyjamas with a towel wound around her head, cradling a purring Sampson. Her suitcases were already stacked neatly in the corner, and her wet clothes hung up on the curtain rod to dry.

'They're all asleep. I just checked,' said Libby, handing her a mug of tea. Libby was dressed in her tartan PJ's, and Ugg boots.

'Thank you for taking Colette tonight. Thank you for also taking me in,' said Carol. She held her elbow out wide as she sipped her tea, careful not to disturb Sampson. 'I want you to know my plan tonight was to find somewhere for us to stay for the next week or so, and then tomorrow I was going to pick up Colette.'

'Of course you were,' said Libby, soothingly.

'Now of course I can't understand what I was thinking,' sighed Carol. 'I certainly never dreamed I'd wind up here tonight. In your lovely guest bedroom,' she added, looking around.

'You did exactly the right thing.'

The walls of the little room were whitewashed brick, and the floor just tiles with rush matting. Red-and-white gingham curtains shut out the rainy night outside, and the bedside lamp cast a rosy glow on the thick wooden beams of the ceiling.

'Steve's phoned. Twice actually,' Libby said reluctantly, sorry to break the cosy mood.

'I thought I heard it ringing. He must have just got home.'

'He wants to come over, but Ben's persuaded him to give you a few days. To clear your head.'

Carol closed her eyes for a moment and took a deep breath, before opening them again. 'You're so kind. And I'm so sorry to put you in this position—you and Ben.'

'Oh Carol, please don't worry about that! I feel honoured that you thought of me. Ben wasn't sure what else to tell him, though. He said Steve seemed very surprised.'

'Yes. Well.' Carol looked down at her hands.

'Is it that, maybe, you just need a little break? Steve said something to Ben about what a hard time you had coming out here, on the boat.'

'He did?' replied Carol, her face becoming an even whiter shade of pale.

'Do you ... I mean, would you like to talk about it?' Libby asked gently.

Wordlessly Carol shook her head. Her fingers were white as they clutched her mug.

'Of course, that's okay, too.' Libby forced herself to smile to cover her pang of disappointment. She'd promised herself she wouldn't ask nosy questions, but it was so warm and intimate in here. 'Has it been very terrible? It must be for you to come here like this, in the rain,' she rushed on. 'Oh Carol. I had no idea!' She'd been planning to follow Ben's advice, to mind her own business, to wait for Carol to tell her what she wanted, when she wanted— but now that seemed like a very cold resolution to have made. 'I'm always here for you, if you want to, you know, to talk.'

'Thank you, Libby, truly, from the bottom of my heart, but I don't think I can at the moment,' said Carol, dabbing the corner of each eye with her lace-trimmed handkerchief, which someone had embroidered with an elaborate 'C', surrounded by tiny pink roses. 'Least said, soonest mended.' She flashed Libby a brave smile.

'All right then. I'm always here if you need me,' said Libby, impulsively leaning forward to kiss Carol goodnight on the cheek, before closing the door quietly behind her.

'I think Carol should stay here,' said Libby breathlessly as she walked into the living room. 'I mean, for more than just a few days.'

'In this madhouse?' Ben yawned. He'd changed into his red velour tracksuit and was lying down on the floor, stretching out his back on the beanbag. 'We shouldn't take sides. Besides, she'll probably just go back to him anyway. It's what women in these cases nearly always do.'

'*In these cases?*' The way he was just lying there, looking so carefree—she suddenly felt the urge to go over and kick him, but she kept her voice calm. 'She's my friend, Ben. And if she did go back, it would most likely be because she literally has nowhere else to go.'

The beanbag rustled as he turned over onto his stomach. 'I'm just saying I don't think we should interfere.'

'Interfere? She came to us, in a thunderstorm.' It made Libby's heart hurt, to think of what that must have been like for Carol.

Ben groaned as he stretched his arms above his head. 'Those bloody seats.'

Typical Ben. Libby had just had her mind blown at that concert, and he was whingeing about the seats.

'What are you talking about?' she said, trying to keep her tone light. 'You were only sitting in them for one song.' He'd been gone for almost the whole concert, only returning, all smiles and mouthed apologies, just before the finale.

'I was sitting in one next to the phone booth,' said Ben, sounding slightly wounded.

And suddenly Libby could feel all the peace and goodwill she'd been tripping out on all evening fade away. 'Gosh, that must have been hard for you.'

'It was fine.' He shrugged stoically, ignoring her sarcasm. 'What's been the matter, anyway?' he asked curiously. 'With Carol, I mean?'

'I don't know,' said Libby cautiously. 'I think she's been very unhappy.'

'Unhappy.' Ben snorted.

'Yes, Ben, unhappy. ' Libby felt another surge of irritation flash through her. 'Why? Is happiness a bit much to ask?'

'Steve seems okay to me,' he shrugged.

'But you're not married to Steve.' There was no mistaking the acid in her tone.

'You said she drinks a lot.'

'No, I didn't! I said she was drinking a glass of cider, that one day.'

'You said she was very emotional, and that you wondered if maybe she had a problem.'

'Well, and so what? Now I wish I hadn't told you!'

'What is your problem?' Ben climbed to his feet, the picture of injured innocence.

'What business is it of yours to sit here and judge her, or her reasons for leaving?' Libby hissed. 'If she decides to go then it's her right to go and it doesn't matter what you or anyone else thinks about it.'

'Okay, all right? Seriously, Libby, you need to mellow out.'

'You know, whenever you say that to me, you can count on it having the opposite effect.'

Libby turned on her heel and stalked out of the living room. This kept happening between them, she thought as she climbed the stairs. A simple conversation could suddenly become charged and electric, making her chest flutter and her forehead prickle with anticipation.

'All the same, I think a child needs her father,' said Ben, following her into the bedroom a few moments later, as though there'd been no pause in their conversation and they hadn't just been fighting.

'If that's true,' said Libby, rounding on him, 'then why weren't you at the concert with us tonight?'

'What are you talking about?'

'What was your call about?' She went to stand in front of their full-length mirror and began roughly brushing out her hair.

'You mean at the concert? I told you. It was work. I'm not having an affair, if that's what you're wondering,' he said quietly, coming to stand close behind her.

'I wouldn't think you would be,' said Libby tartly, moving away from him. That part of their life together had always been good. 'That's not what I'm asking,' she said. 'What was the call about? Tell me honestly!' she added, because she could see from his face that he was about to lie.

'Okay, if you must know, I had an idea for a new project.'

'A new project,' she said wonderingly. *So there was no emergency.* 'It couldn't wait until Monday?'

He looked away, and suddenly, without warning, Libby's anger turned into grief.

'It could,' said Libby, her voice breaking. 'Of course it could. You just didn't want to be there.'

She pressed hard with the heels of her hands against her eyes, to staunch the tears that were suddenly gathering there.

'I did, Lib. Really I did!' He was panicking now, as taken aback as she was by the rush of her emotion. 'I just had the idea while I was sitting there and thought I should tell Parker about it before he got caught up with something else!'

'It's Friday night,' she said finally, once she'd managed to catch her breath. She blew her nose, balled up her handkerchief and threw it into the laundry basket. 'You thought he might get caught up with something else before Monday?'

He looked away, shamefaced. 'I'm sorry.'

She shook her head at him, lost for words as she changed into her nightie. He wasn't doing it on purpose, realised Libby, as she emerged from behind their Japanese changing screen. She knew enough about his heart to know he didn't mean for her to feel this way. But none of that mattered anymore. He was doing it anyway, and nothing she did or said would change that.

She sat down on the bed heavily. 'Well, you missed a great evening. It was a huge experience for me. For our whole family, really. It was one of those nights I'll always remember.'

'Really, Lib?' He sat down next to her on the bed and took her hand. 'Well in that case I'm even more sorry. Will you tell me about it, in the morning maybe, with the kids?'

'You won't be here. You told me you had to see Parker about that other thing, remember?'

'Bloody hell,' said Ben. 'That's right. I'll cancel.'

'No, you should go. It doesn't matter anymore,' she said, flapping her hand at him.

Libby lay down and searched for the hot water bottle, which she'd placed there earlier, with her feet. She was glad that Carol was downstairs with Sampson, all safe and cosy in this driving rain. It was nice to think they'd be together in the kitchen in the morning, and that it wouldn't be just her usual Saturday morning alone with the children.

A moment later she felt Ben's arms stealing around her waist, and his warm breath against her neck as he moved closer, the whiskers of his beard making her earlobes prickle. So he felt it too, thought Libby, as she allowed herself to be held by him. The electricity in the air all around them, like a cable arcing, just waiting to make contact with something flammable and burn.

5

Anna

ANNA RIFLED THROUGH THE DRAWERS OF her antique cedar tallboy. Not the leopard print, and never the sequins. Whoever thought sequins on fancy underwear were a good idea didn't have skin. Not the satin, even though it was beautiful. She let her fingers linger over the coffee-coloured handmade lace for a moment before nudging it aside. Too modest. She needed something different. Wait, how about . . . Her fingers found the box she'd bought a few weeks ago, still in its brown paper wrapping at the bottom of her drawer. She'd seen the ad in the back of another of those women's magazines they kept in reception, and she'd sent away for it as a surprise. She stifled a giggle as she pulled off the string.

'Honey?'

'Shh, sorry, darling.'

'What are you doing?'

'Nothing.' She giggled again. 'A surprise!'

Myles switched on his bedside light, rubbing his eyes as he peered at her across the room. 'What are you wearing? Is that an ABBA dress?'

She looked down at her breasts, jutting out pertly between the folds of the simple blue cotton wrap dress she'd bought on impulse earlier this evening at the concert.

'It might be.' She flashed herself a foxy glance, narrowing her eyes and touching her tongue to her lip as she lit the three candles on top of the dresser with a cigarette lighter, and tripped over to Myles's bedside in her fluffy mules, putting a hand out to steady herself as she struck a pose next to where he lay on the mattress, folding one leg over the other, and placing her hands on her knee like a cartoon fairy. 'Look,' she said, arching her back a little and placing both fingers on one nipple. '*Wow*, it says. See that? And this says *Sexy*.' Delicately she traced her fingers over the other.

'Hang on.' Myles reached for his glasses, peering at the red cloud decals cut out in a starburst pattern. 'So it does. Is that suitable for children, do you think?'

'No, Myles, I told them where to iron on the decals. Anyway, do you like?' She arched her back again, slipping back into character.

'I like,' he grinned, leaning back in the bed and placing his hands behind his head.

'You're a very attractive man.' She leaned forward and put her hand on his chest. His skin felt soft and the hair covering his muscles rough. As she stroked her hand down his chest she felt a flutter of desire for him. Faint, like an echo, but there.

'And what do we have under here?' she asked, pulling at the sheet with the tip of her finger. 'Oh!' she exclaimed, starting back and then looking again, putting up a hand as though to shield her gaze. He grinned again, his eyes warm, his hands still folded behind his head. He was wearing blue cotton underpants, somewhat faded, and . . . black cotton socks. She sighed.

'I know! James Bond doesn't wear socks,' Myles said.

'Well, he doesn't,' said Anna reprovingly. 'But you know, that can be easily . . . rectified.' She slid her hand down his strong, muscular legs and slipped her fingers underneath the elastic. She fumbled as he put his foot up to help her while she tried to pull it off. 'It's okay, I'll do it,' he said, leaning down to efficiently take off one, then the other, and folding them into a little ball and placing them in his bedside-table drawer. She slumped a little, wishing he hadn't rolled them into that little ball.

'Now,' he said, folding his hands behind his head again, 'where were we?'

'I was about to seduce you,' Anna rallied, but a change of tempo was in order, she decided, so she got up off the bed and stood with her back to him, her arms and her legs spread wide. 'Rip it off!' she commanded.

'The dress, you mean?'

'Like the ABBA girls do, on stage. It does up with a bow at the side here, see? You have to rip it!'

She felt his hands untie the bow at her waist and then she sensed him hesitate. She was teetering now, on the verge of finding this whole scenario ridiculous.

'Like this?'

She glanced down to where he was holding up one of the sashes.

'No, Myles!' Anna was frustrated now, but she tried to make it a part of her act. She put her hands on her hips and pouted. 'You have to rip it!' She took hold of one of the sashes and pulled it so hard that she smashed her hand against the edge of the bedside table—but no matter—and twirled away from him dressed just in her mules, her bra and undies.

'Wow!' said Myles. 'I mean, wow.' He sat up, and pulled his glasses down to look at her. 'Smooth move, and you look beautiful, darling. So, you had fun tonight, I take it?'

'Yes, I had fun. But that's an understatement. I had—' She put her arms up in the air and twirled, 'a revelation.'

'A revelation?'

'Yes. But I don't want to talk about that now. I want to . . .' She ran her hands down the sides of her body, her head cocked as she looked at him. 'You know.'

'Well, I'm flattered,' he said.

But he didn't make a move. He didn't do anything. In her fantasy of how this would go on the way home in the car, he ought to have pounced on her by now.

Not that he'd ever pounced. She tried to look gracious as she sat down next to him again on the edge of the bed. He was more of a cuddly lover, usually. Undressing her underneath the sheets, and asking her 'Is that good?' and 'Is this okay?' like a doctor, pressing first this and then that experimentally.

'I want to drive you wild,' Anna said now, tickling him delicately under the chin.

Myles caught hold of her fingers and kissed them. 'You do drive me wild.'

'With desire,' she clarified.

He smiled, and gave her fingers back to her. Nothing obvious. Nothing mean. But clear.

She took a deep breath. 'Myles, I . . . what can I do to please you?'

'You do please me.'

'No, you know. I mean, *please* you.'

'Why don't we lie down?' he suggested, reaching to turn off the light switch. 'Why don't you let me—'

'No!' She stopped his hand. 'I mean, not tonight,' she said, making her voice more gentle. 'I want to do something different. The girls are away at Libby's until the morning, and I thought we could . . . try some new things.'

Was that a frown that momentarily crossed his forehead? 'But you're tired, maybe,' she added quickly. 'I mean, I just woke you up. Maybe you . . .'

'No, no,' he said, shaking himself and sitting up more. 'What did you have in mind?'

'Well, I thought we should leave the light on, for a start. And you should let me seduce you, for a change, instead of you always . . . taking care of me.'

'Sounds good,' he smiled gamely.

The trouble was, the mood was wrong, Anna decided. She'd been feeling so confident, so exhilarated. *You could look like Agnetha!* she'd told herself on the way up the stairs, flashing herself one of those shy yet utterly enchanting glances Agnetha specialised in. But now she felt it all trickling away, along with that stirring of desire for Myles that was becoming ever fainter now.

'I know!' She stood up and padded over to the dresser drawers and brought back the brown parcel. 'Look what I've got.'

His expression changed, his eyes widening and his frown deepening.

'You're right to be worried,' she said, tearing at the taped edges. 'This is going to blow your . . . What is it?'

'Where did you get that?' Myles's voice was rough as he tore it out of her hands.

'What? This?' Anna stared at him. 'It's ... it's my parcel,' she stuttered. What was going on? His face had paled, and the package between them, the size of a shoe box, seemed suddenly as incendiary as a bomb. 'It's my mail order.'

'No, it isn't.'

'Yes, it is,' said Anna, pulling at the strings and tearing off the paper. Myles had surrendered now, his hands sitting limp on his knees. 'I ordered some sexy lingerie, you'll see, crotchless, very dirty.' She flashed a half-hearted smile at him. 'Along with a—' She took off the top of the box. 'A lace-up bra,' she whispered, staring. 'And a . . . a . . .' Her voice died away. 'What's this?'

'Magazines,' said Myles. His arms were crossed across his chest, one hand covering his mouth, his expression studiously neutral, just the widening of his eyes signalling things weren't completely as normal.

'I can see that.' Leaving them in the box, she flicked some of the pages. 'These are men's magazines.'

Their eyes met and he nodded.

She swallowed. *Hot hot hot!* it said in big white writing across the top. A tanned blond man, naked except for a horned helmet and a pair of studded leather straps across his chest, was looking down his gorgeous Viking chest at . . . another man, who had his head buried in the Viking's crotch. 'For men.' She swallowed. 'Right?'

'Right,' Myles croaked.

'Are they all?' Still keeping them in their box, she lifted one and then the next, and then the next, seeing at a glance that they all featured men doing explicit things—oh god, from behind, one of them, which was something she'd never seen a photo of before—and it made her flush again, just the shock of seeing something on the page like that, which she'd heard about and knew about, of course, but never actually seen.

'But why did the package have my name on it?'

'I'm sorry,' said Myles, still neutral and serious. 'It was careless of me.'

They could have been discussing a situation at work.

'I should have intercepted it,' he went on. 'I wasn't sure where it had gone, and I assumed it had gone missing somehow, at the post office, I mean. That happens sometimes. And of course I couldn't really enquire.'

'Of course you couldn't. You could have been arrested if they found you with this. You could lose your job at the tax department. You could be sent to prison! I could be sent to prison!'

Myles smiled sadly. 'I don't think they'd take it quite that far.'

She felt dazed, but thoughts were coming back to her. Unwelcome thoughts, from far away. Like the echo of her desire earlier, but now with the hot flash of something sulphurous.

'It's just porn, Anna,' said Myles, softly.

'Then why isn't this about, I don't know, Big Boozies, or Hot Pussy? Why is this full of naked men?'

He shook his head, still covering his mouth with his hand. Because this is what he wanted, Anna realised. Because this made sense of everything.

'Before me. Were you ever with a man?' Her voice sounded faint to her.

'No. I would have told you, if I had been.'

'Did you think about it? *Well?*' she insisted, when he wouldn't answer. 'Did you fantasise? Did you look at gay porn before we married? Did you go to those movies?' He kept shaking his head, his hand still covering his mouth.

Because he was lying. She knew from her job, what the signs were to look for.

'Myles,' her voice dropped to a whisper, 'what are you doing with me?'

'I love you.' He took his hand away from his mouth at last.

'Did you ever love a man, though? Before me?'

'I told you. You know.'

They both looked up at the framed black-and-white photograph of a man smiling, with a hint of Frank Sinatra about him—that same cheeky happiness, his ears the only clumsy thing about him, sticking out on either side of his military cap. It had occupied pride of place on Myles's dresser for as long as she had known him. They had met as new recruits for the war in Vietnam, Myles had told her, on their first date. The first time she and Myles had slept together he'd shown her the bracelet he kept of his friend, with his army identity tags on it, in his bedside-table drawer.

'Were you a couple?' she asked now.

'What? With John? No! No, Anna! We were fighting a war!'

'Do you think he wanted to be, though? In a couple, with you?' Suddenly whole vistas of information were opening up before her. Explaining missing pieces and mysterious feelings, and putting them into place.

'I don't think so. I don't know. He was married.' Myles shrugged, hopelessly.

'Did you talk about it? Did you touch each other? Or anything?'

'Anna!' Myles covered his face, and when he took his hands away she saw that he was crying. She had never seen him cry, not even when Michelle had a febrile convulsion once, as a baby, and turned blue. 'I can't talk about this. You know I can't!'

'I know he died,' said Anna softly. 'And you know how sorry I am about that.' He'd been killed by friendly fire, two weeks before the end of the war, during a final training exercise. Myles had talked with her about it just the once, speaking rapidly, the first time she'd stayed with him in his little bedsit, and then he'd asked her never to talk about it again.

'But . . . I need to know what this means for me, Myles. Can't you see that?' She shivered, cold suddenly in just her underwear and mules, and she reached down for the ABBA dress and draped it around her shoulders.

'It means I loved him,' he whispered. 'And then I fell in love with you.'

'But what about these?' She looked at the magazines. They'd shocked her at first, but now they merely looked like people, hopefully happy in their work as porn actors, hopefully turning each other on. But it was harder for men to fake that, wasn't it? She cringed, thinking of the way she'd run her hands down Myles's legs, and twirled in front of him. Thinking of how the bulge in his underpants had remained resolutely flat. 'Is that why you always want the light off?' She tried to keep her tone gentle, not wanting to scare him with the feelings that were threatening her. 'Is that why you stopped wanting me, after the girls?'

'I didn't stop wanting you, Anna. But after seeing that . . . you went through so much! I knew I had to be gentle.'

'Oh, will you please shut up about gentle? That's what vaginas are for!'

'Don't speak like that. It's not like you.'

'It *is* like me! It's like me now. I want to be real about things, Myles. I want us to be truthful.'

'What's real is that I only love you, Anna,' he said, putting the cover on the box, and putting it to one side. 'I only want you.'

'But you don't,' she said, taking the lid back off the box again and pulling the magazines onto her lap. Now the sight of the men, so into it and unselfconscious and absorbed, reminded her of what it had been like at the ABBA concert, when she, along with everyone else in the crowd, had been so carried away with delight and joy. They seemed to symbolise everything that she'd never had, but wanted, so badly.

'You don't want me,' she said flatly.

'I love you, Anna. I love you. And we're happy. And we're good.'

'No, we're not.' She thrust herself away from him and looked around at the candles on the tallboy, and the drawer filled with lingerie, and everything she'd been taking such pleasure in. 'We're fake. Look. All of this. It's fake.' She picked up the box and threw it on the floor with such force it split apart, the magazines sprawling. Anna picked one up and threw it in the bin, and then she kicked the other two underneath the bed. 'It's all fake and I can't stand it!' She put her hands to her mouth.

'Anna, don't do that,' Myles said, standing up and coming after her.

She felt like she might be about to scream. This feeling inside, so strong and huge, as though the top might blow off her head. But then she caught sight of herself in the mirror, her hair mussed now and her mascara running and she looked fake, too, like an actor, doing a not very good job of chewing up the scenery.

'Oh, to hell with it,' she said, picking up her nightie and walking into the bathroom.

'Anna!' Myles called, knocking roughly but half-heartedly, and after a few more taps on the door she heard him walk away.

She stood in the shower for a long time, letting the water run down her hair and between her breasts, the way it had tonight at the concert, when it had started to rain halfway through 'Tropical Loveland' and she and Libby and Jasper had all grabbed each other's hands. Before tonight, she had always thought of it as a sublimely silly song, but as the plunking chords came lilting out, she felt the walls between herself and everyone else in the crowd—and every other being in the universe, maybe—melt away.

Anna had made a decision in that moment: she would never pretend to be something she wasn't ever again. She would never refuse to acknowledge reality, just because it didn't fit in with her perfect picture, because reality had the potential to make her happy in a way that a perfect picture never could. *I am going to be real*, she had vowed, tears streaming down her cheeks and mixing with the rain, as the two angels on stage—one from the dark side and one from the light; both necessary, both beautiful—serenaded the crowd.

6

Libby

'I WISH YOU COULD STAY HERE. For longer than a few days, I mean,' said Libby the next morning, recklessly, to Carol. 'The kids would love it. And so would I,' she added in a rush. 'Honestly.'

'But Ben would never allow that, would he?' Carol was up and dressed already, in tight, high-waisted jeans and a pink angora sweater. 'I mean *like*, he wouldn't like that,' Carol corrected herself quickly. 'And I could never intrude.'

Libby sighed, both relieved and disappointed that Carol guessed the score.

'Well, at least let me lend you some money,' said Libby. She'd been going to say give but at the last minute something about Carol's expression checked her. 'I can take it from a little nest egg I have, from my dad.'

'That might come in really handy, thank you,' said Carol softly.

She wasn't going to cry again, was she? worried Libby, pressing on. 'I could help you look for a little flat, if you like I could drive you around with the kids once they're up; check out the real-estate listings.'

Phew, no tears. Carol smiled, and this time her expression was soft and sparkling. 'I've always dreamed about my own little flat. Nothing grand or anything. Just mine.'

'I wish I could do more . . .'

'No, really,' said Carol firmly. 'And please let's not talk about it anymore. I wouldn't have left if I didn't have to. You've been such a help to me, Libby. Truly. I don't know what I would have done without you.'

'But I've done nothing, really.'

This brave, heroic Carol only made Libby feel more protective when she walked into the kitchen a few minutes later saying, 'Now tell me, who doesn't like pancakes?'

Anna arrived to collect Michelle and Leanne when Jasper and the girls were only halfway through breakfast—chatting and singing and flicking tightly wadded balls of pancake at each other—and so the women went out into the hallway to talk.

'Carol, we missed you last night,' said Anna, after she and Libby greeted each other with shy smiles. 'Are you feeling better?'

'It was just a cold, wasn't it?' said Libby quickly, keen to shore up Carol's alibi.

'I've run away,' said Carol, at the same time. 'I've left Steve,' she added firmly.

'Really?' said Anna, tilting her head.

Libby frowned at Anna. Why didn't she say something sympathetic like, *I'm so sorry*, or *That's rough*? It's not that hard to commiserate, is it? 'We're off to find Carol a little flat after breakfast,' she said brightly. 'Somewhere close by, hopefully.'

'Just a little bedsit, or anything, really,' said Carol, following Libby's lead, 'as long as it's safe and clean.'

'You know, that's actually quite odd,' said Anna.

'It's not, really.' Libby should have known, from the way Ben was last night, how Anna might react. But she still felt disappointed.

'Huh.' Anna regarded Carol thoughtfully.

Libby braced herself for the next thing she was probably about to say. Something like, *I know divorce is terribly trendy these days*, or, *I always think the kids of single mothers have it especially hard*, which was a favourite of her mum's. But Anna didn't say anything. She just kept studying Carol.

Carol and Libby exchanged glances.

'Anna, are you stoned?' said Libby, finally. 'You're acting weird.'

'I'm sorry.' Anna laughed, a deep husky laugh that Libby had only heard for the first time yesterday. 'It's odd, because I've also left my husband, and because I'm also moving out.'

'But why?' Libby choked a few minutes later, after the children had come pouring out of the kitchen in a swarm to inspect a butterfly house Leanne claimed to have found in the back garden. Libby, Carol and Anna had pulled up chairs around the table in the wreckage of the kitchen.

'My marriage is a sham. We've only had sex four times in the last six years.'

Libby gasped. Anna of the perfect husband and the perfect house and the perfect family? Who was good at everything? Or wanted you to think that she was, anyway. Libby knew it was awful of her, but she felt a flash of satisfaction to have something, at least, that Anna didn't have.

'And then last night I discovered Myles's stash of homosexual pornography.'

Libby gasped again. The way she just came out and said these things, as though she wasn't the kind of person who sent out printed dinner invitations on scented paper, and carried fresh grapes around in sealed containers. As though this wasn't something to hide.

She must have taken drugs, Libby decided. She used to see people at the pub tripping out on acid who behaved like this, trying to fool you that they weren't off their heads by being more proper than any normal person could ever possibly be. It was her matching chunky jewellery that was the giveaway. Who makes sure their earrings match their necklace before 9 a.m. on a weekend, except someone trying to pretend they're with it? But Anna didn't seem like the druggy type, though. Unless someone had spiked her Tab last night, maybe?

'It's not just the lack of sex, though,' said Anna. 'It's that I haven't even missed it.'

'Well, everybody's different,' said Carol kindly, not missing a beat.

'But I *miss* missing it,' said Anna. She banged her fist down on the table like a three-year-old. 'I want to miss it!'

'Anna, are you drunk?' asked Libby desperately.

'Libby! Will you stop? I never take drugs, and I've never felt more sober in my life. Although I have to admit, since the concert last night I've been feeling kind of . . . enchanted.'

Now that Libby thought about it, Anna had been behaving strangely last night as well: hugging them all for that few extra moments too long when they said goodbye; and playing game after game of hide-and-seek with Jasper in the carpark while Ben was off getting the car, until Jasper was the one who finally had to say he was too tired—which was unheard of for Jasper. Libby had appreciated it, of course, but surely that was out of character; and when it came to dealing with all of her camping paraphernalia Anna had brought, she said they should just leave it in a pile next to the entrance for a needy person, and it had been Libby who had neatly folded up all the plastic ponchos and made sure all those frighteningly expensive little Tupperware containers came home.

'What are you going to do about the girls?' Carol asked.

'I'm moving into our investment property—it's on Avon Street, so just around the corner really—so they'll still see their dad all the time.'

'Aren't you worried about how they'll cope?' Carol frowned.

'They're going to have an even better life,' said Anna breezily. 'It's much better for children to live with two parents who are happy and separated, than together and miserable. All the latest research backs that up.'

'But what if the research is wrong?' Carol's hands were clenched into fists, noticed Libby, and her shoulders held almost rigid.

'Wrong?' laughed Anna. 'It's in published peer-reviewed scientific papers. I doubt they could be wrong.' Anna shook her hair out, like a girl in a shampoo commercial, and lifted up her chin. 'But if, for some reason, we are a statistical anomaly and it is bad for the children, this is just an experiment—that's what I said to Myles—and we can always go back.' She looked at Carol. 'Just a thought: why don't you and Colette move in with me?'

'But you two don't even know each other,' objected Libby, before she'd even had a chance to think. 'Do you?' She looked from one to the other, unsteadily.

'Just at school,' said Anna, smiling at Carol.

'Just to say hi,' said Carol, with a friendly nod back at Anna.

'But wouldn't this be a little ... premature?' asked Libby. A knot was tightening in her stomach and her heart was fluttering in her chest.

'Well, I hardly know you, Libby,' Carol pointed out, 'and I've wound up in your guest bedroom.'

'Anyone I find to move in with is bound to be someone I don't know very well,' said Anna philosophically. 'And the beauty of this arrangement is that the girls can support each other, as friends, at such a time of big transition in their lives.'

'Colette's been very lonely,' said Carol, her voice lowered, as though it must be some big secret, thought Libby, her irritation rising.

I think this is all moving way too fast, Libby was about to say, but now the children were approaching from the back garden, their voices high and animated, their feet thundering in the passageway.

'Kids, why don't you go and watch some cartoons in the living room?' called Libby, diverting the girls off down the hallway, but Jasper stood still in the doorway of the kitchen, looking at her. 'You too, Jasper,' she said meaningfully, but he stared stubbornly right back. He could always tell when something big was going down.

'We can move in tomorrow morning, if we want, as soon as the fumes from the pest control have cleared,' said Anna, her voice lowered.

'And the rent?' asked Carol quietly.

Did Carol realise how cheap it was? Libby wondered, as Anna ran through some numbers. Anna was basically offering Carol charity, or else the place must be a dump. But Libby could tell, by the way Carol was nodding seriously, that whether she understood that or not, she was accepting it.

'Carol, I thought you wanted to find a place on your own,' said Libby, thinking with a pang of regret of the little flat she'd been imagining for her.

'I didn't know something like *this* might be on offer.' Now Carol was looking at her as if *she* were acting strangely. 'But are you sure there's going to be enough room?' asked Carol, turning back to Anna.

'My god, yes,' said Anna. 'There will still be three bedrooms spare, off the hallway, even after we've all moved in.'

'I thought you said it wasn't a mansion!' said Libby.

'Believe me, it's not,' Anna laughed. 'The rooms are tiny. It used to be a boarding house before we gutted it. But as Myles likes to say, it has good bones. We can look for another tenant when we feel like it,' she said, including Libby in her smile.

At that moment Jasper chose to put a leaf into his mouth.

'I'm so happy for you, Carol. I'm so happy for you both,' gabbled Libby, grabbing Jasper by the hand and pulling him over to the pantry, where she discovered the girls had spilled a fresh batch of pancake mix all over her cork tiles. It wasn't until ten minutes later—after she'd directed the commencement of clean-up operations and performed a leaf extraction—that she was able to sit down.

'Libby, are you all right?' asked Carol. 'You look pale.'

'I'm fine,' said Libby, forcing herself to smile gamely up at them all.

Don't leave me here! she wanted to say to them. The words felt as if they were bursting out of her mouth, and she clenched her teeth tightly to hold them in.

~

'Finally,' said Libby that evening as she walked into the living room. Autumn had swept in with the rain last night, and this was the first chance she'd had to wear her new dressing gown, made from the wool of Peruvian mountain goats, which she'd hand spun and knitted last year. With its long black threads hanging out everywhere and the way it had turned out a little lopsided, she felt a bit like a wild woolly mountain goat herself.

Ben was sitting in the Eames chair, which he'd pulled over to the stereo. That chair had been his big centrepiece gift to her for their tenth wedding anniversary, thought Libby, but he was the only one who ever used it. She was more of a beanbag person.

'Hey, hon.' She tapped him on the shoulder and he smiled, lifting up one of his headphones. The tinny sounds of harpsichord music came pouring out. One of the things she'd liked about Ben in the first place was that he didn't watch sport, but it turned out Radio National was just as bad. 'Can we talk?' she asked him.

'Would you mind if we didn't, tonight, darling? It's been an exhausting week.'

She watched as he reached over to the stereo and carefully readjusted the volume.

'I have to tell you something,' she said conversationally, reaching over to turn the volume back down again.

'Huh?' He lifted up one of the headphones again.

She leaned down to aim her mouth at his ear. 'I said we need to talk!'

'Ow! No need to shout at me!'

'Take off your headphones, then!'

He watched her warily out of the corner of his eye as he slowly removed them and balanced them carefully on the lid of the record player.

'So sorry to disturb you,' said Libby, flashing him a glittering smile.

'Is this about cleaning up the kitchen?' asked Ben suspiciously, peering up at her. 'Because you said you didn't need help.'

'No! Ben!' They weren't one of those couples who almost came to blows arguing about the housework. 'Ugh!'

'It's just that it's a live performance,' he said thinly.

'Oh stuff it, then. Listen to your music.'

Libby watched as he blew her a kiss and put back on the headphones.

So much for her fancy speech about her feelings and his feelings and the differences between a man and a woman which she'd been preparing for all day.

'I've just decided,' said Libby, moving around to stand directly in front of him and drawing herself up so that she was towering over him. 'I'm leaving.' She reached over to the stereo and turned up the volume. 'No, no. Don't get up,' she said, as he ripped off his headphones. 'There's nothing more to say really, except that I am so sick of this.'

He followed her out of the living room and up the stairs to their bedroom, where now they would have to conduct their argument in whispers or risk waking the kids. Libby wondered wearily if it would be too ridiculous to go back down to the living room, where he would surely trail after her, to finish their argument there.

'What on earth has got into you?' he hissed, closing their bedroom door.

'I don't have to do this either,' she said, tearing off her bracelets and rings and dropping them into her bedside-table drawer. 'I don't have to live this way.'

'What way? What's wrong with the way you live?'

'I have been trying to tell you,' she said, ripping off her skirt so roughly that the zipper broke.

Ben sat on the edge of the bed and leaned over to pick up one of his architecture books. 'I'm trying, too, Lib. I'm trying my hardest,' he said resignedly. 'What more do you want from me?'

'For you . . .' *To want to be with me*, Libby was about to say, but she refused to be drawn into another pointless fight. *No more begging*, she promised herself.

'Look.' She tried to make her voice sound kind and reasonable. 'Anna and Carol have that house down the road I told you about. I'm going to move in with them if they'll have me. They've got three bedrooms going spare—it's like a miracle, really—and I really don't want to miss out.'

He was still frowning at her the way he had been downstairs, as though seconds had just passed since she interrupted him listening to his music. 'Look, Lib, I'm sorry for what happened downstairs, okay? But we're both tired, and this is crazy.'

'I know, I get it, and I'm sure you're right.' Suddenly she felt unbelievably weary. 'Please don't make me argue.'

'Make you argue? Are you out of your mind?'

'That's trying to make me argue,' she said, feeling for her hot water bottle with her feet. 'Can you please not sleep in here tonight?'

He slowly put his architecture book down, as if he was only just now understanding that this was real. 'But we've never not slept in the same bed.'

'Ben, please, I can't talk about this anymore, okay?' She rolled onto her side and pulled the doona up to her chin.

'Anymore?' His voice echoed plaintively around the walls of their bare bedroom, like a child's. 'I still don't understand what we're talking about.'

'Which just goes to show,' Libby muttered, adjusting her pillow with some loud thwacks. She had thought she would be too wound up to feel sleepy, but the effort of their late night last night and then her big day today washed over her as soon as she closed her eyes.

'Let's talk about this more in the morning,' she managed to say, just as she was dropping off to sleep. Dimly she heard him shuffling out of the room. But there were no words left to be said, she reminded herself dreamily. She just had to do this, before she lost her nerve.

~

'Summer. Jasper. You know your dad and I love you very much.'

She needed to do it before she could change her mind, Libby had told herself again as soon as she woke up. But then breakfast had taken ages, and Ben had yet another work emergency which meant he had to spend ages talking on the phone—Libby secretly wondered if he might be procrastinating, hoping that if he waited long enough she might change her mind—and so it was almost midday by the time they were all gathered in the living room.

'I know what you're going to say,' said Summer, fixing her with that look which had terrified Libby ever since Summer was a baby.

Ben was standing beside the children, who were perched on the green velvet pouf. Libby was facing them, sitting on the edge of the Eames chair next to Ben's aquarium. She wouldn't have to remember to feed the fish anymore, she realised, in that strange, disconnected way she'd been thinking ever since she woke up this morning, knowing that she had to do this. Or maybe ever since Anna had appeared in the hallway yesterday, like a fairy godmother, offering them a house. Or maybe ever since she'd been so drunk with delight when Jasper started to whirl in front of her at the concert during 'Dancing Queen'. Or maybe ever since she and Ben had been to that couples' consciousness-raising group and she had felt that 'click' of understanding, as if a light had been switched on, which cast an unflattering glow over everything as she listened to the other women talk.

'You're going to say you're leaving Dad, and moving in with Carol and Anna and the girls,' said Summer laconically. 'Colette already told me.'

'But, sweetie, how could she know, when I didn't even know myself until last night?'

Summer tossed her hair over her shoulder, importantly. 'She heard you all talking about it, in the hall.'

'Honey, just because we were talking about her mother doing it, doesn't mean I was going to do it, too.'

'But you are.'

Libby rubbed her temples, defeated by her logic.

'I told you, kids know everything,' added Ben, casting her a black look, as though this was also somehow her fault.

'The most important thing to know is that we love you very much, and that's not going to change,' she rallied, sticking to the script she'd cribbed from her ancient *Dr Spock's* this morning. 'Your father and I still care about each other, too, and that's not going to change either.'

'So why are you splitting up?' asked Summer, already bored apparently, picking at the seam in the leg of her corduroy jeans.

'It's complicated,' Libby began.

'You're going to say one day I'll understand. And then you're going to say it's not our fault.'

'Where do you get all this?' Libby burst out.

'From school.' Summer shrugged.

'Well, anyway, it's true,' said Libby, winded.

Jasper was sitting on the pouf in the middle, gazing around at them all, not yet understanding what was going on but definitely interested.

'Are you done now?' asked Summer.

'Well, yes. I suppose I am.'

Summer stood up and went to rest her head against Ben's chest. He put his arms around her, his dark head lowered over hers so Libby couldn't see either of their faces.

'Oh god, I'm sorry!' gulped Libby. 'I'm sorry, kids. Ben, you too. I'm so sorry!'

'That's okay,' said Jasper, lifting his head to look at her. His eyes were dark pools, impenetrable and serious.

'Does this mean you've changed your mind?' asked Summer, raising her head.

'No!' cried Libby. 'No,' she said again more calmly, throwing a reassuring smile at Jasper, who wasn't fooled. He didn't smile back, as he usually would, but continued to watch her carefully. She had to be a hundred per cent clear now, she told herself, so that what he didn't pick up in the nuance of her words he would pick up clearly in her tone and feeling. 'I'm sorry I couldn't make this work. But we're still all going to see each other all the time. And this is going to be an exciting new chapter for our whole family. Isn't it, Ben?'

He shook his head implacably over the top of Summer's head at her, *No*.

'When are we moving?' asked Summer, stepping out of the circle of her father's arms and scratching her ponytail. She looked out the window, already bored again, then went back to sit beside Jasper.

'I'm not sure,' said Libby. 'There are still a few things to work out.'

'Why not today?' asked Ben. 'You said the other two are moving in today, right?'

'Well, yes, but . . .'

'I can help you pack the car, seeing as I've already taken the morning off work.'

'All right then,' said Libby, hardening. 'Seeing as it's the weekend anyway. Let's.'

'That's soon,' said Summer dourly. She wasn't going to give her mother anything more in this conversation, Libby could see. And Jasper was looking around at them all dazedly, over-stimulated by the complication of the three of them talking like this.

The most important thing for Jasper was that he was here, with his family, and now she was breaking that. A hiccup leapt out of her, before she could catch it and stuff it back down again.

'In some ways this is very sad,' she choked, 'but in other ways it's very exciting.'

'For you, maybe,' said Summer.

'No, Summer. Not just for me. For you. And Jasper,' she said in her strictest tone, and both of the children sat up straighter. 'It's always sad for the children when their parents split up.'

Why wasn't Ben helping? She looked at him furiously, before remembering that he'd had only a night to prepare for this, as she had, but he'd spent most of it snoring. She'd heard him through the wall.

'But in other ways this is a new beginning,' she floundered on. 'And you're going to see your dad whenever you want, and he's going to see you. And I'm going to be much, much happier, and so will your dad, in time, and won't that be a wonderful thing?'

'Oh brother,' muttered Summer.

Suddenly, unreasonably stung by their lack of pity or understanding, Libby snapped. 'You know mothers are people too, right, Summer?' she retorted, knowing she was making a tactical mistake here, but suddenly too overwhelmed to know what else to do.

'You just want me to say yes,' said Summer.

'I know the feeling,' muttered Ben.

Libby sat there as Summer stood up and walked out of the room, followed by Jasper, with Ben trailing after them a moment later. She looked around at the new velvet sectional couch she'd only just taken off layby, and her spider plant in its hanging pot and Ben's aquarium with its tiny iridescent fish sailing in and out of the rock caverns and seaweed. She felt deflated, and small. Yet even more determined, somehow, as though all her yearning had crystallised into a very dense and tiny black ball.

~

'Okay, kids,' Libby called out, as she unlocked the driver's side door. 'Let's go.'

'If it makes any difference, I wish you wouldn't,' said Ben, as he helped her pack the last of her suitcases into the car.

'If it makes any difference, I wish I didn't have to.'

'You don't have to!' he exploded, slamming the boot. His eyes were wide and his hair wild, his big black beard particularly bushy-looking. He was dressed in his King Gee shorts with his chest and his feet bare, so he looked like some kind of crazed caveman, standing in the gutter.

'I do. This is my chance, Ben.'

'To do what? To live nearer to the fish markets? Or to leave me?'

'To fulfil myself,' said Libby, looking into his face intently, willing him not to laugh. He didn't, though. He looked back at her, just as intently. 'You know how lonely I've been, I told you,' she said. 'I want to live differently, and if I don't do this now, I might never get another chance! It's not just about leaving you,' she added, as an afterthought. She wanted to be as honest here as possible. *I still love you*, she almost said, but stopped herself just in time. He felt it anyway. She could tell by the way his cheeks were reddening as he looked down.

'All right then. I'll quit.' He rocked back on his heels, like a boxer who'd just delivered the killer blow.

'What?'

'I'll call Parker right now at home and hand in my resignation.' He looked dazed.

'Really?'

'Yep. We can buy a donkey and hire it out for joy rides, because god knows that's all the money we'll have.'

Libby felt wrong-footed for a moment, and almost breathless at the possibilities. 'But you love being an architect. You said that's all you've ever wanted to do.'

'Yep.' He smiled at her a little grimly. 'We can move to the country, or to the moon for all I care. We can live any way that you want.'

Libby leaned against the car door. She had power suddenly, simply because she was leaving, and it touched her how much he was willing to offer to change her mind. But the women were already waiting for her, over in Avon Street, and it felt to Libby like that moment when a cake is rising, and if you open the oven, or disturb it in any way, it won't get there.

'I'm sorry, Ben.' Her head swam and her stomach heaved, as if she might throw up. 'But I have to go.'

'No, you don't.' He blinked at her, as if he was having trouble focusing too. It felt frightening and enormous and so different, suddenly, for this not to be ultimately up to him.

'But I do,' she said. If she didn't get out of here now she never would. This felt as urgent as childbirth. 'I have to.'

He dropped his head and ran his hands over his face and through his hair, scratching his scalp vigorously, the way he did sometimes when he was frustrated, and when he stepped back away from the car, he had changed.

'I can't believe you are doing this,' he said, 'but if you have to, then you have to, I suppose.'

Libby looked around, taking in the sounds and the colours of the quiet street. Her stomach had settled and her mind had cleared. 'You can come and visit. Pretty much any time.'

'Never,' he said solemnly. His face wore a grim expression as slowly he shook his head. 'I promise you I will never come over.'

'What?' She recoiled. 'But, Ben, that's ridiculous! What about the children?'

'What about them? You do what you want, okay? And I will be as cooperative as I know how. I'll have them on Saturday nights and Wednesdays, according to your instructions. But I'm not coming over to be a part of your new gang.' He paused to catch his breath.

'*Gang?*' That smarted. That was not at all what was happening here, whatever he might think. 'You're not being very fair.'

'I don't care. I'm not going be a groovy separated couple,' he continued. 'We're not going out for pizza or sharing special occasions as though nothing went wrong. And I'm never ever going to say that now we have an even better relationship, and that this was the best thing that could ever have happened to us, and that we didn't fail, and that in the Olden Days one of us would have died by now and so it's actually only because one of us has lived too long that our marriage hasn't been a huge success. I'm not doing any of that crap.'

'You're just angry, you don't mean that,' she said softly, as the kids came running out.

He bent down to give Summer a kiss, and to hug Jasper. 'See you, mate,' he said, squeezing Jasper's arm.

'Goodbye, Libby,' he said, looking at her over the roof of the Kingswood once he'd finished strapping Jasper in. Their eyes met and Libby felt a wash of an even greater chill come over her, which she quickly thrust away, like dry ice, both too hot and too freezing to bear.

She put the car into gear, swinging the wheel so abruptly out of the gutter that she bumped into the car parked in front of her. 'Shit, shit, shit,' she muttered to herself. She closed her eyes and breathed in deeply. The seat felt firm against her back and legs, the wheel and gearstick solid underneath her hands. 'Oh well, Daddy's going to have to deal with that,' she said lightly over her shoulder, to reassure the children. She reversed a little, and then took off down the street, the gearbox shuddering as she moved jerkily into third gear.

Her legs felt like dead weights as she followed the children up the stairs to where Carol and Anna were waiting for them on the front verandah. As they ushered her in through the narrow front door, Summer and Jasper joined the other kids thundering up and down the hallway, claiming rooms and asking if they could put rainbow stickers on the windows.

'Absolutely,' said Anna, just as Libby was about to say *No way*.

'You can do whatever you like to them,' added Anna, offhandedly. 'They're all going to be replaced later on, anyway.'

She was walking around in a long tan skirt, polo-neck skivvy and high-heeled boots, as breezy as a real-estate agent rather than a woman about to start a new life in a half-renovated slum. That moment of wild strangeness in the hallway yesterday had evaporated, and Libby wished she'd had time to talk to that woman a little more before this more elegant, poised Anna returned. *How did you tell Myles?* she wanted to know. *What did you say to the girls?* But they were surrounded by the children now, and Carol was busy looking into cupboards and taking measurements, so Libby took Jasper by the hand and they set out to explore.

It was a long narrow house built with the same grand aspirations as Libby's, but with meaner proportions. Just one storey, it had a steeply sloping front garden, terraced into dry little patches of soil, and a meandering flat concrete backyard. The ceilings were high, though, and the windows in each room large and well proportioned, even though they had been fitted with security bars and looked straight into the neighbours' homes. There were eight rooms in the main part of the house, as well as an old Victorian bathroom with a deep claw-footed tub. The hallway led into a long and narrow living area with sliding glass doors leading out to the backyard. In one corner were the beginnings of a new kitchen, with a gas cooker, a restored wooden dresser and a ceramic sink.

'It starts modestly, picks up steam and then falls apart again,' Libby said to Jasper, who was throwing sidelong looks at the dresser, in that way he had when he was formulating an evil plan. She clutched Jasper's hand tightly as she made a mental note to check those drawers for rat traps or poison. The wooden floorboards were new, and the walls had been freshly painted in tasteful cream, and the ceilings in bright white. There were cornices and skirting boards in every room, and ornate plaster roses.

'The previous people didn't wreck it at least,' said Anna self-deprecatingly, when Libby complimented her. 'What do you think?' she asked, smiling at Carol who was standing in the doorway.

Carol looked as exhausted as Libby felt. The roses in her cheeks had faded since yesterday, and her skin had a sick-looking pallor underneath her heavy make-up. She nodded and whispered, 'I think it's great.'

'I create worlds,' Libby murmured to herself, thinking of the Empress card in the Tarot pack that Strauss had given her, as she looked around the empty kitchen.

7

Anna

ANNA SQUINTED THROUGH HER POLAROID SUNGLASSES, marvelling at the clearness of the water which slapped against the sand in a long slow rhythm. The girls were playing in the rockpools with Libby supervising, but Jasper had chosen to stay here with her on the picnic blanket, crunching on pieces of apple as he lounged against her legs. She lay back on her elbows, lifting her face to the sun. The storms and winds that had hurtled around the city for weeks had been blown away by an unusually warm front over the past few days, and now the autumn sun was soothing her and melting her like brie.

'Which reminds me.' She sat up, adjusting Jasper so he was leaning with his back against hers now, and began to unwrap the cheeses and set out the picnic that Libby had packed so carefully this morning.

It still surprised her, what a fuss Libby could make about food. That had been one of the biggest shocks so far about moving in together. Along with the loveliness, the perpetual loveliness, of having adults she *liked* to do things with, along with the company of the children. Like today: a picnic on the harbour with a ferry ride thrown in. What could be simpler? Yet somehow with Myles it was the kind of thing they could never do with another family without weeks of negotiation needed first. And if they went just on their own, Leanne and Michelle might get bored and squabble, and the whole thing could become a slog. This morning all that had been required was a quick conversation over breakfast, and then a cry had gone up around the table. 'To the beach!'

She wished they were having fish and chips for lunch instead, but this was healthier, it was true, and so sophisticated. Who would have thought you could make tzatziki just by mixing yoghurt and cucumber and lemon and garlic? And who would care? Anna smiled wickedly. It was a wicked thought—practically heretical— in this new world she shared with Libby, and one she would never share with her, despite having shared so much recently.

'Just make what you like,' Libby had said on their first night in the house together, when Anna recklessly offered to cook.

'Like what?' asked Anna nervously. She'd been feeling so close to Libby since the ABBA concert, but at the same time she kept worrying that any minute now she might say or do something which would bring that to an end.

'Whatever you think would be good,' said Libby carelessly. 'I mean, we're here to live as we want to, after all. Oh, and if it's all right with you I thought I'd invite around a few of the neighbours.'

She was going to be entertaining visitors, *tonight*? Anna looked around wildly at all the mess. But this was Libby's way, she reminded herself. It was a part of what she'd liked so much about her in the first place.

'It will be our first party,' said Libby. And then, perhaps sensing Anna's dismay, she added quietly, 'It'll help break the ice, for all of us, and it's important for us to get to know the neighbours, so that they can help to keep an eye out for the kids.'

Anna would never have thought of that in a thousand years.

As it happened, only two were home, but they both said yes. Mrs Georgiou, an elderly widow from next door whose children had moved away, and Michael, a very serious young anthropologist from across the road.

Anna toiled all afternoon on spaghetti Bolognese, which she burned on the bottom, and garlic bread. For dessert she made a spectacular apple crumble, which, just as she was taking it out of the oven, slipped from her hands and smashed onto the floor. 'It's ruined!' she moaned, just as Libby walked into the kitchen.

'Hang on a tick,' said Libby, squatting down and sweeping it all back into the tray.

'That's unhygienic!' protested Anna, appalled.

'I won't tell anyone if you won't.'

'But what about germs?'

'Oh, what about them? People go on way too much about germs.'

Anna gave them all small portions at first, though, just in case, but no one died, or even vomited, and in fact everyone said it was delicious and asked for second helpings, and by the time their visitors stood up to leave it was all gone.

'Told you,' said Libby, as they were doing the dishes. Carol was watching TV in the living room, and the children had all gone to bed. 'Scrumptious grub, by the way. Is that one of your regulars?'

'Oh god, no!' said Anna, trying to imagine regularly going through that trauma. 'I don't cook.'

'Then why did you?' asked Libby, stopping her washing-up to look at Anna, her hands still in the water. 'I would have been more than happy to, you know that. I just worry about being bossy, and taking over. You really only just have to say.'

'I wanted to please you,' said Anna, before she could stop herself. Maybe it was the unaccustomed intimacy of doing housework together like this, something she had never done with a friend before. Or maybe it was the wine at dinner. Normally she never drank.

'You wanted to please me? Why on earth?'

Even now the memory of it still made Anna cringe. How she'd turned to Libby and started mirroring her body language, to build rapport, while at the same time the voice in her head began to scream, *Whatever you do, don't let her see you.* She wanted to be real, now, but it was so hard sometimes to resist that little voice. 'I know you don't like me. Summer told Michelle, who told Myles, who told me. Last term.'

'Oh Anna, I'm so sorry.' Libby staggered over to the rickety wooden chair they'd brought home from the tip that afternoon and sat down. 'I hate that Summer overheard me say that. I'm sure I was just sounding off to Ben about something else. And I'm so sorry that I put Michelle into that position, too. And it's not that I didn't like you. It wasn't that.'

'What was it, then?' Anna asked, before that little voice could make her change the subject. She desperately needed to know.

'It's hard to remember, now that everything's so different. Not now, lamb chop!' she added, as Summer wandered into the room, dressed in just her underpants and arm-length satin gloves.

'But Jasper's annoying me!'

'Jasper's asleep, I checked. Now, go to bed and I'll come and tuck you in again, in a sec.'

'You were saying what it was about me that you didn't like,' prompted Anna, once Summer had trailed out of the room.

'Honestly, I can't remember anymore. I was probably just having a bad day.'

'Please, Libby!'

When people want to tell you something, make sure you keep quiet and listen, Anna told her graduate trainees, but this silence was going on and on.

'I think I just thought you were a little bit exhausting, maybe,' said Libby finally. 'As though we were at an everlasting cocktail party, where I had to be on my best behaviour.'

But Anna had been trying so hard to be nice! Or was that what had been so exhausting?

'And you know what? It's probably all me and my stuff.' Libby leaned towards Anna, eagerly. 'I just felt inadequate, probably, and was projecting that onto you.'

Anna tried to smile reassuringly, even though her heart was pounding too hard for her to speak.

'It must have been weird for you when I asked if I could move in.'

'It was. A bit,' Anna managed. She'd been half thrilled and half terrified, but her instinct warned her not to mention that, in case it might be exhausting.

'And the way you've been these last few days,' Libby was saying. 'So confident and strong for us all at bargaining with the men at the tip. And Jasper just loves you,' she added, in a rush. 'I've never seen him take to someone so quickly.'

'I just love Jasper. I don't usually take to someone so quickly, either.'

'So tell me honestly, I'm curious.' Libby ashed her cigarette into a saucer and fixed Anna with a mischievous smile. 'If it was just an ordinary Saturday night chez Anna, what would you have made us for dinner?'

'Myles would have cooked if I had work to do, or the nanny might have left us something. But if I *had* to, then anything quick and easy, I suppose, like Spam with baked beans, and junket or jelly for dessert. But that's wrong, isn't it?' she cried, as Libby winced. 'You don't like it.'

Libby was laughing at her openly now. 'No. Well, I mean, no one could! Apart from food, though, hon, I think we're going to get along very well.'

~

Anna smiled now at the memory as she pulled her sheer orange caftan over her head. She'd bought this for an exorbitant amount at the hotel gift shop last year in Hawaii, where she and Myles had gone for a tense week's holiday without the girls. She'd worn it lying next to an extraordinary clifftop pool, and then out to dinner, where she made Myles try sashimi, because someone had told her it was an aphrodisiac, and they drank Dom Pérignon. They always had the best of everything when they went on holiday, as if, mused Anna as she adjusted the caftan's neckline, they were trying to compensate for the lack of just one thing. It was strange to think how much had changed since then. She looked around at all the families picnicking near them on the grass. Now striped-zinc noses, Frisbees and drinks made with Cottee's Cordial were the backdrop for her fancy caftan, and it fitted in perfectly. She shaded her eyes as she checked on the girls, who were still playing in the rockpools.

Summer was sitting cross-legged at the edge of the water. Her body looked sturdy and strong in Leanne's bikini, the delicate frill of the neckline at odds with her no-nonsense approach to life—so protective of Jasper, and impatient with everyone else. She looked like a tomboy, and Libby couldn't seem to help wanting to dress her as one. 'This is so groovy, darling,' she'd overheard Libby saying that morning as she tried to persuade her into a green one-piece Speedo. But Summer would have none of it. 'My ambition is to get married and have babies when I grow up,' she'd announced on the ferry over here. Her dark hair was cut in layers around her face, and she had a sprinkling of adorable freckles across her nose. If you were going to cast the girls in a movie, Summer would be the capable lead. Except in this group, oddly, she wasn't. It was Michelle who was—plump and fair, with hair so fine it wouldn't even go into a ponytail. In the cruel rankings of young girls, her attributes scored dismally. Worst of all, she was a terrible dancer. But there was something so playful and generous about her, and Anna could see why the girls allowed her to be in charge. Summer was too stubborn about what she wanted to be an inspiring leader, like that completely inappropriate bikini. 'I don't care, I'm wearing it!' she'd snapped at Libby this morning. 'There's not a thing I can do with her,' Libby had sighed, giving up. But Anna thought she'd be okay. More than okay. She had that careless entitlement of a child who knows they are cherished. Anna hoped her girls did, too.

Leanne, who was sitting opposite Summer and making a trench for the seawater to go into, was what Myles called 'a real girl's girl'. Her fingers often in her mouth, she was still such a baby in so many ways, even though she was eight. The other girls could have eaten her for breakfast if they'd wanted to. Passive and without guile, she trained her big hazel eyes on you when she wanted something, and waited for you to do the rest. Like Michelle, she had fair skin, and a sudden toothy grin that she bestowed on you at unexpected moments, along with flashes of wit that shocked Anna sometimes with their insight. Leanne took after her father, Anna had always thought. In a group with potentially too many leaders and not enough followers, it was easy to see why they included Leanne.

And finally there was Colette, who, even sitting on the beach with wet hair and covered in sand, looked elegant. She put together outfits, and wore heels and full make-up around the house, as insouciantly as a model. She obviously took after Carol, not only in her looks, but in her love of all things artificial and sparkly. If only Carol had some of Colette's confidence.

Carol was standing with her back to them all, just knee deep in the water, her white skin almost fluorescent against the orange crochet of her bikini. She shuddered each time a wave gently slapped at her.

'You need to go in, Carol,' shouted Anna, making a megaphone with her hands. Jasper was sitting up now, too, making that clucking sound he made with his tongue when he was amused.

'It's blooming cold,' Carol shrieked.

Her accent was just as clipped and lilting as ever, thought Anna, even though her daughter's accent was becoming more Australian every day.

She relaxed onto the picnic rug, picking up and tossing back a ball that Jasper was taking turns throwing and then rolling to her. There was something about Carol, which she couldn't quite put her finger on yet. It was in the way she wore her clothes—all those satins, sequins, and tight, tight blouses, which, let's face it, were right out there, even for Sandgate. And the way she'd taken Sampson along, when she ran away that night. Like her clothes—it was so impractical. But Colette loved him, and Steve would have put him out on the street, Carol said, and so far it was turning out very well, for all three of them. Beneath that shy and gentle manner, there was a daring and a faith in life which Anna envied and wanted to emulate.

Suddenly Carol collapsed at the knees and disappeared into the water.

'Carol?' called Anna, looking around to see if any other adults were nearby. She could see Carol's shape bobbing under the water. Had she fainted? Carol couldn't swim, she'd said. Should she call out to the girls? The shape moved, and then Carol popped back up again, like a jack-in-the-box.

'Oh my god, it's cold!' she wailed, helpless with laughter as she plunged back into the water again.

This time when she popped up Anna was ready for her, and she began applauding and making wolf whistles. Carol looked up at Anna and beamed. The girls, meanwhile, continued playing, as though their mothers carrying on like this was irrelevant, if not embarrassing, and best ignored.

~

Steve had been around this morning. Anna had answered the door, expecting it to be Mrs Georgiou bringing mulberries over for Libby to make into a pie, and so when she opened it, she got a shock.

'Where's Carol?' he asked roughly, before she'd even managed to say hello.

'She said she doesn't want to see you.' Anna moved to close the door, but he put a hand up and leaned his weight against it. 'You can't come in,' she said.

'Fine. I'd like to speak with my wife, please. Or my daughter. Out here.'

'They're out. But in any case,' Anna stepped forward and lowered her voice, pulling the door behind her, 'she's not ready to speak to you.'

'When will she be?'

'I don't know.'

Anna followed his eye as he looked around, taking in the house's ugly brick frontage, steel-framed windows and arid garden beds, with two savagely pruned roses on either side of the path to the gate, barely clinging on. He peered over her shoulder, openly curious about what lay back there. Anna quickly glanced behind her, but it was just the empty hallway, with its wooden floorboards and bumpy brickwork painted white.

'It's my house. Mine and Myles's,' she said, giving in a little.

'Yours and Myles's.' Steve's face twisted, and Anna realised he must know that she'd left her husband, too. Had they talked to each other? Had they held some kind of a manly meeting in one of their living rooms, the three of them workshopping what had just happened to their lives? The thought of it strangely moved her.

'Doing it up, are you?' asked Steve.

Anna nodded, speechless. He had thick reddish hair combed back from his forehead and long to his shoulders, a lean angular body and a beaky nose. He was taller than she'd realised the night she met him at the ABBA concert, with a kind of dynamic energy running through him that she did remember. She felt it flowing towards her now, like a charge.

'What's the rent, for Carol?'

'Not much.'

He smiled, humourlessly. 'I'm sure. That's just the kind of thing rich people say. She scrounging off you?'

'Carol doesn't *scrounge*,' said Anna crisply, galvanised by his animosity. 'I wouldn't let anybody scrounge off me, either.'

'What about food and clothing and what-not? How's she paying for that? Because I'm not giving her anything. Do you understand?'

'It's hardly *giving*, is it, when everything you have is half hers? And if Carol wants you to know her business, she'll tell you.'

Their eyes met, and Anna felt that charge again, like an electrical current going straight down her back like a shiver.

'Tell her I came around then, would you?'

She watched him go back down the stairs, his shoulders straightening as he approached the gate. By the time he was out on the street again he was whistling, and she briefly wondered where he was going, before she stepped back and closed the door.

'Who was that?' Libby asked, appearing at the end of the hall.

'I'll tell you later,' Anna called out, aware of the kids scattered around the house, and determined to find Carol and tell her about Steve's visit privately.

What was that charge about? That moment of attraction—if that's what it was—and that shiver down her back? Anna sat up, suddenly uncomfortable. Sweat was dripping down the back of her neck underneath her ponytail, and there was some kind of scratchy thread woven into this caftan which made it suddenly unbearable. She ripped it off, bundled it into a ball and thrust it into her bag. It couldn't be attraction, because it hadn't been there on the night of the ABBA concert, and attraction wasn't that inconsistent— surely. Not that she could remember the last time she had been attracted to anyone, so she was hardly an expert on these things. But she could never be attracted to a man like Steve, who was so pushy and arrogant. Let alone to Carol's ex. Just the idea of it made her feel nauseous.

~

Jasper was putting balls into a bucket now, pulling one out and then throwing it in again, listening for the satisfying thump. Anna picked up a ball and thumped it into the bucket next to him. He glanced at her and gave her a quick smile, and pointed diffidently to the picnic basket.

'Would you like a biscuit, Jassie?'

'How are you guys going?' called Libby, walking up the hill towards them, wearing a white halter-neck bikini with a pink hibiscus tucked into her thick brown hair. Everything about her was flowing and abundant and feminine. Even though it was autumn now, she still had a deep and glowing tan. 'Jasper, are you having a good time?'

'We're going well,' said Anna, after a pause while she waited for Jasper to speak.

'Jasper is happy,' he said, and Libby's eyes filled with tears.

'Really, Jassie?' She knelt down to blow a raspberry on his leg, making him giggle delightedly. 'Really?'

'I'm happy,' said Anna, smiling at Libby.

Libby sat back on her knees and smiled back at her. 'I'm happy, too.'

When the girls finally came up the hill from the beach to eat, Anna and Carol sat back as Libby served them, slapping together sandwiches made from the dips and salads and cabanossi that she seemed to have conjured out of thin air that morning. They all dug in, except Michelle who sat hesitating.

'Does this have parsley in it?' she asked, her chin trembling threateningly.

'Only the tiniest bit,' said Libby, whipping it away to scrape off the tabouli, and popping in an extra piece of cabanossi and handing it back. 'There, now it's just like a sausage sandwich, only nicer.'

'You love sausage sandwiches, don't you, darling?' Anna smiled at Michelle encouragingly. 'They're your favourite.'

'I can't eat where the parsley has been,' said Michelle firmly.

Anna was afraid that Libby was about to deliver a lecture on adventurous eating, the way Anna might have done if she didn't know better, but instead Libby picked up Michelle's hand and kissed it. 'I didn't used to like parsley when I was a young girl, either. When I was your age I didn't eat anything *but* sausages!'

'Really?' replied Colette, feigning polite interest just like an adult might.

'Michelle eats way more than sausages,' said Leanne, interested that this might be a source of praise.

'She certainly does,' said Anna, almost limp with relief. *That Libby had passed this test?* she wondered uneasily. *Or that Michelle had?*

'Are we going home now?' asked Leanne, as they began to pack up their things. She'd only had a few bites of her sandwich, and just a few sips of cordial.

'Of course,' said Anna, trying to sound matter-of-fact as she rinsed out their swimming costumes under a tap, and wrapped them up in a towel.

'I mean home-home,' said Leanne. 'Where Daddy lives.'

'You'll be staying with your dad next week,' said Anna, carefully. 'You know that. You're going to be staying with him exactly half the time, and exactly half the time at Avon Street, with me.

Now, why don't we sneak a chocolate, quick, while nobody else is looking?'

But Leanne had started to cry, and for the next miserable half-hour nothing could stop her silent tears. Not hot chips once they got to the wharf, or Carol's soft woollen scarf, which she tried to wrap around Leanne's neck as they waited on the windy jetty.

On the ferry Anna sat with her arms around each of her girls, staring at the water. It looked dark and cold and bleak now, not beautiful and warm as it had this morning on the way over. She was trying to protect the girls, and to help them through this in every way she could think of, but what if it just wasn't enough?

She and Myles had agreed to split custody fifty-fifty, and keep the arrangements with their nanny—who picked the girls up from school and spent the afternoons with them until dinner—just the same. All the logistics of their separation had gone remarkably smoothly, considering how abrupt it had been. Emotionally, though, it had been a rollercoaster. Every time they saw each other Myles found a way to take her aside and tell her she was crazy, before begging her to come back.

'Anna, please, be reasonable,' he'd pleaded with her this morning when he dropped off the girls. They were standing in her new bedroom, which had just a bed and some suitcases in it, and was the only place they could find any privacy, while they waited for the girls to go racing around the house, checking that they had everything they needed for the picnic this afternoon. 'The three of you setting up house together like this, on a whim?' His face screwed up in outrage. 'It's irresponsible.'

'It's not a whim, Myles,' Anna had managed to calmly reply. 'I'm not saying this is the best decision I'm ever going to make, and

I'm not saying that this is necessarily forever. But I need to work this out. On my own.'

'It's hardly on your own, though, is it?' he hissed. 'You've turned this place back into a boarding house!'

She refused to rise to the bait. 'Please, Myles. Won't you try to understand?' '

'We should work this out together,' he insisted stubbornly. 'That's what married couples do.'

Anna thought of all the conversations she'd tried to initiate with him, and the holidays she'd booked for them, and all the times she'd purposely drunk too much—and she hated being drunk—and done just about everything she could think of to change the way things were between them.

'I don't see how we can,' she said.

'Look,' he stepped back, opening his hands as if he was releasing something, 'if sex is so important to you, why don't we just decide to make love more often?'

'More often?' He made it sound as simple as getting an oil change. 'You mean ever!'

'Oh Anna, I can't help the way I'm wired,' he sighed.

As if *he* was the one who had the right to feel exasperated. 'So why didn't you tell me that?' she cried.

'Because, I keep telling you, I didn't think it was important—especially not after we had the girls. To be honest, I didn't think it was important to you, actually, either.'

'Gosh, you really know how to make a girl feel attractive,' she snapped, stung, because he was right. Sex had never been important to her, except as a means to an end. It was only recently, in the last year or so, that she had begun to put that together with the pervasive and unsettling feeling she had that something crucial was missing. Not just from their relationship, but from her whole life.

'This isn't just about sex,' she whispered. 'It's about me, about what *I* want.'

'Well, what do you want?'

He was gazing at her eagerly—as if she was about to pop out an answer! 'I don't know, Myles! I keep telling you.' She tried to curb her frustration. 'That's what this is all about.'

'But what about the girls?' His expression was pleading now.

'They're partly why I'm doing this,' Anna whispered, pleading back at him—for patience and understanding. 'I don't want them growing up thinking that this is all they should accept.'

'Accept?' His face had been scrunched up in confusion, but now his eyes flared angrily behind the thick black frames of his glasses. 'A loving home? A devoted father? A successful mother who has always, always had my support to go out to work?' He counted them off on his fingers.

As though, thought Anna, there was a limit.

And then Leanne came storming in, waving her goggles in triumph, and Michelle followed, wailing that she couldn't find anything because everything was still in boxes, and Anna and Myles agreed to meet for lunch in the city as soon as possible, where they could talk in peace.

'What am I supposed to tell everyone?' asked Myles, as she was seeing him out.

'Just tell them the truth.' She sounded as offhanded as she felt. The idea behind all this was to be real, after all.

'But what *is* that?' he asked. The pain in his voice was unmistakable.

'I don't know yet, Myles,' she said, softening towards him. 'I keep telling you. I need time.'

'But how *much* time? This is very difficult for me too, you know.'

He was still her Myles, thought Anna. She still felt love when she looked at him.

'I'm sorry,' she said gently. 'I don't know.'

~

'Are you okay?' whispered Carol over Colette's sleeping head, once they'd transferred to the bus that would take them back through the city centre, to their new home. Libby was sitting next to Carol, with Jasper on her lap and Summer collapsed against her, surrounded by shopping bags and wet towels, looking like a mother hen in a very bedraggled nest. Jasper alone of all the children was still awake, his finger on the window, tracing over the lights of the passing cars.

'Just wondering if I'm doing the right thing,' said Anna. She felt too wrung out by Leanne's tears to soften it.

'I'm sure you are,' said Libby, and Carol nodded, but the expression in her eyes was sad.

Anna looked through the window at the darkening city streets. There was no script for this; no certainty. There were no milestones to measure her progress against, or key performance indicators to be ticked off. For the first time in her life she was flying blind, and there was no way to predict how it would unfold.

8

Carol

'THERE NEEDS TO BE ONE MORE thing,' said Libby, once they'd agreed on a fixed amount the three of them would contribute to the weekly budget, with a clear understanding that if one of them fell short, the other two would make it work.

'One more thing for what?' Carol felt almost light-hearted now that they'd sorted this out. It was the same feeling she'd had when she'd swum in the ocean for the first time ever at Fairlight the other day, and put her whole head in the water. It was pure relief, if short-lived, from the usual grinding worry she felt. Normally she could only bear the stress with the help of her pills, but not today. Today she had her friends.

'We need one more thing to make us a proper group.'

They were sitting at the kitchen table, children all tucked up in bed, and Sampson was the only one left who looked ready for an argument, staring up at them accusingly as he prowled around in front of his bowl in the kitchen.

'Like a coven, you mean?' laughed Anna, and Carol couldn't help but smile. Anna was in such a good mood lately, always smiling and laughing—a surprising laugh, loud and guttural, which didn't match her usual elegance at all. 'We could prick our thumbs and share our blood. The girls did that, you know, last term.'

'With cordial,' Libby snorted. 'But they're onto something. Maybe we need to tell each other a secret. Something special, that we've never told anyone before.'

'But secrets can be dangerous,' frowned Anna.

'Jeez, Anna!' Libby groaned. 'Shall we just get plastered, instead? Or how about we all guess Sampson's weight? Oof!' Libby laughed, picking up a reluctant Sampson.

'Okay, okay, I get it. I want to play,' said Anna, reaching for her glass of wine. Her accent was more refined than Libby's and hard to place. If Carol had met her overseas somewhere, like in London, she wouldn't have even realised she was Australian.

'Carol, you start.'

'But I don't have any secrets like that!'

'Yet you're blushing.' Libby winked.

'And I would tell you my secret, but you already know it,' said Anna.

'You mean about never having sex?' replied Libby. 'That blew my mind.'

'Well, that too, but I mean about Myles being gay.'

'But is he, really? If he doesn't want to be?' asked Carol, cocking her head to one side. 'I mean, there must be *something* he can do about it, surely?'

'Like take two Aspro?' said Anna drily.

'Like talk to a minister, or see a psychologist, or something,' Carol muttered.

It bothered her, what small reasons they had for leaving, when she'd had no choice. Carol's mother and grandmother had been single mothers, each of them widowed by a war. Compared to that, it didn't seem like too high a price to pay to put up with Myles's and Ben's quirks. And so much else about this set-up could bother her, if she let it. The children running around near-naked, with no shoes on half the time, and the shabby furnishings, from the tip of all places! And the cold. The fog came right up from the harbour some mornings, and not even direct sunshine could get rid of it until midday. She'd never been this cold inside a house before, and it wasn't even winter yet. They didn't seem to care about heating in this country. But at least now she was climbing up instead of sliding down further into the pit, Carol reminded herself as Libby poured them each another glass of wine. She was grateful to have a guarantee for Colette's sake that the electricity bill would be paid, and that every night there would be food on the table and the company of other children.

'I don't believe that Myles could change in such a fundamental way, even though I know he wants to,' said Anna. 'Where I grew up, there was a couple who lived upstairs in the front room, both men. It was hard for them. People were horrible to them. But they really loved one another—even as a child I could see that—and they never changed.'

'You grew up in a boarding house?' asked Libby. 'I'm sorry, that wasn't your point,' she added quickly, as Anna frowned and looked away.

'No, that's okay.' Anna raised her chin defiantly. 'I grew up in a boarding house that my mother ran in return for free accommodation, after my dad left. Down near the fish markets.'

'You mean you grew up right here, in Sandgate? But Anna,' exclaimed Libby, her eyes shining, 'that's so interesting! Why didn't I know that about you?'

'No one knows except for Myles.'

'But why?' asked Libby. 'I would have thought that would be something to show off about.'

'Because we were poor,' said Anna bluntly.

'Oh,' said Libby, obviously caught by surprise.

Carol was surprised that Libby hadn't realised. Anna had a carefulness that reminded Carol of some of the girls she'd gone to school with, from the orphanage up the road—as if everything she did would have consequences.

'I always thought if people like you knew how I grew up, you wouldn't like me.'

'People like me?' responded Libby, uncertainly.

Anna's face twisted in a half smile. 'You were the girl who had everything: nice house, nice parents, nice car, right?'

'That's true.' Libby nodded and sipped her wine thoughtfully, before carefully placing it down on the table. 'I'm sorry, Anna,' she said, looking her squarely in the eyes.

'It's all right now,' said Anna, shrugging it off.

'No, I mean I'm sorry you thought I wouldn't understand. I probably wouldn't have. And I'm sorry about that.'

'Oh, it's fine. My god, it's all so long ago,' said Anna lightly. A moment later she excused herself to get something from her handbag.

Carol stroked Sampson while Libby sat, lost in her own thoughts, until Anna came bustling back in and pulled her chair up to the table. 'Who's next?'

'Okay, my secret,' said Libby. 'I've written half a cookbook.' She blew out her cheeks and stretched her arms, as if that had taken a lot out of her.

'Wow,' said Carol. She hoped that was the right thing to say.

'Only half?' asked Anna. 'Why only half?'

That was typical of Anna, Carol was learning. She'd never met anyone so focused on work.

'Oh, you know.' Libby shrugged. 'Time, energy, all that. It's probably just a silly dream. I mean, who actually gets to publish a cookbook anyway? Apart from, like, famous authors, or people who are well connected?'

'I've got the Margaret Fulton cookbook,' said Carol tentatively.

'Yes, but she's an expert,' said Libby. She seemed deflated, as though she'd expected a different reaction.

'What's it about?' asked Anna.

Libby rolled her eyes. 'Cooking,' she said faintly.

'No, honestly, I want to know.'

'Really? It seems stupid now.'

Carol had never seen Libby this uncertain before, not even when she arrived that morning with the children, after she'd left Ben.

'You have to tell us,' said Anna levelly, glancing at Carol.

'Yes, you do,' Carol quickly chimed in.

'Okay, here goes,' Libby muttered to herself. 'It's called *One Pot Wonders of the World*.' She rolled her eyes.

'But that's great,' said Carol.

'It's the working title anyway,' said Libby. Her cheeks were flushed. 'The theme is meals you can make for your family and friends, using only the one pot, and only the one dish in the middle of the table, preferably, too.' She was warming to her topic, sitting up a little straighter and smiling as she spoke. 'I began writing it in my share houses, where there were never any pots and pans, or not clean ones, anyway, and the recipes are great for kids, too. And then, when Ben and I went to Indonesia, I realised it must be the same for housewives and roadside stall holders, or anyone short on time and resources, anywhere. And so that's been a dream of mine, ever since, to collect recipe ideas from all over the world, so that whoever wants to make something simple and delicious and adventurous can find it in my book.'

'Now that is a very good idea,' said Anna, 'if your Teriyaki Pork with Pineapple *en flambe* is anything to go by.'

'Wait . . . you actually made it?' asked Libby.

'Myles did. He's a subscriber to *Epicure* magazine. He said he loved it.'

'Wow,' said Libby. She looked stunned.

'It's a brilliant idea for a cookbook, Libby, I'd buy it,' Carol said. 'Everything you think of to cook is so good.'

'Thanks guys,' said Libby, seemingly absorbed in scratching Sampson in the exact place he preferred it, on the very edge of his chin. She looked radiant.

'I was pregnant and I lost the baby at five months on the boat on the way over here,' said Carol, taking herself by surprise. She wanted to give them something of herself in return for their secrets, and this seemed like the most personal and intimate thing she could tell them.

'Oh *Carol*,' said Libby, her face crumpling with sympathy, and Carol almost couldn't go on.

But Anna was looking at her steadily, with a strength that felt to Carol like a guard rail that she could lean against, as she continued. 'When I found out I was expecting, I told Steve we should stay at home and wait another year, but he said he was sick of waiting, and that it was up to me if I came or not. But the ship was so uncomfortable, and I got seasick, and there was only one doctor on board.'

Libby's hand crept out and took hold of Carol's.

'After that, everything changed, and we started fighting all the time. And well, I can't help wishing that I'd stayed home.'

'Of course you do,' said Libby. 'Now it all makes sense.'

'What makes sense?' Had she been behaving strangely? Carol wondered, as she put her guard up. She still sometimes thought about the day Libby had found her drinking cider on the step.

'You being so anxious for Colette, and not wanting her to be alone,' said Libby.

'Oh.' Carol relaxed. She'd never met people who weren't family as generous as Libby and Anna, and it was taking her a while to get used to it.

'You did the right thing, risking it to come here,' said Anna. 'Being a single mother is no joke,' she added in an undertone, which made Carol think about her childhood in that boarding house. The fact that Anna had an idea what she might be in for made it even more extraordinary to Carol that she thought it could have been worth it to have broken up with Myles.

'Says us,' said Libby, laughing as she refilled Carol's glass, which sat next to the cup of tea she'd just made her. Everything about Libby was abundant, but it was quite obvious to Carol that she had no idea.

'Says us,' replied Anna gravely.

'I look back sometimes, and, well . . . things certainly haven't turned out the way I'd hoped,' said Carol. 'I suppose nothing does. I'd been wanting to have another baby for so long, ever since Colette was born.' Sampson jumped into her lap, and she put her nose to his soft head as he bumped her, closing her eyes for a moment and focusing on the softness of his fur. 'I thought maybe it was all finally coming together for me.'

'Maybe it still is,' said Anna.

Carol snorted. She couldn't help it. 'I doubt that.'

'You could have another baby now,' said Libby.

She had been afraid someone might say that. It's why she'd never talked about it before

'But I don't want another one,' said Carol simply, letting her hands fall into her lap. 'I wanted that one.'

'Carol, don't say that,' Libby exclaimed.

'But it's true. That part of my life feels over to me.'

'We could help you,' said Libby.

Now, for just a moment, Carol let go of all her rules about this, and allowed herself to imagine it. That she wasn't really all alone out here, and that a baby could be possible again, one day.

'I suppose I could, couldn't I?' She sniffed. 'Except that in that scenario I would need to talk to Steve.'

'Carol!' Anna smiled.

'What?'

'You just made a dirty joke!'

Carol had to think for a long moment before she clapped her hand over her mouth. 'I didn't mean so we could make a baby,' she cried, struggling to be heard over their shouts of laughter, but feeling somewhat proud. 'I meant to get the separation sorted out. And then that I would meet someone new.'

'We know what you mean,' said Libby, patting her on the arm.

The old kitchen felt like a nest into which the three of them had dragged all their sparkling treasures. Anna's blue enamel coffee pot sat on the shelf above the stove, holding a bunch of sweet peas Libby had brought home from her old garden, and Carol's satin-edged table runners had been draped over the rickety side-board, and her lace doilies placed on the armrests of the sagging floral couch they'd wedged into the corner. She felt privileged for these women to know this thing about her, and for her to know those secrets about them. For the first time since leaving England, she felt safe, and as if some kind of future might be possible.

~

The next morning Carol checked her reflection in her bedroom mirror: her tailored denim suit looked crisp and neat, her orange chiffon neck scarf toning perfectly with her nail polish. She adjusted her matching denim cap to a slightly rakish angle, and set off up Sandgate Road.

A fruit shop, a milk bar, a pub with TVs blaring and a shop devoted entirely to sheet music filled the first block. Carol couldn't play an instrument or sing a note to save herself, but she loved the idea of a shop filled with nothing but songs.

On the corner opposite stood a bookstore called Bilitis, devoted entirely to lesbian literature. A huge oil painting featuring water nymphs filled the window, and next to that was an Art Deco cinema showing old movies her mother would have loved—Mae West was her personal heroine—and midnight screenings of *The Rocky Horror Picture Show*.

Carol's favourite shops, though, were the second-hand clothes stores at the top of Ada Road, which sold clothes by weight. So far she'd bought blankets and an old angora jumper she planned to unravel and knit into a cardigan for Colette, but she had her eye on a sequinned skull cap. Not today, though, Carol told herself. Anna had been paying for all the groceries, and it was scary how much food they could all go through. Libby was a genius with the cooking, making everything stretch further than you ever would have thought possible, and creating dishes from the cheapest cuts, which even the children loved, but she was down to her last twenty dollars, and if she didn't find a way to earn some money soon, she was going to have to phone Steve. Colette had been talking to him regularly and visiting him, thanks to Libby, who handled all the logistics. Carol hadn't seen or spoken to him since the night she left four weeks ago, and just the thought of it made her palms clammy and the skin on the back of her neck sweat.

Now she had arrived at the top of Sandgate Road, where the large curved windows of Mr Harold's House of Hair took up the entire corner. She paused on the step and said a quick Hail Mary before she pushed open the door.

'You're here for the interview,' said the man standing behind the counter, as she walked in. He wore tight black stovepipe trousers—which did his middle-aged body no favours—and a tight black buttoned-up shirt.

'Are you Mr Harold?' He was the only man in here, but she didn't want to seem presumptuous.

'The one and only.' He reached out his hand, waggling his fingers at her.

'Excuse me?' Carol stepped back.

'Your résumé?' He smiled thinly, waggling his fingers again.

'Oh! Here.' Carol forced herself to smile brightly at him as she took it out of her bag.

He flicked a glance over it as he motioned her into a corner. 'Let me explain how we do business and then you can tell me if you think this is the right place for you.'

'That sounds fabulous,' said Carol faintly, forcing herself to smile at him again.

'I'm talking about taking the initiative,' Mr Harold was saying, five minutes later. Carol had kept her eyes trained on his face, like a snake charmer, as he talked about What People Don't Realise, and The Problem with This Country. As he launched into Teamwork—'which you would have no experience of, because you don't play football or rugby'—she snuck a look around.

A line of women's legs in pantyhose and pumps stretched out along one side of the salon, their owners' heads disappearing into hairdryers, while on the other side another line of women reclined back into sinks. Each sink had a woman in a white coat stationed behind it. None of them were laughing or talking to each other the way they'd used to at her old salon, in London. These women kept flicking anxious glances at Mr Harold, to check he wasn't watching. This was called work, after all, her mother would have said. It wasn't called fun for a reason. The styling stations, with their oval mirrors and little trolleys of equipment, were arranged along the back wall, where Carol saw that the hairspray and hot rollers were out in force, as though not a day had passed since 1965, when all anyone wanted was a perfectly solid beehive.

'Is something amusing?' Mr Harold was staring at her.

'Oh no. Please go on. This is fascinating,' Carol said, but his friendly mood was gone now, and he launched into Rules and Expectations and The Customer is King.

'Most of our clients have children, of course, and they'll want to get their hair done and dusted before the children get home from school. You have one, don't you?' His eyes flicked down at her résumé.

'A daughter.'

'She's not going to get sick, is she?'

Carol felt sick herself at the thought. 'No. She's, um,' she stuttered. 'She's very healthy.'

'Well, good. The hours are ten until four, with a half-hour break, and staying until five on a Saturday, as needed.'

'Until four?' stammered Carol. 'I thought the ad said until three.'

'That was a different position. It's not going to be a problem, is it?'

She was about to say no, she couldn't do it after all, but then she remembered Libby casually mentioning this as a possibility this morning, and offering to look after Colette if she ever needed her to. 'She can muck in with Jasper and Summer. It's really no big deal.'

'That will be fine,' she managed to say to Mr Harold.

'You turned down an interview here the other day, didn't you?'

Carol's heart sank even further. That had been weeks ago. She had hoped he might have forgotten, or that somehow he hadn't realised.

'I was in difficult circumstances.'

'Well, I'm sure we don't want any trouble. All our clientele are married ladies, and they wouldn't feel comfortable . . .'

'There won't be any trouble.'

Mr Harold inclined his head, staring at her heavily, his gaze filled with meaning. 'The way some young women are living these days . . . I've had to show more than a few of them the door.'

'Oh no!' said Carol, trying to look suitably appalled.

'I'm glad to see you're not one of those types.' He nodded at her hand, where the square-cut diamond and rubies of Libby's engagement ring glittered She had left her own rings behind on the dressing table at Church Street.

'Anna thinks I don't understand about being a single mother, but I do,' said Libby, as she slipped it onto Carol's wedding finger this morning. 'Or I'm learning, anyway,' she added wryly. 'I've been getting some funny looks.' Carol had been planning to say she was a widow, but this was so much better. Mr Harold was the kind of person who would be nicer to her if he thought she had the backing of a real live man.

'Well, good!' Mr Harold clapped his hands. 'You can get started today, if you like. Mrs Watson rang in asking for an appointment today, on a Friday, I ask you! I told her we're full with our regulars but if you can get started now . . .'

'Of course, Mr Harold,' said Carol, relief washing through her like a rainbow. She could at least find out how much that sequined cap cost, she told herself, as she put away her handbag and took her scissors out of their special case.

~

Two letters were sitting on her dressing table when she arrived home—one with an airmail sticker and her mother's even hand-writing, addressed to the old house. Steve must have been around to drop it off here, Carol realised, her heart fluttering in her chest. The other said just *Carol* in big block letters. She set them both back down on the dressing table and went out to the back of the house. Colette was eating Chinese fried rice with Jasper and the girls in the kitchen and barely looked up to kiss her, even though Carol had been longing for a hug all day. 'So you got the job,' said Libby, who was standing at the stove. Carol had phoned her from the salon to tell her she'd be coming home later than expected. 'Clever clogs. Not that I thought you wouldn't.'

'It's great,' said Carol wanly, rubbing her feet, which weren't used to standing all day anymore. The thrill of the money had worn off pretty quickly once she started working under Mr Harold's exacting gaze, and now she was exhausted.

'Why don't you slip into something more comfortable?' asked Libby, guessing, as always, how she was feeling, and taking care of her.

'But aren't you exhausted?' countered Carol. She had found Libby in the kitchen at six this morning with the paper, circling 'positions vacant', even though she had heard Libby murmuring quietly to Jasper very late last night. 'Why don't I take over here, and you go and have a bath? Or you could sit down and let me serve you a glass of wine, while you tell me about your day,' suggested Carol.

'Oh no you don't!' teased Libby. 'We're about to make chocolate sauce, and I intend to lick the bowl. I saw you have some letters,' she added, under the children's shouts of protest.

'One's from Mum,' Carol whispered back.

'I thought it might be. I know you're desperate to read them. Go on,' said Libby, giving her a little push. 'And take your time,' she yelled out after her, as Carol hurried back down the hall.

Carol closed her bedroom door and eased her shoes off her feet. She took off her girdle and bra, and put on her old pink-and-blue kimono, before sitting cross-legged in the middle of her bed, an envelope on each knee.

Her mother's first, she decided.

To Dear Carol. Hello Pet.

She leaned back against her bedhead and closed her eyes, picturing her mother sitting in her tiny kitchen, a pot of tea stewing at her elbow, her feet in their quilted slippers crossed neatly at her ankles, a pile of coins stacked on the meter, and the African violets nodding on the windowsill next to her, half dead from her smoke.

I was that sorry to get your letter saying how difficult things have been.

She wrote just the way she talked. Carol could almost hear her mother's voice speaking in her head.

I suppose I should say you have made your bed and now you must lie in it. But the truth is, I don't think the Harrington women know much about men. I wish I could advise you, but you haven't been set an example of how to make a good marriage, and neither was I. I know I missed your father, but then again, I never had to consult with anyone else, did I? At least your nan and I could say, Drat that dratted war. *We'll just have to say,* Drat that dratted Steve, *now, won't we?*

Carol laughed out loud.

Which is to say, it's not your fault.

This had been underlined twice, and Carol had to pause to catch her breath before she could keep reading.

I know this might not be the right thing, and I'm sure I don't want to cause more trouble, but I have saved some money, and Aunty and Uncle both wanted to give you something towards birthdays and Christmas too, and so taking all of that into consideration I think you and our girl should come home. I have enclosed funds.

This was underlined twice as well.

Carol had thought it was another letter nestled in there. She gasped as she unfolded it. It was a money order, able to be cashed only by Carol, for more than enough money to buy her and Colette's passage back to England.

She felt the weight across her shoulders—which had been getting heavier and heavier every day, so that some mornings she wasn't even sure if she could get up anymore—lift, and a feeling of warmth and love and comfort envelop her. It was a feeling Carol had never realised she might have to do without, because she had never been away from her mother for more than a day before, until the day she left home for good.

If you come back alone, Father, I'm sure, will disapprove, but we can go to a different church—or no church at all if it comes to that. I sometimes wonder why we bother. Everyone will be that happy to see you, and Steve must do as he thinks best.

And then, written in a different colour blue, as though it were an afterthought, although Carol was sure her mother would have been stewing about it all night before she added it to her aerogramme: *We all deserve a better life, but it broke my heart your leaving, and what is the point if it's not? Love, Mum.*

Carol tucked the money order into the back compartment of her purse, behind the school photograph of Colette, and the lock of her father's hair in tissue paper, which he'd given her mother just before he was deployed.

And now there was nothing for it. With the side of her thumbnail, long and sharp and painted Cherry Bomb red, she tore open Steve's letter. It was a single piece of paper, typed—which meant he must have done it at work.

Babe.

Enough is enough. You know it's your duty to come back. Not just to Colette. To me.

Here the typing ended, and in blue biro he had scribbled more.

How are we meant to sort this out if you're doing no talkies? I'll drop by on my way home tonight. We have to speak.

Carol's heart kicked in her chest as the doorbell rang, and for a moment she looked around wildly for an escape. But if she didn't answer, Steve might keep on ringing, and she didn't want to create a scene. She grabbed the sash of her kimono and wrapped it tightly around her waist as she walked down the hall, wishing she'd had time to put on a bra. The door pushed open as soon as she unlatched it and there he stood, in his tan slacks and green shirt, and for a moment so familiar and dear to her that she walked into his arms.

'Are you alone?'

'They're all out the back,' she said, forcing herself to pull away. 'What do you want?' She positioned herself in the doorway, where hopefully, half a foot away from where he was standing on the verandah, she could ignore the physical pull of him.

'What do you think?' He sounded cocky but in his eyes she could see his hurt expression. 'You've made your point. Now I want you to come home.'

'I can't do that.'

'Why are you doing this to me?' His tone changed.

'What do you mean?' She looked up at him.

'Have you lost the plot? Is that it? Disappearing like that to run off and live with these lezzos?' He smiled down at her shakily. 'Has my Carol finally gone completely nuts-o on me?'

He was still her Steve, with that handsome face and that feeling of home, but her skin was crawling and she felt dirty, whereas a moment ago she had felt lit up and happy just to be in his arms.

'No, actually.' She forced herself to step away, casting her eyes down. If they met his, she would dissolve into a puddle of weakness.

'What is it, babe?' Steve edged closer, snaking his hand back around her waist. 'What's got you acting so upset and crazy? You can tell me.'

She shook her head. She didn't have words to describe what it had become like, living with him.

'I know I was short sometimes, but that's normal between a husband and a wife. It doesn't mean they don't love each other. We've both been off our game.'

Carol remembered the way he was on the boat, after her miscarriage; she had put the way he was treating her down to nerves and anxiety. And then at the hostel where they'd stayed until they moved into their own place, where he'd become worse. Then moving into their own place, and setting it up, and how she'd learned to walk on eggshells by then, and was crying all the time, afraid to show him how she was feeling. She was always worried about what mood Steve would be in when he woke up or came home, and how bad he could make her feel, so that she felt worthless, waiting for him to decide what she should do.

'What am I expected to do, living all alone?' He rubbed his stomach where a non-existent role of fat was meant to be. That wall of muscle and smooth skin that used to make her heart melt, just to touch it. 'Come on, babe. I need you.'

She hated to think of Steve like that, in a bare kitchen and empty house, so stark and uninviting compared to her own.

'I got a job today,' she said, to change the subject, but the moment the words left her lips she regretted them.

'Well, that's just wonderful!' He beamed. 'That's what I kept saying, didn't I? We should celebrate! Leave Colette with this lot one more night, and go out on the town. Things will be easier now. The pressure will be off.'

Carol blinked. The idea of them dressed up and out having fun the way they used to was so easy to imagine—it was difficult to believe she was really standing here, deciding that she didn't want that.

'Steve, I want to go home,' she said, trying to keep the begging out of her voice. If this went on for a few more minutes, how was she going to be able to resist him? And how could she go back, knowing what mornings and evenings and weekends with him had been like, and knowing it might happen again, and she and Sampson and the suitcases would have to get into another taxi. Let alone what that would do to Colette. 'I mean home-home. To England home.'

'Ah.' He nodded, as though he had been expecting this. 'With Colette? Yeah. No. You're not doing that.'

'Why not?' she replied, feeling stronger every moment at the thought of returning. 'You should come home, too. I know your work isn't going as well as you hoped. Why don't you come, too? You can find a little flat near Mum's, and we can live near each other. Maybe we could try again, if you like. Why not?'

She was amazed at herself, at the way these plans were popping out of her, even though she hadn't even begun to think this through.

'I'm telling you, you can't leave.'

'Why not? We can live with Mum to start with and—'

'You're not leaving, because you don't have a passport.'

'What are you talking about? Of course I do.'

'I've cancelled it.'

Her blood ran cold. 'I'll get a new one, then,' said Carol. 'I'll apply.'

'No, you won't. No wife can get a passport without her husband's permission.'

'What are you talking about? Does it go the other way? Can I cancel your passport? If you want a new one do I have to sign?'

'No, silly. I have to sign your application, as your husband. It's just the same here as it is back home, I checked.'

'You checked? Why?'

'Because I don't want you to go.' He smirked. So he had read her mother's letter. Even with her nest egg and the contribution from their family and friends, it couldn't take her home.

'Mummy?' The front door pushed against her legs.

Dressed in just her blouse and tunic—no shoes, no cardigan, dirty face and hands, her hair falling out of the plaits Carol had done for her that morning—Colette looked like a little street urchin.

'How long have you been standing there?' Carol asked, her heart sinking.

'Pumpkin!' said Steve, squatting down to Colette's height.

'Daddy!' Colette screamed, throwing herself into his arms.

He looked at her triumphantly over Colette's head.

~

'I can't see him again, not for a while, at least,' said Carol, after the children had gone to bed. They were sitting at the kitchen table, drinking peppermint tea. Libby was dealing out cards for Gin Rummy, Carol's favourite game, but she could hardly focus, and kept forgetting to follow suit.

'Why not?' asked Libby, busily rearranging her hand.

'Because I can't think when I'm with him. All I want to do is give in. But I don't think I can go on, if I go back to live with him.'

'Then you don't have to,' said Libby, jumping in. 'She doesn't have to, does she, Anna?'

'No, she doesn't,' said Anna, placing down a card. It was the queen of spades, giving her a full flush, which she fanned out in front of her on the scarred wooden table top, matter-of-factly.

'But how can I stop him?' asked Carol, lowering her cards, the game forgotten. 'He knows I live here, and he'll work out any minute now where I'm working. And Mr Harold won't like that.'

'Anna will talk to him. Won't you, Anna?' prompted Libby.

'Me?' Anna paused, her pencil poised above the scorecard. 'Why me?'

'Because you're good at negotiating with people like that.'

'Like what?'

'Men. Telling them what they're allowed to do and what they're not. I remember the way you ordered the dads around at the Christmas fête. *Do this, put that there, not there, there!* You were terrifying. In a good way,' Libby added.

'I wasn't ordering. I was asking,' said Anna stiffly. 'And if I remember rightly you were pretty good at it, too.'

'With the food. For anything else, I'm hopeless. None of them take me seriously. And you work near Steve, don't you? He works in town, for Channel Seven, right? You can explain to him why he can't see Carol for a while. Except on neutral territory. It has to be you, Anna.'

'It has to be,' said Carol. 'Or else he's going to come to work and ruin everything. Oh, me and my stupid big mouth!'

'Don't say that,' said Anna, sharply. 'He would have worked it out, anyway. He's not stupid, is he?'

'He's very smart, actually,' said Carol. 'He won a scholarship to go to technical college, before he dropped out.'

'I'm not sure why you think he'd listen to me,' frowned Anna.

'There's no one else.' Libby opened the freezer and drew out three bowls of ice cream. She stuck a stick of homemade honeycomb into each one and pushed them in front of the women at the table, before sitting back down again and taking a bite.

Anna took off her glasses and looked at her bowl sternly, before pushing it aside—she never indulged herself, Carol had noticed—and then with the same steely expression, she looked at Carol. 'Is this what you really want?'

She still had the money order from her mother, like an insurance policy, Carol told herself. And a job. And now she had allies, too.

'Yes.'

9

Anna

'GOOD DAY?' ASKED MYLES AS HE sat next to Anna on the grass.

'Yes, thanks.'

Office workers and schoolchildren were picnicking all around them on this strip of parkland between the rivers of city traffic. The War Memorial loomed down one end of the promenade, and the chilly-looking fountain at the other. Anna had found a grassy spot for them to sit in a spare patch of sunlight.

'Is it just me, or are you dressing differently?' asked Anna, looking him up and down. 'That shirt. Those shorts. They're very . . .' She frowned, searching for the right word. 'Bright,' she said finally, although that wasn't it.

Myles looked down at himself. His long socks featured a dramatic sunrise in black and orange, and his green short-sleeved shirt contrasted with his wide purple tie.

'These are my Tuesday socks and shorts.'

'You wear the same socks and shorts every Tuesday?'

'I have a bit of an outfit I wear for each day of the week, for each season. This is autumn. It makes getting ready in the morning easier.'

'Myles, what if people at work notice? They'll laugh at you.'

'They have noticed. Don't forget they're tax auditors.' He shrugged. 'They say it makes it easy to remember what day it is. Anyway, it's nothing new, I've been doing it for over a year.'

'A year? How could I not have noticed that?'

He let her question dangle in the air.

'I'm sorry I wasn't more observant,' Anna sighed.

'It did often feel like your mind was somewhere else,' he said gently.

'It was on work,' she said shortly. 'But I'm sorry I didn't notice your rotating outfits. It seems very efficient. Mental, maybe, but efficient.'

'Thanks. I'll take that as a compliment.'

'I knew you would.' Anna sighed again.

Myles had always been different, and that's what Anna liked about him. In the world she'd grown up in, where tradesmen and footy players were kings, he seemed gentle and sophisticated. Unlike the other domineering professionals-in-the-making she'd met at university, Myles was a good listener, and she felt when she was with him that she could actually breathe. And he was manly. He'd been a lifesaver, and served in Vietnam before they met, and he carried an air of sadness that she longed to take away. He wore corduroy and tweed with elbow patches in those days, like a vague professor, and yet he could put up a drywall or dig a hole as well as any he-man you put him up against. But should it have been obvious to her, somehow, that he played for the other team? Was it quite clear to everyone who knew them? Was she the only one who hadn't been in on the joke?

When Anna met Myles, she had already been working for three years. In that time she had learned to keep her colleagues at bay, and had earned a reputation for being an ice queen. *Frigid*, some of the men she'd rejected called her, or *stuck-up bitch*. Anna hadn't much minded. Of course it was offensive, but she would rather that than to have accidentally fallen pregnant, or to have been led astray by her female hormones—which she learned about in psychology—and married to someone she didn't truly love.

'You seem more serious than the other girls,' Myles had said, walking up to her at a university reunion, as soon as the principal of her college had finished her welcome speech.

'Oh dear,' Anna sighed, bored already at the good-natured ribbing she was about to be forced to endure.

'I meant it as a compliment, actually. You're not married?' He glanced at her hands. 'Oh, how terrible! How terrible!' he smiled, doing a wicked impression of the women she'd just been talking to from her college.

'Well, don't you get all cut up about it.' She smiled back, feeling much less pitiable now that she was talking to the most handsome man in the place.

The restaurant he took her to that night after the reunion was one of those plain-looking places, where the high price is always a surprise. Their steaks were charcoal black on the outside, red on the inside and must have weighed two pounds apiece. They always had the best of everything when they were together.

When they first made love, she had thought of nothing but passion. He was more affectionate than ardent, but once he had got her going, she took over, and he always seemed pleased by her reaction. Afterwards, on Sunday mornings, they would read the papers together on the verandah of her little apartment, with

French toast, freshly squeezed orange juice and coffee on a tray in the sunshine. It really had been perfect, remembered Anna now. Until it wasn't.

Why didn't he tell me? she wondered. She wouldn't have fallen in love with him the way she had if she'd known. She wouldn't have expected anything that he couldn't give. And she wouldn't have looked for that missing piece inside herself the way she had been for the past few years. Although maybe it had been missing from the beginning, and that's why he had chosen her, and that's also why she had chosen him. Maybe, in some awful twisted way, they had found each other.

Their marriage ceremony had been held in the Sandgate Registry Office, where two giant lions carved from local sandstone guarded the chamber's doors. Anna had worn a cream wool skirt and peplum jacket which she'd sewn herself on her trusty old Singer sewing machine. Myles had worn his only suit. The long emergency of her childhood was over, Anna realised, as they recited their wedding vows in front of their families and friends. Posing for photographs afterwards, she had never felt so safe and happy as she did standing with Myles between the lions' paws.

~

'Do you think you're going to sleep with someone?' Myles asked miserably, once they'd talked children, houses, bank accounts and plans for the holidays.

'I suppose so.'

Anna looked around at the people surrounding them on the grass. It was hard to imagine being attracted to any of them, but then that had always been her problem, hadn't it?

'I mean, it *is* the seventies,' she amended. 'You should, too, Myles, surely. With a man, I mean. Why not?' She was trying to sound enthusiastic, but instead she sounded hard and brittle.

'Because I love you,' said Myles. 'Because I'm happy—I was happy—with you.'

'I don't believe that.'

'Oh look!' he cried, pointing over to the fountain, as though she hadn't spoken. A group of young people with long hair like hippies were stripping off naked to jump in. 'That looks fun.'

'Very fun,' echoed Anna, as she wrapped up the remains of her sandwich. She had lost her appetite. His clothes were definitely more . . . out there, though, Anna noted as she watched him eat. The trouble was that all the men were dressing more flamboyantly these days. Even dressed for what were obviously corporate jobs, half the men in this park looked like peacocks in their paisley blouses and bell-bottom trousers and wide patterned ties. And they couldn't all be gay, could they? She felt almost dizzy as she looked around at them all. Sometimes, when she got into one of these moods, she began to feel as if she didn't know anything anymore.

~

'Steve, it's Anna Wotcek,' she said briskly into the phone as soon as she arrived back at her desk. 'I wondered if we could meet up after work this evening for a quick word? Carol's asked me to speak with you.'

'Tonight?'

She could hear people shouting, and heavy machinery in the background.

'All right then,' he said. 'I can't argue with Carol.'

They agreed to meet in the shopping arcade underneath Anna's office building, which was as cosy and warm as a rabbit warren, while still public and busy. Her bus stop also happened to be right out the front, a fact she was very glad of that evening when she looked up from her desk and realised it was about to storm.

She took the sheaf of tables she'd been working on all afternoon out to where her personal assistant was still sitting, under a single fluorescent light.

'Gilbert! Shouldn't you be gone by now?' The rest of the huge open-plan office was deserted.

'Just finishing off a few things.' He barely looked up as she put the papers down on his desk.

Anna was starting to think her affirmative action in hiring a man had been a mistake. He always knew too much and had all the answers, according to him, and she'd started to notice how much her other, male, partners praised him—despite the fact that he was, at best, a mediocre secretary.

'Well, don't stay too much longer. You know, if you're unable to get your work done in normal office hours, we should talk about getting you some extra training.'

He did a bad job of hiding his irritation as he smiled his thanks. 'By the way, I keep meaning to ask you,' he piped up, as she turned away, 'how are the children?'

Next thing he'd be asking if she was thinking of quitting soon, thought Anna, as she stepped into the lifts. She had been good enough at her job not to get sacked the moment they realised she was pregnant, but she'd only just scraped by the second time, with Leanne, and now she felt as if she were always on trial, making up for her big mistake.

She was getting there, though. Last year she'd made capital partner, the first woman in the hundred-year history of the company to ever do so, and if she could keep billing at this rate, soon she would move into a suite.

'Is it because I have a good job?' she'd asked Myles at lunch. 'Does the fact that I earn more than you interfere with your sense of masculinity somehow?'

'No! You know how proud of you I am.'

But she still wondered. What if being successful was a turn-off, like hairy armpits? Not just to Myles, but to lots of men?

She had never questioned any of this before, because Myles had always been so supportive, but now she wondered where that came from. Was he compensating for her? As she stepped out of the lifts, she thought of all the secretaries at her firm. Apart from Gilbert, they were all women. Was it possible they were purposely not pushing harder for promotion because they knew you couldn't have everything, and they were choosing to be loved instead? She was the only female capital partner. Was it possible—what a sickening thought—that they all felt sorry for her?

The lift arrived at the basement floor and she stepped out into the arcade.

'Anna.'

Steve stood a few feet away from her, his feet apart, dressed in jeans and a simple white T-shirt, his hands in the pockets of his tan leather jacket, bouncing lightly on the balls of his feet, like a sprinter at the start of a race.

'All right?'

'Of course.' Carol said it too, sometimes—it must be an English thing—and Anna had stopped wondering why it wouldn't be.

'So . . .' He cocked his head to one side as he looked at her.

'Carol asked me to talk to you.'

'You're her union rep,' he smirked.

'Well, yes, actually, that's a perfectly good way to think of it.' She gestured to a bench that had been parked in front of some ferns and a miniature palm tree in white plastic tubs. 'Shall we?'

'What? Here?'

'It won't take long.'

'We couldn't go to a bar?' His voice rose incredulously.

'It's not that kind of conversation.' She sat down, clasping her hands together, her silver cuff bracelets clinking. *The ball is in my court*, she reminded herself. It worked like a mantra, whenever she had a difficult pitch to make to clients. *I am in my element.* 'You can't just turn up at my house, Steve.'

'Says who?'

'Says me. And Carol,' she added quickly. 'She doesn't want to see you.'

His shoulders sagged, and his face dropped. Carol had left him on the night of the concert with no warning, remembered Anna. She'd just packed up and gone.

'When will she?' he asked.

'It's only been four weeks. Give it some time, won't you? And some money.' The minute she said this, Anna knew she'd made a mistake.

'She still bludging off you, then? I knew it.'

'She has a job, as a matter of fact.'

'I know that. And I bet I know where, too.'

Why remind him? Anna cursed herself.

'*Oh, I'm too scared, blah blah blah*,' he said in an ugly voice. 'Hasn't stopped her from leaving Colette alone now after school, has it, when it suits her?'

This time Anna managed not to rise to the bait.

'Is that it, then?' he asked.

'What do you mean?' She had been going to talk about the fact that none of their husbands could just turn up without calling, even though the truth was Myles did, and Ben refused to come around at all. But the conversation seemed to have died, somehow, and the opportunity to push for more advantage had gone with it.

'Right, then.' He stood up and began to walk towards the escalator.

'Hey!' Her voice rang around the empty space. 'Wait!'

'What now?'

'Are you going to keep coming over, or not?'

He walked back and stopped, just half a foot away from her. Too close—but she forced herself to keep standing there, and not to give him any ground.

'You asked me to come here, to tell me not to come to the place where my wife and daughter are living. I've heard you. What else do you want?'

'An answer! Carol needs to know for her peace of mind. She's very vulnerable, you know.'

Steve put his finger under his nose and breathed in deeply with his eyes closed, as though deep in thought.

Anna looked on incredulously. It was an effort not to laugh.

'I'll tell you what,' said Steve, opening his eyes, 'there's a bar upstairs which I passed on the way in. If you come and have a drink it will give me a chance to think.'

Anna knew that bar. She went there with clients sometimes after evening focus groups. 'No.'

'What if I say that on condition of you having a drink with me I won't come to the house anymore?'

'Really?' She thought of Carol's face. 'All right. One drink.'

It was dark inside the bistro, the black-and-gold banquettes and low-hanging chandeliers reflected in the mirrored wall decorations and gleaming black countertop of the bar.

'What are you drinking?' he asked, leading her to the bar as though she were his guest.

'I'll just have a Tab, thanks, bartender,' she said, avoiding Steve's eyes as she took off her coat.

'You agreed to a drink,' he said belligerently. 'Have a real drink.'

'That's not what I agreed,' she said crisply, 'but all right then.' She was about to ask for a glass of the house red—her usual—when on impulse she changed her mind. 'I'll have a whisky on the rocks,' she said daringly. 'With a splash of water.' After all, Anna reminded herself, she was doing things differently now.

'You know, you're different to how I thought you'd be,' said Steve, once they were sitting down facing one another in a banquette.

'Meaning what?' Anna put her handbag on the table and drew out her pack of cigarettes.

'That you're not stuck up,' said Steve, smoothly flicking his lighter as she drew a cigarette to her lips, and then slipping it back into the upper pocket of his shirt.

'Charming.' Anna took a long drag of her cigarette. The man was crude. So obvious and dull. 'However, you're not.'

'What?'

'Different.'

'Touché.' He reached over and took one of the cigarettes from her pack. Once he'd lit it, he glanced at her, his eyebrows raised, ironically asking for permission.

She would go straight home after this, she decided, even though she'd been intending to go back to the office for a few hours.

She would buy a lasagne from the deli on the corner, which she could pop in the oven tomorrow night when the girls were back from staying with Myles. She jumped as she felt a touch on her wrist.

'Sorry.'

'For what?' Anna replied lightly, moving her hand away.

'For getting at you.'

Their eyes met and Anna felt a jolt of recognition. Steve was testing her, she realised, and testing this situation, looking for information and points of weakness he could use later to gain the upper hand. She did that at work sometimes, in a much more subtle way, of course.

Their drinks arrived in thick crystal tumblers on a silver tray.

'That's better,' she said, as she let the first wash of liquid warm her throat, followed by another and then another, taking quick sips to help her relax.

'Hey! That's not how you drink whisky.'

'It's how *I* drink whisky,' she said, trying to hide her embarrassment.'

Steve smiled sceptically, his eyebrows raised, as if he was in on her childish deception, and before she could stop herself she'd given him a half smile back.

'That's better,' he said, his gaze holding hers for a moment longer than was strictly necessary. Anna tilted up her glass for the dregs, closing her eyes to break the intensity, but when she opened them again his eyes were still on her face, watching her.

'I have to go,' she said abruptly, gathering up her cigarettes and handbag.

'I'll see you out,' Steve said, jumping to his feet.

As lithe as a cat, noticed Anna reluctantly, with a twisting feeling, both pleasurable and sickening, in her abdomen. What was this feeling she kept having around him?

'No. That's okay,' Anna said, shying away from his hands as he moved to help her put on her coat. 'Here, let me,' she said when the bartender brought over the bill, reaching for her purse.

'You can't be serious.' His lip curled.

Anna froze, watching helplessly as he paid. It was three times what it would have cost in the pub across the street. Not to mention almost double the tiny contributions towards the housekeeping that Carol had been struggling to make.

'You don't need to be scared of me, you know,' he said conversationally as they walked away.

'I'm not scared.' Her voice sounded high, though, and artificial to her ears.

'You're a very attractive woman,' he said casually, as they stepped onto the escalator.

She turned up the collar of her trench coat to hide her face and the sickening mix of pleasure and shame which she was sure must be written there.

'Did I just break the rules?' he asked, peering around to catch her eye.

'What rules?' she shot back.

'Shouldn't you be offended? Isn't it sexist or something these days? To pay a woman a compliment?'

She was offended by his arrogance, and horrified by her own response to him, but she tried to sound offhand. 'Well, it happens.'

'That's not what I heard.'

'Pardon me?'

'It's been a very long time for you, hasn't it?' He smirked.

It took a moment for her to get it, but when she did, her insides shrivelled. It was as if she had been groped.

'That's really none of your business,' she snapped.

Steve was laughing now, his face lit up with pleasure. 'You're not the only one who knows things, Anna Wotcek.'

'But how? How would you know something like that?' Surely Myles wouldn't have told him.

'Colette told me.'

Colette? 'She must have overheard something. I'm sorry,' said Anna stiffly.

'Oh, she'll be fine,' said Steve magnanimously. 'Sorry to have embarrassed you.'

'I'm not embarrassed,' she said flatly.

'Really?' He looked amused.

'No,' she said firmly, convincing herself. 'After all, it's not as if we're ever going to see each other again.'

'That's a shame.'

'Not really.' She managed to sound positively light. 'Oh look, there's my bus.'

There it was, steaming and straining towards her, at the traffic lights. She had never been so happy to see it in her life.

'You know, I'd already decided that I wasn't going to go to the house, even if you hadn't agreed to have a drink with me,' said Steve, standing too close to her as she waited in the bus queue. 'All you had to do was ask.'

'Uh-huh.' Anna pretended to be absorbed in fishing her bus ticket out of her bag. She would be gone from here in just a few seconds, she told herself.

'I would have offered you more. I would have said I won't visit Carol at work, either, if you'd asked me.'

Something snapped inside Anna, and she stepped out of the line. 'So all of a sudden it's up to me, now? What you do?'

Their eyes held each other's for a long moment. Like two animals circling one another in the jungle, taking each other's measure. Or more like dogs around an overflowing rubbish bin. She hated this.

'Too late,' he said, and stepped back, as if he were releasing her.

Feeling cross and awkward, she clumped up the stairs onto the bus, her stocking catching on someone's bag and laddering, her hand missing the railing so she was thrown down the aisle when the bus lurched forward.

As she settled into her seat she saw out of the corner of her eye that Steve was still standing by the side of the road in the rain, looking at her intently, as if he were in a spy movie.

'For god's sake!' she muttered, as he slowly raised a hand, theatrically waving goodbye.

~

'Why, Anna, you're glowing,' said Libby, as Anna let herself into the house in a gust of wind and rain. Libby had started laying a fire on wet evenings, mainly to help get rid of the mould, she said, but it created a lovely, cosy atmosphere. The girls were lying in front of it on the battered carpet, cutting out shapes from sewing patterns and pinning them onto felt. Jasper was sitting in Libby's lap on the sofa, as she helped him hand over hand with his scissors.

'With irritation!' said Anna, peering into her Cabaret mirror above the mantelpiece. With mascara running down her cheeks and her red painted lips standing out starkly against her pale skin, she almost looked like the movie's sad and romantic heroine.

'It didn't go well, then?' Libby looked at her over Colette's head.

'About as well as you might expect with that . . . that person.' She glanced at Colette, who was snipping away, seemingly oblivious. But only seemingly, Anna reminded herself, her insides shrivelling again at the thought of Steve's comments as she went into the kitchen and stowed the lasagne in the fridge. She would have to take more care about what she said in front of Colette, and she needed to warn Libby and Carol, too.

'How are you, Jassie?' Anna asked, leaning down to hug him. As usual, the moment Jasper saw her he had made a beeline for her, flinging his arms around Anna's hips. She went around the living room, tickling Colette and Summer on their heads before making her way to Carol's room.

'How did you go?' Carol asked. She was sitting on a stool at her dressing table, and she swivelled around to face Anna.

'He won't be coming over uninvited anymore.'

Carol slumped in relief. 'Did he say anything about coming to my work?'

She looked so vulnerable sitting there, and so alone. Anna's heart twisted. 'I'm sorry, Carol. He wouldn't promise me that.'

Later that evening, Libby sat curled up on the red velvet sofa, her big wooden needles rhythmically clack-clacking, her face impassive above them. Carol sat next to her holding a letter from her mother, staring wistfully into the flames. Anna was sitting in the armchair opposite, her head bent over the latest *Vogue*, examining each photo carefully before turning the page. The one she liked best was of a woman standing with her legs apart on a rock platform, her hands planted on her hips, smiling joyously. She wore a loose hessian skirt and a white peasant top, with slouching reindeer boots. Anna's fingers traced the outline of the woman's smile. She might have just split up with her husband. She might have only just realised he never really wanted her. As she posed in that outfit she might have had to force herself to stop wondering if anyone ever would want her, and to think about another day, maybe her wedding day, and to smile, smile, smile for the camera. A tear splashed down onto the page and Anna flicked it away, stealing a glance at the other two to check they hadn't noticed.

~

The next evening Anna left work early again—early for her, even though everyone else had cleared out ages ago, even Gilbert—and this time she caught the bus in the opposite direction. Today she went east instead of west, down Taylor Street with its gay bars and nightclubs, past the army barracks, the cinema and the old Town Hall to another suburb, very similar to Sandy, of rundown mansions and newly revived little shops. Evening was falling, and as Anna walked down a street of terraces she could see into people's living rooms, glimpsing book-lined walls and Turkish rugs as often as mean little kitchenettes, squeezed in next to narrow cots and primitive bathroom arrangements.

She turned into a stark white three-storey terrace where a small orange tree sat in a wooden tub by the gate. Anna wiped her feet carefully, fluffed out her hair and knocked on the glossy black door.

A small lithe woman opened it. She wore spotless cream stretch pants, the kind Anna used to wear for jazz ballet, and a black cowl-neck sweater.

'You're back.'

'Hi, Nicky.'

Anna sidled past her and turned immediately at the first doorway, where she kicked off her pumps before walking over the polished floorboards to the windows and collapsing into a low-slung tapestry-covered chair. It all felt as familiar as if she'd been here yesterday, even though it had actually been over a year.

'What's happening?' asked Nicky, padding over to sit down opposite. Her blues eyes were sunken in her craggy face, her nose beaky and her fine silver hair hanging in waves around her face.

Anna told her about her dinner party, the ABBA concert, Myles's magazines and moving out. 'And then there's this man, Steve,' she said breathlessly, the words tumbling out of her as she described what had happened between them, last night.

'Well, that's easy, at least. The answer's no—you shouldn't see him again. He's just a distraction,' said Nicky flatly. She sat back in her seat and looked at Anna, openly waiting for her reaction.

Nicky had always been this way, inscrutable when she wanted to be, and outspoken when she chose to be. Anna felt relieved that today she was choosing not to be mysterious.

'Why, *why* does he have to be the first man I've been attracted to since forever?' Anna wailed.

'You shouldn't read too much into this. It's very common, actually, for women. It's about control,' said Nicky, with a little smile. She spoke in the heavy accent and sure scepticism of her tragic central European background. 'All your life you have lived in the polarity of your helpless passionate mother, and the practical, sexless Anna.'

'Not completely sexless,' Anna muttered.

'Even the idea of sex makes you feel out of control and vulnerable, so you chose to marry a man you didn't desire, in order to feel safe. Now you have come to realise that merely being in control of everything isn't all that you want.'

'Wow.' Anna felt winded and a little bit offended by that *merely*—as if it were so easy! 'You think I didn't desire Myles?'

Nicky blinked. 'Now you are allowing yourself to be vulnerable by acknowledging desire. That's good.'

Anna smiled, relieved. It was lovely to feel as if she had done *something* right.

'The key for you is to realise that desire is not about feeling vulnerable or about feeling safe, although for women, it is understandable that it has been. But that is the wrong frame.'

'What is desire about, then?' asked Anna, breathless again at the prospect of an answer.

'Maybe it's about feeling safe and vulnerable. Or maybe it's something else altogether.' Disappointingly for Anna, Nicky had that smile on her face which meant she was done giving out answers. 'That's what you are going to find out.'

'Right,' said Anna. She felt a little as if her head had been opened up, and now just the clear air of enlightenment was rushing past. 'Do you still take Bankcard? Or shall I write you a cheque?'

Nicky laughed, patting her leg. 'It's not your job to deal with this man. It's impossible, in fact. And it's not possible for you to rescue Carol, either.'

Anna relaxed back into her seat, picking up a cushion from the sofa next to her and cradling it in her lap. 'That seems like a bit of a cop-out to me.'

'I'm sure there must be other ways for you to support her than getting caught in this web, no?' Nicky checked her watch. 'We still have forty minutes left. Why don't we talk about something other than this Steve ... Oh, I have an idea! Why don't we talk about you?'

~

When Anna was required to see a therapist as part of her training for her psychology degree, she had imagined it would involve a lot of lying around on a firmly upholstered chaise longue, talking about her dreams. But the woman who greeted her at the door was as direct as a shopkeeper, making notes on a yellow notepad while Anna talked, and then asking the exact question Anna most didn't want to answer, and helping her face the things she didn't want to see.

That she was scared of becoming like her mother, for example, both as a woman and as a mother. That she hated swimming in bodies of still water, and the taste of olives, both for the same reason—they reminded her of something ancient and bitter and murky that she didn't want stirred up, like her childhood. That the panic she felt when she gave birth to Michelle, and as her baby cried until she learned how to settle her, was an ancient panic; maybe it was in the hormonal DNA of all women, or maybe just in Anna's. She and Nicky dissected all of this and talked about it until Anna was able to look after both her girls as lovingly and attentively as she wanted to and didn't think twice about striding out into Myall Lake where they went for holidays, and could eat two olives straight up with a dirty enough martini.

'What kind of therapy do you *do*?' Anna asked Nicky over and over in the early years, wanting to look it up and study it so that she could understand why it worked so well.

'A little bit of everything,' said Nicky, smiling mysteriously.

'So it's agreed: you're not going to see this man again?' prompted Nicky at the end of their session.

'Of course not. I only wanted to help Carol.'

'Then why are you looking so tortured?' asked Nicky humorously, unwrapping a Butter Menthol, which she popped into her mouth.

'It makes me feel sad.'

'Well, it's all tragic, of course. But which part of it, exactly?'

'The idea of not having that feeling again. That I felt with him on the escalator.' And even before that, in the bar, she reminded herself. She had become aware of it from the moment she'd seen him at the front door, just after they'd moved into Avon Street, in fact.

'You mean desire,' Nicky clarified.

'Yes,' muttered Anna. She felt like a traitor to Carol, and to everything she believed in, simply admitting to that.

'Oh rubbish,' said Nicky affectionately. 'You're a woman in your prime. You will feel desire, and find it in many places, if that's what you can allow. But this sadness that you're feeling—you don't think it has anything to do with Myles?' She took off her glasses to peer at Anna. 'That you have discovered an enormous secret about him that has changed everything?'

'But I feel relieved about that. I told you. It explains why we weren't connecting.'

'For him,' said Nicky severely. 'It doesn't explain why, for you. Now, I have a question: you say this has been a problem for years. Perhaps for your whole marriage. So why have you and I never talked about it?'

'Because . . . if I had talked about it, even with you, then that would have made it real,' said Anna hesitantly. 'I think that's why Myles never wanted to talk about it either.'

'But, Anna, your feelings are real.' Nicky smiled with a tinge of barely discernible triumph. 'They exist, whether or not you can admit it, or even whether or not you know it. All you get to decide is how to respond to them. So,' she said, clapping her hands, 'my next question: why weren't you listening to yourself?'

Anna's eyes filled with tears.

'And here comes the true sadness,' said Nicky, as she briskly tore off a tissue and handed it to Anna, who sat with it pressed against her eyes.

'How could I have been such an idiot?'

'No one gets to your age without having made mistakes.'

'I don't think I've ever felt desire, until now.'

'Because why?' asked Nicky, her head cocked to one side. She clearly already knew the answer. 'Why until now?'

'Because of ABBA?' asked Anna uncertainly, twisting the tissue in her hands.

'No.' Nicky smiled again, affectionately this time. 'Because finally you feel safe.'

'And so I decide to blow up my life? That doesn't make any sense.'

'Because finally you feel safe enough to blow up the parts that aren't authentic, so that you can make a life that is.'

'First I married Myles and now I'm attracted to my flatmate's awful ex,' breathed Anna, awestruck. 'I don't think I have what it takes for this.'

Nicky patted her knee encouragingly. 'If it's happiness you want, then from what you tell me you have already found that with these two other women and your children. And if it's desire, also . . .'

'Which it is,' said Anna firmly.

'It might be difficult, but it's not complicated. You must listen to how you feel.'

Anna looked out the windows into the darkness. She didn't feel excited anymore, or exhilarated, or any of the myriad wonderful emotions she'd been experiencing ever since she decided to move out. She just felt terrified.

~

By the time she arrived home, dinner was already over. Her lasagne had been a huge success, Carol reported. She was sitting with Colette snuggled between her legs on her bed, playing with a string with Sampson. Colette's cheeks were tearstained, but Carol shook her head at her, so Anna didn't linger.

'How was school today?' she asked Michelle, who was colouring in a map at her desk.

'Fine.'

'How was it with Dad last night?'

Michelle looked at her distantly. 'Fine.'

'And how are you, darling?' she asked, turning to Leanne, somewhat desperately.

'Fine.'

Well, after all, what did you expect? Anna asked herself, as she changed into her pyjamas and dressing gown. She needed to give the girls time to adjust to this new reality, and to recognise that it might take even longer before they would be able to speak honestly with her about how they felt about it. And the last way she could expect to know was to ask them directly. She would have to be smarter about it, and look for signs. With Leanne that probably wouldn't be too difficult, but with Michelle it was always more complicated.

'Do you think the girls are getting along?' she asked Libby, whom she found cuddling with Jasper on the big old armchair in the living room. Libby looked up at her, and Anna started in surprise. She'd never seen Libby look so drawn. 'What's wrong?'

'Jassie's had a hard day, haven't you, Jassie?' Libby sighed, stroking his hair. Instead of jumping up to hug Anna, as he usually did, he turned his face into Libby's shoulder and snuggled in further, like a bear burrowing into its mother's fur. 'He had an accident, at school.' He shuddered, and Anna saw his little hand, which was holding Libby's, clench.

'Maybe we should talk about this later,' said Anna softly. 'Jassie, why don't I take you to bed while Mummy has a lie-down?'

Jasper nodded mutely as Libby kissed him.

'He's regressed,' said Libby, once Anna had settled him off to sleep, and gone into Libby's bedroom to sit on the end of her bed. 'They said I should expect this, but I didn't think it would be so bad. It's not just toileting. It's his motor skills. Everything. At school they said he's been refusing to do any of his exercises, or help clear away at the end of the day. And today when his teacher tried to make him at least pick up his own bag, he screamed. And you know Jasper—he's usually the sweetest, most helpful child.'

'Of course he is,' said Anna loyally. 'He's wonderful.'

'Well, today they said I should take him back to that child psychologist, who costs an arm and a leg and speaks rubbish. Sorry,' she added.

'I'm not a psychologist, Libby. I keep telling you. But did they think that he might help Jasper?'

'They just don't want to be responsible,' Libby said. 'You know, for the first few weeks of living with us here he seemed to be doing so well. I was hoping that he might even be catching up a little bit. He just loves being with all of us like this, and especially with the girls. There's always something happening.'

'We love being with Jasper,' said Anna. For a child who rarely spoke, and who could be so low-key that you almost didn't notice him sometimes, he had a big impact. Michelle and Leanne were more loving towards him than she'd seen them be to anyone else, and they all did things more slowly and patiently because of him. He in turn was far more tough-minded, tenacious and funny than she ever would have suspected if they hadn't been living together.

'Something's upset him, and he doesn't have the words to explain,' Libby was saying. 'Maybe it's some kind of argument or tension he's been picking up between the girls. Summer mentioned something about Colette and Michelle being at odds the other day. I know it will pass, and that he'll move forward again. He always does. But it's just so hard when it's like this. It can feel . . .' She sighed again, and stopped herself.

'Say it, Lib. You can tell me.'

'Even though we're all together, and it's so much fun, and you're all so helpful . . . when I'm up changing Jasper's sheets every night, and he's so angry with me . . . it can feel as if I'm still on my own.'

'Oh Libby, I don't want you to feel that way. What does Ben think?'

'That it's all my fault. Or that's what he implies, it's not as if we ever really talk. Thank god he's so generous with the child support. That takes a bit of the pressure off, at least. And you and Carol are so helpful.' Libby closed her eyes again, resting her head against the back of her chair.

'You're the most helpful out of all of us,' said Anna. 'I don't know how I would have managed without you.'

Libby was so competent and capable that it never crossed Anna's mind to worry about her, let alone feel an emotion as unwelcome and complicated as pity. But now she thought of how challenging it had been to teach Michelle and Leanne to care for themselves over the years, and get them ready—emotionally, as well as practically—to go to school; and then she tried to double that and then triple that to imagine what it must have been like for Libby with Jasper for all these years.

'They've asked me to do an extra day at school tomorrow, supporting the kids to use the toilet and all that, on top of my usual day each week; but Ben was there all last weekend building special ramps, which just put even more of the childcare onto me . . .'

And to think Anna had felt virtuous helping in class with reading occasionally, and going to P&C meetings! She sat back in surprise, ashamed that she hadn't thought about this properly until now. Even living with Libby, it was easy to take for granted the support she provided for Jasper, both at home and at school, because Jasper was so adorable, and Libby was so loving and uncomplaining. And she must have been hiding Jasper's extra laundry, too, Anna realised. The girls had always hated other people to know when they wet their beds, and Jasper must feel the same. Now that she came to think of it—and she couldn't believe it had taken her this long to realise—Libby had far too much on her plate.

'I'm going to start taking Jasper out with the girls on weekends, and Summer, too, if she feels like it,' Anna said. 'We're going to have proper adventures.'

'You don't know what you're offering,' Libby said, with something between a laugh and a moan.

'Yes, I do,' said Anna. 'Or at least I do a little bit. Please let me help you.'

'It's a nice idea. Jasper would love it, and if I could just manage some proper sleep, maybe I could even get a job.'

'Now, that is an excellent idea,' said Anna. She'd been wondering what Libby's plans were in that department. 'And why don't I come with you, to that appointment?'

'To see the specialist? But why?'

'To support you.'

'But I don't think you're even allowed to do that, are you? To bring a doctor along to a doctor's meeting?'

'Libby, I'm not a doctor! I meant as your friend.'

Libby looked baffled and Anna felt mortified. Maybe this was none of her business. Maybe she was being exhausting, or this was *a bit much*.

Anna saw a look of pure exhaustion cross Libby's face. She would insist on getting up with Jasper tonight, and from now on for at least one night a week, she decided. She would ask Carol if she wanted to do it, too, and that way Libby could have at least a couple of full nights of sleep each week. Libby could stay up late if she wanted to, sleep in, or have more one-on-one time with Summer. And Anna would be so happy to spend more time with Jasper.

'I could just come with you and listen,' Anna said. 'Or I could put in my two cents' worth if that's what you wanted. You might dread it less, if I come too.'

'I'm afraid the psychologist is going to say Jasper would be better off in a home,' Libby whispered.

'What?' Anna started.

'The specialist. They always say it's not fair to him, not to give him the opportunity. And that it's not fair to us.' Her tone was scathing.

'And what do you say?'

'That the only opportunity they're talking about is for him to be out of sight and out of mind. I've been to those places, Anna. They're institutions. The best place for Jasper is with his own family, in his own home. It is for all kids, but especially for kids like him. Oh god. What if Ben's right?' Libby dragged her hands over her face. 'What if I'm making a huge mistake?'

'All I know is, you're a wonderful mother, and Ben is a wonderful father. And living together or living apart, Jassie could not have a better home, or have better parents than the two of you. But, Libby, you have the right to be happy, too. If you don't want to live with Ben, then you shouldn't have to.'

'Why are you being so nice to me?' Libby burst out.

'What do you mean?' Anna recoiled. Had she gone too far again?

'I'm sorry, I didn't mean it like that, I'm just so tired,' said Libby. 'What I mean is, you're so lovely. I keep noticing it. Have you always been this way?'

'Myles says I have a peculiar talent for putting my worst foot forward, which means I don't always make a great first impression,' said Anna shyly.

'Well, I would love it if you came with me to the specialist. As my friend.'

This was the kind of moment where some women would probably hug each other, thought Anna, but she settled for making tea instead.

'I'm sure things will get better, Libby. You'll see, everything will settle down,' she said, as she handed Libby a fresh cup.

'I'm sure,' said Libby, smiling at Anna gratefully, but she didn't seem convinced.

10

Libby

'HELLO, HELLO,' LIBBY CALLED OUT AS she lifted up the corner of the bar and slipped through, lowering it into place behind her. The Stag and Ball Hotel was the opposite of glamorous, but it was close to home—just a ten-minute walk through the backstreets of Sandgate, past the dog track and the fish markets—and Libby was simply happy to have found a job for the first time in ten years.

She took an apron from the pile and wrapped it around her waist, criss-crossing the ties to pull it tight and smooth over the buttons of her skirt, then checked her appearance in the mirror behind the bar. To her intense disappointment, she looked matronly; while the apron didn't help, it was mostly the fault of her breasts. They weren't the pert little apples you were supposed to have— hers were large and full. They looked conventional, somehow, and a bit careless, as if she'd forgotten to say 'when'. Her hair looked good, though, and she swung her head from side to side in satisfaction. Carol now insisted on giving her a weekly blow-dry and so her shag bounced in smooth waves around her face, as if she'd just left the salon.

'Hello, darl. How's tricks?'

'Hello Lois, I didn't see you there.'

Lois was squatting down in front of the bar fridge, ticking things off a list. She wore the same regulation white shirt and black skirt as Libby, but custom-tailored so that it fit snugly to her neat curves. Her white-blonde hair was set in tight waves around her face, and her deep red lipstick made a dramatic slash of colour in her pale and perfectly powdered face. She was sixty if she was a day, Libby had calculated at her interview, but so far she'd never seen her sit down. Lois's only concession to comfort were her thick, white-soled nurse's shoes, which Libby vowed she wouldn't be seen dead in. That lasted until her second day on the job, when she decided it didn't matter what she wore from the waist down anyway, seeing as she was standing behind a bar.

'We're out of rum,' said Lois, over the rim of her spectacles.

'What, again?'

Lois never stopped moving, and Libby tried hard to follow suit. Now she began to wipe down the dark marble bar and lay out the scarlet runners, embellished with the pub's insignia of a ball, a stag and a ribbon intertwined.

'He looks well hung,' was a favourite joke of the customers, Libby quickly learned. Or maybe, for something different: 'Now that's a big ball!'

'Sadly just the one, though,' Libby would shoot back as she filled their orders, barely listening to their answers as she struggled to work out the change. Her brain had become foggier and slower since she'd last been a barmaid, and she didn't remember ever feeling this exhausted at the end of an ordinary day. Why did

I ever think work was so special? she had wondered almost as soon as she started. It was only now that she remembered how happy and relieved she'd been to quit when she got engaged. And that was before she had two children, let alone before she was obliged to 'volunteer' her services in Jasper's classroom one day each week. With Anna's and Carol's help, though, she was somehow managing, and it felt good to be earning some money to add to her nest egg.

A loud knock startled her out of her thoughts. A gnarled old face was peering in at her through the glass of the door. She glanced up at the clock and sped across the old blue carpet to open it. 'Good morning, Bernie. Bang on time as usual.'

'She kicks me out, doesn't she? "You leave me alone now, Mr Murray," she says. "I've got to do my cleaning."'

'Well, she can't do that with a big lump like you underfoot,' said Libby fondly.

'She's not really cleaning,' Bernie harrumphed as he settled himself comfortably onto his favourite stool. 'She's just going to sit around all day, gossiping with her friends.'

'Like you, Bernie,' said Libby, giving the tables a flick with her cloth as she went around the room. 'It's a big day today. We're raffling off the meat tray, and they're running the Empire Cup at Flemington this afternoon.' She cleared a space at one end of the bar for the chicken, which would be displayed on a chafing dish surrounded by cut-up vegetables and pats of butter, and tuned the radio, which would be turned up and down all morning for the races.

Not much had changed in the decade since she'd been a bartender—certainly not the wages—but the hardest thing for Libby to get used to was the quiet. She didn't have the curiosity about her customers she used to, or the feeling that at any minute somebody might walk in who could change her life. It was more peaceful this way, but it also gave her time to think—a pursuit she wasn't exactly fond of these days. She fought it by keeping herself extra busy, running in and out to the bottle shop, and up and down to the salesmen staying in the rooms upstairs, keeping everyone supplied with beer.

It was always a relief when lunchtime came around, and the office workers poured in. They took up their stations at the tall round tables situated as far as possible from the bar, and ordered complicated concoctions, changing their order every time. After a while they would start to speak more loudly, and take off their jackets and the noise level would rise, and soon whenever Libby looked up at the clock, another half-hour would have flown by.

'It's busy today,' said Bernie, as Libby counted the price of his usual cheese sandwich from the pile of coins he kept piled up in front of him on the bar.

'It's always like this on a Friday, Bern.'

'Makes no difference to me what day it is,' he grumbled. 'I'm retired.'

'He's just cross because he didn't win the chook,' said Albert, who was sitting opposite.

'Mrs Murray will be disappointed, will she, Bernie?' asked Libby, glancing up as a new group of people came crowding through the doors. This lot were wearing tennis outfits and had already had a drink or two somewhere else by the look of them. They were laughing and sweaty, and the lone woman's smile was wide and exhilarated. Libby couldn't help but admire the woman's outfit, and her petite frame. Her white tennis dress was neat yet sexy, and she held her racquet against her shoulder with a certain flare. She was speaking animatedly to one of the men who stood with his back to Libby, his red tracksuit jacket hung loosely over his shoulder. They leaned towards one another and kissed, and Libby sighed to think of being so free and easy as to be out kissing at the pub on a Friday afternoon. The woman murmured something and he nodded, turning around.

The shock felt physical.

'Ben?' His beard was gone and his hair was short. He looked so different that for a moment she hardly recognised him.

He paled for a moment, before saying something to the woman and walking over, crowding in between Bernie and Albert to stand in front of Libby at the bar.

'What are you doing here?' she asked. She could hardly breathe.

'Ah, having a drink.' He cleared his throat. 'What are *you* doing here?'

'What does it look like? Who's that?' she managed to add, before her throat closed over.

'Who?'

Bernie's and Albert's heads swivelled from one to the other, as if they were watching a tennis match.

'The girl whose throat you were just sticking your tongue down!' she choked.

'Oh.' He glanced pointedly at the two old men, but this was the most riveting thing to have happened in here in ages, and they weren't budging. 'Just a friend.'

Something about the way he was standing, so tall and square-shouldered, yet still with his jacket draped oh-so-loosely over his shoulder, convinced her that he'd planned this.

'So you thought you'd bring her along, to stage a little kiss?'

'What? No! Can't I go out for a drink on a Friday arvo without it being about you?'

So he was still furious. His consistency shouldn't have surprised her. Nothing could make him stop loving her when they lived together. And nothing could make him soften towards her now.

'You never knock off early,' said Libby flatly. 'Not to mention you don't play tennis.'

'I might have changed.'

'I doubt it. And you've always been a rotten liar.'

Ben had been cold and hard with her since the day she left. Their pick-ups and drop-offs and conversations about the kids went smoothly, but he was always chillingly polite. A chunk of his salary appeared like clockwork in her account every Thursday, but he refused to share anything else. And now this, obviously, was the next step in the way he'd decided they would conduct their separation.

She cleared her throat and looked around. Bernie had gone to the bathroom—bless him—and Albert had buried his head in his newspaper, following the form. Now someone turned up the volume on the radio and a horse race came blaring forth.

'Are you going to keep punishing me forever?' she asked, under the cover of the announcer.

'What?' He pointed at his ear. 'I can't hear you.'

'Are you going to keep punishing me forever?' repeated Libby, leaning over the bar to speak directly into his ear.

His face was ashen when she straightened up again.

'I should get back to work,' she said. The race was ending, and Bernie was heading back across the room. Ben's mouth was moving, but she couldn't make out a word.

Please don't cry, Libby begged herself. Not in front of Ben and that woman, let alone Bernie and Albert and all the other regulars whom she had to face again on Monday.

'Libby, listen to me,' said Ben, reaching across the bar for her hand.

'Don't touch me!' She jerked backwards, bumping into Lois.

Ben backed away, staring, his arms floating back helplessly to his sides. 'I didn't mean . . .'

'You can't touch the barmaids,' said Bernie, nodding piously as he sat back down.

'No, you can't,' said Albert, in a rare moment of agreement.

'Are you all right?' Lois asked Libby in a low voice. 'Sit down.'

'I can't do that!' said Libby, scandalised.

'Yes, you can. Now sit.' She thrust Libby down by the shoulders onto the folding stepladder they used to reach the bottles on the top shelf. 'And you'll all just have to wait,' said Lois, raising her voice at the crowd of customers who were gathering. 'Now, sir, what are you having?' she asked Ben, who fumbled for his wallet and recited his order, his eyes fixed miserably on Libby the whole time. His shoulders were slumped as he shambled back to where his friends waited, the drinks balanced on an aluminium tray.

After a few minutes Libby forced herself to start serving again, shrugging off Lois's objections but watching Ben out of the corner of her eye the whole time, clocking his every move.

His tennis buddies hadn't noticed anything was up, evidently, from the way they were slapping him on the shoulder and expecting him to join in their jokes. He was silent, though, and stunted in his movements, taking cautious sips of his beer, and the woman in the tennis dress kept throwing him anxious glances as they stood side by side, no longer touching. A man in their group asked something, gesturing at Ben's glass, and she saw her estranged husband shake his head and point at his watch. They laughed and groaned in protest as they gathered their sports bags and headed for the door.

Except for Ben, who was coming over to the bar. Libby turned away and pretended to polish the spirits bottles, until his stare on her back became unbearable and she whirled around.

'Can't you see I'm busy?'

'I know you are,' he said, every feature etched with misery. 'But can I talk to you later? At the end of your shift?'

'You've got the kids tonight. Remember?' she replied, trying to sound extra stern.

He closed his eyes. 'Please, Libby.' This was the first time since she'd left that he'd asked her for anything. Maybe there was a chink in the armour he'd put on the day she left him; this was the first hint of human emotion or caring she'd seen in any of their interactions since then.

'I'm off at five,' she said. 'Now go.'

He stared at her for another long moment before turning away. Libby stood watching as he walked out the door.

'Who was that?' asked Lois.

It was the first direct question Lois had ever asked her. In the two months since Libby had started working here, the only personal subject they'd ever spoken about was the children, and that was only because the two of them came in with Carol to pick up the house keys one day.

'He's my husband.' Libby was crying openly now that Ben wouldn't see.

'What a dog.' Lois handed her a bunch of paper napkins from the pile they kept beside the beer taps. 'Out at lunchtime with another bird. Good looking, too. Although not as good looking as you.'

'Thanks, Lois,' said Libby, blowing her nose—which was another big bartending no-no, but she was long past caring now.

'What a low-down, lying, worthless, scumbag dog.' Lois cast her gaze around the emptying room, balefully. 'Men!' she said. Bernie and Albert shrank down into their beer coasters. 'Bloody men!'

'Ben's not a dog,' protested Libby weakly.

'I just saw him! Kissing that little girl in broad daylight. She must be half his age, too!'

'No. Actually—' it took every last ounce of courage Libby had to say it '—we're separated.'

'Separated?' Lois took her glasses out of her cleavage to stare at Libby's wedding finger, which still bore her matching diamond and ruby engagement and wedding rings. 'Was that his idea or yours? Speak up, girly! I can't hear you.'

'It was me!'

'So he cheated,' Lois sighed. 'All the same, it's not very nice to come parading that girl around. It's worse, actually.'

'He didn't cheat. He didn't do anything. I just wasn't happy, that's all.'

'Hell's bells! You mean you left him?'

Libby flinched. In all her weeks with Lois she had never heard her swear, not even when they left the meat tray out and had to sell tickets at half price. The older woman stood with her hands on her hips and her head stuck forward like a chicken's.

'With two young kids you left to be a single mother and work in a bar?'

'It's not like that,' said Libby miserably.

'Oh, my dear.' Lois folded up her glasses and slipped them back into her cleavage, shaking her head sadly. 'You silly, silly girl.'

~

Ben was waiting for her, slumped against a street light, when she emerged.

It wasn't just the lighting inside—although he would be the first person in the universe it actually flattered, he did look good.

'Where are your friends?' And by that she meant the woman in the tennis dress.

'They've all gone home.'

'Where are the kids?' she asked sharply.

'They're fine.'

'Where are they?' she asked, her voice rising. She would be sick if that woman was with Jasper.

'In the car. Over there.'

Libby peered around the corner to where the Kingswood was parked, facing in the opposite direction, illegally, next to a telephone booth. With stern self-discipline, she resisted the temptation to point that out.

'I told them we were stopping off here because I had to pick something up for you, from your work,' said Ben. 'I don't want them to know you're here, if that's okay. It will just get them all worked up.'

Normally she would have insisted on seeing the kids anyway, but she didn't want them to see her like this, especially Jasper. 'Okay.'

'I'm sorry, Libby.'

'For what, exactly?' She tried to sound unconcerned, even though she was hanging on every word.

'For how I've been. Today especially. For coming here, with Antonia, and . . . and kissing her like that.'

So the woman had a name. That wasn't good. Libby wanted to be liberated, but that didn't mean she felt good about someone else kissing her husband. Her ex-husband, Libby reminded herself.

Let alone the idea of Ben going out with her. If he had to be touched by another woman—the idea was almost unimaginable, although now Libby could see she had been crazy not to realise it was inevitable—why couldn't it be casual? A crazy episode after which Ben would never see her again, and Libby would never have to learn her name? It seemed very hard, so soon after separating, for all this to be going on.

'I don't have a good excuse for it,' Ben was saying. 'Summer told me you worked here and . . . and I still felt angry, I suppose. But it was wrong of me. I realised that as soon as I saw you. And I'm sorry.'

'Okay,' said Libby hoarsely again.

'Thank you.'

'So who's Antonia?' She tried out an encouraging smile.

She saw him about to cut her off—by now she could tell by the smallest muscles in his face—and then he changed his mind. 'She's a colleague.'

'Is she an architect?' For Ben to fall in love with a fellow professional who shared his passion for housing—that was Libby's greatest fear.

'No, Antonia's an engineer.' For Ben to fall in love with a fellow professional who was a technical expert—actually, that was worse.

'On placement,' said Ben. 'She's only just graduated.'

Libby blinked. That meant Antonia was even younger than she looked. Oh god! Where had Libby's consciousness-raising-group wisdom disappeared to? Right when she needed it the most?

'We haven't slept together.'

'Oh. Well. Groovy, I guess,' said Libby lamely. *But why hadn't they?* She and Ben had slept together the first night they met.

A shout rose from the car.

'Has um, Antonia met the children?' Libby's voice shook a little. It was hard to believe they were already having this conversation. It had only been four months.

'Not yet. We're just getting to know each other.'

'Oh. Groovy.' Where was her rich vocabulary, which she was usually so proud of? Libby despaired. 'Cool.'

Another shout rose from the car.

'Just a sec.'

Libby watched as he walked around the corner to the car, bending over to say something through the window, and then throwing in a bag of chips, which he drew from his jacket pocket.

'They're going to go everywhere,' warned Libby, when he returned. 'Is the floor clean? Because you know they'll eat off it.'

'Lib.'

He hadn't called her that since she'd left. And he had his possum eyes back again. That soft expression she hadn't seen for so long, all liquid and melty, when he looked at her.

'I won't let anyone you don't know near the kids until I have your approval, okay?' he said.

'How did . . .' She shook her head, speechless at the enormity of what was happening. 'How have we come to this?'

'You wanted it.'

He wasn't stiffly holding himself apart from her anymore. He was being grave and kind and sober—just like her old Ben. This was worse.

'But, you know,' he continued, 'I've been thinking, maybe it's for the best.'

'How's that?' she managed to ask.

'It was all just getting too complicated.' He scratched his head. 'You weren't happy. I wasn't happy.'

'Weren't you?' This was the first she'd heard of it.

'I was stuck.' He shrugged, smiling ruefully. 'Now I'm going out, trying new things—like tennis—and I've lost some weight.'

'You look good.'

'Thanks, I feel good.'

He looked great, actually. Libby was suddenly able to see him for a moment with new eyes.

'You've cut your hair.' Her voice was coming back to her. In a minute she might start to breathe normally. 'And shaved your beard. I almost didn't recognise you.'

'Finally,' he said, putting his hands up to his face as though searching for it. 'Listen, I should get the kids home. It's feeding time at the zoo.'

'Chish and Fips?' Libby smiled to make it clear she wasn't going to disapprove.

'No. I have a woman who comes in now, remember? Mrs Guest. She'll have made something. Chops and veg, I think she said, and she always makes something fancy for dessert.'

'That's right.' Libby had failed to update her mental picture, and she'd been imagining him stumbling and fumbling around the house like a kind of stone-age caveman dad.

'It's certainly a lot more work than I realised, though, keeping those kids fed and entertained. Man!' He shook his head. 'I don't remember anyone entertaining me when I was their age.'

'Maybe you didn't notice.'

'You're right,' he said thoughtfully. 'I probably didn't. Anyway, my hat goes off to you, Lib. Even more so than before.'

Libby smiled back at him, reluctantly. He was being kind to her, she realised, and appreciative.

'What about work?' she asked curiously. She had been wondering.

'Work's good, actually. I've had to become a whole lot more efficient, and that's probably a good thing.'

'Probably,' she said drily.

'All right then,' said Ben awkwardly. Their cheeks brushed against one another's in an air kiss, something they had never done before, and Ben strode around the corner to the Kingswood, opening the kids' door and half climbing into the back. Unwinding a mangled seatbelt, probably, guessed Libby, or scooping up the remains of the exploded chip packet. Libby took one last look over her shoulder as she forced herself to walk away. The last glimpse Libby had of him were his legs sticking out like a bear with its head in a tree trunk, or a winter den, maybe, seeing to its cubs.

~

Libby walked home slowly through the winter afternoon, stopping to pat stray cats and pick up some cans someone had left in the street. She turned in at their gate and checked the letterbox. No letter from Strauss, but she would be arriving for her annual visit next week, so she probably hadn't bothered to write. This garden was barren in winter and the rose bush still wasn't blooming, noticed Libby, as she dragged herself up the stairs, even though Mrs Georgiou from next door kept promising her that any day now it would.

'Hi, girls!' Libby called out as she walked down the hall. Colette and Michelle and Leanne were each in their own rooms to judge by the firmly closed doors, and possibly in bad moods, to judge by their silence.

'Are the girls all right?' she asked as she entered the kitchen.

'Colette told me they're playing some kind of game where they're pretending not to speak to one another,' said Carol.

'Oh,' said Libby, even more relieved that Summer was with Ben tonight. 'Funny girls.'

She'd started calling them The Girls—they all had, because they moved around in such a different way from Jasper, eddying and flowing around him the way a school of fish might around an octopus. He was a boy for one thing, but also as a person he seemed so much more open and willing to engage with the adults around him. The girls had become so closed and secretive, as if they moved in their own world—a different world, which had its own rules, that Libby couldn't see into or understand anymore. And when she did catch a glimpse of it, like now, it disturbed her. They had their own private in-jokes and ways of speaking, their own ways of fighting and relating that she couldn't trust that she knew.

Jasper, on the other hand, was still young enough to be transparent. She knew it wouldn't last. He probably wasn't even as transparent now as she thought. But Libby felt as if she knew where she was with him in a way she almost never felt anymore with Summer, and she wondered if Anna and Carol felt that with their daughters. Then again, thought Libby a few minutes later, as she dumped her apron in the laundry, what did their husbands think of them? She knew she'd always moved in ways Ben didn't understand, and vice versa. Perhaps as we grow older we're all increasingly impenetrable, thought Libby, looking out into the garden, and then she shook herself. If she didn't stop ruminating she'd keep going down this rabbit hole, and soon she wouldn't believe that anyone could really understand or be understood by anybody else, and we may as well all throw ourselves in the ocean.

'Carol's made sangria,' said Anna, looking up from the TV guide. 'I've bought some French onion dip and crackers, and Pierre Trudeau's on after the news.'

'Cool,' said Libby faintly.

'Sampson's excited, at least,' said Carol, lugging him into the living room.

'Bloody Ben.' Libby plumped herself down on the couch, and eased off her shoes.

'Oh my god!' said Anna, as she and Carol exchanged significant glances.

'What?' asked Libby.

'We've never heard you say a word against him in all this time,' said Carol. 'That must be some kind of record.'

'He used to think me wearing a seatbelt was an insult to his driving, did I ever tell you about that?'

Carol and Anna shook their heads.

'And if I asked him to pick up some bread on his way home from work, you'd think it was the martyrdom of St Stephen.'

'Huh,' said Carol, diplomatically.

'He never asked questions, and he was never, ever wrong about anything.'

'Well that's just sheer bad manners,' said Anna.

'He'd started wearing those bow ties to work that architects wear, even though we always used to laugh at that, and after dinner he'd go around the table and push all the chairs in exactly one inch away from the table.'

'Do you miss him, Lib? It's okay to, you know,' said Carol, underneath the sound of the blaring TV.

'How did you get to be so wise?' Libby stared at her.

'I'm a hairdresser.' Carol shrugged.

Libby lay down on the couch and exhaled properly for what felt like the first time in months. 'Bloody, bloody Ben.'

~

'You did it!' cried Strauss, striding down the hall. She had just had a shower, and now she was transformed from the crusty black-clad lump Libby had collected from the airport that morning into a sunny ball of energy, in a yellow skivvy, no bra and khaki overalls, her short bleached-blonde hair freshly spiked and her rosy round face radiant with pleasure. The strong coffees Libby had kept pouring into her over breakfast must have helped. 'You said you wanted to live differently, and now you are.'

'Now I am,' said Libby wanly, following her into the living room. Everyone else was off at school and work, so she and Strauss had the house to themselves.

'You have a real gift for this kind of thing, Lib. I've always said so. You're the Queen of the Good Share House.'

'It's not just me,' said Libby modestly.

'Whereas every time I join one, it falls apart.'

'That's just because you're so political,' said Libby, patting her on the arm.

'It's more because someone leaves the milk out of the fridge and someone else leaves a snotty note.'

Libby shivered and drew her dressing gown more tightly around her. What would she do if this household fell apart?

'Oh, I'm not worried about you lot,' said Strauss. 'You're all far too nice and sensible. In a good way,' she added, over Libby's retching noises.

'It definitely helps to have the kids,' said Libby, sitting down on the other end of the couch. She was still in her pyjamas, which she'd worn out to the airport with a coat over the top. Of course the moment Strauss saw her, standing at the top of the ramp in the Arrivals Hall, she'd shouted, 'And what do you think you're doing, greeting the international traveller in your jim-jams?'

'It makes it harder, though, after, when the house breaks up,' said Strauss sadly. 'Hey Lib. I've missed you.'

'I've missed you, too.'

Although she hadn't as much as she thought she would, Libby realised, when Strauss got up to answer the phone. She hadn't missed her in that gut-wrenching way she had after Strauss first left, saying, 'See ya, chick,' at the airport, and leaving a hole in Libby's life that she had worried might never be filled. She didn't have time, for one thing. Her need for everyday company and companionship were being met now, and so it was purely a Strauss-sized hole that Libby had to grapple with, rather than a gaping chasm of her own need. Now, if Anna or Carol needed to be alone, more often than not the other would be around and keen to chat, or just sit quietly together, reading and knitting or listening to something on the radio, which didn't feel like an affront, the way it used to sometimes with Ben. And Libby was seeing other friends more often, now, too. She could be looser about arrangements, knowing she could ask Anna or Carol to help with the children, and so she could more easily be spontaneous, and say yes.

'Any word from Mags?' asked Libby, once Strauss had hung up the phone and reappeared in the doorway of the living room. Strauss shook her head. Her radiance had disappeared, and now she just looked devastated.

'Oh hon.' Libby took Strauss's hand. It was small and strong, like Strauss. 'I'm sorry it didn't work out.' Mags was Strauss's Great Love, whom she had been living with for the last ten months in London.

'Yeah well.' Strauss fished around in the bib of her overalls for her tobacco tin and papers.

'Maybe she'll be there waiting, when you get back.'

'I don't think so.' Strauss put down her durry and let her head fall back against the couch. 'She's lovely. I wish you could have met her.'

'Maybe I will,' said Libby, stroking Strauss's hair. 'Maybe you two will work it out when you get back, and you'll bring her out here next year for a visit. Or maybe we'll all come to London for a holiday. Now that would be something, wouldn't it?'

'Maybe,' said Strauss, but she had that look about her, which made Libby think that a new Great Love might soon be on her way. 'What about you? Ben's got a new chicky-babe, you said.'

Libby smiled bravely. 'Don't mention it in front of the others, will you?' She'd had a few days to get used to it, and now she could almost think of him kissing that woman in the pub without wanting to throw up.

'What? You mean don't say, "Hey kids, big news—your dad's shagging around" at dinner tonight?'

'He hasn't slept with her,' said Libby sharply. 'He told me.'

Strauss sucked back on her durry, exhaling finally in a cloud of smoke. 'But he will.'

Libby stared down at her hands. Every time she thought about Ben she felt seasick. Putting out a hand to support her against the wall when she was walking down the hall, and pulling her head up sharply to take a breath sometimes when she was knitting, or pulling a beer at work. 'Are you all right, darling?' Lois kept asking, and suggesting that she sit down.

'Oh Lib.' Strauss opened her arms.

The brass buckles on her overalls were digging painfully into Libby's shoulder, but Strauss's familiar vanilla smell made her feel safe for a moment in a world that seemed to be whirling faster and faster.

'You don't still love him, do you?' asked Strauss.

'You don't stop loving someone just because you move out.'

Strauss sat back and put a gentle hand under Libby's chin to look at her. 'In my experience—vast in the ways of humanity—you do.'

Libby was crying openly now, sniffing and snorting into the tissues Strauss kept handing her. 'I hated living with him, Strauss. I just hated it.'

She couldn't stop picturing him standing by the car on the day she left him, begging her for another chance. But what was she supposed to do at that point? she kept wondering, her thoughts taking her around in a loop. Just keep living there with him gone all the time? Everything about this situation was better for her, except that she didn't have him.

'Ben's one-track minded,' Strauss was saying. 'He thought it was all about him getting you and the kids there safe and in one piece, like a hero. But where the hell is there? And in the meantime you were suffering, and he didn't want to know.'

'Exactly!' This is where Strauss excelled, thought Libby, as she loudly blew her nose. For Strauss a crying woman moaning about her marriage was just another day at the office. Literally.

'Now that's a good sign that you're laughing.'

'Is it? I was just thinking about your work at the shelter.' Libby started crying again afresh at the idea of it. 'My problems must seem pathetic to you.'

'You're wonderful, Lib,' said Strauss firmly. 'I'd marry you.'

'Except I'm not your type,' Libby sniffed. 'You'd leave me for one of your bikie say-nothings.'

'You could be my first wife. Christ, I'm an idiot,' Strauss groaned, as Libby flinched.

'It's okay,' said Libby. 'I mean, it's true. I am Ben's first wife. I may as well face it.'

'Oh, Libby, in the future . . .'

'Will you please shut up about the future!' Libby cried. 'I don't care about the future. If I did I would have stayed with Ben, wouldn't I? I want to be happy now.'

'I know, Libs. I know that,' Strauss soothed. 'I just meant I have a joint in my pocket and in the future you could smoke it with me. Like in the next five minutes.'

That night they threw a party. Old and new friends all turned up. Ben was invited—on principle, Libby insisted—but to her relief he said no. He offered to take the children, though, and Strauss insisted that Libby accept. In a miracle of timing, all the kids went to stay with their dads, so the women had the house to themselves. They filled the bath with ice and Libby made chickpea and apricot couscous in a giant soup tureen, and it was like those parties they used to have before the children came along, thought Libby, surveying the wreckage the next morning.

At some point she'd gone to bed, simply waving into the living room and then closing her bedroom door, confident that someone would see their guests out, and make sure no one crashed out in any of the children's rooms. There had been some attractive men at the party, Lois kept exclaiming, but Libby couldn't imagine being attracted to anyone, let alone being attractive to anyone in that way ever again. When she went to collect the children in the morning

Ben gave her a long look, and she gave him a long look back, but they didn't say anything. She wanted to tell him something about Strauss's visit or ask him something about his new girlfriend to try to bring some normality to their new situation, but Libby's words froze up in her throat. She had moved out and Ben was single and had a girlfriend now—she forced herself to accept it. There was no turning back.

11

Carol

'YOU LOOK VERY PRETTY, MRS DEAL,' said Carol, tucking a comb into the hair of the woman sitting in front of her, and twisting a little spray of jasmine into it. 'Now, you can take this out tonight and, in the morning, why don't you put one of your pins with the rhinestones in?'

'What a nice idea,' said Mrs Deal, giving her hair a quick glance in the mirror before gathering up her hat, gloves and handbag. 'You always make my hair look so fresh.'

Mrs Deal favoured a beehive style, even though she had thinning hair, and nothing Carol said could talk her out of it. Carol had found, though, that if she used very strong anti-dandruff shampoo, it would last the week until her next appointment. She watched discreetly as Mrs Deal paid Mr Harold—he was the only person in the salon allowed to handle money. Carol could tell from the saccharine smile he gave Mrs Deal, that, as always, she had left Carol a generous tip.

Haircuts were cheaper here than back in England, and expectations were lower, too. Her clients always seemed far more interested in catching Carol up on what had happened in their lives since their last appointment, than in what she was doing to their hair. 'Just the usual,' they'd sigh, sinking into her chair, and nothing she could say about the new easy-care styles or the way a fringe or a side parting could take years off would budge them. No matter how it turned out, if Carol applied enough hairspray they were pleased.

'Your four-thirty's cancelled,' said Mr Harold to Carol, his smile evaporating once he'd shown Mrs Deal out the door.

'Oh, I hope she's all right,' said Carol. Mrs Harman was a shy, kind woman with hair so fine it was like cat fur, and Carol could do almost nothing with it. Nevertheless, she turned up like clockwork every Thursday for a wash and blow-dry.

'It's her mother,' said Mr Harold heavily. He disapproved of his customers having unpredictable family members almost as much as he disapproved of that in his staff. 'Which means you've got an early mark,' he said, turning away. Since her interview he had pretty much ignored her, preferring to give all his attention to the customers, over whom he preened and fawned, and none of whom, as far as Carol could tell, were fooled for a second. No one, not the customers nor any of the hairdressers, paid him any mind.

Carol shrugged on her coat in the little hallway behind the shop, belting it tightly and doing up the big buttons to her neck, and she let herself out into the back lane. It was a still, sweet spring afternoon and the sky was washed with a pinky-blue haze that looked as pretty and unrealistic as a landscape spray-painted onto the side of a panel van.

She tried to go home a different way every day, just in case Steve might be lurking about. At this time he'd be at work himself, though, and in any case it had been months now and she hadn't heard a peep out of him. Libby handled Colette's drop-offs and pick-ups, which all went smoothly, every other weekend and Wednesday night. There had been no more notes or phone calls. It felt like a reprieve, rather than an end, but for now whatever Anna had said to him had worked.

She walked along past the back of the fish shop and the timber yard, neatly skirting around the overflowing bins and boxes of stinking garbage, and then crossed over to walk past the women's shelter on Parnell Street. It looked rundown and frightening from the street, with its boarded-up windows and iron-grille over the front door. Carol had shuddered with pity and a kind of deep dread the first few times she'd walked past. But now and again she saw children arriving home from school, and women going in and out, and they looked so comfortingly normal that she no longer noticed the building's intimidating exterior.

Further on down the road and around the corner was the salon she used to walk past all the time when she first moved here. Velvet and Lace, said the sign, in curling gold running writing on a black wooden background. It couldn't have been more different from the white plastic lettering of Mr Harold's, which lit up fluorescent green at night. She stopped to peer wistfully in through the window.

Black velvet drapes framed the edges of the window, which had a large gold-framed mirror in the middle of it, facing out into the street, and a vase as tall as her thigh displaying a spray of peacock feathers to one side. Zebra-print wallpaper covered the back wall, and an old drop-crystal chandelier hung low over a table covered in black velvet, holding six large white candles in gleaming glass holders and neat piles of magazines. At the back of the little space sat two hairdressers' chairs, and in front of that, taking up nearly all of the floor, lay an enormous caramel-coloured Afghan hound, spread-eagled over the tiles. He lifted his head slightly to look at her.

'May I help you?'

Carol jumped. A short, stocky woman dressed in a red cheong-sam and gym boots stood next to her. Her black hair was cut very short, and lacquered to make it gleam, like the silent movie stars of the 1920s, who Carol's mother adored

'Is this your shop?' Carol asked timidly.

'Yes, it is. I'm Velvet. There is no Lace,' said the woman, sticking out her hand. 'You're a hairdresser, aren't you?'

'How can you tell?'

'I'm a Pisces. Just kidding. Your hair.'

The girls at Mr Harold's had been experimenting and it had evolved into a complete mess. Today they'd slicked it down at the front so that the back sprang out like a fluff ball. And they'd tried a new dye, which had turned her honey-blonde an unfortunate orange.

'That's Red,' said Velvet, nodding her head towards the dog inside, who had hauled himself to his feet now and was swaying slightly as he peered at them through the window, as though making up his mind whether or not he was supposed to bark. 'Come here, handsome.' He pushed the door open and padded down the steps to join them. His nose was soft as he pushed it into Carol's hand. 'He likes you.' The two women smiled at each other, as though they were sharing a joke or some rare good fortune, even though neither of them knew yet what that might be.

When Carol arrived home, Anna was kneeling by the bath washing Leanne, who was singing tunelessly and pouring water from one cup into another as her mother sponged her back. Jasper was sitting on a low blue stool, looking through a book, crinkling and crunching the pages back and forth.

'Good day?' asked Anna, half turning around to smile.

'Wonderful. Fantastic. Amazing. And you?'

'So-so. The girls have been squabbling again, and Sampson brought a decapitated rat in for afternoon tea. But it's all good now, isn't it, darlings? How are you?' Anna sat back on her heels to look at Carol. 'Carol, you're beaming.'

'I've found a new job.'

~

'It was Velvet's half-price students' night tonight so she let me audition on two of her customers,' said Carol, once the children had gone to bed. They were all in the laundry, which felt warm and cosy on this early spring night. Anna was ironing blouses for work, and Libby stood next to her, separating the washing into piles on the concrete floor. Carol stood leaning against the doorframe, holding a bowl of carrot soup. 'She says I have real promise, and that if I can attract the clientele, we can expand into the shop next door and be partners. But, for now, she says I can be her assistant.'

'Her assistant!' exclaimed Libby. 'But that would be a demotion.'

'I won't be earning much less than at Mr Harold's,' said Carol quickly, in case Libby might be worried about her contribution to the housekeeping.

'But where you are now is a sure thing.'

Carol frowned down at her dinner, which she still felt too excited to eat. 'It is a risk,' she conceded. 'I might have to use Mum's money, if I fall short, to see me through.'

'But that's your only security, and your only way to get back home!' Libby's voice rose. 'Steve still hasn't given you your share of your money, has he? What if the business fails? Or you can't attract enough clientele?'

'Then I suppose I'll lose it.' She felt tired suddenly, and shrunken, as though all of her excitement had been sucked into the cold concrete floor.

'You'll be completely stuck.'

'Libby! What's got into you?' Anna had been ironing quietly, but now she put the iron down with a clang.

'Carol's always said she wants to be independent,' said Libby. 'At least at Mr Harold's she's getting a secure wage.'

'But this is a job I want,' said Carol. 'And I love being there.'

'You're the one always saying that we make too big a thing of independence, Libby,' said Anna. 'You're the one always saying that it's natural for us to rely on one another, and to help each other, to go for what we want.'

'Of course, you're right,' said Libby, but her horrified expression remained.

Libby seemed heavy and low, thought Carol, as she began sorting laundry. And it had been ages since she had let Carol do anything with her hair. Libby wore it dragged back into that scraggy ponytail nearly every day now, even though it was meant to be worn loose and brushed forward around her face.

'I think you should go for it, Carol,' said Anna, picking up the iron again. 'But don't use your money from your mum. I'll lend it to you. As an investment.'

'No, I couldn't—'

'You need to back yourself,' said Anna firmly, cutting her off. 'You'll never get anywhere in life if you don't. And this is your dream set-up, right? Which has landed in your lap?'

'Pretty much,' admitted Carol. Anna made it all sound so simple. 'I never dreamed I could actually have it.'

'That's a good thing about being here, then, isn't it?' replied Anna.

'There are lots of good things about being here,' said Carol loyally, but it had been no secret to any of them how homesick she had been.

'Don't miss out on this opportunity, because it might not come again,' said Anna earnestly. 'And once you're making a fortune, and you and Colette have all the clogs and platform wedges you've ever dreamed of, you can pay me back.'

'I just have a very funny feeling about this,' muttered Libby as Carol and Anna shook hands.

'Oh Libby,' Anna snapped in response. 'Ever since Ben got that girlfriend, you've had a funny feeling about everything.'

Libby flinched, and Carol frowned at Anna. They were all being so careful never to mention it.

'Oh god, Libby, I'm sorry,' said Anna, stricken.

'You know what? You're right,' said Libby. 'I'm sorry, Carol.' Before Carol could say anything, Libby turned the taps on hard and began scrubbing clothes and rinsing them in the bottom of the old stone sink. 'It was bound to happen sometime,' she said over her shoulder.

'But so quickly,' said Anna, with that talent she had for inadvertently pressing down right where it hurt. 'I mean, what's it been, six months?'

Libby had become completely absorbed in her scrubbing, and didn't reply. It had actually only been four months since they'd split up, the day that Ben had come into the pub, but Carol, at least, had the good sense not to say anything.

'There's something else,' said Carol quickly once Libby finally turned the taps off, before Anna could repeat her question. 'One of the customers gave me an invitation to a party. It's very exclusive, he said.'

They all looked down at the piece of paper she placed on the ironing board between them.

Grab your love beads and get on board the love train, for a Very Exclusive Gathering, it said, in fancy lettering surrounded by hand-drawn hearts and stars. The more humdrum details had been typed underneath.

'This reminds me of Summer's christening invitation,' said Libby.

'Velvet said it's famous, locally,' said Carol proudly. 'They have it every year.'

'Then how come I've never heard of it?' retorted Libby.

'Maybe because this is a different kind of party,' said Anna, her eyes sparkling with amusement. 'It's the kind where everyone turns up single. Even the couples, if you know what I mean. Me and Myles used to get invites sometimes, back in the day. Somehow it transpired that we could never go.'

'You mean . . .' Libby's mouth fell open.

'It's the kind where you go and you can sleep with anybody you feel like. Velvet told me,' said Carol airily. 'Like free love.'

'Carol, that is so sixties of you,' Libby gasped.

'Well, I never did anything like that in the sixties. Did you?'

'God no,' said Libby, shuddering.

'Nor me,' said Anna, laughing in open admiration of Carol now.

'And is this woman—Velvet—is she going?' Libby asked, looking even more worried, if that were possible, than she had a few minutes ago when they were talking about Carol's job.

'No, god no!' Velvet had said those exact words, in fact, when Carol asked her. 'She said love ain't free,' Carol added, putting on a voice like Dolly Parton's.

'But why on earth would *you* want to go to a party like that, Carol?' asked Libby.

'Well, for one thing it's been ages since I've . . . you know.'

'Had sex?' guessed Anna encouragingly, ignoring Libby's grim expression.

'Well, yes,' said Carol. 'I just think it's unhealthy not to.'

'You mean like drinking orange juice?' Anna laughed, and Carol appreciated her trying to ease the tension that had suddenly sprung up between her and Libby. 'I'd say I'm a walking ad for the fact that you can live very well without it. Or not get scurvy, at least.'

'Plus, I've never had an orgasm,' said Carol defiantly. She'd never said the word aloud before, but she'd been wanting to, for ages.

'Seriously?' replied Libby. 'Oh Carol . . .'

'I'm not sure if I have either,' said Anna, and Carol instantly felt better.

'So, will you come?' she asked the two of them.

'Never, not in a million years,' said Libby, folding her arms across her chest.

'Let's see what you say when I invite you again next year.' Carol winked. 'What about you, Anna?'

'I told Myles I was going to have sex with someone, and I suppose this is the perfect opportunity.' Anna picked up the invitation and peered at it, lifting up her glasses. 'How exclusive can it be if they've Xeroxed it?'

'Obviously it's exclusively for a lot of fab people,' said Carol, pulling her lipstick and compact out of her handbag and reapplying it, even though they would all soon be going to bed.

The next morning Carol handed in her notice. 'But this is a very good wage for a married woman!' said Mr Harold, sacking her on the spot. That afternoon she went to work for Velvet.

12

Anna

ON THE NIGHT OF THE PARTY it was Carol's turn to make dinner, and so it was sausages and mash with overcooked green peas again. Afterwards the kids all watched TV, which they seemed to be doing almost every night lately. They were also eating too much processed food, and sugar, too. All Anna's standards seemed to have gone out the window, and while on some days she felt relaxed and good about it, on other days, like today, it filled her with anxiety. Michelle's teeth, Leanne's weight, their mood, their learning . . . Or maybe she felt anxious because she'd seen Steve again this evening. Twice in fact. First outside her office, and then again at the bus stop, just as she was getting on her bus. It rattled her, even though she wasn't positive that he'd even seen her; and he lived in Sandgate, too, she reminded herself, and so surely it was simply a coincidence. After all, lots of people would be knocking off work around that time, and Anna made a note to take the later bus.

She'd arrived home determined to take all the kids outside to do something active this evening before she left for the party, but they moaned when she suggested it and put up such a fuss that in the end she relented and agreed to five more minutes in front of the TV, and then another five. They wound up watching the entire program, which was about a blended family who fitted together seamlessly, like pieces of moulded plastic. Anna sat with them on the couch, transfixed.

'What do you think, girls?' she asked when the program ended. Jasper had wandered off down the hall to find Libby halfway through. 'Do those people seem like anyone you know?' If they could at least have an intelligent conversation that would redeem the hour they'd just wasted watching it, but they gazed back at her mutely.

'It's earth calling! Can one of the girls please respond to me?'

'You need to say which of us specifically you want to answer,' said Michelle finally, glancing around at the others, who all smirked.

'Why don't you each take turns?' replied Anna sharply. 'Leanne, you start.' But the ads had ended and now the credits of a whole new episode were rolling.

'I'll tell you later,' said Michelle faintly, and once again they were lost to her. Anna sank back into the couch, defeated.

'Ready,' said Carol at last, standing in the doorway of the living room.

'Pretty,' said Jasper, appearing in the hall beside her.

Carol's red dress wound around her shoulders in a giant ruffle, coming in at the waist and then flaring out again below her knees in another ruffle. Fine gold chains dangled from her ears, and a matching gold chain snaked around her waist.

'You look beautiful, Mama,' said Colette, though Anna sensed disapproval in her tone. 'Are you going on a date?'

'No, honey bunch. I'm going to a party.'

Anna was wearing tight designer jeans, chunky-heeled burgundy boots and a white satin blouse with a thin black leather tie knotted loosely at her throat. Maybe it wasn't the kind of casual outfit some people would choose for a swingers party, but that was why she'd selected it. The only way she could bring herself to go through with this thing was to help herself feel very formal and protected.

'Okay, kids, just ten more minutes,' said Libby, walking down the hallway to see Carol and Anna off.

'Are you sure you don't want to come?' asked Carol. 'I bet you Mrs Georgiou would come over to look after the kids in a heartbeat.'

'I promise you, I am thrilled to be left at home,' said Libby. 'Now, you two have a great time, all right?'

'Don't worry, we will,' said Carol, blowing Libby a kiss and skipping gaily down the stairs, with Anna following her reluctantly.

~

'We should have a safe word.'

Anna grabbed Carol's arm as they followed a bunch of barefoot hippies up the front path of the rundown two-storey mansion. They were only a few blocks away from her old place, and it looked a lot like the 'before' to her house's 'after'. No War in Vietnam stickers were pasted all over the front windows, which were broken in places, with boards pushed behind them to fill the gaps, and mismatched old couches were crowded onto the bedraggled verandah.

'What if it's just an orgy?' asked Anna. 'Or something even weirder?' The whole time on their walk here she'd been thinking of new ways that it could go wrong.

'Anna, you are spinning out.'

'Of course I am. Why aren't you?'

'I have an idea,' said Carol. She pulled out a Revlon lipstick from her tiny Glomesh handbag—which held a handkerchief, a box of Tic Tacs, three condoms in their wrappers, and a ten-dollar note. 'We're going to make a pact,' said Carol, drawing a red line with the lipstick on her palm. 'The rules of the pact are, if we don't like it here, then we'll leave. What else?'

'What happens at the party, stays at the party,' said Anna, and then she drew a blank. 'I guess that covers it.'

'Good. You draw a line, too,' said Carol. 'And now smoosh.' They rubbed their palms together, until they looked as if they had been lightly smeared in blood.

'Oh, and another thing: no details,' said Anna, as they were walking up the path. 'I don't want to have to listen to who did what to whom.'

'I'm down with that.'

Was there anything Carol *wasn't* down with, these days? wondered Anna enviously as Carol walked up the stairs, her red dress rippling behind her as if she was walking onto the yacht from that Carly Simon song.

Throbbing psychedelic music greeted them in the entry way, which was painted midnight blue. 'Hello, ladies.' A man dressed in nothing but his underwear and a hat and sunglasses approached, offering a hand-rolled cigarette. 'Here, have some. It's first-class grass.'

Anna needed something if she was going to make it through the next five minutes, and so she forced herself to say yes. 'I'm Keith, by the way. Sagittarius. Would you like to join me?' he asked, opening the door to the front room as they each took a few puffs.

Anna peered through the smoky gloom into what looked like an adult version of a high-school make-out room. Wall-to-wall mattresses lined the floor, populated with couples—some of whom were vigorously enjoying each other's company. She felt faint as she leaned against the wainscoting.

'No thanks!' Carol giggled, tripping on her heels as they made their way down the long hallway, the sickly sweet smell of grass wafting after them. They pushed their way through the crowded kitchen into a living room, which, Anna realised as she looked around in relief, seemed much more her speed. The first thing that was obvious was that she wasn't the only one here who felt nervous. 'There are a lot of first-timers tonight,' someone in the kitchen had said, and, once she'd regained her bearings, it was easy to pick them out. On one side of the room were groups of women in sparkly mini-dresses and men in unbuttoned shirts, chatting easily over their paper cups. On the other, isolated couples stared around wildly like trapped animals, along with the occasional solitary man. Anna sat down awkwardly on a couch next to a couple who were sitting rigidly side by side, staring straight ahead. She saw Carol approaching from across the room, dragging a young man who could not have been more than twenty-five years old behind her, but then again, Carol was quite young too.

'Anna, this is Declan, Declan this is Anna,' said Carol, her voice sounding extra bubbly.

What? Already? They'd only been here ten minutes.

'Declan's studying medicine at the university. Oh, Anna's drinking red wine,' Carol told him.

'That pretty much covers it,' laughed Anna, returning Declan's courteous smile.

'And what about you?' he asked Carol. She looked at him sidelong, her head tilted, with just the hint of a smile playing about her lips. 'I'll have a lemonade.' She threw it down like a challenge; the first test of the young hero who might, or might not, win the fair maiden's hand. Carol raised a long red fingernail, placed it in the middle of his chest, and gave him a little push. 'Go.'

'He's pretty,' she said to Anna, as they turned their heads to watch him plunge into the kitchen.

'He can't believe his luck.'

Carol giggled, and Anna could see why anyone in this room might want her. 'I need to get on with it. Otherwise I'll lose my nerve.'

The couple who had been sitting on the sofa next to Anna for the last ten minutes, without talking or doing anything as far as Anna could tell, suddenly stood up and walked off purposefully, hand in hand.

'Oh god, do you think they're going to . . .'

'I certainly hope so,' said Carol, reaching up to accept the glass a newly materialised Declan was offering. She put the straw into her mouth and gave it a little suck before licking her lips, maintaining eye contact with Declan the whole time. 'Yum.'

Where had Carol gone? wondered Anna, equally horrified and transfixed. *Who was this playful vixen?*

And then, like an actress coming out of character, Carol burst into laughter. Declan laughed along, too, obviously confused but happy with how things were progressing.

'Now, duck, will you be all right if we leave you for a little while?' she asked Anna, as naturally as if they were on a bus. 'Declan wants to show me around.'

'Please. It would be a relief,' muttered Anna, slumping in her seat.

A man with a long beard nodded at her meaningfully from the other side of the room, and she kept her face as blank as possible as she swivelled her head away. As she refused another drink, this one offered by a man who possibly was wearing a toupee, she was reminded of her university days, when the men who were attracted to her always seemed, frankly, a little off. The fact was, Anna concluded, some women are sexy and some women are not, and she happened to be one of the nots. She folded her arms across her chest, and after a moment the man with the maybe-toupee moved away.

Although it was difficult to see how this kind of thing suited any of the women here, really, thought Anna, as she looked around the room, noticing how carefully the women were presented compared to the men, some of whom had barely even bothered to get dressed. Women always had to put in more effort. And now, on top of everything, they were expected to put out, without a ring on their finger or even a steady boyfriend. And meanwhile these men found themselves at an all-you-can-eat buffet, without needing to have a home or even an income to share, let alone a personality. Anna rolled her eyes at a man dressed in a black velvet suit who was pointing at her and smiling.

What was going to happen to the girls, if this was the world they were going to inherit? What would happen to her? The image of Steve leaning against the street light outside her building that evening flashed before her eyes, and she shook her head to chase it away. A good man would turn up for her someday, Anna told herself firmly; a good and attractive man. After all, her therapist had pretty much guaranteed it.

'Hiya,' said Carol, thumping down into the seat next to her, which all this time had remained vacant.

Anna jumped. 'Back already? Where's Declan?'

'He's around,' said Carol carelessly. 'I told him we might meet up with him later. Then again, we might not.'

'Did you have sex with him, Carol?' Anna whispered. 'Oh my lord,' she sighed, as Carol nodded. 'What was it like?'

'Quick.' Carol shrugged. 'But what about you? Have you seen anyone you like?'

'I'm way too old for this.'

'What are you talking about? Look,' Carol pointed at the man in the black velvet suit who was sitting on the other side of the room now, talking to a group of young people who could have been actors they were so good-looking, in that actor-y kind of way. 'He's even older than you.'

'I'm too old for this *myself*, is what I mean,' said Anna frostily. But the truth was she wouldn't have liked this party even when she was Carol's age, not even if anyone even faintly appropriate had been interested in her. Her younger self would have thought it was a waste of a wonderful building and she would have spent the evening working out how much she would offer for it, if she had the money, and how she would renovate it.

'I thought you were desperate to have sex,' said Carol, her brow furrowed.

'Will you please shut up?' Anna hissed, but no one could hear them over the sitar music which had started blasting over the sound system anyway. 'I never said I was *desperate*. And certainly not like this.'

Even if she did see someone she liked and got up the courage to disappear with them upstairs somewhere, it wouldn't be sex. It would be a performance—on her part, anyway—and getting away from that had been the whole point.

'Well, what did you think it would be like?' asked Carol, craning to smile at a man over Anna's shoulder, then her nose wrinkled, as though she'd smelled something bad. 'Too hairy, and he's wearing shoes without socks. And don't look at me like that, Anna! Let me ask you something, Mrs Always Has An Answer For Everything: what do you think is the point of this party?'

'Is it a meat market?'

Carol laughed with that champagne laugh she seemed to have invented just for tonight. 'Well, I think it's wonderful,' she said, popping a chip into her mouth and gazing around contentedly. 'Like a treasure hunt, for grown-ups.'

Why am I so cynical? Anna cursed herself, as Carol, adjusting her shoulder ruffle, excused herself from Anna and boogied on over to join a woman in a belly-dancing outfit who was beckoning to her from the makeshift dance floor.

She couldn't just leave Carol here, Anna decided, but she couldn't bring herself to explore any further either, and so she sat trapped on the sofa, nodding to people and tightly smiling, like an old-fashioned chaperone. Surely Carol would return any moment, reeling from the horror, and they could go home.

An hour later, she still hadn't emerged and Anna had fallen asleep, drooling lightly on her snakeskin handbag.

~

'Anna Wotcek, from Swenson Davis?'

She woke with a start. Her mouth was horribly dry and her neck had a crick in it. A man was kneeling in front of her.

'I thought that was you.'

She blinked. It was the man in the black velvet suit.

'Simon Lieber,' he said, picking up her hand, which was resting in her lap and shaking it. 'I have to say, this is the last place I would ever have expected us to bump into each other.'

'Doctor Lieber?' The taste of red wine and chips and old cigarettes sloshed around in the space between her eyes and her mouth. 'From my focus groups?'

'The role of lipids in identifying novel treatment areas for cardiovascular events.'

She jumped up out of her seat, her knees screaming in pain—how long had she been sleeping there anyway? 'It's been very nice to see you again. Goodbye.'

'Anna! Ms Wotcek! Wait!' he called out, following her through the crowd.

It had got so full in this room, suddenly.

'I didn't know what kind of a party it was, either!' he called after her, as she pushed her way towards fresh air.

She waited for him on the stairs going down into the garden, where groups of people were huddled, passing cigarettes back and forth and singing softly along to an out-of-sight, badly tuned guitar. She would have to face him sometime, and better here than at work.

He was laughing as he caught up to her, somehow now with two glasses of wine—one white, one red—in his hands.

'Here. Take your pick. I couldn't remember which one you drink.'

'Because at work I don't,' she said acerbically, taking the red. 'I'm sorry, I'm afraid I didn't recognise you.'

'I know you didn't. I couldn't work out why you were at a party acting so frosty with everyone. And then I kept getting stuck in weird atmospheres. Finally I went upstairs looking for the bathroom and . . . let's say the penny dropped.'

'You mean you really didn't realise what kind of party this is?'

'Not until about an hour ago. Which must have been around when you fell asleep.'

So he had been watching her for all that time. The thought of it gave her a funny feeling in the pit of her stomach that wasn't entirely unwelcome. She tried a sip of the wine. 'This is actually quite good.'

'Beaujolais Bin No 17. I brought my own.' He shrugged. 'Back in my day, that's how you prepared for a party.'

'Those misty far-off days,' laughed Anna, taking a proper appreciative gulp.

An hour later they were sitting, smoking Anna's cigarettes and drinking more of his Beaujolais on two metal chairs they dragged out onto the lawn, next to a stand of jasmine and wisteria that was tumbling its sweet scent all over them on this warm early spring night. There had been no sign of Carol. They discussed his daughter, who was going to New York to study acting, and Anna's latest research project, as well as recent advances in identifying key contributors to the cascades of lipid disease. At some point in their conversation he had put his hand casually on her knee to make a point, and she had been letting it sit there, radiating heat, for about as long as she could stand.

'That's a very pretty outfit you have on, by the way. You look like an even more beautiful Diane Keaton.'

Anna glowed. She couldn't help it.

'This is the first time I've ever seen you without a clipboard,' he added.

'I must have left it on the couch in there,' Anna smiled.

'Will you score me once we're done, and grade it on the curve?'

'That depends on what we do.'

Anna's heart started to thump as she put her glass down next to her chair. The noise of the party seemed very far away, suddenly, and the smell of jasmine and wisteria became very strong. She put her hand on top of his where it lay, still, on her knee. She glanced into his eyes, and then at his beautiful, shapely mouth. She leaned forward to kiss it.

And then she lost her balance and lurched forward in her seat towards him. He caught her and pulled her to him, one hand gripping her shoulder, and the other tangled in her hair. It was as if a wave was toppling her over and sweeping her towards him.

'Oh Anna,' he breathed, his voice husky.

So this is what it's like to feel wanted, thought Anna as they started kissing again. This was like swimming in a midnight sea, sparks of light glinting and flashing behind her closed eyes as the current swept her further and further out.

'No. Wait.' She pushed him away, gasping for breath. She could hear him breathing heavily, too, and she could see the rise and fall of his chest, where a salt-and-pepper mix of hair peeped out from the neckline of his shirt. 'This is unprofessional.' Really she meant, *I'm scared.*

'We're not at work.' His arms were still around her shoulders, holding her tightly to him.

'Well, how about the fact that I'm still married?' she asked, breaking free from the circle of his arms. Really she meant, *This is too fast.*

'You're married?' His tone changed, and she forced herself to look up at him. He didn't seem any different than he had before they started to kiss, which was a relief, even though she wasn't quite sure what she had been afraid of. That he might have turned into some kind of sex god? Or a hanging jury?

'I'm separated,' she said, coming back to dry land with a thump. 'I should have mentioned it earlier, I suppose.' Anna silently cursed herself . *Poor Myles.* 'It's only been six months, though, and I don't know what I'm doing.' Anna groaned. 'I'm sorry.'

'No, no, I get it.' He reached down underneath his chair to retrieve his glass of wine. 'For the first year after my separation I didn't know what I was doing, either.'

Simon was so kind. She remembered now how intelligent his comments on her focus-group sheets always were, and how gracefully he participated—never domineering but not retiring either—in the doctors' groups.

'But then you did?' Anna asked, curiosity getting the better of her embarrassment.

'She went on a trip to Turkey for three weeks with my best friend without telling me, and so that helped to clarify things.'

'I'm sorry, that's awful.'

'It was.' He smiled, ruefully. 'I think it's great that you're taking it slow. Respecting your old relationship, and giving yourself time to work out what you want.'

'You know, I did know it was one of those parties,' said Anna, shamed by his honesty. 'My housemate is in there now, going crazy with it, I think.'

'So why did you come?' he asked curiously.

'I guess I thought of it as field research,' she said miserably.

'And what's this, then? An in-depth interview?'

'More like mystery shopping,' she managed to lob back.

His eyes were amused as he lit a cigarette, but Anna was cringing inside at the change in the mood between them. Cool and defensive now, instead of warm and open, the way it had been before. She was the one who had pulled away from the kiss to make excuses. But he was the one leaning back in his seat now, and rocking it back and forth, all of his body language telling her that he wanted to get away. Or was that just him reacting to what she had just said?

Anna felt hopelessly muddled now, and she was glad it was dark so he couldn't see her disappointment.

'Anyway, it's been lovely catching up with you,' she said, idiotically offering him her hand to shake, the way she would have at work.

Relieved he didn't want to walk with her back into the party, Anna picked her way slowly across the buffalo grass, leaving him sitting there alone. She was checking the couch for anything that might have fallen out of her handbag while she was sleeping when Carol walked in looking as fresh and lovely as when the party had started.

~

'Now I get why you left Myles,' laughed Carol, as she twirled and sashayed down the street. Her feet were bare, and the gold chain which had hung around her waist at the start of the evening wasn't there anymore. 'I couldn't understand it before,' said Carol. 'What's the big deal? I kept thinking. It's just sex. But *good* sex—sex like *that* is amazing.'

'Watch out you don't step on a needle,' said Anna, trudging after her.

'It doesn't need to be about love, or closeness or intimacy, or all that stuff I always thought about with Steve. It's just fun!'

'Oh brother,' Anna sighed. It seemed so unfair that she couldn't allow herself so much as a kiss, while Carol had been going at it all evening, apparently, and had emerged dewier than ever.

'Anna, can I ask you something?' Carol stopped dead in front of Anna, blocking her path, so that Anna was forced to stop walking. 'Will you give me your professional opinion? As a doctor?'

'I keep telling you, I'm a market researcher, not a psychologist. But go ahead.'

'Could I be a nymphomaniac?'

'Carol, no.' Anna looked around to see who might have overheard her, but of course the streets at this time were deserted. 'That's a myth.'

'Well, at least now I know I'm not frigid, right? No matter what Steve used to say sometimes.'

'Bloody Steve,' muttered Anna. She pictured him leaning against the street light again, and she shook her head, chasing the thought away. 'But Carol, just out of curiosity, how many people did you sleep with?'

'Well, it depends on how you define "sleep with",' Carol giggled.

'You don't know?'

'Well, after Declan I decided I wasn't interested in the usual.' Carol grimaced. 'I had quite enough of that with Steve, thank you very much. I did other things, you know, with that woman with the amazing hair, and . . .' Her voice dropped, and she grabbed Anna's arm. 'Can I tell you about something that happened tonight?'

'If you must,' Anna quavered. Pact or no pact, she was about to hear some details.

'It was on those corduroy couches in that room off the kitchen.'

'Please, don't remind me,' Anna shuddered. She couldn't imagine how you would ever get them clean.

'I was sitting there with these two men, and—'

'You know, Carol, I am not nearly as open-minded as I look.'

'You wore cufflinks and a tie tonight,' said Carol affectionately, 'but it was nothing like that.'

'Oh god, what, then?' Anna cried.

The moon had long faded from the sky, and the horizon was turning pink.

'Tonight, I had an epiphany.' Carol's voice dropped to a whisper. 'And I think it's going to change my life.'

'So?' prompted Anna, after a long silence.

'Hmm?' said Carol, mock-innocently.

'So what was it?' Anna snapped, way too tired to be tactful.

'That's for me to know and you to find out,' said Carol, bursting into peals of laughter.

They really were two different species, Anna realised as she persuaded Carol to put her shoes back on. Men like Simon Lieber were making a basic error when they mistook an Anna for a Carol, or even a Libby for that matter. An Anna was destined to feel foolish, and miss all the boats, and stumble from disaster to disaster, while a Carol, for all her vulnerability and weakness, was destined for . . . well, who knows? It was like watching a butterfly pulling out of its cocoon, mused Anna, and suddenly the thought of Steve's head turning to watch something, or someone—was it her, maybe?—flashed before her, and this time she couldn't shake it. His shadow seemed to follow Anna, as she followed Carol, shimmying and shaking her whole body to silent music as she boogied on down the street.

13

Carol

THE TRIMMER'S MOTOR HUMMED AND BUZZED pleasurably against Carol's scalp on Monday morning as she turned her head one way and then the other underneath its claws.

'Hi, hon,' said Velvet, walking into the salon and hanging up her coat. Red came padding in after her and flopped down onto the floor. 'How was the—' She gasped and whirled around. 'What are you doing?'

'What does it look like?' replied Carol, without pausing.

'But your hair!' shrieked Violet, falling to her knees on the tiles as she tried to gather up Carol's locks.

'It was dead and you know it.' Carol set down the trimmer. 'Will you help me with the back?'

'It was better than nothing,' moaned Velvet, climbing to her feet and taking up the razor. 'Let's focus on how big your eyes are going to look after this.'

'And my pimples,' said Carol, leaning closer to the mirror to examine her hairline.

'What pimples?' asked Velvet, turning off the razor.

Carol stared at her reflection, her ears pounding in the sudden quiet. Her neck looked extra-long and her head looked almost regal. Her ears seemed very small, though, and her mouth and her nose looked huge.

'I look like an alien,' Carol laughed.

'What came over you?' asked Velvet.

'You were here. You saw.'

'You mean that's when you decided? Just now?'

'Velvet, I need to tell you something.' Carol spun around in her chair to face her. 'On Saturday night, I had a vision for the business.'

'Ah.' Velvet nodded, satisfied. 'When a woman shaves her hair off, it's always something big.'

'I'm going to make my side of the salon for men only,' said Carol as they began to mix up lotions in the wet area, standing side by side.

'Men don't pay enough, and they don't do colour,' objected Velvet. She was wearing a long floral tea dress this morning, with a brightly coloured embroidered wool jerkin, so that she looked like a cross between a shepherd and a Russian Princess, circa 1905. 'All they care about is the price and the time. Plus, they're sleazy.'

'We're going to call it The Stallions' Stable,' said Carol breezily, undeterred. 'We're going to tell them that they're not to lift a finger, or do a thing. They're here to feel cared for. It's going to be full service—moustaches and beards, as well as hair. We're going to offer them hand and head massages, and eye masks, and aroma-therapy, to help them mellow out.'

'They're going to think it's a brothel,' Velvet said.

'We're going to make them feel cared for and confident, inside and out, so they can go out and charm the ladies in their lives. Or the gentlemen. And they're going to pay a lot for it, you'll see.'

'From a big bald baby?'

Carol ran her hands over her scalp. It felt rough yet soft, like a kind of silky stubble that you would never find on a man. Each time she caught a glimpse of herself in the salon mirror, she'd think, *Who's that?*

Velvet sighed, looking at Carol with regret. 'It's no good for a hairdresser to be bald. It sets the wrong example.'

'This way the focus is on my customers.'

'If you have any,' Velvet sniffed.

'They're going to come pouring in. You'll see.'

It had surprised her at the party, how the men's faces had changed when they submitted to her, allowing themselves to lay their heads in her lap and give themselves up to her as she massaged their scalps and played with their hair, agreeing to everything she suggested. They hadn't been flirting, or wanting anything more from her, Carol realised, as she held court at the party on the brown corduroy couch off the kitchen. All around them, men were straining to be charming and attractive, competing with one another for the women, who—equally nervously—were straining to be charmed. When they came to sit next to Carol, though, and she asked them about their hair, they relaxed, and became as pliant and vulnerable as boys. She'd never had a brother or a father, and so the only man she'd ever been this close to before was Steve. She'd never even had any male clients. Steve wouldn't have liked it, for one thing, and no man dared venture into Mr Harold's territory. But she loved having this opportunity to take care of them, she realised, sitting there, without the pressure of them wanting something from her she didn't want to give. And they wanted to be looked after like this, too, she understood on the couch on Saturday night. The only time they had ever been touched like this, one of the men had told her as he reluctantly got up to give the next man in line his turn, was by his mum.

~

With the help of Anna's investment, Carol and Velvet put in saloon doors and white wooden palings, on which they nailed a row of iron hooks, for the reins and bridles and Stetson hats they hung there. With just a few flowing black lines, Velvet painted a silhouette of a stallion's head on the far wall, so that it was the first thing a client would see when they came through the door. Compared to the lush luxury of Velvet and Lace it looked clean and spare and elegant. Next they installed two black barbers' chairs that folded right back to horizontal, so that Carol could give her customers a shave and a facial massage while they were waiting for their colour to sink in. She would encourage them to close their eyes and put themselves entirely in her hands, the feeling of power thrilling her, especially when she was giving them a close razor shave.

'When you suggest a new style, you need to make them say yes to you three times. That way they'll feel like they really want it,' Velvet coached. 'You need to push for colour. That's where the money is. You'll never get anywhere just cutting.'

Her customers were students and lecturers from the university, and businessmen and actors who lived nearby. The prices she charged were higher than at Mr Harold's—they needed to be—but she did a better job than she'd done at Mr Harold's, too.

These weren't weekly haircuts. They were all about the colour, and the cut, and lasted for six weeks. Under Carol's expert guidance, her more adventurous clients began investing in mohawks and corkscrew perms, surfie manes and blow waves.

Soon after opening, Carol added skincare to her services, as well as scalp care for her clients experiencing hair loss; and soon her customers were leaving with pots of beard balm and face and hand moisturiser, as well as shampoo and conditioner specific to their hair type, to keep themselves looking good at home. 'Accentuating the layers is crucial'; 'You can air dry or use a diffuser'; 'Apply a soft-hold mousse, focusing on coating the layers,' she'd say, and the next minute they were asking her if she could order products in for them, and encouraging her to take a modest profit.

At first she felt a complicated kind of guilt when it came to telling the customer what they owed, but now she positively looked forward to it. *You are becoming shameless*, she'd tell herself, as she folded the bills into the till. *You are a shameless hussy*. It's what her mother used to call her, in tones of undisguised love and affection.

'You're a hoyden,' her mother would also say, and that's what she now sometimes called Colette.

'What's a hoyden?' Colette would ask.

'A shameless hussy,' Carol would reply, her eyes twinkling merrily. She always felt merry these days, especially when she was adding to the pile of bills she kept stored in the safe at the back of the salon.

She liked choosing what she would wear each day, with no one to comment or criticise—except, of course, for her hair. From the first day she arrived home, everyone commented on that.

'Your head looks amazing, Mama,' Colette had breathed rapturously the first time she saw it. Anna had burst into applause, and

Jasper kept wanting to touch it all the time. Libby seemed disturbed by it, though, as if it were another symptom of a worrying trend, and some of the other mothers at school had shaken their heads in disappointment when she dropped Colette off, refusing to look her in the eye. Carol didn't care. She liked seeing more eyes and more smile and more expression on her face whenever she happened to catch her own reflection, and she was sure her profile looked more elegant.

Carol also liked leaving her room messy, or tidy, as she chose. She liked talking to Colette with no one to chime in and correct her. And she liked making decisions—even tiny ones, such as what to feed the children, or what she would do with her free time when she found herself on her own without wondering what Steve might have to say about it. She used to be so afraid of being on her own, overwhelmed by such difficult feelings of panic and anxiety. But now she found she liked solitude more and more. Perhaps because she wasn't ever alone if she didn't want to be—there was always someone in the living room or the kitchen or garden, working or doing something with the children, or simply hanging out. And becoming more confident in these small decisions was giving Carol the confidence to make bigger ones, like trying to open her own bank account. They wouldn't let her—of course, it's what she'd been told would happen—without her husband's signature, but she had walked into the local branch and asked for the necessary paperwork, just like any other grown adult.

Dear Steve, she wrote on a piece of scented notepaper she cadged from Anna. *Can we please meet soon to discuss paperwork and whatnot? I have started my own business and need your signature on some papers.* She signed it and slipped it into Colette's suitcase. The next morning she found an answering note in Colette's bag.

I'll be there tomorrow at 6, it said in Steve's blocky handwriting. *It will be good to look around and see if it's a good idea.*

~

Later that morning she and Velvet were flipping through a sample book when Carol stopped on a page showing a woman smiling with her hair in an old-fashioned bouffant.

'That's how I used to look,' she said.

'That colour—H14.' Velvet narrowed her eyes as she looked from the magazine to Carol and back again. 'It's good for you.'

'Fresh and lovely,' read Carol from the caption.

Velvet sighed. 'If only you had hair.'

Velvet was the best salesperson Carol had ever met. She moved faster, and was more efficient and service-oriented than anyone Carol had ever dealt with before. But—perhaps it was her Singaporean–Chinese background, or being with Carol who was a new immigrant herself, or just the core of Velvet—she was also the most breathtakingly honest.

'Bald is not a good look for you,' Velvet sniffed, making notes and pulling bottles forward from her trolley, ready to refill Carol's supplies of dyes and treatments. 'But twice more you've shaved it.'

'I can't help it,' said Carol, running her hands over her head. She had become addicted to feeling the tiny tufts of hair turning over against her palm, and the feeling of freedom she felt every morning when the only decision she had to make was between her sequined skull cap, which she'd finally bought herself, or the multicoloured beanie that Libby had specially crocheted for her. Even though it was springtime now, the mornings were still sometimes cold.

'What I really need is a wig,' said Carol as she looked at the picture.

'Hey, I can get that for you!' said Velvet, her eyes widening in delight. 'Pure polyester, from the factory.'

'I can't afford a wig,' said Carol, holding up a sample of H14 next to her cheek and examining it. 'This does bring out my warm tones,' she said wistfully.

'Yes, you can. My friend works there. I have three,' said Velvet.

'Really? Why?' asked Carol, looking up curiously.

Velvet's hair was always worn short and gleaming, lacquered in tight waves around her head, like a 1920s dandy.

'Oh, you know,' said Velvet vaguely. 'It's good for when you want to look more feminine.'

Carol assumed Velvet liked women, although she wasn't sure why, exactly. She'd never seen her so much as flirt with anyone since they met. Not that Carol had either. She had a strict no-romance policy when it came to her clients, and outside of work, she hadn't had time to meet anyone. She was planning to, though. She wanted to know if some tentative discoveries that she'd made at the party—aside from her calling, of course—might be true. Like, how much had she ever enjoyed the missionary position anyway? Compared to other . . . things? And might she prefer being with women than with men? So far, with so little experience, it wasn't possible to tell. *That will all just have to wait, though*, she would tell herself firmly, and she did so again now. She had much more important things to think about than sex. She was going to be seeing Steve for the first time in nine months tomorrow evening, and she had to make sure she was prepared.

~

That night Carol took extra care with her beauty routine, making sure every inch of her was worked on and buffed and presented to perfection, so that when she put on the wig the next afternoon, it felt like the crowning glory.

'It looks good,' said Velvet, once Carol had wound a comb in the back to raise it a little, in the sixties fashion the style demanded. 'Old-fashioned, but good on you.'

'Wish me luck.'

'It's not luck you need. It's a cricket bat. You do!' she insisted, as Carol shook her head at her. Velvet had learned enough from Carol's hints and only half-completed stories to have formed a very firm opinion about Steve. But at Carol's insistence she left, driving away in her van at 6 p.m. exactly, with Red riding shotgun beside her. After waiting for fifteen minutes on the street, and then another fifteen minutes sitting tensely in one of the barbers' chairs, Carol went into the kitchenette that ran along the back of the salon and began cutting foils for a full head of streaks she had booked in for tomorrow.

'Carol?'

Steve's voice still sent a shiver down her back.

'Won't be a second,' she called out, her hands fumbling as she untied her apron.

'Well, look at you,' he said, coming to stand in the doorway.

'Shall we get out of here?' Carol suggested lightly as she edged past him. It hadn't occurred to her that he would come to find her out the back, where it was all so makeshift and tatty. She had planned to greet him in the gorgeousness of the salon. But now it looked tatty, too, and she almost couldn't bear the thought of what Steve must be thinking as he looked around, squinting and peering at the fixtures as though he'd never been in a salon before. 'You look good, at least,' he said finally.

'So do you,' she replied automatically, although she hadn't been able to look at him yet. She stole a glance. He was wearing his usual uniform of jeans and a leather bomber jacket, and his hair was still in that feathered style she used to manage for him. Who did it now? she wondered, staring at the floor.

'Wait.' He was peering at her closely now. 'What have you done to your hair?'

Carol had to stop herself from backing away from him as he stepped closer to examine her hairline.

'Cor, blimey. Is that a wig?' His eyes gleamed in amusement. 'Colette told me you'd shaved your head. So you regret it now, huh? Your butch haircut?'

'No, Steve ...' She shook her head, that familiar buzzing in her mind when he began to mock and circle threatening to overwhelm her.

'Is it even going to grow back?' he asked sympathetically as he walked around her, his hands in the pockets of his jeans, his neck craning for a better angle.

'Push back,' Velvet had said to her, just before she left that evening. 'If he starts serving it up to you, push back.'

'No, I don't regret shaving my head!' she snapped, startling them both with her vehemence.

'Okay! Sorry.' He shrugged after a second, retreating towards one of her barbers' chairs. 'No need to get your knickers in a knot.' He leaned forward to examine himself in the mirror, lowering his head to look at his hairline, the way Sampson pretended to be distracted with some urgent grooming whenever he needed time to regroup.

It had worked! Carol watched him in amazement. He had laid off.

'But you *are* more butch.'

'Oh.' Carol sighed. Just when you thought it was safe to go back into the water.

'I asked Colette if you were a radical feminist now, and she said not. But you would never have talked like that to me before.'

'It's just a haircut.' She shrugged. 'Excuse me.' She went out to the back area, where they had hung a mirror over the sink. She looked herself in the eyes as she carefully peeled off her wig and slid it into its silk storage bag. Clearly, it wasn't going to be any use. 'For god's sake!' Steve jumped to his feet in horror as she walked back in. 'What's got into you?'

'Colette told you already, so I don't see what the big deal is.' She walked over to lean casually against the other barbers' chair, as though none of this was that important to her. 'Here, would you like to feel it?' she asked, before he could say anything more insulting, *which was probably a mistake*, she told herself as she reached for his hand and guided it to her scalp. But all she felt was the warmth of his fingers underneath hers, travelling first one way and then the other over her head. Being this close to him, she could smell his aftershave, musky and familiar, reminding her, like a smell from childhood, of something good but long gone.

'Babe,' said Steve, his voice breaking.

Carol looked up. His voice was tight, and his face closed in. This was not her confident, presuming Steve. His skin was pimpled around his forehead, and he'd lost weight. His hair was oily and had been cut roughly, she realised, almost as though he'd done it himself.

'Steve, are you all right?' she asked.

'Not really.'

'What is it?' she replied quickly, alarmed. For Steve to admit that meant that it must be something big.

237

'I lost my job.'

The pain she felt, hearing this, was as bad as if she'd lost her own job, or maybe even worse. Steve's work had always been the most important thing to him, and to her. 'What happened?'

'Same old, same old.'

'Oh babe.' This was the man she'd seen hurt when he lost his job back home, and then again by all the rejections and setbacks they'd endured since they got here. 'I'm sorry.' She walked into his arms, her head fitting where it always had, one hand pressed against his chest and the other sliding its way around his waist, hooking her thumb into his belt. She could hear his heartbeat, and feel the strength of him against her, like a rock she could lean against.

'I've missed you,' he said.

Her breathing was short and shallow against her chest, like a swallow fluttering, unable to get free. She had forgotten the reality of him.

'I've missed you, too.' Being without Steve was like trying to do without an arm or a leg. It was like trying to breathe on the moon, where there was no oxygen. And all those days she'd spent without him seemed empty and meaningless by comparison.

'I've been thinking,' Steve said. 'This is all about what happened on the boat, isn't it?'

Shock gave her the strength to step away. 'What?' Not once had he ever mentioned that awful night.

'That's when you began going completely strange on me.'

'Strange on you?' She shook her head in confusion.

'If I'd had more patience and been willing to let you yammer on, it would never have come to this, would it?'

'I don't know.'

His tone was still bearable, but his words made her back prickle, her body remembering how things could move and change between them before her mind could quite register it.

'It made you nervous, and on top of the stress of the move and all that—' Steve rubbed his nose thoughtfully '—you lost your balance somehow. I get it.' He squeezed his eyes shut for a moment. 'I get it. I should have been more understanding, but I've had a lot of time to think these last few months and I've been to see Doctor Jorgensen.'

'You've been to see Doctor Jorgensen? About me?' To think of the two men sitting there in that clinic, talking about her . . . Her skin goose-pimpled and her back tightened. To think of Dr Jorgensen, whom she had been to see about getting a diaphragm fitted, discussing this.

'It was hard on me, too.'

'You never said,' whispered Carol.

'We should have talked more. About everything, I can see that. From now on, I promise you, things will be different.'

'From now on?' She shook her head in confusion. 'Steve, what are you talking about?'

'This.' With the air of a magician pulling a dove from a hat he pulled an envelope out of his pocket and placed it on the table underneath the mirror. Carol picked it up and pulled out a thick long card. It was a ticket to England, with her and Colette's and Steve's names on it, dated a month from now.

'What's this?'

'It's a one-way ticket for all three of us home. On a Jumbo.' He smiled proudly as she gasped. So this is where the money that she should have been getting for child support had gone, thought Carol.

'I'll admit it. You weren't wrong,' Steve continued, 'although maybe you were a little bit melodramatic, shall we say, in making your point. I just needed time to get used to the idea.'

'You expect me to just pack up Colette and come too?' Carol was blunt with surprise. 'I can't do that.' Although, even as she was saying that, with the ticket in her hand, Carol could see a whole new future blossoming before her.

'We could get a little flat, near your mum but on our own, and try again for a baby like you wanted.'

She could picture it already. Shining in front of her, like a promise.

'But I've made a life here now,' she stammered. 'The house, this business and Velvet.'

'These aren't our people, babe. You know that. You saw it before I did. They're not our kind.'

Suddenly it all seemed foreign to her, too, as she looked around. Especially herself. Who was her kind, now, anyway? The question gave her a sense of vertigo. A single mother and a hairdresser, with nothing and no one of her own, apart from Colette.

'But we moved,' she said desperately. 'We left all of our people behind.'

'It was a mistake.' Steve shrugged. 'But luckily,' he waggled his eyebrows at the ticket, 'we can change it.'

So he got to decide that they should come here, and he got to decide when they should go, she realised bitterly. She and Colette were just pieces on his chequerboard, to be moved around at his whim.

'Steve, I have a home,' she said, almost pleading with him. 'I have a life here. I have a business; look at how well it's doing.'

'You've done well, Carol. It's impressive. But things don't always stay going well, believe me.'

'What are you talking about?' She heard something in his tone, something she didn't like.

'Well, for example, I know Anna's backing you. You won't have much money if she withdraws that, will you?'

How did he know these things?

'Colette told me.' Steve shrugged, reading her thoughts as usual. 'And your house won't last. Women always fight.'

'No, they don't!' She felt sullen now, and exhausted. 'We don't fight.'

He smiled secretively, as though he knew something she didn't, and her skin crawled. 'I bet you will.'

'I bet we won't,' she said, more firmly now, her confidence rising.

He tapped the envelope with the ticket in it with his knuckles, and blew her a kiss. 'Time will tell,' he said, pulling on his jacket.

'How can it not?' she muttered sulkily.

'You know, Carol, it's not right for Colette to be raised by a single mother,' he said, just as he was leaving. 'I wouldn't wish that on a dog.'

Carol kept looking at the envelope as she closed up the salon. She could be home in a month. There would be snow on the ground. She and Colette and her mum could go into Piccadilly Circus to see the Christmas lights, the way they always did. Colette could slot right back in at her old school, and Carol could start her own salon there, too, now that she had more confidence. Why not? Maybe she could even make it work with Steve.

14

Anna

'GOOD DAY?' ASKED MYLES AS HE walked up to the picnic rug Anna had laid out for them on the grass. Spring had burst into full-blown summer in the last few days, and women were sitting with their skirts pulled up to their thighs, their stocking-less legs stretched out in front of them, while the men had unbuttoned their shirts to their navels, soaking up the sun. The fountain in the middle of the lawn splashed merrily, giving the day the feeling of a party.

'It's a great day,' said Anna, even though before she saw him she would have said it was only average. 'You're looking very handsome,' she said, as he sat down.

Myles had let his hair grow longer, and now it curled around his ears in gentle waves. He'd swapped his thick black-framed glasses for frameless ones, which showed off his long eyelashes and flattered his olive skin. By 5 p.m. he'd have stubble, but at lunchtime it was just a shadow over his jawline.

'You're looking rather splendid yourself,' he replied, unwrapping his sandwiches. 'That's a lovely outfit.'

'Thank you.' She was wearing a khaki jumpsuit today, with a leopard-print handbag and matching scarf tied like a cravat at her throat, and high-heeled espadrilles imported from the South of France.

'How did the girls seem to you this morning?' asked Myles, as he opened up a bag of chips.

'Fine. I think.' Anna sipped her coffee—no sugar, black. 'I had to leave early, breakfast meeting, but they seemed fine when I left. Why?'

'No special reason.'

'Myles.' She put her hand over the packet to stop him eating for a moment. 'What is it?'

'They seemed a bit off yesterday, that's all, and Nanny says they've been acting that way with her for a while.'

'What way, Myles? You're being very vague.'

'I know. I'm sorry. They were reluctant to go back to your place, that's all. They didn't want to get in the car, refused to pack their things . . .'

'Okay, I get it, Myles.' She shook her head in disappointment. 'I thought we were over this.'

'You think I'm making it up?'

'Not on purpose. But you're very sensitive to how they're feeling when they're staying with Mum in a way that I don't see you worrying about when they're with Dad.'

'Point taken,' he sighed.

'Look,' said Anna. She hated to see him worry. 'We both know they're bound to have their ups and downs, whatever their living situation. I'll have a talk to them tonight, okay? If there's anything there I'll get to the bottom of it.'

'Sounds good.'

'Personally, I think they're adjusting better than we could have expected. Did you see their end-of-year report cards? Their marks haven't gone down in one subject in the last nine months since we moved out, and for maths and geography they've gone up!'

'Great,' said Myles, obviously still worried.

Anna gave up and snuck a chip, allowing it to rest on her tongue and dissolve there, flooding her with bliss.

'Anna, I have to tell you something.'

Myles's voice interrupted her reverie.

'I . . . I met someone.'

Her heart plummeted as she gasped, and she felt a flush of heat go right through her body.

'Not serious . . . not real . . . we've only seen each other a few times,' he stammered. 'I thought I should. Like you said, it's 1977, and this might be my only chance and . . .' His voice trailed away.

'No, it's good,' she said, trying to catch her breath. 'I'm glad you did. I mean, we agreed. I just wasn't expecting it, that's all.'

'I'm sorry. I didn't know how I should tell you.'

'No, no, it's fine, really.' She waved away his apology. 'It's fine,' she added firmly, convincing herself. 'Was it, um . . . was it a man?'

'Yes.' His face was blank.

'Well?' She smiled at him brightly, trying to sound upbeat. 'Was it fun?' As if they were talking about going on the rollercoaster.

He looked down into his lap and a private expression—half smile, half frown—flashed across his face. 'It was . . . interesting.'

'Interesting? Come on, Myles. It's me, remember? I want us to be honest.'

'No, you're right. I want us to be honest, too. It just takes some practice.'

'Let's try again. How was it?' This time, amid the dread, she felt a little curious.

'It was good,' he said simply. He opened his hands out wide, as if he was giving something up, or setting something free. 'It was what I wanted.'

Her heart twisted at the thought of someone lucky enough to be wanted by Myles.

He raised his eyes to hers. 'But nothing like being with you.'

She was about to make a wry joke about that, at her own expense, when she saw that his eyes were filled with pain.

'I've been with someone, too,' she said abruptly. She hadn't been planning to say anything, but obviously this was the moment. 'I met him at a sex party.'

'*You?*' This was the first time in their lives—no, the second time, the first time was the night of the ABBA concert, when she came over to the bed with that shoe box—that he looked genuinely shocked by her.

'It wasn't as much fun as it sounds.'

'Yes. Well.' He relaxed back onto his elbows. 'You see, to me that doesn't actually sound like fun.'

She was beginning to enjoy this, Anna realised. What could have been an excruciating conversation for some couples—like Libby, for example, when Ben told her about his new girlfriend— was making her feel much closer to Myles.

'You know, with us, I thought, because we loved each other, that it would all come good,' said Myles. 'I never meant to deceive you. Oh, Anna, I'm sorry!' His voice, too, was tinged with pain.

She leaned forward across the picnic blanket and threw her arms around his neck, pressing her cheek against his.

'I promise you, I wanted to be everything you wanted me to be,' he whispered, his voice muffled by her hair.

'Oh Myles,' said Anna, breathing in the familiar scent of him, 'you were.'

'Please come back,' he said gravely, as they stood up and folded the picnic blanket then put the remains of their sandwiches in the bin. 'This is not what I want.'

'Do you think it's what I want?' replied Anna, trying to keep the bitterness out of her voice.

She missed him, she realised. She missed his unique and particular Myles-ness, which was something she knew she'd never find in anyone else, woman or man.

'I used to think sex said, "You are more important to me than anything else in the world"', said Myles, as they waited at the traffic lights. 'But now I don't believe that's true.'

'I don't think so, either,' said Anna, resting her head on his shoulder.

They walked arm in arm back to her office through the city streets splashed with sunshine.

A block before they reached her building she began to walk faster, craning her head around and scanning the faces of the people they passed. What if Steve was watching them? The thought of it made her shoulders twitch. What if he popped out from behind a doorway and started walking down the street in front of her, the way he sometimes did?

'Do you feel weird about being seen with me?' asked Myles, picking up on her tension.

'Oh, it's not that,' said Anna, flustered that he'd noticed. 'It's . . .' She thought about telling him, but then she shook her head.

'Too complicated,' said Myles, smiling understandingly. 'We've fallen out of touch.'

'We have,' she agreed sadly. Obviously he thought she was thinking about work.

'I miss our vodka tonic catch-ups.'

'I do, too,' said Anna, with a lump in her throat.

There was nothing she would have liked more than to be able to talk to Myles about this, curled up on the sofa in their beautiful living room, with the girls tucked up safe and sound upstairs in bed. Although if that were possible then none of this would be happening in the first place.

He released her arm as they stopped outside her office building.

'Sure you don't want to tell me about it?' He narrowed his eyes and looked at her searchingly, tracing her cheek tenderly with the edge of his hand.

She grabbed it and kissed it lightly, before firmly giving it back to him. 'I'm sure.'

What if she told Myles, and he got involved—which she knew he would do, no matter what she said—and then Steve started showing up at Myles's work? What if they got into an argument? Myles had been in the army, and even though usually he was the gentlest of men, he would never back down from a fight. Anna shuddered at the thought of it as she watched him walk off down the street. Then she turned and quickly pushed through the revolving glass doors of her office building, looking from side to side out of the corner of her eye as she hurried to the lifts.

'Wait!' she cried, thrusting her hand out to stop a pair of doors closing. 'Thank you,' she said brightly to the disapproving stares of the other people returning from lunch as she squeezed herself in, even though it was already overcrowded. 'Phew,' she muttered, taking off her sunglasses and pressing her fingers into her eyes.

~

Steve was now showing up regularly, too often for it to even possibly be a coincidence, and Anna was in the unprecedented position of not knowing what to do. Should she tell Carol? Or would that make it bigger than it already was, and destroy some of Carol's newfound confidence into the bargain? And she could hardly explain to Carol that, as well as the awfulness of having Steve showing up at random times, she also couldn't stop thinking about him, in an uneasy, unsettled way that hummed along inside her all the time no matter what else she did. So it wasn't even that she was being disturbed by him a number of times a week. It was a total disturbance that was affecting her whole system.

He'd shown up once every three days on average, for the last three weeks, according to her office diary, where she noted his appearances with a little mark. Before that it had been only once every couple of weeks. She would see him waiting near her bus stop in the evenings, or sitting casually in the garden plaza where she usually ate her lunch. The first few times she ignored him, but by the fourth time it had become obvious that he knew that she knew he was there. Still, she did nothing to acknowledge his presence, and simply walked faster to the bus stop, jumping into a taxi if she was going to have to wait, or getting up and hurrying away from her lunch and back into her office building, where she knew he couldn't follow her. Not that he'd ever tried. She had worried at first that he might climb onto her bus one day, or try to corner her at lunch. But he just watched.

Which was almost just as bad, she realised, after another week of that. What did he want? What was he planning? It only ever happened in the city, it seemed, and so each time the weekend came around, she felt some relief. Every time she went outside now on a weekday, she carried a burden of suspense.

'You have to stop doing this,' Anna had said to him a week ago, finally acknowledging his presence. Steve was leaning against one of the steel girders which supported the huge glass atrium inside her office building's reception area. Up until now he had always waited just outside. He stood out in his desert boots and jeans.

'I could have security throw you out, you know,' she said. 'This is private property.'

'Fine, then. I'll wait on the street.'

'Wait for what, though?' she replied, curiosity overcoming her determination to project strength.

'Not sure, exactly.'

'You're not *sure*?' For one crazy moment Anna almost wanted to laugh at him. He felt it, too.

'Had time on my hands,' he muttered, looking down.

'So you're bored? Is that what you're saying?' She needed to follow up on her advantage while she had it. 'So you thought you'd come and harass me?'

'It's a free country.' He looked away.

'Don't you have a job?'

He flinched.

So that's it, thought Anna, relaxing momentarily. 'Do you want me to tell Carol you don't have work anymore?' she asked.

'I don't care, really.' He shrugged. 'Better not.' He looked up, and their eyes met in unwelcome complicity. 'You know she'll worry.'

Anna knew very well. That's why she hadn't told Carol, or Libby, about any of this.

'If you don't want me to tell Carol, then what?' she asked, trying to reason this through. 'Is it something you want to get from me? Like—I don't know—help finding you another job?'

He wrinkled his nose. 'Nah,' he laughed, not giving her the chance to refuse. 'That'll be the day when I need some sheila to find a job for me.'

'Is it money? It must be expensive paying the rent on Church Street on your own.'

'Tell me about it! I've got some other things going on.'

'You mean you're gambling,' said Anna flatly. She'd had enough experience with her father to recognise the signs. 'All right, then, I give up. What do you want from me?'

'I don't know, really.' He looked around curiously at the men and women streaming past. 'It's just something to do.'

'Seriously, Steve, you're behaving like a creep,' said Anna, running out of patience.

'Am I? Is that what I'm doing?' He dropped the surly indifference and seemed to be genuinely asking, as though it were her responsibility to work him out.

Genuinely lost for words, Anna picked up her briefcase and walked off. Two days later he was back again, standing in precisely the same place.

'So what is the problem, exactly?' the manager of her building had asked, when Anna finally decided to complain. He had been friendly and respectful as she introduced herself, but now he was looking at her doubtfully as she explained. 'Look, ma'am,' he interrupted, 'we're here to deal with bomb threats and kidnappings, that kind of thing. Frankly, I don't see what is so threatening about a man waiting for you sometimes.'

'Because I don't want him to. And, frankly, I would have thought you might be able to help me with this, in the event of there not being a hostage situation happening right this minute.' His eyes fluttered. She shouldn't have put it like that.

'You don't want him to.' He looked at her thoughtfully, up and down. 'Have you told him that?' He sounded sceptical.

'Of course!' snapped Anna, but all her authority and confidence, so carefully cultivated and practised in this building, seemed to have been stripped away. Now, suddenly, it seemed possible that she might be the crazy one.

'He hasn't followed you home, has he?' asked the manager. He seemed bored now, and was shuffling through his rosters. 'He hasn't threatened you or done actual physical harm?'

'No.'

'Are you worried that he might?'

'No, no,' Anna dully replied. The games Steve played were mental ones. She was sure of that.

'There's the question of *his* rights, you see,' said the manager, deadpan, but she could see it in his eyes that he disliked her. 'I suggest you take the back lifts. Problem solved.' He flashed her a smile, and even though she was a partner in the firm that took up three floors of this building, paying astronomical rent, she knew that if she took this any further up the food chain, she would be the one who lost.

'If you feel that you absolutely have to talk to me for some reason, then you should phone,' Anna said, trying to sound reasonable the next day when she found Steve waiting for her again, this time in the street just outside her building.

That was a mistake.

'All right,' he'd said flippantly, 'I'll phone.'

That had been a week ago, and now he was phoning her office at random times every day. He hadn't shown up again in person, at least.

~

The lift slowly emptied as it carried Anna up to her floor. She felt much better about things, actually, after that lunch with Myles. And she always felt better up here, anyway, as if, so high up in the clouds, nothing could really touch her.

'Any messages?' she asked Gilbert as she swung past his desk. 'With any luck I can get the whole analysis completed this afternoon if no one interrupts me,' she told him. 'Just my luck,' she sighed as the phone began ringing the minute she sat down at her desk.

'It's Steve Ball calling,' said the telephone operator.

It seemed awfully like perfect timing for him to be calling at this minute. Had he been watching her?

'Put him through.'

'What do you want?' she asked harshly, as soon as she saw that operator's light switch off. Being with Myles had given her strength, and now she felt capable of being very definite with him, whereas too often lately she'd stayed silent on the line, feeling helpless.

'You said I should call.' Steve sounded sullen.

'No, actually, I didn't,' she snapped into the receiver. 'I said if you absolutely had to speak to me, you should call.'

'What if I do absolutely have to speak to you?'

Anna watched, appalled, as goose-bumps formed down her arm. No matter how self-confident she was feeling, it seemed that he could take it away in seconds.

'Listen, stop calling. Okay?' She spoke quietly, glancing around to make sure Gilbert was nowhere in earshot. He was sitting at his desk outside the clear glass walls of her office, typing, as though it were just any ordinary day at the office. 'I have work to do.'

Steve remained silent.

'If you need to talk about money or whatever, then you and Carol need to sort it out.'

'All right,' he said agreeably. There was a click, and the line went dead.

Anna felt faint for a moment with the strength of her relief. She sat back in her swivel chair and looked out her window, feeling nothing except a little tired. She reached for her handbag and found a cigarette. She didn't usually do this until the end of the day—she thought it looked careless to smoke at work, although the men seemed to believe it only made them look more masculine—but today she decided she deserved it. It had taken a lot of courage to talk to him like that But why? *Why?* she asked herself. Why did it take so much out of her and ask so much of her to deal with such a . . . a pipsqueak? Why did it feel so big?

It's creepy, Anna told herself. This is what creeps did, wasn't it? The tension she sensed hovering around him when he made his appearances was almost unbearable, like a brewing storm. She hated it, and she already knew that she hated him. This new behaviour of his would have been quite enough to make her feel that way, even if she didn't love Carol. Most of all, though, she hated herself for not being capable of putting a stop to his ridiculous behaviour, when surely it ought to be easy. Especially for Anna Wotcek, who—everyone agreed—could do anything she set her mind to.

Is it because I used to be attracted to him? she kept asking herself over the next few days. What she felt now was too dark to be mistaken for attraction. She had lost five pounds in the past two weeks—five pounds she actually needed, her hips and cheekbones were starting to look too pronounced—and the whole thing was wrecking her sleep. She thought about Steve sometimes as she lay in bed. She thought about his voice on the phone, when he told her he absolutely had to speak to her, forming a loop in her brain which went round and around. The twin feelings of fear and curiosity he aroused in her, revealing a whole new way of stopping time.

Should I tell Carol? she wondered again. But what could Carol do? Except stress out about it, and that would interrupt all the wonderful things she was achieving. *Should I tell Nicky?* But Nicky would make it all about Anna's self-development, and ever since Anna had decided to have nothing to do with him, eight months ago now, she didn't think that approach made sense. She didn't believe she had invited this into her life, no matter what Carl Jung might have said.

As she travelled down in the lift that evening, Anna felt relieved he hadn't called again, and maybe, even, a little bored. Perhaps that meant it might be ending, for her at least, she thought hopefully. Perhaps Myles had inspired a kind of breakthrough. After all, if she could manage to stop caring so much, then it wouldn't matter what Steve did.

The lift had almost reached the second floor when she remembered she was supposed to be leaving by the back way. But the bell had already dinged, and the doors were already opening, and even before she turned to look, somehow she knew he would be there. She forced herself to walk towards him, the click of her heels ringing out on the marble floor.

'What is it you absolutely have to speak to me about?' she asked loudly.

He wasn't dressed immaculately, for once, she noticed. His T-shirt was crumpled and there was a smear of mud on his jeans.

'Well, go on, then.' She crossed her arms.

'It's Colette.'

'Has something happened?' She felt adrenaline flooding her as he hesitated. 'Oh god.'

'No, she's all right.'

'Oh.' She was always flooded with adrenaline when she saw him, remembered Anna, yet more irritated. 'Look, I want you to stop doing this, all right? I told you.' *You are wasting my time*, she wanted to say to him. *You are disturbing my sleep.* But that would make it too personal.

'I mean, physically she's okay,' continued Steve, as if he hadn't heard her. 'You're the only person I can talk to, who knows her. Please!'

'I need to sit down.' Suddenly Anna felt unsteady on her feet. 'Let's go over to those chairs.' She pointed to one of the black leather lounge suites scattered around the atrium.

'No, let's not sit there.' Steve glared at her. His eyes were red, as if he'd been crying. 'I need to talk to you, properly, about the kids. Colette's been telling me stuff that you need to know.'

'You think there's something you can tell me about my own children?'

'And I need a drink,' he added, in a heartfelt way that neutralised any hint of a threat.

'All right,' sighed Anna, drained of the will to resist. Maybe it would be possible to hash this out with him and get to the bottom of it, so she could get on with her life.

He was shorter than her, she noticed, as she guided him down the escalator into the bowels of the building where she had her keys cut and her dry cleaning done. It just seemed so ridiculous that she could be so affected by this wisp. There, in one of the little doorways, was an Irish bar, done up inside with green felt bar runners and four-leaf clovers.

'What are you drinking?' she asked, as they walked in.

'A double whisky,' he said, leaning against the bar and shoving his hands in his pockets.

He was even going to let her pay this time. What the hell could be the matter?

'I'll have two, thanks, bartender,' Anna said, before carefully putting her briefcase on the bar between them, so there could be no chance of them accidentally touching, and sitting down next to him.

Steve pulled out a piece of paper and thrust it over to her along the bar. 'She wrote me this yesterday.' Spiky handwriting crawled down the page, which had obviously already been folded and unfolded many times.

Dear Dada, how are you? I am well. But, I don't feel good. I miss you. The girls are mean. Summer is mean and Leanne is mean. And Michelle is stupid. I miss you.

'Well,' said Anna, unnerved. 'That's, um . . .' She read it again. *Michelle is stupid? Leanne is mean?* That couldn't be right. 'I mean, um . . .' She cleared her throat and had a sip of whisky. 'Colette sounds very sad.'

'She's not okay,' said Steve, his voice husky with emotion as he stared at it.

'I'm sorry,' said Anna, reading it again, and this time she was moved by Colette's laborious handwriting, and the obvious trust she felt in her father. 'Has she . . . has she mentioned anything like this to you before?'

'Never. This is not like Colette.'

'Have you told Carol about this?'

Steve flinched at the mention of her. 'She won't listen.'

'Really? I thought you guys saw each other about a bank account, a little while ago . . .' Anna's words died in her throat as he looked up at her, his face flushed deep red.

'She won't *listen*,' he repeated.

'Okay.' Anna paused for a moment to regroup. 'Look, Steve, I really don't want to get in between you guys.'

'It's a bit late for that now, isn't it?' he sneered.

'What?'

He met her gaze. 'You know.'

'Know *what*?'

He put his hand over hers where it was resting on the bar and leaned towards her. 'Living like this, it's not good for her.'

'Living like what? With me and Libby, you mean?' Anna snatched her hand away. 'This is all about Carol, isn't it? This has nothing to do with Colette.'

'You're wrong.' Just as suddenly as he had turned on her, he turned back into the other man—the one with the eyes filled with sadness, who had persuaded her to bring him to this bar. 'I wouldn't do that to my own kid.'

'All right,' said Anna, her eyes flicking to her watch. Just five more minutes, she decided. She eyed the peanuts the bartender had placed in front of them in a little white china bowl. They might not be clean, she reminded herself, even though her stomach was grumbling. She was shivering slightly, too. It was air conditioned so fiercely in here that she wished she had a jacket with her.

'I need you to tell me honestly what you think is going on with Colette,' Steve was saying. 'She's the only thing I have. The only person who I've ever loved, apart from Carol.'

'Uh-huh.' Anna nodded blandly, humouring him. The whisky was making him maudlin.

'Tell me honestly, Anna. Do you think that she's all right?'

Anna was about to say yes, anything to get her out of here, when something stopped her—a question that was unfurling in the pit of her stomach. 'I don't know, really,' she said reluctantly, taking a sip of her drink.

Would her own girls write to Anna like that if they didn't get to see her nearly every day? She hated to admit this to herself, but she didn't think they would. They had become inscrutable lately, to her, at least. They were such good and obedient little girls—everyone commented upon it. But she didn't entirely trust all that obedience and goodness, realised Anna, as she stared down into her whisky. She had looked at Leanne and Michelle a few times lately and wondered, somewhere in the back of her mind, could it be real? They were so different now from how they used to be, when she and Myles lived together. They used to squabble and cry and complain constantly. They used to be boisterous, too, she realised, sitting there. They used to scream with laughter. When she and Myles lived together there used to be so much drama: laughing and fighting, happiness and despair. Now, they seemed so much calmer—or was it that they had just learned how to be self-contained? Her heart twisted at the thought. 'The kids are all handling it so well,' she and Libby and Carol kept saying to one another, but was that because the alternative was just too awful for the women to contemplate? Or were they simply doing as Anna had learned to do—at the same age as the girls were now—and putting on a front?

'Are you all right?' Steve was looking at her curiously.

The whisky had melted in her head like liquid amber and suddenly she could see right to the heart of things.

'I have to go,' Anna said, tilting her head back to finish her drink and pushing back her hair. It felt suggestive, of course, she realised irritably as she climbed down from her stool, like everything she did when she was around Steve—as though her intentions would be decided by his interpretation of her behaviour.

'What is it?' asked Steve, alarmed.

'My children are turning out just like me,' she said grimly, unable to hide her misery. She tensed as she felt him move closer to her, but when she looked up, ready to defend herself, to her surprise his face had softened in sympathy.

'I see things about myself that I don't like in Colette sometimes.'

'Really?' She wasn't used to a person who kept changing like this: from hard to soft to scornful to tender in seconds, turning like a disco ball in the light. She scooped up a handful of nuts and began eating them quickly, one by one.

'Thank you for staying and talking to me,' Steve said.

But I've hardly said anything, she was about to reply, when he lowered his head towards hers. *Carol's a wonderful person*, she wanted to say, but her tongue had just discovered a piece of peanut stuck in her tooth, and so she nodded instead.

'You're really beautiful, did you know that?'

Who was he talking about? Anna wondered. And then he leaned forward and kissed her. She stood frozen as his lips pressed against hers, and remained frozen as he sat back on his bar stool, watching for her reaction. *Beautiful?* She put her fingers to her lips to touch where his lips had just been, and then looked at him, trying to understand what had just happened. His hands grasped hers and he leaned forward as if he was about to kiss her again. Anna stepped back just in time, bashing her ankle painfully against the leg of her bar stool.

'Oi! Oi!'

She looked up, blinking.

The bartender stood in front of them, beet red and waving his tea towel at them. 'You can't do that here, missy.'

Anna gaped at him. 'Me?'

'This is a respectable establishment. Take him out into the street if you want to do that sort of thing. Get a room!'

'What sort of thing?' She looked at Steve, expecting him to stand up for her. 'Are you going to let him speak to me like that?' she demanded.

But the man who had just kissed her was gone and in his place was the detached, disdainful Steve, sullenly gathering up his cigarettes and lighter, and leaving the letter from Colette stained and lonely looking on the bar.

'You're a feminist, aren't you? You can look after yourself.' Steve winked at her. 'It's okay. She's leaving,' he said to the bartender in an undertone.

Anna felt the shock of humiliation strike deep. She grabbed her briefcase and pushed her way to the door and out into the cool silent whiteness of the mall, which was blinding after the darkness of the bar.

'Anna. Anna, wait!' She heard his running footsteps behind her.

What happened? What just happened? Anna asked herself as she stepped onto the escalator, which began to take her—oh, the relief of it—back up into the street, where buses and cars were roaring past and the hubbub of the world rose to greet her.

'You looked so pretty standing there and I just . . . I'm sorry.' He shrugged, taking up a position next to her. 'I lose my head with men like that.'

'Men like that? He's a bartender!' she said incredulously.

Steve shrugged and looked away. 'To you, maybe.'

'I come from the same place as you come from, Steve. Or worse, maybe. So don't tell me I'm too middle class to understand.'

'I know. I know you do. That's why we like each other, isn't it?' He edged closer to her, so his arm was touching hers.

'Like each other?' she echoed, moving herself away. 'I've never *liked* you, Steve.'

'Whatever you want to call it,' he muttered, running his hand through his hair. It all fell back perfectly into place.

You're a woman in your prime, Anna pictured Nicky saying. *You will feel desire, and find it in many places, if that's what you can allow.*

Kissing Simon Lieber had been like catching a wave, or being swept up in one, she realised then, with startling clarity, on the escalator. With Myles it had been like a fire they were struggling to create. With Steve . . . with Steve whatever it was he made happen between them was like a competition—but she had no reason to compete.

They rose to the top of the escalator and Anna stepped off, walking quickly towards the street with Steve keeping up with her. Here were the pot plants and the ashtrays and the lifts, all just as she had left them—Anna glanced at her watch—thirty minutes ago. Being with Steve had changed all the rules of her universe for a little while, tripping her up and confusing her. But not anymore.

'Please stop,' she said.

'Stop what?'

'Whatever it is you think you're doing. Stop waiting for me. Stop calling me.'

He shook his head, smiling. 'I always told myself that if you said please, that I would.'

'Well, that's just ridiculous. But okay, I've said it.' Anna shook her head to clear it, but it already felt clear. The whisky was just sugar now, which she could use and metabolise any way she chose. It was just a source of energy, like Steve.

'What are you going to tell Carol?' he asked.

'What? Oh.' The smile playing around his lips set a cascade of understanding running through her, flipping over her assumptions like cards, and answering all her lingering questions. 'You're trying to get at Carol, aren't you? You're not worried about Colette at all.'

'I was,' he replied swiftly—too swiftly.

'You'd really go to this much trouble to wreck her home?'

'I just wonder how she'd feel about that kiss.' He put his hands into his pockets and rocked forward on his heels, cocking his head to one side.

'Are you threatening me?'

It seemed unbelievable, out here on this warm summer evening, that their lips could have actually touched. As if, having happened four floors below in the freezing underground, it had taken place in a different dimension.

'I won't tell if you won't,' he said playfully.

'You never quit, do you? I'm certainly not leaving it up to you.'

'Might not be such a happy home, now, hey?'

'Steve, seriously.' She turned to face him, holding her briefcase against her chest like a shield. 'Why won't you let Carol have this?'

'So she hasn't told you.'

'Told me what?'

'We're going home to England.' He sounded triumphant.

'Carol's not,' said Anna automatically. 'She would have said something.' Her words died on her lips as he smiled smugly. 'Carol's built too much, she's made too much, to leave it all behind,' she added uncertainly.

'Why don't you tell her about what's been happening between us, then, and find out?'

'Steve, I keep telling you, nothing's been happening between us,' said Anna coolly, but she was shaking as she turned and walked away from him, and when she thought about telling Carol how he'd kissed her in the bar this evening, she felt sick.

15

Libby

LIBBY HEARD A HIGH KEENING SOUND, on a frequency that was almost like a bird calling, as she walked home from her shift at the pub.

Jasper made that noise. When he was upset.

Libby took off her shoes and began to run. She threw herself up the stairs, dropping her handbag and the shopping bags by the front door and walked, breathless, down the hall.

'Jasper? Where's Jasper?'

Colette, Summer and Leanne were sitting in the living room in front of the television, their chins resting on their hands, almost mimicking one another in their bored detachment.

'He's in the garden,' said Anna, from the armchair. 'I promised the girls we could watch half an hour of the worst thing possible and then they can get on with their homework. Michelle's already started.'

Libby dashed through the kitchen and out to the backyard, where she found Jasper sitting on the concrete, banging a shoe against the ground. He looked up at her, and quickly looked down again, seemingly totally absorbed in his shoe and making that rhythmic hooting sound again, but more quietly this time.

'Hi, my darling.'

He was wearing just a T-shirt and shorts, and she could see that he was shivering. Even though it was early summer, it still was cool at night. 'Hop up, come on.' His legs were stiff as he unfurled himself. Libby closed her arms around him, pressing her cheek against his, which he kept averted, everything in him straining towards that shoe. Libby could feel how much he wanted to keep banging it on the ground. 'No more shoes,' said Libby, peeling his fingers away from it while with the other she hung onto her glasses, which he was staring at now, about to grab them at any moment.

'How long has he been sitting out there?' Libby asked Anna sharply as they came back through the living room. Anna was standing up, her hands twisting together anxiously. 'Summer, get up and run a bath,' snapped Libby. 'Why was he out there alone?' she demanded, turning back to Anna.

'He wouldn't come in when I asked him to, and I didn't know what to do.'

'So you just left him?'

'I thought he was happy! I thought those sounds were happy sounds. He loves those shoes.'

'No, they're not happy. And he loves those shoes the way you love cigarettes and how would you feel if you came home and Michelle was sitting out there alone, chain-smoking?'

'I'm sorry, Libby, but how was I to know?'

And yet Libby was supposed to know that Michelle didn't like parsley and so she made sure it wasn't in any of their meals. And she was supposed to know that Leanne needed to have first bath, and . . . oh, what was the point?

If they talked any longer, she would say something she would regret, and so she marched out, still holding Jasper, her eyes filling with tears, and into the bathroom, where Summer was already dumping salts and oils into the bath. 'You can get in, too,' she told Summer, raising her voice over the sound of the running water. 'Quick sticks.' She knelt on the tiles to help Jasper, who was clumsy as he climbed out of his clothes, his knees and elbows tight as he tried to bend them. 'There we go,' she said, easing off the tap so the noise of the running water wouldn't be so loud, and pressing down hard on Jasper's shoulders to help him feel grounded in the water. His face was still blank, but she felt the muscles in his shoulders relaxing as the water level rose.

'Why didn't you say something?' Libby asked Summer, once she'd stripped off and joined Jasper in the bath. This was the first time Summer had been willing to brave the embarrassment of a bath with Jasper since they'd moved here. The other girls all apparently only found it acceptable to bathe alone. 'Why didn't you tell Anna he was getting too cold?'

'She was busy on the phone about something to do with a survey meeting until just before you came back.'

Libby took a deep breath to calm herself. It was quite possible Summer was exaggerating, she reminded herself. She had been known to fan the flames of controversy in the past. 'Why didn't you do something, then? Why didn't you bring Jasper in to watch TV with you guys? Or do something with just the two of you in his room?' She went on, raising her voice over Summer's interruptions.

'You need to look out for him, Summer. You need to look after him if there's nobody else to.'

Libby had sworn to herself, when Jasper was diagnosed, that she would never make Summer responsible, or give her the job of parenting him. 'Nothing's ideal or necessarily fair, okay?' she said as Summer opened her mouth to argue. 'The three of us love each other more than anyone, okay? And sometimes we need to pull together as a team.'

Summer reached over and kissed Jasper on the cheek. He looked up, and smiled at her—a true, gap-toothed smile of delight. Something deep inside Libby unknotted as she looked at them.

'All right, Mummy,' said Summer solemnly. 'I promise.'

'I'm sorry, Libby,' said Anna, as soon as Libby walked back into the kitchen. She was sitting at the table, smoking, with a purring Sampson on her lap, obviously lying in wait for her. Libby walked over to the stove, took a pot from the rack they'd strung above the benchtop and began to fill it with water. 'I shouldn't have left him in the garden, and I should have put a jumper on him.'

Libby didn't trust herself to speak as she lit the flame underneath the pot. She opened the fridge to see if there was anything she could use to make a sauce. The shelves were empty—of course, her top-up shop was still in the hall—except for some old containers of onions and dhal.

'I've had a hard day,' said Anna quietly.

'I get it,' said Libby, turning on her. 'I know what that's like, believe me. You just needed to veg out, right? But that can't be the case with Jasper. If you're looking after him, then he has to be your first priority. No matter what,' she said, thumping the packet of pasta she found at the back of the cupboard down on the benchtop so hard it split open.

'Oh, don't bother cooking,' said Anna, taking another drag of her cigarette. 'I'm sorry, I should have said. I'm going to treat us and order in.'

Libby sighed. Of course. Anna could sit around on a week-night at dinner time because she was just going to pay to make the problem go away. 'In that case you need to order it now. We have to eat by seven if Jasper's going to be able to get to sleep by eight-thirty.' *And that's already an hour too late*, Libby managed not to say.

'Of course.' Anna stubbed out her cigarette and reached for the phone. 'Is that Ricky's? We'll have six serves of fish-and-chips, thanks. Yes, and scallops—potato. And, um, why don't you throw in six pineapple fritters? Cool.'

Which might not be bad for the girls, who could manage their own appetites and food intake admirably, it seemed to Libby, but it would be irresistible for Jasper not to gorge. Let alone her.

I wish I had my own kitchen. Libby quickly quelled the thought before she let herself think it for too long. *I wish I could have come home and been alone with my babies tonight.*

'So how was your day?' asked Anna.

'It was hard,' said Libby, standing uselessly at the stove. She didn't know what to do with herself in a kitchen if she wasn't cooking. She wished Jasper were here, hugging her legs the way he liked to while she was preparing meals, but Summer had begged to be allowed to help him dress—as penance perhaps? Or just a very rare moment of responsibility?

'Look, Mummy,' said Summer, appearing in the kitchen doorway with Jasper. 'Jasper dressed himself, I just helped a little bit. Didn't you, Jasper?' Libby could tell, just from the way he was standing and making eye contact—as loose and relaxed as any child—that he was feeling as good now in his body as he had been feeling awful before.

'I'm so proud of you both,' said Libby, her voice breaking. God, she probably sounded pathetic, thought Libby, glancing at Anna. 'We think it's an achievement, anyway,' she said, defiantly lifting her chin.

'Of course, it's a huge achievement! I was thrilled when the girls learned.'

But Libby didn't believe her. The girls had probably been dressing themselves since they were two, and being generally precocious in every way; and now she could tell that Summer was picking up on the way she was feeling, as well as Jasper. She hated the idea of the kids becoming self-conscious about who they were. She shrivelled inside at the thought of it as she put her arms around them. *Bloody Anna with her perfect children.*

'Now let's make the sound a water dragon makes, when it's catching a fly.' She began to make kissing noises with Jasper and Summer, so that the three of them together made a smacking kiss. *I wish we lived on our own.*

'Libby I'm sorry again about this afternoon. I'm sure if I hadn't had such a hard day I wouldn't have dropped the ball like that,' said Anna once the kids, finally, were all in bed. Carol was still out with Velvet—she'd phoned home just before dinner—even though she'd said it was for just one drink.

'Jasper's not a ball.'

'No, of course not. I should have managed it better. I should have realised he was stressed. He kept pushing me away, though.'

To her shame, something in Libby felt better at the thought of this.

'Lib, if you think it would be better to do fewer shifts at the pub I would be happy to, you know, make it up to you, financially,' continued Anna. 'To stay at home with the kids, I mean. If you think they need more attention. I mean, I think they need more attention, too.' She was obviously flustered now, her words falling over themselves. 'I mean, it's quite obvious you're so much better at this than me.'

'It's not that I particularly like my job at the pub,' said Libby slowly. 'It's rotten pay, and I'd much prefer not to have to do it, actually. But if you're suggesting that, just because I'm not head of some marketing company, it makes more sense for me to be here . . .' *Warning, warning*, flashed a sign in Libby's brain. It had already been a horrible day, and she had come home exhausted. *Go to bed. Do not pass go. Do not get in a fight with your housemates about the children.* Strauss had warned her.

'Libby, please.' Anna touched her arm, and Libby had to fight the urge to slap it away. 'I'm not suggesting anything like that. I know you love your job, at least some of the time, and you do it excellently. I'm just saying I know I don't do this well enough. Please. Don't pull away.'

'I don't have to love working just because you do. It's not my *career*.'

'Of course not. But you know, I've been thinking—you make such beautiful food. But not just that, you make it in such a lovely way. So simple and informal, and yet everyone feels taken care of. If you ever wanted to cater my focus groups, as a business, I mean, that would be so wonderful.'

'Wonderful for who? For me?' Libby snapped. 'Anna, seriously, don't lay your career-girl bullshit on me. I already work quite hard enough.'

'Libby, please! That's not what I was saying at all. I'm not Ben!'

'I know that. Why would you say that?'

'It's as if I can't say anything right!'

'You . . . you . . .' Libby bit her lip, refusing to indulge the tears pricking behind her eyes.

'You know how much I admire you.'

Anna was right, Libby did know, but there were still wisps of hurt trailing around like cobwebs in the breeze. 'I saw that look on your face when I said how proud I was of my children,' she whispered.

'What? No!' exclaimed Anna. 'You misread it entirely. I was thinking how much I wish I had a bond with my girls the way you have with Summer and Jasper.'

Libby forced herself to take a breath. Anna was her friend, she reminded herself. 'Really?'

'All the time,' said Anna. 'I see it all the time between you guys.'

Libby took another deep, shuddering breath and wiped her hands on her jeans. 'You're right. I'm sorry. Part of it is just that I'm exhausted.'

'I know I'm not a natural mother,' said Anna miserably.

'Oh, Anna, what even is that?' replied Libby gently. 'Everyone has to learn.'

'But I've always told myself, just because you're not a "natural" at it, doesn't mean you still can't excel.'

Excel, thought Libby. What a perfectly Anna word. 'You can't excel at motherhood.' Libby smiled, trying to jolly Anna out of it. 'That's like excelling at meditation. Or sex.'

'Well, you can fail at it, anyway. Like marriage,' said Anna grimly.

'You haven't failed as a friend, at least.' Libby nudged her, annoying Sampson, who jumped down off Anna's lap.

'But that's just it, Libby. I have.'

'What are you talking about?' asked Libby, looking around for the teapot. What she really needed now was a very strong cup.

'I have to tell you something,' said Anna. 'And Carol. I should wait until she gets home, but it's something to do with Steve. To do with me and Steve,' she clarified.

'Oh. Okay,' said Libby, uneasily. 'But what could there be between you and Steve?'

'Something inappropriate,' said Anna grimly.

'Oh.' Libby's horror mounted as all the conclusions she was jumping to were confirmed by the shame on Anna's face. 'Oh Anna! How could you?'

16

Anna

'I KISSED STEVE,' SAID ANNA, AN hour later, as soon as Carol sat down. 'I've been attracted to him since we all moved in together, and tonight I kissed him in a bar. Or, rather, he kissed me . . . I don't understand it. But I'm sorry.' Determination made her words blunt and shocking, instead of forming the careful explanation she'd planned. All she was capable of now, though, was raw description.

'You just take,' said Libby, her voice low and trance-like, staring into the glass of wine in front of her. She'd been drinking steadily for the past hour, refusing to speak to Anna.

'What are you talking about, Libby?' Carol was still rain-fresh and dewy from her walk home, holding the mug of tea she had insisted on, even though Libby had tried to talk her into a glass of wine.

'Anna takes everything.'

'Well, sometimes it seems as though you already have everything!' said Anna, stung.

'You're very good at helping yourself, though, aren't you?' replied Libby.

'And, Libby, you're very good at making it all about you!' snapped Carol.

Libby stared at Carol, and then down at the table, ashamed.

'But, Anna, I didn't know you and Steve were even talking,' said Carol, turning back to her.

The way Carol looked at her was still so open and trusting, marvelled Anna. How was it even possible that she hadn't screamed at her, the way Libby had when Anna told her, or run away, the way Libby had shortly after she'd screamed at her? Libby had stayed in her room until Carol came home, leaving Anna to agonise alone in the kitchen. Carol sat quite still and poised, while Libby, meanwhile, was opening a fresh cask and filling her glass to the brim with cheap red.

'We weren't talking,' said Anna. 'I haven't had anything to do with Steve since I went to talk with him about you, way back in April. I haven't even thought about him since . . .' She thought of all the meals they'd shared, and their outings, and conversations, and her strange bitten-off conversations with Myles, and, weirdly out of nowhere, her kiss at that party with Simon Lieber flashed through her mind. Whom she also hadn't thought about for months until this afternoon. Now why was that? she wondered fleetingly. 'Since our life has been so full. But then about six weeks ago, out of the blue, he started showing up outside my office. I swear I haven't wanted it. I've told him to go away over and over but he just kept contacting me.'

Libby snorted.

'It's true, Libby,' said Anna, offended now as well as upset. 'Just because I was attracted to him doesn't make me responsible for what he does.'

Libby turned away, obviously not ready to give her the benefit of any doubt.

'I didn't tell you, Carol, because I didn't want to worry you,' Anna continued. 'I wish I had now, because this afternoon he told me . . . he told me something about you . . .' She glanced at Libby.

'What?' asked Libby, instantly vigilant. 'What?'

Carol's eyes widened as Anna looked back at her. 'Oh.' She swallowed, her fingers lacing together tightly in front of her chest. 'I wanted to decide before I told you,' said Carol. 'But Steve wants me to go back with him . . . to England.'

Libby looked incredulous. 'After all that he's done?'

'Colette's been very unhappy lately,' said Carol in a very small voice, 'and Steve's saying everything will be different if we go back.' She sighed. 'We were happy in England, you see . . .' Her face took on a dreamy expression as she looked out the back window. 'Or maybe I just didn't know any better,' she added, with a hard little shake of her head. 'I should thank you, Anna, because Steve's just made it very clear to me that I shouldn't do it. But I'm sorry he's been bothering you. I'll go over and have a little chat with him this weekend.'

'No, Carol!' gasped Libby, almost jumping out of her seat in horror. 'Not after this. It's too much. You said you mustn't see him, remember?'

'Really, Libby, it's fine.' Carol's words still had that sweet and easy delivery, but her smile had an edge to it now.

'I do think he's stopped, now. After we kissed . . .' Anna coughed, sensitive to how just saying these words might make Carol feel. 'Somehow I think he will.'

'You gave him what he wanted, I expect,' said Carol, removing a piece of tobacco from her lip.

'What's that?' asked Anna, enthralled by her unshakable cool.

'To bring us down. He thinks if I can't live here, that I'll get back with him.' Carol shook her head with a grim expression as she stubbed out her cigarette, looking over to Libby, who was now lying with her head on her arms. 'Mainly, though, he's just jealous.' She lightly kicked Libby's chair. 'He's jealous of what I've got with the two of you, and so he wanted to spoil it.'

'Well, he's succeeded, hasn't he?' burst out Libby.

'What *are* you on about?' Carol stared at her, puzzled and wary.

'There are just some things, like husbands, that you are not allowed to take!' Libby slammed her chair back from the table and stalked out of the room.

Anna and Carol sat in stunned silence.

'I always knew she didn't like me,' said Anna eventually.

'She does like you.' Carol leaned forward to grab her hands. 'She loves you. She told me, last weekend.'

'Really?' replied Anna, both hopeful and disbelieving.

'Don't you comfort her!' called out Libby from the living room. 'Don't you!'

Carol stood up and walked around the table then put her arms around Anna, leaning down over her shoulders to hug her. 'I love you, too.'

'I don't understand how you can be so sensible about this!' snapped Libby, walking back into the kitchen and opening the fridge door violently. 'I know we're all meant to be into free love now and that no one belongs to anyone but I don't like it when someone else fancies my husband.'

Anna shuddered, but Carol held on tight to her hand as she sat down next to her at the table. 'For one thing, he's not my husband anymore,' said Carol calmly. 'But, for another, he's a ridiculous flirt!'

'Really?' asked Anna, fascinated. 'You've never mentioned that.'

'I've only just realised myself. Working in the salon, with all those guys, I've started to pick it. Not that there's anything wrong with a little harmless flirting, necessarily.' Carol winked at Anna, just the way she had at the party. 'It's only an issue when someone uses it to try to take advantage.'

To Anna, Carol was like sunshine. All those feelings of confusion and shame that had been gathering around her ever since Anna realised she was attracted to Steve had evaporated like mist.

'Well, I'm disappointed in her behaviour,' Libby was saying as she piled leftovers along with a bottle of fizzy water and the remains of a chocolate mousse in the middle of the table, and began to lay out plates and cutlery. 'How will we go on after this?'

'Quite easily,' laughed Carol. She was wearing a flowing sequined top with batwing sleeves, so that when she moved they fluttered. 'You know, Velvet says we don't own anyone,' she said, looking around at her friends with a smile.

'You like Velvet, don't you?' Anna asked Carol curiously, as Libby began spooning up mouthfuls of chocolate mousse straight from the bowl, which she held cradled in her lap.

'She lives life how she wants.' Carol shrugged.

Libby made a noise that at first sounded like another snort but then turned into a sob. 'I'm sorry, Anna. Please forgive me.' Then she said something else, but now she was crying so hard her tears were running into her mouth, making her next words unintelligible. 'And don't you be nice to me, either!' she finished, pointing at Anna with her spoon. 'Not after how awful I've been to you!'

'All right,' said Anna uncertainly.

Libby flopped her head down onto her arms. 'Oh god!' she said, her voice muffled. 'Why am I being such a bitch?'

Anna and Carol exchanged glances as they got up from the table and went around to her, prying the spoon and the bowl of chocolate mousse out of her hands and guiding her out of the kitchen.

'I haven't cleaned my teeth,' Libby moaned as they shambled, like a strange three-backed, six-legged animal into her bedroom.

'I haven't . . . Jasper, I need to . . .' She was hiccupping and stuttering as they helped her into bed.

'Go to sleep, Libby,' said Carol, kissing her hard on the side of her cheek and tucking her in.

Anna leaned over to kiss her, too, in exactly the same spot. 'We'll look after everything.'

17

Libby

LIBBY FELT SURE SHE WOULDN'T BE able to sleep as she rolled over and burrowed her face into her pillow. She felt too dirty and horrible, after all the awful things she'd said, to deserve anything so innocent and helpful as oblivion, but a few moments after the others had left the room, she closed her eyes experimentally, just to rest them—they were so sore from all that crying—and the next time she opened them it was morning. And even though her head ached and her eyes were swollen she did feel somewhat better about things. Friday mornings were usually the busiest in the house, with one or more of the kids packing a bag to be collected by their dad after school for the weekend.

This Friday, Leanne and Michelle were going to stay with Myles. Summer and Jasper would be home, and tomorrow Ben would take Jasper to swimming lessons at the heated pool. Colette was scheduled to be picked up by Steve from school and collected tomorrow by Libby, who'd become expert at keeping it professional and cool with Steve by staying in the car while Colette climbed in and out, like a little traveller between worlds.

Libby kept track of it all with a magnetic calendar on the fridge, with each child represented by a different coloured magnet, which would move from one side of the large white expanse to the other depending on their plans. This was intended to make it easy to see at a glance where everyone was meant to be at any given time, although generally one or all of the mothers would simply shout, 'Who's there?' down the hall at regular intervals, checking up on whoever was not underfoot in the kitchen or the laundry, or lately, sprawled out on the couch in the living room in front of the TV.

At the start, the no-TV-during-the-day rule had worked well under Libby's leadership. She got the kids to work in the vegetable garden, to help with the cooking and cleaning up after meals, and to make projects together with felt and Perkins Paste and old Christmas decorations at the big trestle table she'd set up in the corner of the laundry. She made it fun, too, so that the whingeing and grumbling that usually accompanied these tasks—making them frankly unbearable for Anna—didn't occur.

Lately, though, Libby had been feeling too tired. Too tired to go out and get the seedlings ready and the soil turned over, so that the children wouldn't be kept waiting around when they came out to garden. Too tired to buy the felt squares and art supplies, think up the projects to guide the children in, to encourage Jasper to hold the scissors and participate as much as he was able. Too tired to take all the steps necessary to include the children in the household chores. She believed it was important to train children in the everyday work of life, but lately she didn't have the energy for anything close to that. Their clatter in the kitchen disturbed her and made her snappy, and she felt almost a *hunger* to spend time in her own thoughts as she worked. Which was ironic, considering all those years she had felt too alone. These days, her thoughts tended to revolve around one subject: Ben. Ben. Ben. It was as though her mind had become snagged and she couldn't unhook it no matter how hard she tried.

I think about him more than I ever have in my whole life, she wrote to Strauss.

It's hormonal stop, Strauss replied. *You're missing dick stop.*

To think of the person at the post office in London writing this down! Let alone the woman at the post office in Sandgate who winked at Libby as she handed it to her across the counter. Libby stuck the telegram in the bottom of her bedside-table drawer where it made her smile, for a moment at least, every morning.

But she wasn't—missing dick, that is. She wasn't even actually missing Ben in that way, even though right up until she had moved out she had always loved their physical relationship. Libby felt almost asexual now, as though she'd stepped out of those kinds of feelings the way you might step out of a dress. She was probably very old-fashioned and stodgy in that way, and the thought made her sad as she listened to some of the other single mums at the school gate talk about their love lives. Everyone was having sex, it seemed. Not just Ben and the other mums, but even some of her old friends from Park Ridge, whose marriages were also collapsing. 'There must be something about this age,' said Libby's mother. Although whether that was Libby's age, or the kids', she didn't say.

Anna kept offering to introduce Libby to some of her doctors from work. 'Not to marry, Libby. To have a drink with. To experiment. To get back out there again.'

'You're a fine one to talk. What about that guy you pashed at the party?'

'I can't mix the personal with the professional. Besides, it's scary out there.'

'I'm not scared,' Libby had said. 'I'm just not interested.'

She was such a disappointment to herself, all round.

'You poor duck,' Carol said when Libby confided all this to her, lying on the end of Carol's bed that Friday morning, after the explosion in the kitchen the night before. Carol sat propped up against her pillows, sleepily cradling the cup of tea Libby had brought in for her. Libby found it intensely comforting to be in Carol's room, and was always looking for an opportunity to go in there. The pink-ruched influence of Carol's choices of furnishings felt like going back to the womb, or the half shell that Venus was born into on the waves maybe, which Carol, ever changing, ever growing, would step out of each morning as dewy and rosy as a Botticelli. 'Is that why you were so upset with Anna last night?'

'I feel rotten about that. Ugh.'

'She knows,' said Carol, taking another sip of her tea. 'You two just rub each other the wrong way sometimes, that's all.'

Libby increasingly appreciated Carol's way of looking at the world, particularly her unfussy approach to shocks and reversals like her own.

'Do you think he loves her?' Libby asked. These were words she wouldn't have felt safe enough to utter anywhere else except here, where all the frills and frippery seemed to soak them up.

Carol looked up at the ceiling, considering. 'From what Anna said, there's definitely some kind of attraction, but I wouldn't call that love.'

'I'm sorry, I don't mean Steve. I mean Ben. Do you think Ben loves that woman, Antonia?'

'Oh Libby, even if he does, it doesn't mean he doesn't still care about you, too.'

'Why not?' Libby almost felt like a child with Carol sometimes, these days.

'Because he loved you. And love can't go away, or become something else, just like that.'

'No, it can't, can it?' replied Libby, immensely comforted. 'Do you still love Steve?'

'I was actually thinking about that this morning, when you came in,' said Carol comfortably, dunking a biscuit in her tea. 'I'd like to say yes. I mean, it sounds awful otherwise, doesn't it? I want to always love Colette's dad. But I'm not sure. I mean, last night I really didn't feel that bad when Anna told me. And this morning, I feel quite cheery!'

'You do seem cheery.'

Carol was wearing a man's white singlet and satin boxer shorts. Her face without make-up glowed, as fresh as a girl's. Libby envied the way she could throw herself into things, and the way she could recover from hard knocks. Carol had a bounciness to her that Libby could never imagine regaining.

Once everyone had left the house that morning Libby went back to bed, taking Sampson to sleep on her feet like a hot water bottle. Hours must have passed, because the afternoon sun was streaming in through the window when she was woken by the telephone.

'It's Erica, from Sandgate Primary School.'

'Erica, how are you? Did you get the raffle money I dropped off on Wednesday?'

'First of all, I just want to assure you that Summer is absolutely fine.'

'Oh good . . .' said Libby faintly.

'Mrs Swift wants to know if you can drop by this afternoon.'

'To the principal's office? But Ben's picking the kids up today. He's dropping them around to my place later. Is something wrong?'

'It's nothing too serious, really,' said Erica, suddenly confiding. 'Summer's been acting like a little ruffian, along with some of the other girls. My goodness! In my day we wouldn't have dreamed of behaving that way.'

'*What* way?'

'You see those ads on the buses saying girls can do anything, and I'm sure that kind of thing's to blame. But Mrs Swift needs to talk to you, as well as the parents of the other girls.'

'Which girls?' Libby rubbed her hands over her face, trying to wake up.

'Leanne and Michelle and Colette. You live with them, don't you? Mrs Swift says if we don't throw the book at them straight off the bat, then the situation will only get worse.'

'About *what*, though?'

'It seems that just before the end of lunchtime they had an argument, the upshot being that they all punched each other in the face.'

~

Libby was parking the car in the lane outside the school when she saw Anna climb out of a taxi.

'Anna, wait up,' she called out, hurrying over. 'Can I help you with that?' asked Libby, picking up Anna's briefcase as Anna wrestled with her umbrella and handbag.

'Thanks.' Anna pushed her tortoiseshell glasses to the top of her head, and they smiled at one another shyly.

It was a start. Libby had been longing to throw herself at Anna's feet in apology ever since she woke up that morning, but with Anna in such a rush to get to work early for a presentation, she hadn't had the chance.

'What's this all about with the principal, anyway?' asked Anna. 'My secretary took the message.'

'The girls have had a fight, I think,' said Libby. She didn't want to say anything more until they had the full story, which they would have soon enough. Libby sighed—her heart had felt even heavier in her chest since she put the phone down, making it even more difficult to get a really good deep breath. 'I'm glad you're here, too. Shall we go in together?'

They set off across the playground. Anna, dressed in a pants suit with high stiletto heels, tottered a little as she tried to keep up with Libby, who was striding forth in her trusty old Birkenstocks.

'You know, we shouldn't expect them to be friends just because it's convenient,' said Libby, slowing to match Anna's pace.

'Well, it isn't convenient now, is it?' replied Anna, smiling wryly. 'It sounds like they hate each other.'

'No, surely not!' protested Libby. 'It was just a playground dust-up, Erica said.'

'But they might,' said Anna. 'And why shouldn't they have strong feelings? We do.'

'You're right.' Libby swallowed, thinking of last night. She felt lucky Anna was willing to even talk to her. 'I know we can't just add water and always magically get along,' she continued. 'I mean, it's not as though it's automatic for us to be friends, just because we're women and have some things in common, is it?'

'No. No, I'd say it's most certainly not automatic,' said Anna drily. 'Especially not for me.'

'We need to be able to talk about difficult things and to argue,' insisted Libby. They were almost at the school office now and she needed to get this out. 'We need to be able to be wrong sometimes. Or even a lot of the time, maybe.'

'Are you talking about the Carol and Steve thing?' asked Anna, wincing as she stepped on a stone. 'Because I know that was wrong.'

'No! I'm talking about me. About you and me.' She stopped walking and turned to face Anna, stopping her in her tracks. 'I'm trying to say sorry for last night.'

'Oh,' said Anna.

'It was none of my business, and I was awful. Oh god, I was awful. I just hope that you can forgive me.'

Anna pulled her glasses back down onto her nose and looked through them at Libby, her magnified eyes enormous. 'I forgive you.'

Anna wobbled a little as Libby threw her arms around her, and, once the hug had ended, she kept leaning on Libby to slip off her shoes. 'That's better,' she sighed.

'No matter what's happened between the girls,' Libby went on, 'I still want to be your friend.'

'Oh. That's good, because I still want to be yours, too.' Anna smiled, her relief shining from her face like sunshine.

'Phew,' said Libby. 'There's no script for this, is there?'

'Nope,' said Anna, taking hold of Libby's hand as they walked up the stairs. 'We have to make it all up.'

~

The full heat of their estranged husbands' disapproval greeted them as they walked through the swing doors, directed at them in a laser beam.

'Myles? Ben? What are you doing here?' asked Anna.

'We were called to come here from work,' said Ben heavily. 'I was in an important meeting.'

'I was called from home,' Libby snapped. 'I was having an important rest.'

'I told you Mrs Swift wants to see all of you, remember?' said Erica brightly from behind her counter.

'Sweeties!' cried Anna, going over to where Michelle and Leanne sat next to Myles on a wooden bench, and kneeling in front of them on the carpet. 'What happened?'

'Hi, pussycat,' said Libby softly to Summer, who was sitting next to Ben on a row of miniature green plastic chairs against the opposite wall. She had a pad of white gauze taped across her nose and was pressing a bag of ice to her face. All three girls did, in fact, Libby realised, looking around at them in wonder. 'Far out,' she said. This was much worse than she had thought.

'Michelle punched me,' Summer said indistinctly through her bag of ice.

Libby had trouble understanding her, but Anna had no problem.

'Well, then, who punched Michelle?' she asked, resting her hand protectively on Michelle's head.

'I did,' said Summer, closing her eyes for a moment in quiet satisfaction.

'But wait a minute, where's Colette?' asked Anna, and at that moment Carol came swinging through the doors, still wearing her apron from the salon. 'I was halfway through a perm,' she panted. 'Where's Colette?'

Ben looked at Myles, who solemnly nodded as though agreeing it should be Ben who would be their spokesperson. 'Steve just left with her. He said it was his afternoon anyway and he wanted to take her to the beach.'

Carol sat down, her elbows on her knees, and took a deep breath.

'He got here first and spoke to the principal on his own, so he didn't want to wait,' Myles said. 'But she's fine, he said. Going to have a bit of a bruise for a while, like these guys here, but it will heal.'

'A *bruise*?' echoed Carol, starting.

'And maybe a little bump,' called out Erica, ever cheerful.

'She punched me first,' said Leanne defensively from the other side of the room.

'We offered to pass on the message,' said Myles, frowning at Leanne, who slumped in her chair and pressed her ice pack more firmly against her nose.

'That's not a problem, is it?' asked Ben anxiously. 'He said you were going to pick Colette up tomorrow afternoon, from his place.'

'I am,' piped up Libby. 'It's at four o'clock.'

'That's right. I'll do it, thanks anyway, Libby. Steve and I need to talk.'

'It's at four,' repeated Libby a little desperately, though she didn't know why.

'I know,' said Carol firmly. 'But the girls,' she said, turning to look at them all wonderingly. 'What's going on?'

'That's what none of us can understand.' Ben beckoned all the parents over to the entry way, where they stood in a huddle, out of earshot of the girls. 'We've been trying to get it out of them, but no dice. What are you women doing over there at that house, anyway?'

'Excuse me,' Libby whispered back. 'Why are you assuming it's our fault?'

'Well!' huffed Ben, nodding at the girls sitting behind him, and Libby could just hear him thinking, *There's your answer.*

'Well, what?' asked Libby, smiling sweetly.

'No one's blaming anybody, okay?' replied Ben, hastily backing down.

Even though, of course, Libby felt it was entirely her fault. Just looking at Summer's eye hurt her physically in the chest, in a way she knew it didn't hurt Ben. And Libby knew she would worry about this, and torture herself over it for weeks, maybe months, in a way that wouldn't occur to him. He took a completely different form of responsibility for their children than she did, and it had nothing to do with how they felt. Fathers were so lucky, she reflected for about the millionth time.

'The point is, what's happened to the girls?' asked Ben, turning back around to face them.

'Was it a misunderstanding?' Libby asked, turning back around too.

'Michelle, are you jealous of Colette, maybe?' asked Carol.

'For what?' asked Michelle.

'Steady on,' said Anna.

'I didn't have anything particular in mind,' said Carol, biting her lip.

Libby sighed. One of the girls must have heard her arguing with Anna and Carol in the kitchen last night, causing it to be twisted and replayed between them today, except with an awful outcome. She looked at them all ruefully as they fiddled with their bags of ice. It was just as Ben said: kids knew everything. But, equally, they didn't know anything.

'I'm sorry it's been hard lately,' she said, including them all in her gaze.

Ben caught Libby's eye as they started to walk into the principal's office, and they smiled at one another in mutual apology. Was that a good sign or a bad sign, she wondered, that now they could have a complete argument, without either of them having to say more than a few words?

~

'Four young girls in a fist fight, in the middle of the playground!' said Mrs Swift, looking at them severely across her desk. The girls, utterly bored from all that time in the waiting room, had barely seemed to register when the parents were called into the office, even though in Libby's day, if she had been in Summer's place she would have been terrified. They must have already been given their lecture, Libby assumed, as Mrs Swift told them how shocked she was.

'What would you have done if they had been boys?' asked Anna.

'Five of the best, with the cane of course. It's just so much more complicated with girls.'

'And you're not concerned that might have something to do with the epidemic of male violence?'

Libby admired Anna's moxie, but she couldn't help but feel herself shrink a little inside as Mrs Swift launched into her lecture on the perils of a broken home. She'd heard it before, from various people, of course, a few times, but today with the thought of Summer out there, and the other girls, all with swollen eyes, Libby realised it was true. Their children were at risk of going off the rails. They were going to face problems the other children in their classes, from 'intact homes', as Mrs Swift put it, would never face. *How could this be me?* Libby asked herself, suddenly seeing it all through her mother's eyes, including her own unironed skirt and messy hair. *How could this be happening to my daughter?*

'Oh really?' replied Anna, once Mrs Swift had finally concluded, with a heavy, 'I've never seen anything like it before in my life!'

Libby felt ready to throw herself down on the carpet in front of the principal, begging for official forgiveness, whereas Anna was fiddling with the clasp on her handbag, looking supremely irritated.

'When I came here,' said Anna, 'kids that age were fighting all the time, and by kids I mean boys *and* girls. Not that I think it's a good thing,' she added hastily, as Ben frowned and Carol opened her mouth to object. 'I'm just saying it was not uncommon.'

'You came here, to Sandgate Primary?' Libby asked Anna, feeling even more disoriented as they stood up to leave.

'Back when it was even more of a dump.'

How could I not know that? she wondered, watching Anna curiously as she stalked back to reception.

'I mean, really! That level of simplistic thinking is just not going to cut it,' Anna was saying to Myles, when Libby caught up. Libby always felt as though nothing could go too wrong at school, whereas Anna obviously felt just the opposite—questioning Erica now about her contact details, and telling Myles that they ought to have kept that tutor.

What difference would that have made? Libby wondered.

'The girls have their own tutor?' Carol asked.

'Had,' said Anna. 'Just for maths.'

'Even though Michelle's only in fourth grade?'

Libby looked at Anna in further confusion. They had been so intimate and talked about so many things, but in many ways Libby still knew so little about Anna. Maybe she would ask her about these things, later. Or maybe she never would, Libby realised with a feeling so dark it was like a presentiment. Maybe she would never have the chance to ask Anna about anything so personal as that, ever again. Maybe this was it, she told herself, looking around at them all. Maybe this was the end of things. It had been feeling like the end—well, for a while, she admitted to herself, ever since Strauss had gone to England, or since Summer was born. But the end of what? She was desperate to know. That despair she thought she had outrun by leaving Ben was now creeping back again, perhaps even worse than before.

'Come on, kids,' said Myles, once they returned to reception. 'Let's get you all home.'

'But you can't go back to your dad's place this evening,' said Libby to Leanne and Michelle, horrified at the idea of them being separated. 'We all need to go back to Avon Street. We all need to talk about this properly, and work it through.'

'Summer's saying she won't do it,' said Ben quietly to Libby, sympathy gleaming in his eyes.

'What do you mean *won't*? She doesn't have a choice.'

'She's refusing to go back there, Libby. She says if you make her, she and Jasper will just run around to my place when you're not looking.' He lowered his voice further, glancing around to make sure none of the girls were listening. 'She's saying from now on while you're living with the other girls, they're going to stay at home with me.'

'Colette's been saying that, too,' said Carol quietly.

They looked at Anna, who nodded sadly. 'Yep.'

'But they don't have a choice,' repeated Libby, her voice rising and turning to the girls, who were still slouched sullenly on their chairs, as far away from one another as possible. 'This is not some kind of collective. We are your mothers and we are telling you!'

'Let's leave it for tonight, Lib,' soothed Ben. 'Why don't you come home with me and help to settle them, just for this evening? We can discuss it all again in the morning. But, for now, I think we need to accept that this is how they feel.'

It broke Libby's heart to see them walk out, each of the girls refusing to look at one another as they trailed like a ragtag bunch of strangers through the corridors and out into the carpark.

~

'Libby, can I have a word?' asked Carol as Ben went to pick up Jasper and fetch the car. 'Velvet says I can move into the little flat above the salon on Monday. I'd like to do that today if that's all right with you, so that I can pick Colette up from Steve's tomorrow and take her home there, if she likes.'

'I don't suppose there's any point saying this is all an over-reaction?' replied Libby, staring at her toes.

'I know we were playing it cool in there, but they attacked each other,' said Carol. 'And Steve says Colette's been telling him how much she hates it at Avon Street for months.'

'But how will you afford it on your own?' Libby sighed. 'I could ask Ben—'

'I'll be fine,' said Carol, cutting her off with a smile.

With her head shaved, Carol's eyes seemed even larger, and looking more closely Libby saw that she'd applied fake eyelashes to heighten the effect. *Fake eyelashes!* Libby marvelled. When she was still mucking around that morning in her old nightie and

Ugg boots, Carol must have been sitting at her dressing table applying them. What a mystery other people were. And now she had already found a new place to live . . .

'But the drop-offs and pick-ups with Steve!' Libby felt like bursting into tears. 'How are you going to cope?'

'I'm not going to tell you anything more unless you stop feeling sorry for me.'

'But I don't feel sorry for you,' Libby finally managed to say through her tears. 'I think you're amazing. I think . . .' She stopped and blew her nose, squeezing her eyes shut and opening them again. 'I feel sorry for myself.'

Carol put her arms around Libby's shoulders, and for a moment Libby allowed herself to snuggle her face into Carol's neck.

To think that she had been planning to make toffee apples this weekend, and to shout the women to a movie to make amends. She had been wondering what they might do for Christmas, which now loomed alarmingly just three weeks away, and which suddenly seemed unimaginable in a house without Carol in it. Although of course, when she had been lying in bed, thinking about those things, that would have been around the time the girls had been beginning to fight.

'I thought we had made a whole world! And now look at it. Gone in less than twenty-four hours.'

'But it was always temporary,' said Carol, her voice gentle but with a quizzical expression in her eyes.

'Was it?' asked Libby, stepping away from her. While she had been nesting, Carol had been perching. It made sense.

'Of course,' said Carol, brushing Libby's hair tenderly away from her face. 'I've always wanted my own little flat. I told you, remember, on my first night.'

'That's right,' said Libby. Somehow in her excitement about their household she had let herself forget that. 'But what if you're lonely, all on your own?' she whispered, looking out into the school yard, which had that creepy, deserted feeling empty playgrounds always get.

'Well, I won't be alone, will I? Because for a start I have Colette. But, in any case, I'll always have Sampson. He's going to have a whole new career as a salon cat. I wonder how he's going to get on with Red?'

'Who? Oh,' Libby remembered, 'Velvet's dog.'

It seemed to Libby that the world just kept on expanding, with more and more people and animals and options for what to do and how to live thronging in.

It was as though the moment she stepped outside the fortress of her marriage, change could happen so quickly and turbulently in any area, Libby realised with a kind of awe, as the men brought the cars around, slamming doors and calling out instructions to the children as though nothing huge or terrible was happening. She had longed for change for so many years, feeling as though nothing could be moved no matter how hard she tried. Now it was as though she had walked through some kind of portal where everything was the opposite, and now the question was, how could she hold on?

'We'll still be close, won't we? After you've moved, I mean?' asked Libby.

'What are you talking about? Of course we will. You helped me when I was desperate, Libby. I'll never forget that.'

Desperate. Libby looked around at Carol and Anna and the girls. There were so many different forms of desperate.

18

Anna

SIMON LIEBER HAS A NICE BODY, Anna had been writing in the margin of her notebook earlier that day. *A good body.* She thought about drawing it. If you could draw it, you would sort of make a bubble, the way she'd learned to draw a cat. And then you would draw arms on, and muscles, the way you put in whiskers, and then you . . . She looked up, distracted by the sudden quiet. The circle of doctors were all staring at her, including—oh god—Simon Lieber, who was looking politely amused.

'We've just discussed the relationship of lipids to statins in the bloodstream . . .' said one of the doctors.

She checked that the note taker was busy and that the reels of the recorder were working.

'Yes?'

'Do you have another question?' asked the doctor closest to her, who—oh god!—could see what she'd been drawing. She snapped her clipboard shut and stood up.

'No! Thank you. That will be all for today. Thank you so much for coming out during your lunch break.'

'Anna, it's good to see you. Are you okay?' asked Simon as the doctors all rushed to the buffet set up at the back of the room.

'Hello, Simon. Of course. Why wouldn't I be?' She flashed him a smile, just in case that sounded defensive. 'No, I'm great, actually.' But she wasn't, so why had she just said that? 'Anyway, enough about me.' She sounded unhinged! 'How are you?' The last time she'd seen him had been in the springtime midnight garden. And now here they were in a carpeted, furnished, over-curtained and upholstered room. It seemed like a symbol of everything that was wrong with her life.

'I'm well, thank you. Everything going well with your, um—' he stepped a little closer, and Anna thought she saw some of the doctors at the buffet notice, although maybe that was because a waitress had just walked in with some fresh meatballs '—divorce?'

'Oh, we're not divorcing! I mean . . . not at the moment, not yet,' she amended, reacting to the confusion on his face. Why had she panicked and said that? 'We're still deciding,' she finished lamely.

'Right.'

Oh god, he was attractive. His warm eyes, heavy eyebrows and fine wool suit that looked good quality yet rumpled, as though he'd slept in it. On second thought, there was nothing particularly attractive about the way he looked, she decided, looking at him more analytically. But he was attractive. She felt attracted to him, and that was a completely different thing.

'Anna?' He was looking at her quizzically. 'Are you okay?'

'Simon, um, can we talk for a moment? Please?'

'We are talking, aren't we?'

His smile had stopped being indulgent and was becoming tense, it seemed to Anna. All of his body language was wrong. Well, so was hers. She'd dressed especially for today in her best Carla Zampatti suit, but what made a suit impressive was not necessarily what made her sexy—she should have asked Carol! But it was too late now.

'Outside,' she said, motioning with her head and leading him straight behind the curtain that didn't go anywhere. Oh, this was a symbol of her life, all right. Trapped in the curtains, going nowhere. They were heavy taffeta, at least, so there was no way anyone else would overhear.

'The door's in the other direction,' said Simon, bemused. 'But I should be getting back to work now, in any case,' he said apologetically. 'I have a one o'clock.'

'This will only take a minute.' She checked her watch. 'Half a minute, in fact. We have to be out of here by 12.45. I just wanted to tell you how much I enjoyed meeting you at the . . . at the party.'

'I enjoyed it, too,' he said, visibly relaxing, which pleased her. 'Phew! I thought maybe you were going to tell me I shouldn't come anymore.'

'Are you that committed to market research?'

'I think you know the answer to that,' he said, smiling a little nervously, and looking deep into her eyes.

'We also do have excellent meatballs,' she replied.

He frowned in confusion and she kicked herself. She had just gone and lightened the atmosphere when she'd wanted to be more real. This is what she had become so good at: deflecting, glossing over, pretending nothing was happening when it was. It *was*. Standing here behind this curtain, what was stopping her from kissing him, right now?

'It's been more than two minutes,' he said regretfully, looking at his watch. 'My patients will be getting restless.'

'Listen, Simon,' she said as he began to feel along the dark brown taffeta, looking for the break in the curtains. 'The truth is, I've been looking forward to seeing you. A lot, actually. But I wanted to explain something. About me, I mean. About my strange behaviour. At the party, and now probably.' Oh god, now she had twenty seconds left before the staff would come in to clear away. 'You see,' she said, her words falling over themselves in a rush, 'my husband, Myles, well . . . the reason our marriage didn't work is because, well, I think . . .' She paused to wonder if this secret was all right to tell. But she trusted Simon, she decided. And so hopefully Myles would, too. 'This is confidential, obviously, but . . . he might be gay. Sometimes. Or somewhere. In another life he would have been. Or something like that, anyway.'

She had never said that outside the house before. Apart from Libby and Carol, she had never told anyone. She felt a wash of shame covering her, but instead of mockery in his eyes, she saw pity.

'Sometimes? I don't understand.'

'He never did anything. I mean, he never acted on it. He . . . it's a long story. And he says he loves me. And I love him. But the point is, it's knocked my confidence a little bit.'

'I can see why it would.'

'But it wasn't just that.' She was determined to be honest, but now she had fifteen seconds in which to do it. 'It wasn't just him, though. It was me, too. Anyway, he says he wants to get back together, and that it can change. And the thing is, I'm not even sure if I would like that. I mean, if it's possible even. He says it is, but . . . I'm confused.'

He nodded, his eyes full of sympathy. 'You sound confused.'

She felt exhausted suddenly. 'I am,' she said miserably, and she began to pull at the curtains uselessly. They seemed like a solid wall of brown taffeta and white gauze, trapping her, and she would never get out.

'It's okay,' he said gently. 'Call me, okay? When you're less confused?' And he reached for her hand, picked the curtain up by the hem and showed her the way out.

~

Now, as Anna drove the girls home from their meeting at the principal's office in Myles's station wagon, she kept stealing glances at them in the rear-view mirror, worrying about what they might be thinking. They weren't asking any of the questions she was sure must be at the top of their minds. *Was their mum ever coming back to live with their dad? Were they ever going to all live at home again? Were they ever going to be a normal family?* She knew she should be asking these questions for them and eliciting their answers, or even raising them as general topics of conversation. But for now all she wanted to do was drive quietly, with one hand on the steering wheel and the other resting lightly on the gear stick, next to Myles's thigh.

As for Myles, he was quiet, too, answering the girls' questions about what's for dinner and can we have ice cream and what if I need to go to the toilet in his typical desultory fashion. Taking time to make sure they understood everything he was telling them, and handing over tissues to the back seat.

Michelle seemed okay, as Anna glanced at her again in the rear-view mirror. The white plaster tape looked shocking across her nose, but otherwise she seemed utterly recovered from the drama.

She wouldn't be, of course, Anna reminded herself as they drove down Sandgate Road. There was a lot to talk about, but for now she wanted her daughters to think about happy things.

'I thought that tonight we could write our Christmas lists,' she said, as she turned into their old street.

'Yay! Presents!' yelled Leanne, bouncing around in the back seat.

'What we'd *like* to get, not what we *will*,' Michelle corrected Leanne. 'But why?' she added, frowning suddenly, looking from her mother to her father and back again. 'Is this because Summer broke my nose?'

'It's not broken. It's bumped,' said Anna firmly.

'Is it because you and Dad are splitting up?' Michelle's face looked dangerously as if it were about to crumple.

'No, silly. It's because soon it's going to be Christmas, and Santa doesn't know what to get you. And, besides, you bumped Summer's nose, too, so that wouldn't be right, would it?'

'No,' said Michelle, and something about the way she wasn't sucking on her fingers or even letting herself twirl her hair made Anna realise she was feeling really bad.

'It's because no matter what happens I think we all deserve to think about something fun and lovely, like Christmas,' said Anna, more gently now. 'And because on Monday you're both going to apologise to Summer and Colette.'

'I'm not,' whispered Leanne.

'No way,' said Michelle.

'Yes, you are,' said Myles, backing up Anna.

'You will, and it will be fine. Okay? You have to trust me,' said Anna.

But why should they trust her about anything, Anna asked herself, *after what she'd put them through?* After not realising how complicated and out of control their relationships had become, and how upset they all were? This was going to take years and years of therapy.

~

It was a warm summer's night, and the French doors in the living room were open onto the garden, just as Anna had imagined when she and Myles had first walked into this room all those years ago. That day of the viewing, she and Myles had been one of a horde of curious couples, some wealthy-looking pairs who arrived in nice Volvos and even a Mercedes and others just strolling up, obviously from around the neighbourhood and curious, rather than in the market to buy. She and Myles weren't buying, but as they walked through the rooms, seeing the devastation rats and poverty could bring in the fine plaster arches and decorative ceilings, something in Anna had stirred. After all, she had just been promoted at work, and these grand houses were still extraordinarily undervalued.

'The girls are getting bigger,' she'd said to Myles as they stood together, staring at this same outlook on that day. Plasterboard had been nailed across the whole back wall where bricks would once have been, and the broken windows stuffed with paper and blocks of wood. 'Watch out for black snakes,' the real-estate agent had warned as they ventured out to where a giant block of concrete sat in the middle of the overgrown garden.

'It's a lot of work,' Myles had said, turning to her, and something zinged between them. It had been the first zing since the girls were born, Anna remembered, looking back. Maybe they'd both seen the possibility for the same thing: a fresh start.

That's what this could be now. The two of them an even stronger couple, perhaps, after all that they had learned about themselves, during this last year. With the girls becoming more independent and with more money to keep renovating, they could even add a conservatory out the back here. That would be really something. She and Myles worked so well together. Everyone said so. They didn't fight. They didn't compete with one another. They made things and did things and kept creating more. She sighed in satisfaction at the thought of all they had achieved together, and what they could still do.

'What are you sighing about?'

She jumped and turned. She hadn't heard Myles come into the room.

'This room. It's just what I was dreaming of when we walked in that first day.'

'When the agent said it was deceptively spacious?'

Anna giggled. 'Not so deceptive now, is it?'

They had chosen wood as the feature for this room leading out to the garden, and it gleamed and glowed from the love seat they'd bought and restored, and the large farmer's table they'd found in the Southern Highlands and brought back on a flatbed truck. The wooden chairs were chosen in antique shops and bid for at auctions, carefully mismatched and quaint, some still with their paint not yet stripped off. Anna's hands itched to get going on them. She looked forward to that slow process, which made her feel safe and confident about the future. She liked knowing what restorative tasks awaited her in the months ahead. Those long hours listening to documentaries on the radio, mesmerised by the action of her own hands, stripping back and repairing, then painting and polishing the wood.

'Next stop, the back garden,' said Myles, slipping his arm through hers and resting his scratchy chin on top of her head.

'You scratch,' she protested as she rested her hand on his arm. He felt so good to touch, his skin as warm and comforting to her touch as the girls'.

'You can't feel it through your hair.'

'I can,' she complained good-naturedly as she leaned back against him.

'Let's dance,' said Myles, rocking her from side to side.

'Is this dancing?'

'Now it is!' he exclaimed, spinning her and raising her arm above her head. Although taken by surprise, she adjusted quickly, and when he swung her around into his other arm, she was ready for it, anticipating his moves and walking backwards on her toes like Ginger Rogers.

'Didn't we have fun?' he sang, in his surprisingly beautiful baritone. 'Rollicking and rolling, through all those salad days?'

They stopped, flushed and panting.

'Those definitely aren't the words,' said Anna.

'I can't remember the moves, either,' said Myles. 'Dance school was so long ago!'

'We did pretty well,' said Anna.

'This room is a vision of beauty,' said Myles, 'and you're the most beautiful thing in it.'

Anna nodded, acknowledging his compliment but chilled, somehow, as he dropped her hand and walked away in search of the paper. As he sank back into the sofa, sighing loudly, she turned and looked at the back garden

It was slowly coming good. Flowers were appearing where she had cleared away the undergrowth last summer, beating a path to the shed where she planned to restore her furniture. The concrete block had been jackhammered away, and the pavers were in the process of creating a herringbone pattern for the patio. Soon another long dining table would be set up out there, constructed out of a single curving piece of very expensive Swedish metal, and a trellis built, with jasmine and wisteria trained to spill over it. The plan was to have Sunday breakfasts out there and host big boozy lunches in the dappled afternoons with friends and colleagues, while children ran in and out.

Anna swallowed, pressing her hand against her chest.

In a few years the girls would bring boyfriends, or girlfriends, home. They would get a dog, probably—she couldn't hold out against their pleas much longer. Hopefully a small one. Something fluffy and soft, she decided. A little friend, rather than a guardian of the house.

She sighed heavily.

'What is it?' asked Myles, glancing up from the paper he was reading on the sofa. 'Anna! What is it?' he repeated, jumping up in alarm at the expression on her face.

She looked around at their living room, with its carefully mismatched furnishings, and the photographs from their wedding day and the children's birthdays and assorted Christmases arranged neatly on the coffee table, gleaming in their silver frames.

'We can't keep going like this,' she said simply, turning to him and folding her arms.

'Like what, darling?'

'Like married people. We need to divorce.'

He sat back down and picked up his newspaper. 'I was afraid you were going to say that.'

'I'll move in around the corner. I saw they've put that row of terraces up for rent. The girls will each have their own en suite, and it will be easy for us all to pop back and forth. We can get back to our vodka tonic catch-ups, and what would you think of us also sharing custody of a dog?'

'But what will we say to people about our relationship? What will we tell the girls?' asked Myles, his face frowning behind his glasses.

'We'll tell them the truth,' said Anna. She went over and sat next to him. 'We'll tell them that we're not married anymore, but that we still love one another and that we're still working it out.'

'This is probably going to take years and years of therapy,' sighed Myles.

'Let alone years of therapy for the girls,' Anna smiled.

He laughed kindly at her little joke. She was already planning how to fit regular visits with Nicky into their schedules. As well as working out dates for the girls and her to spend time with Jasper, and phoning up Simon Lieber, whose surgery number she happened to have learned by heart. Maybe she should try calling him now, in fact, before she lost her courage, just in case he was still at work.

'Shall I book us in for relationship therapy, too?' she asked Myles. 'I mean, how would you feel about me going out with someone? Or you going out with someone, for that matter, too?'

'You don't need to worry so much, sweetheart,' Myles said comfortably, shaking out his paper.

'But how would you feel about me asking someone out, tonight?' After all the time she'd already wasted, she didn't want to lose momentum.

'I'm positive that will be all right,' he said simply.

And somehow, as she walked up the stairs, Anna knew that no matter what happened, or who they did or didn't wind up with, Myles was right.

She sat down on the edge of the bed, next to the telephone, and opened up her notebook.

'Good grief!' she said out loud to the empty bedroom. Someone had written a phone number with *call me* written above it, and on the opposite page, where she had written *Simon Lieber has a nice body*, along with a perfectly terrible drawing, frankly, of a muscular cat, someone had written *thank you!* with a smiley face. That someone was obviously Simon Lieber, thought Anna, cringing. He must have done it while she was speaking to the catering staff, just before he left.

'What if he thinks I only like him based purely on sexual attraction?' she moaned. 'Oh god! What if he thinks I just want to use him for sex?' But then she thought of the warmth and the energy she'd felt flowing between them today behind that curtain. 'And so what if he does?' she answered herself airily, tossing her hair back as she picked up the phone.

19

Libby

'HOW AM I GOING TO EXPLAIN this to Jasper?' asked Libby as Ben steered the car out of the carpark. 'He's already been through so much this year.'

'Actually, aside from that hiccup a few months ago, he's been managing incredibly well,' said Ben, his eyes on the road. 'It's obviously Summer we need to watch.'

'Should we move schools, do you think?' she asked quietly, checking in the rear-view mirror that Summer was wearing her headphones.

'No!' said Ben as he drove through Sandgate's darkening streets. 'That's the last thing we should do. They need to learn to work through this. They need to learn to stay and face the consequences.'

What a Ben-ish kind of thought, old-fashioned and sensible. And he was right about Jasper. Apart from yesterday, he had been quite bright and sunny. Much more easygoing than he used to be, and more able and willing to move from place to place, with a trust in others and in new situations that he hadn't had before. Just this morning Jasper had proudly showed Summer the new hand-mirror Anna had given him. Summer in turn had done a beautiful job of being politely admiring.

'We're going home, Jassie, that's right,' Summer had said as he put on his seatbelt and looked thoughtfully out the window, and Libby had felt a stab of fresh guilt, because Summer was not the one she had ever worried about. Not in a serious way. Jasper had taken up all of that. But Ben was right. Summer was the one who had been finding things most difficult this year. She was the one who had taken this hardest, from the start.

'You girls will get along again, I promise,' Libby told her, raising her voice to be heard in the back seat. 'Soon you'll be best friends again.' She knew she couldn't promise this, but at that moment she felt desperate to believe it was true.

'No, we won't. And I don't care, actually,' said Summer, lifting her headphones off one ear coolly. 'I already have a best friend.'

'It has to be all right for the girls not to get along sometimes, Libby,' Ben said. 'Not everyone has to like each other in the end.'

'That's right,' Summer said.

Her sociable Summer! Libby mourned. She watched Summer walk ahead of them into the house, where she hung up her school bag and neatly stowed her shoes. Summer seemed to like reading more than she used to, and only ever talked about playing with Nell, who Colette had made up with months ago, but who seemed to Libby to be such a serious little girl. And Summer was changing physically, as well. She was taller, and less neatly arranged. She wore her hair differently now, too, brushed straight down her back in a waterfall, instead of in playful bunches. She was more sedate; a self-consciousness had developed—and generally she was not the carefree little hippy child Libby had always planned. She was herself, Libby had to concede, stealing a glance at her as Summer sat on the couch with Jasper in the living room, turning the pages of a *National Geographic* magazine. She was her own self. Serious, and composed, and concerned about the world around her in a way that Libby had never been.

'Oh,' Libby gasped, and she started to cry again, and this time they were tears of pure maternal guilt. 'I'm sorry, darling.'

'Stop it, Mummy.' Summer put aside her magazine and picked up Jasper's new hand-mirror to examine her hair.

'This is going to take time,' said Ben, who was sitting in the beanbag and beckoning Libby over. 'You need to give her a while.'

Libby nodded, but the tears kept streaming down her cheeks like twin rivers of grief as she sank down, almost on top of him, into the beanbag.

'Oh,' she sobbed, leaning her head on Ben's shoulder, the cotton material of his shirt quickly becoming quite wet with her tears. 'Oh!' she said again finally, when she was done with crying.

The children were still absorbed in Summer's magazine, flicking slowly through the pages.

'Listen, Lib,' said Ben, once the children were busy with their evening routines. He glanced at his watch in that stealthy move with which Libby was all too familiar. They were standing in the hallway upstairs, Jasper pottering around in his bedroom while Summer lazed in the bath, and Libby braced herself, ready for him to tell her he would have to disappear after dinner in order to get on with some work. 'I need to ask you something.'

He was going to sell the house. Or move in with that woman, Antonia. Or even marry her. Dread gathered in Libby as she readied herself for the next blow. 'Pardon?' she replied. His mouth was moving and his eyebrows were raised but she hadn't caught a word.

Ben took a deep breath. 'I said, I was wondering if . . . I mean, I wasn't going to ask you this. I mean, I haven't. But . . . seeing as we're here. Will you come and make dinner, here, tomorrow night? For the managing partner and his wife? And stay on, for the whole dinner?'

'What on earth are you talking about?'

'They're offering a promotion, for an executive vice director. As long as this dinner goes well I think they're going to give the job to me.'

'What!' exclaimed Libby. 'The whole point of me moving out was so that I wouldn't have to listen to you going on about work.'

'Well, I don't think that was the whole point,' said Ben mildly. 'This is to your advantage, though.'

'Because . . .?'

'Because if I get this promotion, I'll get a rather significant pay rise, which will benefit all of us, especially now that we have two separate households.'

'But Ben . . .' She was about to launch into one of her Lectures From Libby about how women shouldn't just be part of the professional furniture, about how corporations should entertain in restaurants and a promotion should be based on merit not on having a presentable partner. What if your partner was the same sex as you? What about people whose wives weren't in the mood to entertain? Or didn't know how? And what about women like Anna who didn't have a wife stashed away at home to prepare fondue and chocolate cheesecake to make that perfect impression?

'They just want to know the people they're promoting are stable, and will be a good addition to the team,' said Ben, speaking in the monotone he reserved for her lectures, even though apart from 'But Ben ...' she hadn't actually said a word. 'And what's wrong with going to people's houses sometimes?' His voice rose with his enthusiasm. 'You're the one who loves to entertain. Yes, you do! Don't deny it! And, in any case, I'm proud of my home and my children. I like showing them off.'

Neither of them really had the energy for this now, though, as they argued back and forth half-heartedly. Ever since she'd moved out they hadn't really disagreed about this kind of thing much at all, even though they'd certainly had their opportunities. They'd both been too distracted by the demands of their real lives, and too exhausted.

'But what will the children do?' She couldn't count on Carol or Anna anymore, she realised, her heart breaking open another crack.

'This is their home, Lib,' said Ben gently. 'They always sleep here when they're with me.'

'And where will Antonia be?'

'We broke up months ago. In fact, I don't even know if we officially went out.' He shuddered. 'Young people these days are very casual about things.'

'But what about your housekeeper, Mrs Guest? Can't she handle it?'

'Of course she can. But not like you, Libby. She only does the washing, the shopping and the ironing. She doesn't make it feel like home the way you do. And there's no one in the world, I'm convinced of it, who can make something as simple as a dinner such a happy and meaningful event.'

'Wow. You've never said anything like that to me before.'

'Well, it's true.'

Libby stared at the carpet, trying to make sense of this. 'And if this goes well, you'll get that promotion?'

'Yes, the one we've both sacrificed so much for.'

'*We've* sacrificed? What have you sacrificed, specifically?' Libby remembered clearly how much he loved going off to work every day, and how satisfied he always seemed when he returned home—compared to her own lean and hungry self, starving for adult company after a day spent with the children.

'How can you ask me that?' He gaped at her. 'I sacrificed you! I didn't mean to, but that's what happened, isn't it? If I hadn't worked so hard for this, I'd still have you.'

Libby gaped back at him in equal wonder. Ben's promotion had become mythical; something that would keep receding, just ahead of him, into the future as he chased it. She had stopped believing that this day would come, or that it would change anything if it did.

'It's your promotion too, Libby. And if I get it, you'll have more alimony to do the things you'd like to do, quite apart from the children. You could go and visit Strauss. With the kids, or on your own.'

'Seriously?'

'Seriously. Not that what you choose to do with your share of our resources has anything to do with me.'

'I could quit my job at the pub,' Libby mused, her grief forgotten in light of these new possibilities. 'I could start up a little catering business. Just tiny,' she said quickly, glancing at Ben. 'Nothing big, but Anna offered me some work catering for her focus groups . . . It could all go pear-shaped, of course, but it might be fun. And I would like to take the kids on a trip. To France, maybe.'

'To do the Pilgrims' Trail,' said Ben.

'With a donkey, exactly. And to get some more recipes, so I can finish my book. You know, *One Pot Wonders*—'

'*Of the World*,' he interrupted, finishing her sentence. 'Of course I know. I was the one who helped you translate for the nasi goreng that time, remember? In Indonesia.'

Libby frowned, and then her face cleared. 'That's right.'

'So will you do it?' Ben asked.

'Of course I'll do it. But not for any of those reasons. I want you to have everything you want, Ben, and so if you want this, I'll do everything I can to help you get it.'

'It's not everything I want,' he said tiredly, but then Jasper called for him from his bed, and Ben turned away from her and went into the bedroom.

Both kids were unusually relaxed this evening, Libby noticed as she tucked Summer in. They were often tense after the carefully civil handovers Libby and Ben enacted, but tonight, for all her tears and their bickering, the kids seemed happy.

'I predict this dinner is going to go wonderfully, and I predict that you're going to get this promotion, and you will be very happy,' said Libby, walking into the kitchen and sitting next to Ben at the table, once Summer and Jasper had gone off to sleep.

'No, I won't be happy, Lib,' he said, moving closer to her.

The feeling of his skin on hers sent a sigh of relief, like a cool breeze, through her veins. It would not be a smart idea to kiss him, she told herself, even while everything inside her was telling her to just do it. But that would make things more complicated, and she already had quite enough on her plate, what with getting the kids all sorted, and making sure things stayed good with Anna and Carol, and, most urgently, finding a new place to live.

'How am I going to cope, Ben?' she asked, making sure to keep her voice low so that neither of the children would hear.

'Oh Lib,' said Ben, stroking her leg, and the feeling of his hand on her skin almost made her start crying again. 'You'll cope better than anyone I know, no matter what happens. You always make a beautiful world.'

20

Carol

THE NEXT AFTERNOON CAROL LEFT VELVET to close up the salon, and she walked the familiar route up the hill, past the trots and Sandgate School, to her old house. The gutters were clear of leaves and the front path swept and clean, Carol noted as she knocked on the front door.

It flew open, startling her.

'Are you alone?' Steve stood barefoot, dressed in just a pair of tiny denim cut-offs and a skimpy football singlet, showing off his tan.

'Hi, Mama,' said Colette, flying down the hall and disappearing into her bedroom, waving.

'Hi, Cookie,' she called out, straining for a glimpse of her daughter's bruised nose.

'Of course I'm alone,' she said to Steve, stepping past him through the door.

The floor echoed with the squeak of her cork platform sandals as she walked down the hall. 'Shall we sit in the kitchen?' she asked.

It all looked the same. The orange Formica of the kitchen table was smooth and polished clean. The lounge suite and matching mood lamps and bar stools they'd brought with them from England, just the same.

She shivered a little as she took off her lace duster jacket, even though it was a warm day. She looked around to see if Steve would take it for her. He followed her into the kitchen, but didn't offer, and so she tossed it onto the couch.

'Well, hi,' she said, blotting her face with a tissue. Her heart was racing and her palms were sweating as she took off her wide-brimmed floppy hat and sat down at the kitchen table.

'So you still have that butch haircut, huh?' Steve sat opposite her. 'You must regret it now that you've lost your friends.'

'I haven't lost my friends.'

'We'll be home in three weeks' time. They're not going to recognise you.'

Her heart twisted at the thought of it. But then she let it go. 'We're not going home.'

'But you promised!'

She already felt tired at the thought of trying to correct him. 'I know that you kissed Anna.' It gave her a surprising feeling of satisfaction to shock him, and then to watch him search for an answer.

'It didn't mean anything,' he said, after a long pause.

'I know,' she said swiftly, catching him off guard again. 'You were hassling her.'

'Yeah, right, is that what she told you?'

'You know what I'm talking about,' said Carol. 'It gave you a feeling of power, didn't it? Not just over her, but over me.' She felt like a car ploughing through sand, and no matter how much he resisted, she wasn't going to cave in this time. No matter what.

'I hope you're not going to fall for that,' said Steve, recovering fast. 'She's a stuck-up bitch, Carol, and frigid. I want nothing more to do with her.'

'Frigid? As if you would know about that.'

'Huh?' He did a double take. 'What's got into you today, anyway? Is it PMT?'

'*I've* got into me.' Carol longed for a cigarette, but if she lit up now it would appear too friendly, as if she were settling in. She would have it later, she promised herself, once she got out of here.

'Fine, come or don't come.' He shrugged. 'But we're leaving.'

Her heart dropped. 'We? What are you talking about?'

'Colette and I are going home to England and you'll just have to lump it if you're not going to come.'

Okay, to hell with it, she really needed a cigarette. Carol lifted up the flap of her macramé bag and drew out a cigarette and a lighter, all the while keeping her eyes trained on Steve.

'If you try to take Colette anywhere I'll have you arrested so fast it will make your head spin.'

'Oh, really?' He looked amused as he folded his arms across his chest. Carol never argued with him, because he always won, and they both knew that. 'Like how?'

She flicked the lighter and inhaled deeply—there, that was better. 'Like, I'll call the police, who would arrest you,' she said, standing up to fetch the ashtray that sat right where she used to put it in the cupboard in front of the glasses. 'Like, it would be a long time before you ever got to see Colette again.'

'Playing tough now, are you?' There was that mean look in his eyes at last. She actually found it simpler to deal with him these days when he came out into the open. She could defend herself more easily.

'I'm not playing.' She leaned against the doorway, holding the ashtray as she flicked her cigarette. 'Three of my regulars are cops, Steve. From Sandgate.'

He laughed in disbelief. 'Cops come to that . . . that ponce hole, to get their hair done?'

'Mick and Bob get streaks and feathered layers. Everyone wants those, suddenly; I'm calling it the David Cassidy effect. Bruce just gets maintenance on his mullet. He gave me his home number, too, in case I need him for anything.' She shrugged with exaggerated modesty and smiled, wrinkling her nose at the ceiling. 'They all think I'm great.'

Steve stroked his moustache with the back of his index finger, looking at her. As if she weren't looking right back at him. It felt odd to feel so detached from Steve even when they were in the middle of an argument like this. It was like looking at him through one-way glass.

'You can't make me come back, you know.'

'As if,' he said, with a bark of laughter, rolling his eyes scornfully. 'I'm not about to grab you kicking and screaming and force you into the car. If I was, I would have done it by now. What do you take me for? Are you telling those cops I beat you? Are you running around spreading lies about me?' He still had that look in his eyes, the one that used to scare her so. 'Maybe you'd like that?'

'No,' she said, speaking with difficulty past the lump in her throat.

'Some women do, you know, subconsciously.'

'I don't know what you mean.'

'You wouldn't.' He shrugged.

He always did this, she reminded herself. At a certain point in their fights he would say something she couldn't follow, and then he would be the smart one and she would be the dumb one, dependent on him for everything.

'Steve, I'm never coming back.'

They looked at each other. There was nothing left to bargain with. Anything of value had been taken off the table.

'So what are your plans, exactly?' he asked casually, changing tack so fast it left her reeling.

Up until now she hadn't had a plan, except to leave and to take it step by step, and hope that maybe someday Steve might change. But she knew that if he didn't, she and Colette would be okay. Carol had cast herself out into the waters with Sampson and her suitcases that rainy night, and somehow she had managed to find safety. And now the answer to Steve's question came to her, as clear and beautiful as neon signs flashing into the night.

'My mum's going to come out and live with us in the flat above the hair salon.'

He looked at her sadly. 'Babe,' his voice broke, 'she's not going to want to do that.'

'Yes, she is,' said Carol, steadily. 'She would have come before, if you'd let her, and now we don't need to ask your permission. She's going to love it—especially Sampson—and it's going to be wonderful for Colette. But right now,' she continued, gathering up her cigarettes and lighter and putting on her hat, 'I have a date. Cookie!' she called out down the hall as she put on her jacket. 'We have to move it or we're going to be late.' Colette came spinning out of her room, grabbing her by the hand and swinging her little red suitcase by its handle.

'Ta-ta,' called Colette from the doorway, but Steve didn't say anything, and Carol pulled the door closed behind them.

'The swelling's going down,' she said, putting her finger under Colette's chin and turning her head from side to side once they'd walked through the front gate. 'Does it hurt much?'

'Not much,' said Colette valiantly.

'Well, good,' said Carol, smoothing her daughter's hair behind her ears and ducking in to give her a quick kiss.

'Ew!' said Colette, rubbing at her lips, but she was grinning.

'I bet Velvet makes you cheesy toast,' said Carol, as they walked down the street.

'That's my favourite.'

'I bet you have a disco and you both get dressed up.'

'Will Velvet's dog be there?'

'Red? Of course. That's where he lives, remember?'

'And where are you going to be?' asked Colette, skipping a little beside her.

'I'm going to be at Libby's, for dinner.'

They wandered along the street in a companionable silence for a few moments. Then Colette asked, 'What's it going to be like at school on Monday?'

Carol felt relieved. She'd been worried Colette was going to keep pretending, for Carol's sake, to be strong.

'You know, it doesn't matter what they think about you. It only matters what you think about yourself,' said Carol, tucking Colette under her arm as they walked. 'It's important you know that you're a strong person, and that one day you're going to have true friends, who will always be there for you.'

'Like Anna and Libby?'

'Exactly.' Carol smoothed her cheek. 'And Velvet.'

'And what about Dad? Is he your friend, too?'

'No. No, he's not.' She watched Colette carefully to check on her reaction. 'You know I can't control what he does, or doesn't do, right?'

Colette nodded solemnly.

'But I can control what I do. And I do.' It made Carol feel so good to say this that she said it again. 'I do.'

Colette smiled and wriggled out from beneath Carol's arm.

'I've had a great idea, too,' said Carol, taking her hand instead. 'I think you should start dance lessons.'

'Really? You mean like jazz ballet?' Colette stopped dead in the street. 'But we can't afford it.'

'Yes, we can.' Now that they lived above the salon, Carol would start opening until late on Thursdays, she'd decided, and she could offer casual wash and blow-drys to walk-ins, too. 'You'll meet more people, and other girls who are more like you.'

And it would give Colette something to do with her energy that wasn't homework, or boys, which was surely going to be the next thing if Carol's own history was anything to go by. Dancing would keep her busy and distract her, giving her just enough time and energy for homework before falling into bed. Carol wished she'd had something like that.

'Will they wear make-up?' asked Colette, her eyes dancing with excitement as they began to walk again.

'I'm sure. And glam costumes, too,' said Carol.

Colette let go of Carol's hand and performed a little fan kick on the footpath in front of her, then pirouetted and sashayed the whole way home.

'Mum?' said Colette thoughtfully as they reached the salon. 'You're much happier now, aren't you? Without Dad?'

Carol paused, halfway through opening the front door. 'Much happier,' she said firmly.

'I thought so. I'm glad you're not together,' said Colette breezily, skipping inside.

Carol closed her eyes in a silent prayer of thanks as she closed the door behind them.

21

Libby

LIBBY'S MOTHER, THAT FIEND OF ETIQUETTE, used to say that the only question when you were having company was: silk or taffeta? These days it was more: denim or cheesecloth? Or basil or mint, maybe? Both! decided Libby the next afternoon, plucking leaves from the pots she had planted in a row on her sunny windowsill, and chopping them up finely for her four-cheese dip.

She was back in her old kitchen, with her six gas burners and her custom-made racks for her spices, her pots hanging from the ceiling at the perfect height.

'I still love being here,' said Libby to Summer when she wandered in to see what was happening. 'Just because I had to leave doesn't mean that I didn't love it.'

The children went to bed early and easily, to Libby's surprise, excited as they had been at the thought of a dinner party and the threats from Summer that she might possibly sing. But after supper they'd both been content with an After Dinner Mint for dessert, and had gone to bed quietly. This gave Libby time to dress in a figure-hugging brown jersey dress. She put on her chunky silver Moroccan necklace and earrings, and flat sandals that would be easy for moving around in, and went downstairs to put the finishing touches on dinner.

She'd decided to serve a simple buffet: baked fish with rice salad and green beans, and a trifle with homemade sponge cake and summer fruits for dessert. Just as she was arranging the jasmine, which she'd brought in in armfuls from the front garden, the doorbell rang.

'What kind of a monster arrives early?' muttered Libby as she stomped up the hall. But there on the doorstep, instead of the managing partner and his wife, stood Anna.

Libby felt a rush of delight at the sight of her. 'Can you leave the girls with Myles tonight and join us for dinner? I tried to phone earlier but no one answered.'

Anna, of course, immediately looked stressed at the prospect of doing anything so spontaneous, and Libby had to stop herself from apologising. 'Anyway, have a think about it,' Libby added. 'What did you come around for?'

'I've been trying to phone you, too,' said Anna. 'I wanted to ask you about taking Jasper out tomorrow. We're going sailing, and the girls would love it. I also thought we should make a schedule so we can keep seeing him regularly, before it all gets too hectic with moving.' Her whole demeanour calmed instantly as she began to talk about logistics.

'It sounds great,' interrupted Libby, when finally Anna paused to take a breath. 'But can it wait until after? I need to talk to you about that catering gig you suggested, too. I think it's a great idea, actually, and I need to thank you, but I have to get the beans on now.'

'Of course,' said Anna, flushing slightly. 'And I'd love to come.' She glanced over her shoulder, and Libby realised a man was standing on the path, looking around curiously. 'That's Simon Lieber,' Anna whispered.

Libby's eyes lit up. 'From the sex party?' She craned over Anna's shoulder to look.

'From my focus group,' said Anna firmly. 'Would it be all right if he came, too, as my date?'

~

'I told you, Libby, this is your domain. Whatever you think is best,' said Ben, when Libby checked with him.

The decision-making power he was giving her was awesome, and slightly scary. *But this is what I do*, Libby reminded herself. *This is what everyone says I'm good at.* She was going to be starting a little business doing it, after all. She had to trust her instincts.

'You're nervous,' she explained to Ben. 'I bet the managing partner's a little bit nervous, too, for different reasons,' she added when he looked sceptical. 'It's probably hell for him to go to these home auditions, let alone for his wife. With Carol and Anna it will be fun, and interesting, and they'll go home having had a taste of the true riches of Sandgate.'

'Great,' said Ben, nodding.

'You're not worried about making a bad impression?' asked Libby, wanting to check for one last time that it really was okay. She knew neither Carol nor Anna would care if she told them she'd changed her mind.

'Whatever happens, it's going to make the right impression if you're here with me,' said Ben serenely. 'After all, it's our life.'

'Is it?' She was standing in the hallway with her back to the kitchen, where Anna and that handsome Simon Lieber had tactfully retreated to shell peas.

Ben stood in the living-room doorway, bathed in the glow of the mood lamp, dressed in tan slacks and a white embroidered shirt, his arms hanging loosely by his sides.

'Libby, there's something I need to say to you, before our guests arrive.'

The back of Libby's neck prickled. She held herself very still.

'I want you to be at the dinner tonight not just to help get me the promotion, but as my wife.'

'Why?' Libby whispered.

'Because I'm lonely without you. Because the house doesn't feel like home without you.'

Libby felt a wave of happiness and pleasure suffuse her, but she needed a moment to think about this, so she closed her eyes.

'I only want to be married if we can create something new,' she said, opening her eyes again.

'That's ambitious.' He raised his eyebrows.

'I know. I am ambitious. Like you.'

He bent down to pick up a sprig of jasmine she must have dropped on the carpet in her hurry to the door and offered it to her, standing close. 'I want to be your husband, because I want to be a part of whatever you create. And I want to create it with you.'

She accepted the jasmine, inhaling its heady summer sweetness, and tucked it behind her ear. Then she stepped forward and wrapped her arms around him, hugging him tightly. And now they were kissing, and Libby, at last, let herself go.

'Did I happen to mention I love you?' he asked, pulling away to look at her.

'Now that you mention it, I don't think you did,' said Libby, reaching up to stroke one of his sideburns. It felt surprisingly soft. 'But guess what? Good news! I happen to love you, too.'

And now, finally, thought Libby as they began kissing again, that might be enough.

Acknowledgements

A LOT OF SMALL TRIBUTES TO various writers have been strewn throughout these pages, especially Laurie Colwin, the late novelist and memoirist, whose thoughts on the parallels between tennis matches and social life inspired this novel's opening scene. Barbara Pym first wrote about someone having 'knitting pattern good looks,' and an essay by Ariel Levy is the source of the immortal line uttered by Strauss the first time Libby meets her, as well as the way Carol thinks about orange juice. Rona Jaffe's novels of the 1950s provided a compelling glimpse into the sexual mores which informed Anna's outlook, as well as 'There's Something I Have to Tell You,' a compilation of Australian women's stories from the Leichhardt Women's Centre. The Australian author and novelist Ruth Park's essays and memoirs about that time were an especially rich source of insight and information, as was the memoir by Anne Summers, *Ducks on the Pond*.

I would particularly like to thank my publisher Annette Barlow, and editor, Tessa Feggans, as well as Claire de Medici, Christa Munns and Pamela Dunne, and all the wonderful people at Allen & Unwin; Benython Oldfield and Claire Keenan at Zeitgeist Agency; Lou Johnson, Amanda O'Connell, Dana Slaven and Gay Lynch; Stephanie Clifford Hosking for revealing to me how interesting and important the art of hairdressing is, as well as our great conversations and great hair; and Lisa, Jaci, Kyla, Silver, Lesley, Geoff, Maurizio, Stephen and Leo. It always surprises me how many resources, of every kind, are required for the writing of a novel, and I could not have written this one without their extraordinary support.

Finally, I would like to acknowledge the Traditional Owners of the inner city area in Sydney on which the fictional location of Sandgate is based, the Gadigal and Wangal peoples of the Eora nation, and pay my respects to the Elders past, present and future.

About the author

LAURA BLOOM GREW UP IN SYDNEY and now lives with her family in the Northern Rivers Region of NSW, on the East Coast of Australia. She is the author of many critically acclaimed and bestselling novels for adults and children, including *In The Mood* and *The Cleanskin*.

To learn more about Laura, please go to www.laurabloom.com.au.